The lock had been ripped from the door

Ryan grabbed Krysty's shoulder and rolled her over. She twisted bonelessly, and the loose way she moved made him certain she was dead.

The breath caught in Ryan's throat as he stared at his lover's pale face. Then he noticed her breasts rise with a drawn breath. Gently he reached toward her face, cupping her chin in his callused hand.

"Wake up," he urged hoarsely. The one-eyed man patted her cheek tenderly but with enough force to rock her head slightly. "You've got to wake up!"

Abruptly Krysty sat up, her eyes snapping open and into focus like the electronic sights on a war wag. There was another presence. "Do not presume to touch me, whoreson!"

Other titles in the Deathlands saga:

JAMES AXLER

DEATH LANDS®

Starfall

A GOLD EAGLE BOOK FROM
WORLDWIDE®

TORONTO • NEW YORK • LONDON
AMSTERDAM • PARIS • SYDNEY • HAMBURG
STOCKHOLM • ATHENS • TOKYO • MILAN
MADRID • WARSAW • BUDAPEST • AUCKLAND

First edition April 1999

ISBN 0-373-62545-6

STARFALL

Printed in U.S.A.

The night is far spent, the day is at hand:
let us therefore cast off the works of darkness,
and let us put on armor of light.
                              —Romans 13:12

THE DEATHLANDS SAGA

This world is their legacy, a world born in the violent nuclear spasm of 2001 that was the bitter outcome of a struggle for global dominance.

There is no real escape from this shockscape where life always hangs in the balance, vulnerable to newly demonic nature, barbarism, lawlessness.

But they are the warrior survivalists, and they endure—in the way of the lion, the hawk and the tiger, true to nature's heart despite its ruination.

Ryan Cawdor: The privileged son of an East Coast baron. Acquainted with betrayal from a tender age, he is a master of the hard realities.

Krysty Wroth: Harmony ville's own Titian-haired beauty, a woman with the strength of tempered steel. Her premonitions and Gaia powers have been fostered by her Mother Sonja.

J. B. Dix, the Armorer: Weapons master and Ryan's close ally, he, too, honed his skills traversing the Deathlands with the legendary Trader.

Doctor Theophilus Tanner: Torn from his family and a gentler life in 1896, Doc has been thrown into a future he couldn't have imagined.

Dr. Mildred Wyeth: Her father was killed by the Ku Klux Klan, but her fate is not much lighter. Restored from predark cryogenic suspension, she brings twentieth-century healing skills to a nightmare.

Jak Lauren: A true child of the wastelands, reared on adversity, loss and danger, the albino teenager is a fierce fighter and loyal friend.

Dean Cawdor: Ryan's young son by Sharona accepts the only world he knows, and yet he is the seedling bearing the promise of tomorrow.

In a world where all was lost, they are humanity's last hope....

Chapter One

Ryan Cawdor rested his forefinger lightly against the Steyr rifle's trigger as he swept his gaze over the urban shockscape of the ravaged ville. He hunkered in the late-afternoon shadows draped carelessly over the smashed remains of what had once been a concrete-and-steel building in downtown Idaho Falls, Idaho, before a nuclear warhead had nearly blown the city out of existence a hundred years earlier.

He kept the bilious green-tinged sunset behind him, an old gunfighter's trick and the first rule of a predator. His position also carried his scent away from the area he surveyed. The last bath he had taken lay nearly four days' hard travel behind him; he knew he carried a strong musk that an alert animal, mutie or man could detect.

The cold wind, full of the threat of approaching winter, swirled around the big man. He felt it rake through his clothing for a moment, searching across his flesh with frozen skeletal fingers. The touch lingered even after the wind passed on, chilling him to the bone.

Then the scream rent the air again.

The effort sounded strained and thin, as if the screamer's pain had almost crossed the threshold into sensory overload. It keened through the tumbledown buildings, bouncing from the haphazard walls that still stood.

"Lover." The voice was soft, undemanding.

Ryan gazed over his shoulder at the fire-haired woman

hunkered down behind him. He spoke without hesitation. "We wait."

She nodded reluctantly.

The scream died away, winding down rather than getting cut off short. The screamer still lived.

"Mebbe by the time we find whoever's screaming, it'll be too late."

"Better to be late trying to save somebody rather than being early to your own lynching." But the words sounded hollow even to Ryan's ears. Even being intelligent about a play wasn't always easy.

The saying had belonged to the Trader, the man who had finished Ryan's training in survivalism in Deathlands. In his day, the Trader had been a man strong enough, big enough and violent enough to become a legend. His word had been his bond, and a law unto itself. He had saved individuals and once or twice sent a whole community straight to hell when it crossed him or threatened anything that was his.

"I know." The woman grimaced and put a hand to her head. Her other hand held a .38 Smith & Wesson Model 640. "It's just getting hard to take. More than just screaming now. I can almost hear words."

Ryan had nothing to say to that. Krysty Wroth had a gift, inherited from and cultivated by her mother, and it hinged on mutie abilities that Ryan never even pretended to understand. But he did understand her pain and frustration because he saw it etched into her beautiful face, saw the way she carried it in her movements. All the hard years of his own youth, all the carnage he'd seen and caused while traveling with the Trader and the war wags, hadn't completely dehumanized him. But it had hardened his sense of purpose. He was determined to live and to bring his small group through whatever waited up ahead intact.

Krysty was hurting, but she wasn't going to die from it. At least, that was the present thinking.

He scanned the terrain again. The shattered remains of the building they stood on gave him a vantage point almost twenty feet above the ground. If they had been in a forested area or the plains or mountains, the advantage would have been enough.

The blasted remnants of the ville proved to be another matter. Idaho Falls had been a small but thriving metropolitan area back before the nukecaust that had ended the world. In addition to the destruction caused by the bombs, a hundred years of chem storms and nuclear winter raised scars that stood out on the buildings.

Rusted hulks of cars, trucks and buses lined what used to be streets. Acid rain had scoured most of the paint from the vehicles. Windows that had survived the end of the world had been claimed by the survivors.

Looking out over the broken maze of streets and structures, Ryan was certain nothing remained that they could salvage themselves. But the companions had come to the city to trade with the survivors that still lived there, or to take what they needed any way they could. Supplies—especially when they traveled near rad-blasted areas and remnants of unrecovered villes—remained a concern. And they intended to gather any information about the area they didn't already have.

He glanced back at Krysty, worrying about her. For some unknown reason, she had been hearing the screams inside her mind since early that morning after the mat-trans jump that had brought them into the region, long before the noise had become a physical presence to the rest of the group.

"Lot of bastard pain, Ryan," she whispered hoarsely, her sentient red hair curled protectively against her nape.

"You," he asked, "or the other?"

"Gaia, I can't even tell anymore. Me, the other—it's all the same now." She made a gagging noise and tried to cover it with her hand so the sound wouldn't travel. Her shoulders hunched with dry heaves. "No separation."

Ryan looked at her, seeing the way her hands shook. He was a big man, tall and broad, carrying a lot of muscle in his back and shoulders. His curly black hair nearly reached his shoulders. His right eye shone cobalt blue and piercing; the place where his left eye should have been was covered by a scuffed black leather patch that kept infectious material out of the empty socket. A long scar trailed from the corner of his right eye to the corner of his mouth. He reached out and touched her hand. "I'll be back."

She looked at him, her eyes not quite focusing. "Sorry, lover. I know it's all my fault. We shouldn't be shackled to taking something on like this."

"No. It's not your fault. Just how things worked out— that's all." Ryan released her hand and scrambled down the side of the rubble. He thought briefly of leaving the Steyr with Krysty since she had the high ground and could cover him. But he also realized that in her present condition he was better off keeping it.

He dropped from the last chunk of concrete to the street level. His boots rang hollowly against the cracked sidewalk for just a moment. With the wind keening through the debris around him, he doubted the sound carried very far.

A dozen broken-down wags littered the street in front of him. One of them stuck out from the side of the building where it was partially buried under a pile of shattered masonry. All of the wags had long since been stripped.

Three skeletons sat in the wag jutting out from the building. Tattered bits of clothing remained stuck to the yellowed bone. The skeleton behind the wheel had no head, while the one in the passenger's seat had a mouthful of broken teeth and a collapsed lower face. The third skeleton sat in a child's safety seat at a crooked angle.

Ryan didn't let himself dwell on the scene. Too many of them existed across Deathlands. He stared at the building across the street. A sun-faded orange sign sticking up from the debris read Kidwell's Korner Kafe—Ice, Beer, Magazines.

"Jak," Ryan called softly.

"Yeah." The voice barely carried across the small distance.

"Let's go."

"Sure, Ryan." Jak Lauren stepped out from hiding, a .357 Magnum Colt Python in his hand. "Krysty?"

"Hurting." Ryan started forward, aiming in the direction the screams had come from as near as he could judge.

"Find it, chill it. Then move on." Jak moved into position behind Ryan. The teenager had the stark white coloration of a true albino, and the snow-white hair to match. His eyes gleamed like fiery red rubies in the hollows of his scarred face. Iridescent patches of gray and brown clung to his camou-style clothing, and the sharp bits of metal carefully sewn into the material didn't show at all.

SHIFTING SHAPES SKITTERED across and through the debris filling the street. Ryan recognized them as rats, and they were some of the biggest he had ever seen. Nearly eighteen inches tall at the shoulder, they looked like small dogs and hunted in packs like wolves. Coarse brown hair covered their rangy bodies. Their tails trailed behind them, hairless and as thick as Ryan's first two fingers held together. Their behavior patterns drew his instant attention because they didn't act afraid of him at all.

When he had been at his vantage point atop the crumbled building, the rats hadn't warranted much study. Anywhere

people still clung to shreds of civilization, rats were a sure
bet.

But now he gave them his full attention because they
were giving him a big share of theirs.

"Fuckers probably rabid." Jak walked at Ryan's side
little more than an arm's length away. Far enough away
they wouldn't get tangled with each other when they
moved, but close enough they could move together if they
needed to.

"If they decide to attack, a man might not live long
enough to find out anyway." Ryan reached to his right hip
and loosened the thong holding the SIG-Sauer P-226 in the
holster. He took up the razor-edged panga in his left hand,
fingers curled loosely around the haft. The blade was an
eighteen-inch extension of himself, and he knew it intimately.

"Mebbe chill couple. Let eat each other." Jak fisted
some of his leaf-bladed throwing knives.

"No." Ryan kept walking, determined to give the rats a
wide berth if at all possible. He crossed the street, staying
away from the main body of the pack.

After the nukecaust, Mother Nature's hand was no longer
solely responsible for the grand designs of all creatures
great and small. Especially in the rad-blasted areas. Mutie
blood showed up, changing things forever. Sometimes the
rad-burn had created a wholly new creature with no ties to
whatever had originally sired it.

Without warning, the scream rushed through the street
again, echoing within the cavernous vaults left inside the
collapsed buildings. The rats paused, throwing their broad
warty snouts into the breeze.

"Smell it?" Jak asked.

Ryan took a breath. The albino teen's senses were more

developed than most, but he had no problem sorting out the fecund scent of death. "Yeah."

The scream dragged on for a few short seconds, then broke in the middle. For a moment, Ryan thought the screamer had finally died. Before he turned to glance in Krysty's direction to check with her, the voice returned as a snuffling sob.

He couldn't recognize the words, but he knew from the tones that the screamer was a woman.

Ryan stayed close to the crumbled remains. He kept the panga ready in his hand while he followed the barrel of the Steyr forward. Furtive movements sounded inside the building.

With his trained eye, Ryan saw past the ruined facade of the building. Paths had been cleared through the rubble, a sure indication of some kind of habitation.

The Trader had taught Ryan and everyone else under his command to look for signs such as those. Paths around a body of fresh water or a river were understandable and to be expected. Man and beast alike both needed a source of fresh drinking water to survive.

But a path worn into an area where there was no source of water meant something else entirely. Especially when the crossers of those paths were human. At those times, the Trader had pointed out, a smart man knew he had a host of buyers just waiting to be approached. Men or women who made it a habit of crossing other people's paths were looking to get something they wanted from the other party—by whatever means they could get it.

Ryan knew from studying the barren earth worn between the patches of weeds and grass that the area was heavily traveled. It meant either the predators gathered there to attack those weaker than themselves, or that someone had gone into business managing supply and demand for the area.

The big man's curiosity flared into being. Though he had seen a considerable amount of Deathlands, he wanted to see more.

He took up the Steyr in both hands and followed the trail up the steep incline in front of him. He glanced at Jak, watching the youth step into the shadows under some of the broken rock. Jak disappeared within three steps, leaving nothing to mark his passage through the rock.

WRAPPING THE STEYR'S SLING around his forearm to better balance the weapon, Ryan crested the hill. Peering over the edge, Ryan studied the scene unfolding before him.

Over the top of the hill, the land fell away and pooled in a bowl-shaped depression rimmed by stacks of junked cars and the shattered remains of a few warehouses and garages. A rusted fence topped with barbed wire encircled most of the lot. Over the broken remnants of two wire gates, a listing sign with faded paint proclaimed Samuelson's Wrecking Yard.

Nearly two dozen armed men dressed in mismatched clothing and animal skins stood in a loose circle in front of the junkyard around a captive handful of men, women and one child. Three corpses lay stretched out on the barren ground. Two of the dead were women, stripped naked and showing signs of dying hard.

From his position, Ryan could smell the death lingering on the fresh corpses. Another shallow breath brought a different scent to his nose, this one totally animal, ripened with a pungent sourness. He scanned the terrain again, more deliberately this time, and spotted the first of the dogs hunkered down in the spaces between the rusting cars and cracked debris given up by the buildings.

For a moment, Ryan thought the pack of dogs was waiting its chance at the corpses. Urban predators learned to be patient. A wild pack marauding the countryside and coming up on a ville would have a harder time bringing down any of the citizens living within the ville's protection. But tumbledown cities like Idaho Falls gave up their dead as a matter of course. The natural predators living within the bowels of the ruins served the purpose of keeping disease to a minimum by disposing of the decaying flesh.

One of the men stepped forward, taunting his captives. He stood tall and rangy, leaned out to muscle over bone. His cheeks showed great hollows as they sunk in tight against his skull. He wore his black hair pulled back in a long ponytail, which was threaded with finger bones yellow with age. A spotty beard covered most of his lower face under his deep-set eyes. He wore a scuffed and torn leather jacket with a brightly colored patch across its back that Ryan couldn't quite make out.

"This here's Slagger territory," he shouted at the captives. "Man crossing through here better pay up some tribute if he expects to make it across."

"We didn't know," one of the women yelled back. Her voice shuddered with fear. "We're new here. Nobody told us."

"Ignorance of the law ain't no excuse," the Slagger leader said. "Lotta Road Brothers paid the price before skydark. Got no mercy in my heart for you piss-poor fuckers come through here unprepared."

"You've already chilled two of us," one of the men in the captive group said. He was stoop shouldered but carried a lot of weight in his chest, which showed he was accustomed to manual labor. Bruises and drying blood covered his face. He stepped forward, shifting his weight. "How many more you reckon on chilling?"

The Slagger leader grinned. "Gonna chill you all if I've a mind to do it."

Ryan read the stoop-shouldered man's intentions before the man made his move. With nothing left to lose, a person would generally shoot his whole wad on one desperate move. The Trader knew that, and he'd taught the crews of his war wags that philosophy.

Without another word, the stoop-shouldered man leaped at the Slagger member nearest him. A growl of inarticulate rage tore from his throat.

The Slagger struggled to bring around the chopped-down shotgun he carried. He was young, barely into his teens, and scrawny.

"Crain!" one of the women in the group yelled, starting forward. Another Slagger butt-stroked her in the stomach with his weapon. She let out a thin yelp and dropped to her knees, clutching her belly. Before she could defend herself, the Slagger butt-stroked her again in the head.

Ryan watched without making a move. He knew from the woman's voice that she wasn't the one Krysty had somehow linked to.

The stoop-shouldered man backhanded the young Slagger in the face. Blood spewed from his broken nose and covered his face as he staggered back.

Crain came up with the shotgun. Moving with an economy of motion, he lifted the scattergun and pointed it at the Slagger leader. His hand swept both hammers back.

A grin painted the Slagger leader's thin-lipped mouth as he reached for the pistol holstered on his hip. It came free in an eye blink, the coldheart's left hand wrapping instinctively around the cut-down barrel. His right hand dropped to the big lever action under the breech.

Ryan knew instantly that it wasn't a pistol at all. The

weapon was a lever-action rifle that had the barrel and stock cut off, reducing it to something less than two feet long.

The Slagger leader ripped through five shots in quick succession, fanning the lever action.

Crain got off one round. The double-aught buckshot spanged off the rusting wag an arm's span away from the Slagger leader. The pellets slammed through the oxidized metal and unleashed a rust-red metallic fog that coiled over their intended target.

All of the Slagger leader's bullets hit Crain. From the sharp sound of the detonations, Ryan figured the abbreviated rifle was chambered in .30-30. They blew through Crain's chest, punching his heart out.

A ragged cheer punctuated with jeering laughter filled the area. "Halleck! Halleck!" some of the Slaggers chanted in appreciation.

Halleck fed bullets into the rifle's side breech and grinned at his men. "Fucker had it coming. Nobody draws down on me and lives."

The butt-stroked woman lay on the ground, holding both hands over her face as she wept aloud.

The young Slagger recovered his weapon, then quickly turned it and fired the remaining round into the quivering corpse's face. Flesh, blood, bone and patches of hair flew outward, eliciting another cheer from the coldhearts. The Slagger wiped the blood from his face—his own, and his victim's—and reloaded his weapon.

If there had been a way clear, Ryan would have passed by the area. There was too much to risk, and no potential gain in sight.

Except for the voice and screams rattling around in Krysty's skull.

He pulled back from the crest, moving among the broken rubble. Without warning, pebbles and a small wave of dust hurtled down the slope of one of the shattered slabs to gust into his face.

Ryan didn't even try to fool himself into thinking it was caused by the wind. He looked up, his single eye narrowing, and spotted the man-size silhouette that sprang at him.

Chapter Two

Help me!

The voice hammered the inside of Krysty Wroth's skull now. The pain had increased in the short amount of time Ryan had been gone. She blinked back tears and struggled to hang on to her resolve to watch her lover's back.

I'm dying! The voice was a croaked gasp that slashed through Krysty's head. *I don't want to be alone! Please answer me! I know you're there!*

A picture formed in the redhead's mind, washing out the other sights that her eyes brought to her.

The woman stood wrapped in thin gray fog tendrils that obscured her features. She held her arms out in supplication. *Why don't you help me?*

"I can't," Krysty whispered out loud, hoping the woman inside her head could hear her. "I'd get chilled."

No. You must come. Her age could have been anything from twenty to sixty. Her long blond hair wrapped tightly around her head, clinging to her.

"No!" Krysty struggled to see past the woman in the fog, concentrating on the broken terrain of the ville again. Ryan was out there somewhere, and she had his back. "I'm not going to risk getting Ryan chilled."

Who's Ryan?

"Ryan's my lover," Krysty said. "My life."

Impossible! The Chosen don't mate!

Krysty didn't respond. She peered hard into the fog in

her mind, burning holes through it now. The woman's face cleared. Her complexion was nothing short of perfection, a confection of vanilla brushed with the hint of a rose. Krysty had never seen a woman who had looked like her, never seen anyone who looked so unreal. Gaia, was she hallucinating? Had she caused Ryan and the rest of the companions to come out here following a fever dream? She didn't know.

You have taken vows of chastity, the woman said in a stern tone that barely covered the anguish that assailed her.

"No." Some of the pain Krysty was feeling from the woman ebbed, but she felt the woman's confusion in there now.

But your power—everyone knows mating with a man will break your power! How dare you throw your gift away so cheaply!

The vision in Krysty's head thinned and became translucent. The woman's voice sounded more distant in her mind. She saw the broken-down buildings in front of her again, grayed out as though they had no color.

A curious itch trailed through Krysty's mind unexpectedly. She felt chilled by it, and nausea sent burning bile to the back of her throat.

You speak the truth. You are not one of us. The woman's puzzlement filtered through her pain, seeming to become a distraction enough to tear her away from her agony.

"No," Krysty replied, "I'm not." She took a deep, shuddering breath, feeling the pain ebb and flow in her head again. "Who are you?"

Phlorin. I am one of the Chosen.

"What Chosen?"

You do not know?

"No."

But your power? How could you have it and not know of us?

"I received my power from my mother."

The woman screamed as the sound of gunshots ricocheted from the area where Ryan had gone.

Krysty concentrated on the .38 in her fist. It was solid and secure. She had to stay rooted in reality if she was going to help Ryan. She shifted on top of the flattened building, but her equilibrium was distorted and she felt too weak to get to her feet. "What is wrong?"

It is the Slaggers. They think I am a doomie.

Doomies were muties who exhibited paranormal powers, generally hinging on an ability to foretell disastrous events in the near and distant future. Often, they were considered to actually bring bad fortune to those around them rather than to merely predict it. Krysty had worn the label herself. "Who are the Slaggers?"

The men who captured me. Coldhearts of this region. Phlorin's thoughts broke away abruptly.

Instinctively Krysty reached for the woman's voice in her mind. Contact was made, feeling as much like a caress as her sentient hair coiling around her neck. "You are alone?"

Yes.

"Why?"

Because there is no one else.

Krysty felt the woman's thoughts become disjointed, like cold water slipping through her closing fist. She struggled to maintain the contact. As the woman drew away, it felt as though a vacuum opened in her mind, maybe powerful enough to drink down her mind, as well. The thought scared her. "Were you always alone?"

No. The rest of the response was slow in coming.

Krysty waited, her eyes searching through the haze of

her vision to the area where Ryan and Jak had disappeared. Only then did she become aware of how slowly her heart seemed to beat. Then she realized the conversation taking place in her mind had to have been taking place much faster than she realized.

There were others. We never go out alone.

"Where are they?"

Dead.

"How?"

The Slaggers killed Thusella today. Wolves brought Artimys down nearly a week ago.

An image of a rock-covered grave appeared in Krysty's mind. Three women, one of them the blonde she thought was Phlorin, stood above the grave. All of the women wore some kind of white robes. Krysty couldn't believe they dressed in such a fashion while in the rough.

"Three of you?" Krysty asked.

Of course. There are always the Three. There is much power in that number.

"Who are the Chosen?"

There is no time to explain. I am dying.

"Mebbe not." Krysty tightened her hand on the .38. "If there's a way, mebbe we can help."

It's too late for me, child.

"Never too late."

One of the Chosen always knows her time, the woman said. *That is one of our gifts and one of our curses.*

"Give up," Krysty said, "and you might as well cut your own throat." Her head didn't hurt as bad now, but the thrumming vibration filling it changed timber.

I'm giving up only on this hold in the mortal realm. Another life awaits me. One much better than this.

"If you believe," Krysty said.

And you do not?

Krysty didn't answer, though she felt Phlorin already knew. Mother Sonja's teachings about Gaia remained strong in her, provided her a cornerstone of strength and belief.

You do believe.

"Because I have seen what Gaia can do."

Gaia? You worship Gaia?

"I pay her my respects."

How is it, then, that you are not one of the Chosen?

"You know of Gaia?"

All of the Chosen know of Gaia. She is the Earth Mother who binds us all, ties us one to another. Only most are too blind to see.

Krysty didn't know that she agreed with the woman. Gaia was one source of power, but she had seen a number of other belief systems that seemed as strong as her own during her travels with Ryan.

Sacrilege! Gaia is more than a belief system!

Krysty felt properly chastised.

Gaia, give me strength that I have only you to lean on, Krysty Wroth.

"How do you know my name?"

There are many things I know about you now.

Anger flooded Krysty. She knew the woman had somehow ransacked her private thoughts.

You are of the Chosen, whether you admit it or not.

"How can you be so sure?"

Because the Chosen can always recognize each other. It is only one of our ways. If there were more time, perhaps I could explain to you what you have missed.

"I don't know you or the Chosen."

No.

"Do you know about my mother?"

Sonja?

Krysty's heart leaped. Though Mother Sonja had disappeared from Harmony years earlier, even left rumors of her death in her wake, there was no proof that she was dead. "Yes."

Only what I have discerned in your mind.

"She was not one of the Chosen, then."

Perhaps she had another name. I can't see her clearly in your mind.

That was because Krysty had only her earliest memories of her mother. Even those were tainted by wishes and stories she had heard from relatives. "If she had been one of the Chosen, she would have returned there."

She bore you, child. Your mother would not have been allowed back among the Chosen. Now hush. There is much I must do, and I have precious little time to do it.

Another pistol report echoed through the terrain, drawn out long and hollow, giving Krysty fresh indication of how much her sense of time had been distorted by the invasive mind. She struggled to free herself from the hypnotic quality of the woman's thoughts mixing with hers.

For a moment, she believed she was winning, pushing the woman from her mind. Then Phlorin's voice thundered inside her skull, filling her brain with white-hot pain.

Forgive me what I do, Phlorin said. *It is necessary.*

Struggling to hang on to consciousness, Krysty made herself think of Ryan out there without her covering his back. It didn't matter. A lightning bolt burst inside her brain and shut her down, taking her away.

"COMPANY'S COMING, JOHN."

J. B. Dix glanced up from his position on the second floor of the building they'd chosen to wait in and looked into Mildred Wyeth's face. He followed her line of gaze as she stared through the binoculars.

To the east, a broken line of dust scattered across the darkening sky.

"Dear lady," Doc Tanner said, "that dust means only that a few riders travel hither. And there can be any number of explanations for that. They could be venturing here for shelter from the approaching tempest."

"Could be." Mildred nodded reluctantly. Her ebony face remained emotionless, but the dust graying her cheeks and forehead gave silent witness to the wear and tear they had all experienced these past few days. "I suppose the horsemen of the apocalypse wouldn't draw much attention, either. Until their horses were breathing flame up your ass."

Of medium height, Mildred carried a few extra pounds on her stocky frame that even hard living in Deathlands hadn't been able to strip from her. Multicolored beads hung in her hair, holding the locks in braided plaits. Her fatigue-style shirt and pants held ground-in patches of dirt, but the action on her ZKR Czech-made .38 pistol remained clean.

"How many riders, Dean?" J.B didn't bother to study the approaching riders much. Built short and wiry, he didn't look like a man to fear, but he'd been weapons master for the Trader on War Wag One. The steel-rimmed glasses and worn fedora almost gave him the look of a stern schoolteacher instead of a trained killer. He returned his gaze to the area where Ryan and Jak had headed, waiting to see if anything else had happened. So far, he hadn't heard the crack of Ryan's SIG-Sauer or the Steyr, so he knew whatever shooting had been done hadn't involved his friend.

Dean Cawdor shifted at the end of the building. The boy shaded his eyes as he peered at the dust cloud. His stark black curly hair and vivid blue eyes, as well as the rangy build, clearly marked him as his father's child. The holster on his hip was empty because the Browning Hi-Power he carried was in his hand.

"Fifteen, mebbe twenty," Dean called out.

"Riders?" J.B. asked.

"Yeah."

J.B. processed the information. Horses meant some kind of ville. A man out ranging the land with no home would be hard-pressed to keep a horse's belly full. An expert traveler could get by on some ring-pulls and self-heats that he raided or traded for in arid country. Few who regularly traveled Deathlands wandered far from their home twenty on horseback. A horse was a valuable animal, capable of a lot of work and needing a lot of care. Besides being vulnerable to the harsh climate, a horse was also an item worth stealing or killing for.

A dozen or more horses meant whoever was riding them could take care of them. And they wouldn't be out traveling unless it was important.

"Carrying some kind of flag," Dean went on.

"See what it is?" J.B. asked.

"Not yet."

"Let me know." The Armorer kept focused on the terrain ahead of them. Going back and crossing the paths of the riders wasn't a good plan. Better to take their chances losing themselves in the detritus ahead of them.

"John Barrymore," Doc said, shifting close and keeping a low profile, "I fear we are much too far away to offer succor to Ryan should he need it."

"Way Ryan wanted it," J.B. replied. "We got the back door."

"That was then," Doc said stubbornly. "This is now. He surely did not know about the riders closing in on this location."

"We hold." J.B. forced himself to stay at rest, his hands wrapped securely around his Uzi. His Smith & Wesson M-4000 shotgun lay strapped against his back.

"Then someone should be with Krysty," Doc said. When he had been born in South Strafford, Vermont, on February 14, 1868, he had been christened Theophilus Algernon Tanner. He'd earned a science degree at Harvard, then a doctorate at Oxford University in England.

He was tall and lean, and his silver hair blew around his shoulders. His clothing was Victorian, including a frock jacket showing a green patina from age, and cracked leather knee boots. He held a Le Mat percussion pistol in one hand and a black walking stick with a silver lion's head in the other.

Though well over two hundred years old by the count of a conventional calendar, Doc's actual age was much more bizarre than that. He'd been seized from 1896 by a time-trawling experiment conducted by Operation Chronos near the end of the second millennium. Chronos had been merely one facet of the Totality Concept, an organization that had explored arcane avenues for future warfare.

In the 1990s, Doc hadn't given up hope of being returned to his wife, Emily, and their children. In spite of the fact that his transfer from the past was the only known success, and that no one had survived any attempts at being sent back, he worked to take the chance. Ultimately the researchers affiliated with Operation Chronos had marked Doc as a security risk and had trawled him a hundred years into the future. Both experiences had left their mark on the old man, leaving him with episodes of disassociative dementia.

"Krysty's a big girl," Mildred said. "She can take care of herself."

"Still," Doc grumbled, "I would feel better if one of us was with her."

"Dad wanted it that way," Dean said. "So did Krysty.

Less risk to the rest of us if she was kept isolated. Till we find out what's wrong with her.''

Despite Dean's attempts to keep his feelings to himself, his worry was immediately apparent to J.B.

The Armorer said, ''It's going to be just fine.'' But he couldn't help glancing over his shoulder at the approaching column of dust from the riders. Then he cut his gaze to the sky.

It was going to be a race to see what went wrong first: the arrival of the riders, or the arrival of the chem storm.

Then his attention snapped back to the area where Ryan and Jak were as he heard a double tap of shots. There was no doubt that they came from Ryan's SIG-Sauer.

Chapter Three

With the attacker silhouetted in front of him, Ryan stepped to the right and brought up the panga. If possible, he wanted to keep quiet and not draw the attention of the Slagger coldhearts down the incline.

The man landed short of Ryan, coming down hard. His clothes were reduced to rags, strips of material that fluttered around him, caked with filth. If the man hadn't been standing downwind before the attack, Ryan felt certain he would have smelled him before he was able to get close enough.

Rad burns scarred the ghoulie's face and arms, marring the bald scalp with purple blisters of proud flesh. Long black hairs jutted from pustular pockets on his head, and pus wept freely from the affected pores. Broken black teeth filled the rictus of his grin. Still, he was strong enough to swing the homemade club in his hands. A half moon of sharpened metal gleamed at the end of it, turning the weapon into an ax.

Dodging back, Ryan barely avoided the vicious swipe that streaked for his head. Instinctively he raised the 9 mm blaster. He didn't want to fire it unless he had to. The detonation would draw the coldhearts from down in the basin. He hoped the intimidation of the blaster would be enough to turn the ghoulie back.

The ghoulie made gibbering noises and tugged on the club. The half moon of metal had gotten stuck in a mound of earth to the side. Yellow, phlegmy spittle ran from the corner of his warped mouth. With another frantic tug, the club ripped free of the earth. The ghoulie didn't hesitate about carrying on the attack.

"Fireblast!" Ryan swore. He gave ground again, avoiding another hasty swing. While his attacker drew the club back again, he switched hands with his weapons, gripping the panga in his right fist.

The ghoulie growled menacingly and swung again, advancing a step as he did so.

Ryan held his position and stepped inside the club's arc with practiced movements. A man handling a long weapon had to be prepared for his target to attempt to move inside. The ghoulie wasn't.

Blocking the club with his right arm, cursing the fact that he wasn't in a position to use the panga without risking his own safety, Ryan slapped the barrel of the blaster across the ghoulie's temple.

The creature yowled in pained protest as a bloody tear opened up along his temple. Crimson ran freely down the side of his face.

Expecting the ghoulie to be dazed from the blow, Ryan released his hold on the club and lifted the panga for a straight thrust at the creature's throat. Instead, the ghoulie swung the bottom of the club into the one-eyed man's face.

Staggered, Ryan dropped and rolled back, slipping beneath the ghoulie's follow-up stroke. He came up on his knees, ready to dig his boots into the ground and drive himself back to his feet.

Two other ghoulies landed to the right of the first. One of them carried a pitchfork with a broken center tine, and the other held a scythe sporting a ragged edge. The first ghoulie gestured toward them. They fanned out, moving in tandem to quickly circle Ryan.

The movements showed discipline and practice. Ryan

had no doubts that they'd used the strategy successfully against past victims. It was possible that the activity of the Slagger coldhearts drew a crowd, or at least bottled up the trade routes for a time. Then the ghoulies could choose their quarry and escape. Ryan thought they probably lived in the area, existing off whatever they could steal or take from the ville's usual inhabitants. And a ghoulie's favorite meal was meat from a decaying corpse, one they had killed themselves and put away until it reached the proper degree of ripeness.

The fact that the first one hadn't feared the blaster convinced Ryan that they'd had little encounter with them. He chose to rectify that.

Ryan lifted the SIG-Sauer and squeezed the trigger. He put two bullets into the head of the ghoulie who'd attacked him, then turned the blaster on the second mutie, the hollowpoints coring through the creature's chest. The third ghoulie turned to run, screaming in incoherent panic. Without pause, Ryan shot him in the back.

Grimly Ryan rose to his feet and sheathed the panga. He put the SIG-Sauer away, as well, and hefted the Steyr. He strode toward the crest of the hill with the rifle cradled in his arms.

"Jak," he called.

"Here."

Turning his head slightly, Ryan saw the albino teen move into view on the right.

Jak had blood on his face, deep crimson against the pale flesh, but none of it looked like his. His left fist was spiked with a half dozen of the leaf-bladed throwing knives.

"Company?" Ryan asked.

"Some. No more."

Ryan nodded and scanned the broken buildings along their back trail. Now that they knew ghoulies lived among them, the hiding places he'd spotted along the way for a strategic retreat no longer seemed so safe.

"They know," Jak said, nodding toward the basin.

"Hard to miss," Ryan answered.

"Yeah."

"Keep an eye on our backs."

"Sure."

Ryan peered into the basin. The Slaggers had to have bolted at the sound of the first shot. The only ones Ryan saw were taking up positions behind the crumbled structures and the stacks of junked wags. The captives, the remaining man, two women and the child, hid behind a leaning section of splintered fence. Two of the Slaggers closed on them, shouting at them to stay put.

A bullet spanged off a section of brick and mortar to the one-eyed man's right. Ryan drew back, wondering whether to chance going back to face more ghoulies or to attempt to hold the position. J.B. and the others could get clear and retreat to the dry camp they'd made that morning and wait until Jak and Ryan could get free at nightfall.

Then a harsh whistle cut through the air.

Shifting his position atop the crest, Ryan gazed into the basin again, spotting Halleck, the Slagger leader, behind one of the overturned wags. The man put his fingers into his mouth and whistled again, changing pitch this time.

A line of dogs formed along the breaks under the stacks of junked wags. Pink-and-black tongues lolled out of their white-flecked mouths. Their fur was matted and scar-torn, reflecting the harsh existence they were accustomed to.

Another whistle and the dogs rushed out of their hiding places, racing up the incline of the basin toward Ryan and Jak's position.

"Can't stay," Ryan said to the albino.

Jak nodded in agreement.

Ryan pushed up from the ground and stayed low. He ran hard, driving his feet against the earth, choosing a different path back to the building where he'd left Krysty. Getting trapped up on the structure so the ghoulies and the Slaggers could surround them wasn't the choice he would have made, but he was certain they wouldn't be able to outrun the dogs.

Bloodcurdling baying overtook Ryan, summoning awful visions of what the beasts would do to him and Jak if they were caught. His breathing turned ragged, and each gasp was dry and burned the back of his throat.

He stayed close to the buildings, trying to keep himself as small a target as he could in case any of the Slaggers had followed the dogs up the side of the basin. An arm reached unexpectedly from one of the broken windows, and the fist at the end of it knotted up in Ryan's shirt, yanking him off balance.

Surprisingly strong, the arm's owner pulled Ryan up against the window as if he were a rag doll. No glass remained in the windowframe, but the big ghoulie on the other side filled it. Maybe weighing as much as 350 pounds, the ghoulie stood over six feet tall, and would have been even taller if he hadn't been a hunchback. The eyes weren't set properly; the one on the right was almost centered in his cheek and listed inward, looking gray and dead. He crowed in triumph, reaching out with his other hand toward Ryan's head.

The one-eyed man didn't try to fight the ghoulie's incredible strength. He raised the Steyr and rested the barrel against the ghoulie's throat. When he pulled the trigger, the creature's head exploded in a volcano of flesh, blood and gleaming shards of bone.

Covered in gore, Ryan shoved himself back. The baying

dogs sounded closer, but he gave the windows a wider berth as he ran.

J.B. SPOTTED JAK AND RYAN through his binoculars for only a moment before they barreled around the corner of a building and disappeared. He saw the dogs next, baying and leaping over rubble close to the ground.

"Dark night!"

"They have set loose the hounds," Doc said, "or these old ears deceive me."

"Your hearing's fine, Doc." J.B. shifted, checking his weapons to make sure they were all in place. The moves were as natural as breathing.

Doc peered over the side of the building, his face filled with worry. "We cannot leave them to be run down by those foul beasts, John Barrymore."

"Won't do them any good by dying with them." J.B. reseated his fedora on his head and glanced back at Dean. If the boy showed any signs of disobeying his order, and Ryan's orders by proxy, the Armorer fully intended to cold-cock the youngster and pack him out on his back if he had to.

But Dean held his position, his only expression a tight grimace. "Dad and Jak have been up against a lot longer odds than this."

"That's right," J.B. answered, but he knew he'd have been hard-pressed to figure out exactly when at the moment.

"Ryan's going back for Krysty," Mildred said.

J.B. considered that. "Top of the building, they might be able to hold on for a while. Mebbe get lucky and find a way down inside it."

"Could be whatever's inside is every bit as bad as what's outside it," Mildred pointed out.

"Let's not be so bastard hopeful," J.B. said.

"I'm stating facts, John." Mildred turned her accusing gaze on him. "Those are your friends down there. Our friends. We can't just give them up."

"We aren't," J.B. protested. "But we stick to Ryan's plan."

Mildred turned away from him.

J.B. felt himself grow cold inside. Not many had gotten past the hardened exterior he'd manufactured for himself. Traveling Deathlands as he had, he knew acquaintances came and went on a regular basis.

But he cared about Mildred. Their relationship wasn't as open as Ryan and Krysty's because he was a very private person, but it was more open, more true, than anything the Armorer had ever had before. He also cared what Mildred thought about him.

Still, he didn't defend himself. Talking about things wasn't in his nature. He held the Uzi in his hands, letting its familiar hard lines comfort him. He turned his attention to the riders Dean had spotted earlier. Pride touched him when he noticed Dean was still watching the riders instead of peering through the tumbledown buildings trying to spot his father. The boy had learned well that his attention had to be centered on things he could do something about.

The riders had halted some fifty yards away, creating a ragged semicircle of horses and men. Dust kicked up around the animals' hooves, drifting toward the ville on the brewing storm winds.

J.B. studied the riders, reading them as a baron's raiding force. They dressed well and carried armament enough to guarantee few would dare to cross them.

"Anybody know who's a baron in these parts?" the Armorer asked.

Dean shook his head, not looking in J.B.'s direction, either.

Mildred didn't bother to answer.

"The talkative fellow we chanced to have a discourse with yesterday," Doc replied in a quiet voice that barely carried above the baying of the hounds, "mentioned that there were no barons around Idaho Falls that he knew of. This territory was reputed to be free, except for the gangs of coldhearts and clutches of civilians who claimed parcels of it for themselves. But he did also state that he'd seen men reputing themselves to be in the employ of Baron Shaker."

"Shaker?" The name meant nothing to J.B. But then barons rose and fell virtually overnight in the rougher areas out west. The region wasn't anything like the East Coast baronies.

"That is the name," Doc answered. "Unless I do disremember."

"That man say anything about what Baron Shaker might want here?"

"No, just that the baron's men possess the appearance of knowing exactly what it is that they're searching for. And that they don't intend to leave without it."

A baron's business, J.B. knew from firsthand experience, was usually deadly. As he watched, the leader of the group evidently made the decision about what they were going to do.

The riders split into two equal groups and spurred their mounts. The ones who had longblasters brandished them. They rode along the outer edges of the ville, but left no doubt that they were converging on the basin where Ryan and Jak had gone. They numbered nearer thirty than twenty, but J.B. hadn't been able to get an accurate count, either.

Both halves of the group left swirling dust trails in their wake.

"By all appearances," Doc stated, "those riders seem to be in a hurry. They lack even a veneer of quietude."

The Armorer turned his attention back to the building Ryan had chosen as his advance point for the scouting mission. "Yeah, but mebbe they're going to be enough of a diversion to allow us to get the others out of there."

"Chem storm's not going to give us many alternatives," Mildred said. "We stay out here, that storm will strip us down to our bones in minutes. The forest won't give us any protection. Unless we find a place to hole up."

"Only good places to hole up nearby," Dean told her, "are those buildings ahead of us."

J.B. nodded. All things considered, there really was no choice. "Let's go." He was the first one through the broken window, letting the Uzi dangle from the shoulder strap as he climbed down the uneven brick wall using his boot toes and fingers.

Before he reached the ground, a forked tongue of purple lightning slashed across the sky, followed immediately by a rolling cannonade of thunder.

Chapter Four

Ryan slid the Steyr's strap over his shoulder as he rounded the building where he'd left Krysty. A crumpled iron fire escape sprawled over the back of the building, forming a leaning cage of iron bars and steps that allowed him to run up the structure. It would put him near the top of the building.

In the past, the fire escape had hung on the building. Now it was loosely secured, vibrating as he slammed his boots against it.

The dogs raced through buildings as they sought their prey, and they drove more ghoulies out of their hiding places. The ghoulies fought back, swinging their home-made weapons and screaming hysterically in their shrill, gibbering voices. The dogs attacked mercilessly, tearing great hunks of flesh from the ghoulies with their flashing white teeth. The Slaggers trailed behind, getting closer. They cut down any ghoulies who crossed their path, filling the air with the yammering noise of blasterfire.

Jak stayed close behind Ryan, having an easier time scrambling through the lopsided fire escape because of his smaller size and incredible agility.

A pair of curs scampered up slabs of concrete near the fire escape, then vaulted through the bars, landing only a few feet ahead of Ryan, scrambling to regain their balance on the uneven steps.

Shifting with uncanny speed, the lead mutt threw itself

at Ryan, its mouth spread open to reveal the glistening fangs.

Ryan threw up an arm, managing to get it under the big animal's muzzle rather than shoving it into the dog's mouth. The fangs snapped together, missing the one-eyed man's face by inches. The dog's fetid breath swirled around Ryan, almost foul enough to make him nauseous.

The sheer weight and strength possessed by the animal pressed Ryan back as it dug its back legs against the steps. Ryan strained, levering his arm under the animal's muzzle, deliberately putting all his pressure against the dog's throat to close down its breathing passage.

The animal remained determined to reach him. The jaws continued to angrily snap at him, scattering hot spittle across his face. The second dog surged forward, as well, sidling in beside the first.

Ryan slipped his panga free of its sheath, fisting it in his free hand so the blade pointed down instead of up. More of the dogs followed along beside the fire escape now. One of them leaped for the iron structure, but it rebounded from the other dogs and tumbled eight feet to the ground.

Jak's .357 blaster roared to life behind Ryan. The big hollow booms echoed between the buildings. The roll of shots was punctuated by yelps of pain, and curses from men Ryan assumed were Slaggers.

Twisting to put his back against the fire escape, the one-eyed man used it as a brace, then pushed against the lead dog harder. Grudgingly the animal bent, exposing its side. Ryan thrust at once, sinking the panga between the cur's ribs to pierce its heart and lungs.

The dog jerked as if hit by an electric current from a wag battery, then fell back. The one-eyed man closed a fist in the loose flesh of the animal's neck and heaved it over the side through the bars of the fire escape.

The dead dog dropped onto a small knot of curs leaping up at the fire escape, knocking several of them away.

A moment later, Ryan booted the second animal from the fire escape as well, then charged up the steps again. Slaggers scattered around the ground below them, firing up into the iron structure.

Ryan sheathed the panga and drew the 9 mm blaster. He tracked his targets automatically, squeezing the trigger quickly.

The bullets took out a trio of Slaggers, punching them to the ground.

"Too many," Jak stated.

"I know." Ryan kept firing, no longer hitting the Slaggers easily because they'd gone to ground as soon as they realized how well he could shoot. Sparks leaped from the rust-red iron bars of the fire escape, raked by the Slagger gunfire.

Jak dumped the empty shells from the .357, scattering brass across the steps. He reloaded quickly, his nimble fingers searching for bullets in the secret pockets in his clothing.

Reaching the top of the fire escape, Ryan saw that it ended nearly ten feet from the side of the building. From the ground, he hadn't been able to discern that. At the top now, the fire escape also swayed sickeningly from his and Jak's combined weight.

Ryan paused only a moment at the top. The end of the structure was nearly four feet taller than the roof of the building. He scanned the rooftop, wondering where Krysty was and why she wasn't providing covering fire.

Then he saw her prostrate body lying facedown on the roof. Her limbs lay twisted in awkward positions.

Ryan's heart turned cold in his chest, and he stopped breathing as he looked at the woman.

"Ryan," Jak said behind him, "got move. Otherwise, chilled here and now."

Getting the sway of the fire escape locked into his reflexes, Ryan leaped toward the building. He almost made it, but fell short of getting most of his body weight on the rooftop. Gravity pulled at him, dragging him down. He fell, then caught himself with his free hand.

By the time he pulled himself back up to the rooftop, Jak landed in an economical roll and came up on his feet. The albino raised the .357 in both hands, swinging the barrel to cover the rooftop.

Ryan raced to Krysty's side, knowing some of the Slaggers and the dogs were making their way up the fire escape, as well. He knelt beside the redhead and placed a hand on her shoulder, looking her over to see where she'd been wounded.

There didn't appear to be a mark on her.

Before Ryan had a chance to guess at what had happened to her, three growling dogs erupted from the top of the fire escape, jockeying for position. One of them gathered enough courage to fling itself across the distance.

Surprisingly the animal landed almost entirely on the rooftop. It held on with its front legs and whined loudly as its back legs pedaled frantically against the side of the wall below.

Ryan lifted the SIG-Sauer and lowered the sights over the animal's head. He squeezed the trigger, and a hollow-point bullet pulped the dog's head in a bloody spray that whipped over the other animals behind it.

The dog died without a sound and toppled from the rooftop.

Ryan continued to fire, raking the fire escape with the pistol until it cycled dry. Through the haze of blue gun smoke the cheap reload cartridges made, he watched another dog drop in its tracks while others retreated.

Jak ran a quick circuit of the rooftop and came back. "All around us."

Ryan put a fresh magazine into the SIG-Sauer and pocketed the empty. One of the things he'd hoped to find in Idaho Falls was a new supply of magazines for the weapon and military-issue 9 mm rounds left over from before the skydark. He was down to three magazines for the blaster, and in a sustained firefight he didn't have time to keep feeding fresh cartridges into magazines.

He glanced at the rooftop-access door in the center of the building. The air-conditioning units and other HVAC equipment had long since been stripped from the rooftop, harvested for the compressors and other salvageable parts, as well as for the metal itself. A lead-filled pipe was easy to make, and could be a hell of a weapon in close quarters.

"Get the door open," he told Jak.

The albino nodded and hurried away.

During the search earlier, Ryan had noticed that it was stuck. The lock had been ripped from the door, but the collapse of the building had caused the door to jam. He'd left it alone then, figuring it served to contain whatever lurked below. But now it offered a possible escape route.

With the loaded blaster in one fist, Ryan grabbed Krysty by the shoulder and rolled her over.

She twisted bonelessly, and the loose way she moved made him certain she was dead.

The breath caught in Ryan's throat as he stared down at his lover's pale face. Then he noticed her breasts rise with a drawn breath, and he began to breathe again himself. Gently he reached toward her face, cupping it in his callused hand.

"Wake up," he said.

Her eyelids jerked, then flew backward to reveal the bloodshot whites of her eyes. The irises rolled back up into her head. She convulsed, like someone near to drowning just coming back to take his or her first breath.

"Krysty," Ryan said hoarsely. He patted her cheek tenderly but with force enough to rock her head slightly. "You've got to get up."

Abruptly she sat up, her eyes snapping into focus like electronic sights on a war wag. "Do not presume to touch me again, whoreson!"

DEAN RAN POINT for the companions as they sped back into the collection of gutted buildings. He kept the Browning Hi-Power in his fist and worked on keeping his mind clear, as well. Gunfire cracked and echoed between the structures. The hounds' baying sent a chill down his back.

"Slow down, Dean!" Mildred yelled at him from behind. "This isn't a race."

Changing his stride, Dean made for an L-shaped corner of a building foundation sticking up from the weed-covered ground. He hunkered down behind it and studied the broken terrain in front of him.

The baron's riders had closed on the coldhearts, splitting the groups off into miniature battlefields. Both sides knew each other from the sound of the shouted oaths and vehemence they exhibited in their efforts to kill one another. But neither side appeared to be suicidal, taking cover where they found it and trying to get a better position. The dogs also became a factor, charging in under the jumbled mess of broken rock and attacking from the rear. Where most of the coldhearts' weapons were single shot and single action, Baron Shaker's men carried a number of semiautomatic rifles and handblasters.

The coldhearts tried to form a skirmish line, but the best

they could do was slow the advance of the riders. However, as the Slaggers drew more deeply into the ville toward the junkyard of dead wags, they held back the riders' advance with increasing success.

"Damn," Mildred gasped as she reached the foundation remnant. "You call that a trot? I distinctly remember John telling you to strike a reasonable pace." Her words were broken up by her struggles to catch her breath.

Dean wasn't even breathing hard. "I can't help it if I move so quick."

"You run off and get your ass shot up, you won't be so damn proud of being a speed demon," Mildred told him.

A gray furred shape sprang from the other side of the foundation, scrabbling at the irregular surface of the mortar chunk with its black claws. The jaws were open wide, revealing the pink gums and white fangs.

Dean moved without thinking. He grabbed Mildred by the shoulder and shoved her to the side, out of the dog's leap.

The animal hit the ground on all four legs and wheeled to the attack again immediately.

Lifting the Hi-Power, Dean shoved the blaster into the cur's maw and pulled the trigger. The bullet punched a hole in the back of the creature's head, slamming it down to the ground in convulsive shudders.

"Good to move fast, mebbe." Dean didn't bother wiping the dog's blood and spit from his arm.

"Yeah." Mildred took his arm and examined it. "That dog break the skin?"

"No. It didn't have the chance."

"I'm going to check it later," Mildred told him. "If that animal had rabies, you're going to be in a lot of trouble."

Dean didn't worry about it. They still had to see if they lived much past the next few minutes.

Doc and J.B. joined them in short order. The four of them automatically spread out to provide overlapping fields of fire from their position.

"Have you seen friend Ryan?" Doc asked. A pallor had settled over his features from the past exertions, turning his color ashen.

"No," Mildred said.

Dean shook his head, not trusting his voice. Back before he'd learned Ryan still lived, after his mother, Sharona, had died, running had been a lot simpler because there had been no one else to worry about. Now he had a family, and all the anxiety that went with it.

"Top of the building," J.B. said quietly. "Him and Jak made it."

Dean looked back at the building, noting the activity of the baron's riders and the coldhearts swarming the area. Getting to his father and the others was going to be hard. He dropped the magazine from the Hi-Power and replaced the spent cartridge with one from a pocket.

Lightning seared the sky again, and thunder pealed.

"Lot of people between us and them," the Armorer went on. "None of them are going to be considered friendlies. They get in your face, any of them, put them down quick."

"That is one of the liberties of being surrounded by one's enemies," Doc said. He eared back the hammer on the Le Mat blaster. "You can shoot wherever you may without fear of hitting a kindred soul. However, I must hasten to admit I am reminded of General George Armstrong Custer's last words while at Little Big Horn. He gave a wry smile. "Damn, that is a lot of Indians."

"Doc," Mildred said.

"Yes, dear lady."

"Keep your trap shut. I don't know how much of your enthusiasm I can bear."

"Dean," J.B. said before Mildred or Doc could say anything else.

"Yeah."

"Ready to take point again?"

"Yeah."

"Mebbe a little slower this time." J.B. shoved his chin at a building adjacent to the one Ryan had chosen. "We go there first. Set up a line of retreat. Let Ryan know soon as we can. Things go all the way to shit, we dig ourselves in, tooth and toenail, and wait out the storm and the fight."

Dean nodded, then took off. He stayed low, tracking the other combatants out on the field.

FOR A MOMENT, Krysty thought she was caught in one of the nightmares often induced by the mat-trans units. She stood in a hellish land filled with gaping pores that spewed sulfurous fumes and boiling rust-colored water that made her think of old blood.

Her clothes and hair stayed plastered to her body. She felt for her blaster, but her holster at her side was empty. A vague memory twisted inside her head, and she thought she heard Ryan's voice somewhere off in the distance. A chill ran through her despite the steamy heat flooding the land.

She struggled, trying to remember whatever it was she had forgotten. Moving slowly through the hissing geysers of steam and water, she waited for the rest of the nightmare to manifest itself. The jumps through the mat-trans units were seldom easy.

Then she recalled her conversation with Phlorin, recalled how she had seemed to fall into herself.

A nearby geyser exploded, showering her with a deluge of scalding liquid and burning rock fragments that embedded in her flesh. She screamed in pain and began backing away, brushing at her arms and face with her hands.

Instead of feeling the chunks of rocks in her skin, though, she felt only smooth, unblemished flesh. She stared at her open hands in front of her, fully expecting to see them covered with blood.

They were clean.

Even as the realization hit her, Krysty felt the pain leave her body. Only a few heartbeats later, so did the sensation of the burning heat.

She stopped, suddenly realizing where she had to be because there was no other place she could have gone after Phlorin had ripped through her mind. She stared around her, taking in the geyser activity. Marshaling her courage, she thrust her hand into a geyser of steaming water that shot up within arm's reach.

None of the heat touched her. Likewise, none of the water touched her, either. The geyser bubbled and hissed against her hand, jetting through it in streams. As if she were some kind of illusion.

"Gaia!" Krysty said, realizing then what must have happened. "Earth Mother, don't let this be true!"

The burbling geyser continued blasting water through her hand as if it weren't there. She didn't exist. Phlorin had trapped her inside her own mind.

Krysty closed her eyes and concentrated, listening for Ryan's voice again, letting it be her beacon to bring her back to herself. She knew she had to hurry because she could sense what Phlorin was prepared to do to him.

Chapter Five

Astonished by the deep timber in Krysty's voice, as well as by the raw hatred, Ryan barely managed to turn his head to the side as she backhanded him. The blow carried incredible force. On occasion, Krysty was able to tap into a strength much greater than anything human, but only during times of intense stress, or life or death, calling on Gaia's name.

She was tapped in now.

Ryan flew backward, his ears ringing with the impact as his teeth snapped together, slicing deeply into his cheek. The taste of blood filled his mouth. Nearly twenty feet away, his body aching all over, he pushed himself up, gazing at the redhead.

She stood uncertainly, as if getting her land legs after a long time at sea. She gazed at him as if she didn't know him.

"What the hell is wrong with you?" Ryan demanded, barely keeping control over the anger that flooded his vision with fiery red mist. He stood with effort, his legs still weak under him.

"Stay away," Krysty warned in that terrible voice. She drew a hunting knife from her belt, ignoring the pistol on the rooftop beside her.

Bullets chopped into the pebble-and-tar surface, leaving pockmarks behind as lightning flashed overhead. Thunder hammered the dark heavens.

Ryan saw the wild look in his lover's eyes and knew she wasn't herself. He maintained his distance, but he spoke to her in a softer tone. "Krysty, it's me, Ryan."

"Stay away from me."

"Don't you remember?"

For a moment, Krysty's face softened, and uncertainty filled her expression. "Ryan?" Her voice sounded more normal, just strained.

"Yes." Ryan took a step toward her and kept closing. He also kept the SIG-Sauer in his hand. He didn't want to use it, but he knew he wasn't strong enough to take Krysty hand to hand with Gaia's strength fueling her. "What's wrong?"

"Head hurts," she replied in her normal voice. She coiled her free hand up in her sentient hair, pulling at it as tears pooled in her eyes. "Hurts real bad."

"The voice?" Ryan kept moving, getting closer.

"Yes." Krysty gasped in pain. "Said her name was Phlorin. Said she was one of the Chosen. Told me she was dying."

"You still hear her?"

"Not hear her," Krysty disagreed. "She's here with me. Inside my head. Tried to trap me there, tried to make me think I was going through a jump nightmare and wasn't really here, or there, at all. Trying to make me do things even now."

"Make her go away."

"I can't." Krysty shifted, jerking again, a harsh light suddenly filling her green eyes. She took a quick step back, bringing up the hunting knife, the edged side of the blade on top. Giving no indication, she moved into the attack, sending the knife streaking toward Ryan's abdomen.

He batted her hand away with his palm, blocking the

thrust and automatically raised the SIG-Sauer. He stopped short of bashing her in the face through sheer willpower.

She drew the knife back, her features writhing with mixed emotions. Before she could swing again, she collapsed to the ground and lost consciousness.

Jak stood behind her, his .357 still raised where he'd slammed the barrel against the back of her head. "Apologize later," he offered. "If live."

Ryan nodded, his free hand snaking out a short length of leather piggin strings from his coat. A slipknot held a coiled noose ready. He fit the noose around Krysty's wrists and pulled them tight while Jak fired rounds at the fire escape, picking off dogs and sending men ducking for cover.

The Slaggers had abandoned the direct approach up the fire escape, but Ryan noticed one of them had climbed on top of a building adjacent to the one they were on. The coldheart had a rifle and had just settled into a position as Ryan finished securing Krysty's hands.

"Let's go," the one-eyed man said, scooping the woman from the rooftop and slinging her over one shoulder. He staggered for a moment under her weight, still slightly dazed from the backhanded blow his lover had dealt him.

"Door open," Jak called. He picked up Krysty's knife and blaster and tucked them away. "Cover back." He broke open the .357's cylinder and shook out the empties.

Ryan jogged toward the open rooftop-access door. Krysty's deadweight slammed against his back as he stepped inside and started down the staircase.

"JOHN!" MILDRED CALLED out in warning.

J.B. spun quickly and brought up the Uzi. He caressed the trigger and sent a 3-round burst into the chest of the horse closing in on him at breakneck speed.

The horse's rider stayed too low in the saddle to provide a good target, and J.B. knew from experience that shooting a horse in the chest didn't always stop it. The bullets didn't stop the animal now, or even seem to slow it. It charged at the Armorer without pause, bringing its rider close enough to swing at the Armorer with the homemade machete he carried.

J.B. blocked the swing with his Uzi, holding the machine pistol in both hands. He didn't like using the weapon like that because there was too much chance of damage. The impact's vibration ran up his arms, then the horse thundered past.

"Meyers! Dawson!" the rider called out. "Got some outlanders here! Mebbe some of them that Baron Sha—" His head snapped back suddenly, and a fountain of blood gushed from his temple. He toppled from the dying horse, the animal starting down itself now.

J.B. glanced over at Mildred, saw her in the classic Olympic shootist's stance. The Armorer dipped his head and touched the brim of his hat.

Doc ambushed another rider by stepping from the shelter of the broken corner of a nearby building. He lowered the Le Mat blaster and let go with the shotgun barrel. The tight cluster of pellets caught the man full in the chest and blew him out of the saddle.

Moving quickly, J.B. stepped out and grabbed the loose reins of the fear-maddened horse. Lightning strobed across the sky again. The thunderous boom that cracked the air a few seconds later drowned out even the gunshots scattered around the area.

J.B. held on to the reins in one tight fist, watching for other riders. He clucked to the frightened animal out of habit, not really believing it could hear him over the thunder or through the haze of fear that filled it. He let it have its head a moment and ran along beside it. When he had its pace and rhythm, he reached for saddle horn with his hand holding the reins and shoved a foot into the stirrup. He pulled himself up gracefully. Before he'd ridden with the Trader and War Wag One, he'd been accustomed to horses back in Cripple Creek.

He gained control over the animal, feeling the material of his pants sticking to the blood covering the saddle. Pulling the horse around, he reached up and snugged his hat on more tightly.

"John!" Mildred called.

"Find Ryan," J.B. shouted back. "I'm going to cover you."

Mildred stood there uncertainly for a moment.

"Go, dammit," the Armorer snarled. "We're shit out of places to run to." He pulled at the reins again, manhandling the horse and turning it in a tight circle.

Mildred broke into a sprint, heading toward the building where Ryan had been earlier. Doc stayed close behind her, but Dean balanced on a jumble of loose brick and mortar, poised like a young and hungry wolf.

"Go on, boy," J.B. commanded, knowing the term would sting Dean.

Dean ignored the order until hoofbeats neared the area, then he vanished inside the rubble.

J.B. kicked his mount in the sides. The horse bolted again, glad to have its head. He pulled the horse into an intercept course with the hoofbeats. The battle couldn't last much longer, he knew. The storm would see to that.

Two riders came through the gap between the buildings. They both carried rifles, but one of them J.B. identified as a .22-caliber rimfire single shot. It was a dangerous weapon in its own right, but the man carrying the assault rifle next to him was the greater threat.

J.B. leaned forward, keeping himself low, and pushed the Uzi between the horse's peaked ears. He squeezed the trigger, starting the burst at the man's crotch and riding the recoil up.

The rider jerked with the impacts of the bullets. Without a word, he slid from the saddle. The other man got the .22 rifle up quickly enough to loose a shot.

J.B. felt the small-caliber bullet lightly graze his leg, trailing fire after it. He tried to wheel around in the saddle, but the other rider was past him before he could. Pulling on the reins fiercely, he managed to bring the animal's head around.

The man with the .22 rifle levered it open and was thumbing a shell into the barrel. Before he finished, Dean stepped from hiding and fired the Browning Hi-Power at almost point-blank range. The boy had ran along the ridgeline, remaining hidden from his prey until the last moment.

Before the dead man had time to fall from the saddle, Dean vaulted aboard the horse. The animal skittered in fear, almost causing itself to fall. Dean seized the reins and control of the horse. He wheeled it around to face J.B. "Figured two of us might create a better diversion than one," the boy said.

"There's no room for a hero out here," the Armorer said. But inside he had to admire the kid's guts.

Dean didn't respond to the sarcastic remark. He shoved the corpse from the saddle and slid into place. "Got a plan?"

"Stay alive," J.B. replied, "and chill anybody who goes after the others. Pretty simple."

"Going to need shelter," Dean said, pulling his horse onto the same path J.B.'s was following. "That acid rain will come down and strip our bones clean."

The Armorer had no argument for that.

"Staying out here in one of these buildings," Dean went on, "we're just going to trap ourselves."

"Yeah."

"So that leaves only one place we can go and mebbe put some distance from here." Dean nodded at the junkyard ahead of them. "Those stacks of wags will give us some cover to get out of the rain and keep moving at the same time. It's big enough and long enough that we can get lost enough to get away from these people."

J.B. couldn't fault the boy's logic. Dean was growing up, and he'd always been a survivor. "Those coldhearts are nestled up in there like blind rattlers. And they'll know the terrain."

"Figured mebbe we'd bust up their nest." The boy reached inside his shirt. "I know you don't go anywhere without grens if you can help it."

The Armorer kept the thin grin from his face with effort. "As a matter of fact, I have a couple I've been holding back." He reached inside his coat and took out the explosives. Leaning forward, he dropped one into Dean's outstretched hand. "Get in close as you can, then toss it in. And try not to get your ass shot off."

Dean laughed as he wheeled his mount. "It's going to be a hot-pipe ride, J.B." He kicked the horse in the sides and shot off.

Caught off guard, the Armorer urged his horse into a gallop. Dean was right about the junkyard being the only real path to safety, but getting to it was going to be dangerous. He changed magazines in the Uzi, loading up his last full one. The effort was going to be all-or-nothing.

And the rain was going to fall on whoever didn't make it.

RYAN LIFTED THE SIG-SAUER and aimed it at the moving shadow that stepped inside the door.

"Don't shoot," Mildred said breathlessly, lowering her own pistol.

The one-eyed man continued down the steps, hustling, listening to the gunfire echoing around the rubble outside and wondering what it was going to mean for the companions. "Told you to stay back."

"We couldn't," Mildred argued. "The rain was coming. We wouldn't have gotten to safety before it would have been on us."

"Where's J.B. and Dean?" Ryan asked. The floor was covered with rubble from the pockmarked ceiling overhead, and a half-dozen old campfires littered the area.

"John caught a horse," Mildred explained. "He stayed back to cover our retreat from the riders."

Doc cut loose with the scattergun, blowing away a pair of dogs that had slunk close to the building. "Get back, you miserable Baskerville scion." He broke open the Le Mat and reloaded the shotgun barrel.

"What riders?" Ryan asked, crossing to the doorway.

"A dozen or so were approaching the ville," Mildred said. "We got the impression they were a baron's men. They appear to be outfitted well, besides the horses. And they're organized."

"There aren't any barons around here." Ryan glanced out the door and saw three of the riders Mildred was talking about. The air smelled sour with the coming rain, burning the sensitive membranes of his nasal passages. "Where's Dean?"

"My dear Ryan," Doc said, "Young Dean was behind me but a moment earlier. It was not until we arrived here that I found he had departed my company."

"Departed?" Ryan turned on the old man, a red mist spreading before his eye.

Doc shook his head, his craggy face showing discomfort. "Not departed as in dead, dear friend. Just not with us when we—"

"Dean with J.B.," Jak called down. The albino was still on the second story, peering carefully through one of the empty windows. "There." He pointed with his chin, one hand holding the .357 while the other held several of his throwing blades.

Ryan turned in the direction the albino indicated, catching sight of J.B. and Dean bursting free of the clutter and racing across the open space.

Two Slaggers rose up in front of Ryan barely forty feet away, raising their weapons to fire at the Armorer and the boy. Ryan lifted his SIG-Sauer and killed them both before they got a shot off.

"Going junkyard," Jak said.

With the coming rain and the threat of the Slaggers and mystery riders around them, Ryan understood the thinking. The junkyard offered the companions the only real hope of getting out of the area safe from the elements and the hostiles.

"So are we," he stated. He shifted Krysty's weight across his shoulder and started out. The broken terrain proved treacherous, and the extra weight of his lover made it even more so. Even with his skill at staying on his feet, the one-eyed man had trouble with his footing.

Then came the sound of wag engines blasting to life, rumbling from deep inside the junkyard.

Chapter Six

Dean turned in the direction of the wag engines, staring into the depths of the junkyard. The sketchy plan he and J.B. had made had just gone to hell.

Movement drew his eyes to the Jeep that burst out of hiding under a pile of smashed wags, flanked by two motorcycles. All of the vehicles looked as if they'd been cobbled together out of spare parts, stripped of any unnecessary cosmetic parts and reduced to skeletal remnants.

Gunners riding in the back of the Jeep and on back of the motorcycles cut loose at the two riders.

Pulling on the reins, Dean broke off the direct approach. But going back didn't offer any relief, either, because the baron's riders were closing in. A line of bullets chopped into the dirt near the horse's hooves, sliced through the air only inches from Dean's head.

He kicked the horse in the sides again, urging it back into a full gallop toward the oncoming riders. He rode low, presenting as small a target as he was able, and he got past them.

Blasterfire from the coldhearts lashed into the baron's men, emptying two of the saddles. A bullet cut through Dean's shirt, and he felt the heat of its passing. He spotted J.B. to his left. The Armorer exchanged shots with a mounted man, but neither of them appeared to be hit.

Cutting hard to the right, Dean guided the horse in a wide loop back to the fence surrounding the junkyard. One of the motorcycles pulled away from the Jeep and pursued him. Urging his mount to greater speed, the boy raced up a small promontory overlooking the fenced area.

"Go!" he urged the horse, lying low enough that he was screaming in the animal's ear.

On top of the incline, the horse found it had no way to go but forward. Dean felt the big animal's muscles bunch, then it hurled them into the air.

At first, Dean thought the horse was going to clear the fence. But its back hoof got caught in the strands of barbed wire at the top. Coming down off balance, the horse rolled on its side with a grunting snort of pain.

Dean cleared the saddle, rolling himself. He came up on his knees as the motorcyclists made the same jump he'd attempted with the horse. They had more power, though, and cleared the fence with feet to spare.

Spitting out dirt and blood from a busted lip, Dean targeted the motorcycle in the air. He aimed for the center of the men, and for the gas tank. He believed he hit both, but the sudden eruption of the gas tank let him know he'd gotten the fuel tank for certain.

The motorcycle turned into fireball that careened in a short arc, then smashed into the ground front wheel first. The coldheart who'd been driving screamed in hoarse fear and flapped at the flames licking at his crotch.

Dean ignored the man and turned his attention to his second adversary. The man landed in a heap, but he came up with his revolver in his hand, spitting lead. Coolly the younger Cawdor stroked the Browning's trigger and put a round into the man's face, sealing his fate.

Dean fired two more rounds into the burning man to put him down. Pushing himself up, he raced back toward the entrance to the junkyard. Another sonic boom of thunder cascaded over the area, trapped between the stacks of dead wags filling the junkyard.

Movement ahead and to Dean's left drew his attention. He barely kept his finger from squeezing the Browning's trigger as the dirty face of a blond-haired little girl looked up at him.

"Holy shit!" Dean's hand shook as he took the gun sight off her. "What do you think you're—?"

The man leaped at him, a lock-back knife bared in his fist and a look of desperate fear on his face.

"WHAT'S WRONG WITH HER?" J.B. asked, nodding at Krysty. Her tied hands and feet drew the Armorer's eyes as he sat astride the lathered horse.

"Later," Ryan said, swinging Krysty up to his friend.

J.B. grabbed the woman's belt and heaved her over the saddle in front of him. The horse shied at the extra weight, stamping its feet.

"In the meantime," Ryan said, "don't listen to her whatever she says. Keep her tied." It bothered him to say that, but the instructions might keep Krysty and the Armorer alive. He glanced out at the open space in front of the junkyard. The baron's men and the Slaggers had declared all-out war on each other, and it was difficult to tell who was getting the better end of it. Horses and men lay scattered across the torn, bloody earth. "Where's Dean?"

"Saw him get across the fence," J.B. said. "Chilled two coldhearts and a motorcycle."

"Junkyard's the only chance we've got to remain mobile and get out of the rain."

J.B. nodded. "That's what Dean and I figured." He revealed the gren tucked inside his shirt. "We were going to soften them up, get them used to the idea, but they came at us before we were ready."

"We'll do it now," Ryan said. He put away the SIG-Sauer and slid the Steyr off his shoulder. Gazing across to the entrance of the junkyard, he knew it was still a lot of ground to cover. "Get Krysty across first. We'll follow."

The Armorer nodded, but his eyes cut to Mildred.

"It's okay, John," the woman said. "I'll be along."

"She'll make it," Ryan said.

"I'll be holding down the fort."

"Do that. But keep an eye peeled for those bastard dogs. I don't think we've killed them all out yet."

J.B. pulled on the reins and turned the horse. The animal's footing was no longer certain, but it had heart. He put his heels to its sides and charged across the open space.

"Let's go," Ryan ordered. "Jak, you've got point. Mildred, you're after him, then Doc. I'm walking slack, but if you slow down out there, I'm going to kick your skinny ass all the way to that junkyard."

"Friend Ryan, these legs may well be old, but I wager you shall be eating my dust," Doc retorted. "Fear lends this old heart a certain alacrity in nearly every happenstance."

IT PROVED IMPOSSIBLE to run in a straight line. Ryan cursed the luck as they had to dodge dead men and horses, then the combatants.

They were halfway to the junkyard when the Slagger leader, Halleck, pointed to the small group of companions and shouted orders to his men. The baron's horsemen had retreated into the rubble and started picking off some of the Slaggers on foot. The withering fire from the horsemen cut into the numbers of the coldhearts and drove them back to cover.

The Jeep roared off in pursuit, streaking for the companions. Gunners in the back fired at will, but luckily the weapons were semiautomatics and no real time was taken to properly aim.

Ryan knew the companions would never make it before the Jeep caught up to them. He stood and brought the Steyr up to his shoulder, felt the buttstock caress the side of his face. He put the crosshairs over the driver's side of the windshield and squeezed the trigger.

But the uneven ground and the worn springs of the Jeep made the target more elusive. Three shots missed killing the driver, though he felt certain at least one of them had hit the female passenger. Then the Jeep was bearing down on him, taking away all margin for error.

"Fireblast." Ryan turned and ran, watching bullets pockmark the ground around him. The sour stink of the coming rain burned his nose with renewed vigor as he drew it deep into his lungs.

The Jeep bore down on him, and a pair of bullets ripped through his coat.

Ryan threw himself aside at the last moment. The wag's bumper slammed into him with bruising force, clipping him and driving him to the ground. He managed to hang on to the Steyr during his fall, but even as he reached his knees, his body protesting because the wind had been knocked out of him, he saw the wag bearing down on him again.

This time it wouldn't miss.

"STOP, YOU STUPE BASTARD, or I'll blast your triple-ugly face off!" Dean ducked under the man's knife arm and kicked his leg hard enough to topple him. Before the man could get back up, Dean screwed the barrel of the Hi-Power into the side of his neck.

"Don't kill my pa!" the little girl screamed. Tears fell from her blue eyes. "Don't kill my pa!"

If it hadn't been for the little girl's pleas, Dean thought

he might have pulled the trigger. True, the man who'd jumped him didn't look like one of the coldhearts or the baron's horsemen, but the man had tried to chill him all the same.

He hesitated, then cursed at himself because he didn't think his father would have hesitated at all. Survival was self first, not the other guy.

Breathing hard, Dean looked square in the man's frightened eyes. "Your choice, mister. I chill you, I don't chill you, it's all the same to me. But you're going to leave her out here alone."

"You're not one of the Slaggers?" the man asked. He started to get up.

Dean leaned on the Browning more forcibly, making the point clearly. "Don't even know who the Slaggers are."

"They're the coldhearts," the little girl said. "They're the ones that brung us here."

Gunshots still echoed around them, mixed in with the thunder.

"If that's true," Dean told the man, "then mebbe we got a common problem."

"Mister, I just want to get my little girl out of here." Dirt stained the man's face, and it had been days since he'd shaved. His hair was long and his clothes were homespun. "We were on our way north. Got relatives up there. We lost Charity's mom a couple months ago, and I couldn't see a reason to hang around that Fiddler ville anymore. Thought mebbe things would be better back in the lands I knew best. We were following the river, same as some of these other folk, when those coldhearts jumped us and brought us here. That's the God's truth."

"How many are here?" Dean asked. His father had taught him the importance of getting as much information about a situation as he could. His eyes roamed the metallic caverns created by the dead wags.

"Coldhearts?"

"Yeah."

"Must be three, four dozen."

Dean knew it was considerably less than that now. He pulled the Browning's barrel out of the man's neck and glanced at the child. "I'm not going to kill your pa, little girl."

She continued to cry, wiping her face with the back of her hand. She carried a rag doll in the other.

"Okay if I get up now?" the man asked.

"Sure." Dean stepped back, giving himself room to move. He kicked the lock-back knife to the man with his boot toe.

The man pushed himself up and took the little girl in his arms. "I ain't no killer," the man said. "First time I ever drew a weapon on anybody."

"Every man's a killer," Dean said. "Sometimes he just doesn't meet his victim, that's all." He scanned the junkyard, spotting a mongrel hound slinking up beside a pile of wag parts. Moving the blaster, he shot the animal between the eyes, exploding its head. "Pick up your knife. You may need it." Then he hurried toward the entrance, watching J.B. come galloping through with Krysty across his saddle.

Dean's heart thudded in his chest.

RYAN DIVED, no longer able to twist away from the wag bearing down on him. He rolled over the dead horse in front of him, then scurried against the animal's back for shelter.

The wag didn't slow, smashing into the horse's huge corpse and rolling over it. The horse's ribs broke with fierce snaps, and trapped air in its lungs and intestines broke with liquid gurgles.

The tires pushed roughly across Ryan, but the wag's full weight never settled on him because of the horse. He rose to his knees and pulled the Steyr up again. Glaring through the open sights beneath the scope so he could snap-fire, he put a round through the chests of the two coldhearts in the back of the wag before anyone knew he was still alive.

Halleck spun in the passenger's seat, wiping the blood from his face that sprayed from the dead man falling toward him. "The fucker's still alive!" the coldheart leader snarled. "Turn this wag around!"

The wag driver turned hard left, pulling the vehicle around in a tight circle.

Ryan let the man come, narrowly missing Halleck with a shot. Then the driver was full in his sights. He squeezed the trigger and shot the man through the forehead.

Out of control, the wag continued hurtling forward. Halleck grabbed for the dead driver, trying to dislodge him from behind the wheel. It took him a handful of seconds to push the corpse out.

By that time, Ryan had reached the entrance to the junkyard. Dean and the rest of the companions were engaged in a brief firefight with dogs and coldhearts, both of which seemed to be in short supply.

He glanced up at the stacks of crushed wags that reached thirty feet tall. They created a maze across the junkyard. In places, some of them had fallen, toppling like dominoes to bring other stacks down with them. One toppled stack lay across a small building to the right of the entranceway.

Built under the tumbled wreckage, the building had become an armored fortification. Crushed wags covered the top and all sides except the front. Pieces of other wags had been dragged into position in front of the building, creating an armored shell, as well as camouflage.

The companions were scattered, facing the small building with the junkyard entranceway behind them and to the right. Doc and Jak lay hidden behind a wag twenty feet from J.B. and Mildred's position to Ryan's right. Dean crouched over Krysty protectively, the dead horse only an arm's reach away.

"Dark night," J.B. said when Ryan joined them. "Didn't see that bastard fortification until I was almost on top of it. Bastard shot my horse out from under me."

Ryan glanced at Krysty, saw how pale she looked.

"She's okay, Dad," Dean said.

The wag engine approached at high speed, throwing out rooster tails of dust behind it. Grimly Ryan realized that Halleck had left the entrance to the junkyard open on purpose. The horsemen had come hunting him, and he'd evidently been expecting them. The plan had been to drive the attackers into the junkyard, allowing them to think they were getting refuge from the chem storm, while actually they'd be stepping into a cross fire.

It was a good plan.

J.B. finished putting 9 mm rounds in a clip, then shoved the clip into the Uzi. "We can try to slip by them," he said, "but they've got a good position. Some people over there tried to get loose, but the gunners inside the building cut them down before they could get away."

"We can't stay pinned down here," Ryan said. He glanced around, noticing the scattering of human bones around the front of the junkyard for the first time. Most of them were nearly covered by the drifting sand and the flowered weeds that crawled up from the earth. All of them had bite marks on them.

Maybe the dogs were the only ones that ate the victims

that had been trapped in the cross fire before, but Ryan kept remembering the ghoulies.

"How many men inside the fort?" Ryan asked.

"Don't know for sure. A dozen mebbe." The Armorer looked up at him, then out at the wag where Halleck was calling to his men, gathering them to him. "They're not going to wait long out there. The chem storm doesn't give them much choice."

"Doesn't give us much choice, either," Ryan replied. He worked his way to the end of the broken wag, glancing briefly at Krysty. She slept, but her face showed tight lines, as if she was having a bad dream. "What about the people you said were in here?"

"Over there." J.B. nodded toward a recessed area on the other side of the space facing the fortified building. "Looks to be people the coldhearts captured."

"They are," Ryan replied. "Jak and I saw them earlier. Should be a woman among them. Name's Phlorin. I want her found."

"How do you know her?" Mildred asked.

"I don't," Ryan answered. "But she's what's wrong with Krysty."

"I'll find her, Dad," Dean said.

Ryan started to object, wanting Jak to do the search. But he saw the earnest look on his son's face.

"If she's the reason Krysty's tied up now, not being herself, then I'll make sure she's found quick," Dean promised.

"Do it, then," Ryan said. "But stay low."

Dean nodded and seemed to disappear into the ground near the overturned wag.

Ryan glanced back at the Jeep. Halleck was having problems of his own. The Slaggers weren't having much luck getting together without the baron's men shooting into them. The one-eyed man turned to the Armorer. "I'm going to need you to cover me."

"Kick in the door?" J.B. asked.

"I don't see another way." Ryan gestured to Jak, indicating that the albino should circle around the junkyard fort in the opposite direction. Ryan didn't have to tell him what they were going to do.

"If those other coldhearts attack while we're spread out," J.B. said, "we aren't going to be able to hold."

Ryan nodded tightly. "See you in a few." He moved out, finding cover where he could.

Chapter Seven

Ryan crept up on the side of the junkyard fort, the SIG-Sauer leading the way. The structure had enough wood content that he'd considered firing it and burning out the men inside. But that would have left the companions nowhere to go except deeper into the stacks of junked wags, where there were more dogs.

He glanced across the door and found Jak already poised on a section of the car above the fort. The view the men inside the building had was limited. They hadn't planned for a quarry that had time to think and move, or one that was used to moving so quickly.

Two windows, one on either side of the door, looked out over the junkyard. At Ryan's signal, Jak hung from his feet and leaned down to just past the top of the window. The albino opened fire at once, firing through all six rounds in quick succession. He pulled himself up only a second or two before return fire hammered the window's casement.

Spinning quickly, Ryan thrust the 9 mm blaster into the window. A man stood in front of him, his attention on the window Jak had shot through. Ryan fired his first round into the man's temple, emptying his skull in a crimson splash that stained the two men behind him. Two more pairs of shots, and the one-eyed man was certain three men were down inside the fort.

Jak had hit at least three himself, though one man continued to howl in pain.

Ryan's mind took in the details of the fort's interior as he fired, filing the information away. When the SIG-Sauer blew back empty, he was certain no more than three men remained alive inside the room. He spun toward the door instead of the side of the fort, ejecting the empty magazine and shoving a fresh one home.

The interior of the fort was little more than thirty feet to a side. All of it was open space, littered with pallets on the floor and a brace of hammocks in the far corner against the back wall.

Jak dropped into position through his window again and fired the .357 dry. Then he flipped to the ground, landing effortlessly on his feet on the other side of the door. "Two men left," he said, putting the knives away. "Back corners."

Ryan thumbed the slide release, sending it home with a metallic snap. Stepping forward, he turned and rammed his left shoulder into the door, putting all of his two-hundred-plus pounds behind the effort. It had been locked into place, but it hadn't been built strong enough to withstand the abuse he gave it. Hinges gave way, and he followed the door inside.

Smoke from homemade black powder hazed the room and filled it with a sulfuric stench.

A man in the back corner raised his weapon, screaming in rage and fear. His bullets struck the walls near Ryan.

Firing from the point, letting instinct be his guide, Ryan shot the man twice in the heart, relying on the blaster's stopping power to put the man down as he turned on the remaining coldheart.

The Slagger's weapon had evidently jammed. He flung himself forward, trying for one of the abandoned pistols of his comrades.

Ryan shot him through the head, watching in satisfaction

as the body quivered and lay still. He then turned his attention back to the companions outside. He waved them in, stepping outside the door.

Mildred came first, followed by Doc, who carried Krysty's unconscious body gently in his arms. J.B. stood guard as Dean got the coldhearts' prisoners moving. Two of the men carried a twisted old woman dressed in homespun breeches and a curious tunic.

Ryan studied the woman as the ex-prisoners neared. Her hair was as white as snow, and she looked ancient. Black eyes glittered behind the half-closed lids as they settled on Ryan's one blue eye.

Then the old woman smiled. "Ryan Cawdor."

"You don't know me."

"I do now," the woman replied. "Because Krysty does."

"Get her inside," Ryan growled.

The prisoners appeared hesitant to enter the fort. There were only nine of them left—four men, a little girl, a small boy and three women. Phlorin made four women.

"If you people want to stay out here," Ryan said, "that's fine by me. Take your chances with the chem storm and the coldhearts. But if you want to live, throw in with us."

"We get inside that building," one of the men said, "we'll be trapped like rats."

"Your decision," Ryan said coldly. "But when this door shuts, it's not opening again later if you decide you've changed your mind." He stepped over to join J.B., looking at Halleck and his group milling in the distance.

"The man's got a hard decision to make all of a sudden," J.B. said. A smile touched his lean face. "If he comes after us, he knows we aren't going to go down easy. And he's going to leave his flank open to the baron's men."

"Mebbe he'll make the right decision," Ryan said. He

watched the coldhearts. "When he does, the baron's men will follow him."

NONE OF THE PRISONERS decided they wanted to take their chances on their own in the junkyard. They filed into the fort and helped secure the building against the coming attack, using the meager furniture to block the door and partially cover the windows to leave makeshift blasterports.

Ryan started a fire in the fireplace, making sure the flue was open. Jak's preliminary exploration of the fireplace revealed that it was built under a shelf of flattened metal and couldn't be blocked up to smoke them out. They'd recovered two bows and quivers of arrows from the dead coldhearts. Dean had come up with the idea of wrapping pieces of shirts around the arrow shafts and soaking them with fuel they found in a cabinet at the back of the building. The rain might soak most things, but Ryan had noticed that some of the wags had interiors that looked easily flammable. It gave them another weapon in their arsenal.

"Still have two grens," J.B. said.

"That gives us an edge," Ryan agreed, "but that edge will come in the timing, as well." He kept the companions manning the windows and armed his makeshift troops from the dead coldhearts.

Then he put the men in the group to work with Jak and Dean, throwing out the stripped corpses. The bodies lay in front of the building, providing extra protection. The smell of fresh meat drew some of the dogs out of hiding. Two bolder animals approached the dead bodies and started to feast.

"Don't bite the hand that feeds you," Doc said in a soft voice. "But, by the Three Kennedys, what if it *is* the hand that feeds you? And the arm after that?"

After he was satisfied that they were as ready as they were going to be, Ryan crossed over to Mildred and Krysty.

The black woman had confiscated one of the pallets and had Doc place Krysty on it. Before she'd been cryogenically frozen and nuclear winter from the skydark had blown the candle out on the world for a time, she'd been a medical doctor. The problem was, they didn't have much in the way of med supplies.

"How is she?" Ryan asked.

"Still with us," Mildred replied.

Krysty twisted restlessly on the pallet, her mouth working. Doc approached and held one of her hands in his own, patting it gently. "Poor child. Whatever did happen to her, friend Ryan?"

"I'm not sure." Ryan quickly explained how Krysty had attacked him on the rooftop and told him about the woman trying to take over her mind.

"Some kind of psychic attack?" Mildred asked.

"She said that woman got into her mind," Ryan said. "Now I've got the woman."

Phlorin lay on a pallet across the room, bound hand and foot, a gag in her mouth. The woman had been shot in the chest, and Mildred had told Ryan the old woman was going to die. It was only a matter of time until she caught the last train to the coast.

"When Krysty wakes up, we'll see if we can get more answers." Ryan turned his attention to survival again. Saving Krysty only to have them all die in the junkyard was worthless.

"Ryan," J.B. called. "The coldhearts have decided to give it up. They're pulling out."

Ryan walked over to the window and peered out. The rain had started to fall now, coming down in a fine mist that had to be a big factor in Halleck's decision. The wag led the way back into the rubble of the buildings around the junkyard.

As soon as the Slaggers pulled back from the front of the junkyard, though, the horsemen rode through the entrance. Ryan counted over thirty men, then looked at J.B.

"Reinforcements, mebbe," the Armorer said. "The group we saw earlier could have been part of a bigger party. Blasterfire might have attracted them."

"Fireblast," the one-eyed man swore. "We know those men aren't here for us, and they're obviously not here for the coldhearts. Only leaves one thing."

J.B. nodded. "The people in here with us."

Ryan turned on the nine people across the room with the companions. "Any of you know these people out here?"

No one answered and no one moved.

"Get over here to the bastard window and look," Ryan commanded. "If you can't see them from in here, I'll give you a chance to see them up closer when I kick you out of this building." He meant it, too, because his own survival and that of the companions came first. It always did.

Every one of the adults they'd let into the building came up to the window and peered out. And all of them said they didn't know who the men were.

"Mebbe lying," Jak said after the last woman had walked away. "Or mebbe person baron's men look for dead out there and they not know."

"Mebbe," Ryan said, but the thought didn't ease his mind.

A flash of lightning zigzagged through the dark sky, then the heavens opened up and the chem storm howled across the broken face of the ville in wild fury. The acid rain pelted the ground hard enough to leave pockmarks against the dust, and it beat down the weeds that grew around the wrecked wags.

The horsemen spread out around the stacks of rusted wags. They dismounted and unfurled heavy canvas tarps to create tented areas out of the wags. In minutes, they and their animals were safely out of the storm, as well, though Ryan heard pain-filled curses as some of them were burned by the acid rain before they could get to shelter.

He watched the corpses of the coldhearts he and Jak had killed to gain control of the fort. The caustic precipitation ate into the flesh, causing ulcerous boils that burst when they pressed past the elasticity of dead skin. In minutes, the rain began to peel away the flesh, baring it to the white, gleaming bone beneath.

TEN MINUTES PASSED, and the chem storm beat into the ground, whipped against the piles of rusted wags and whistled mournfully through the twisted metal. It showed no signs of letting up. The baron's men remained in their makeshift shelters, but they kept a guard posted.

"We could perforate their provisional habitats," Doc suggested. "Mayhap the rain itself would do what threat of our combined gunplay cannot."

"More than likely," J.B. replied, "it'd just piss them off."

"Break them out of those tents," Ryan said, "gives them bastard few places to go for protection from the chem storm. Most likely place is this place."

"True, friend Ryan. But I heartily dislike feeling like Pooh in the honey jar trapped as we are in this place. No matter how humble an abode this may be, there is no place like home."

Ryan glanced at the old man and saw the familiar signs of dementia at the edges of Doc's gaze. "You just hold steady, Doc. We'll get out of this just fine. We've been in tighter spots than this."

Doc grinned, baring his strangely perfect teeth. "Yes, and Hillary always hated Bill for being reminded of that."

THE ACID RAIN CONTINUED drumming on the metal roof twenty minutes later. The stink of ozone from all the electrical activity mixed with the harsh stench of sulfur and other chems in the air, making it hard to breathe inside the fort.

"There's something else we didn't consider," J.B. said, "that might have brought the baron's men here."

"Phlorin," Ryan answered. "I've already been thinking about that."

The Armorer nodded. "No matter what it looks like now, that rain's going to let up sooner or later. And if we can get those people off our asses now, it would be a good thing."

"I want to make sure Krysty's going to be okay before we give that woman to the baron's people."

J.B. nodded. "Get it done."

Ryan kept the SIG-Sauer in his fist and drew the panga with his other hand. He approached the old woman lying on the floor and dropped into a squat beside her. "You and I are going to talk." He hooked a finger behind the gag in her mouth and pulled it below her chin. He deliberately let the cold steel of the panga's edge caress her throat with enough weight to draw a thin line of thick dark blood.

The woman's black eyes blazed. "There's nothing I have to say to you."

"Good," Ryan told her. "Means you're ready to listen. You've done something to that woman over there." He pointed at Krysty with the panga. "Fucked her head up somehow. I mean to see her back the way she's supposed to be." He freed the woman's left hand, then stepped on her wrist, trapping it against the earthen floor.

"And what are you going to do if I don't?" the old woman wheezed. Her trapped hand moved weakly, like a dying spider trying to scuttle into hiding.

Ryan was conscious of every eye in the room on him. If the other ex-prisoners had any idea what he was talking about, none of them showed it. "I'm going to whittle you down to a more manageable size," he told her roughly. "I know ways that can make your dying a long time in coming."

The woman laughed at him, her spittle laced with the blood from the wound in her chest. "Do you actually think you can frighten me, man?"

"Doesn't matter," Ryan answered in a flat voice. "I'm just telling you how it's going to be."

"Cut me if you wish." Phlorin coughed again, sputtering blood up through her thin blue lips. "I can put myself past the pain. And now that I have Krysty with me, I don't have to be alone when I die."

"I can throw you out there in that acid rain." Ryan stared hard into the woman's magnetic black gaze. "You'll be alone then."

"It won't matter. I've bonded myself with Krysty. She is a part of me now, and I am a part of her. There's nothing you can do to prevent that."

Ryan glanced over at Mildred.

"This woman's dying," Mildred said. "Even if I had all the supplies I'd need and we could guarantee that she wouldn't be moved for a few days, she won't make it."

"You see?" Phlorin taunted. "All you can do is hasten the inevitable. I'd consider it a favor. I don't like lying here, being weaker and more helpless than I've ever been."

"When you die," Ryan said, "mebbe Krysty will wake up and never remember you were even there."

"Do you want to take that chance?"

Ryan gave her a cruel fox's grin. "You're dying, bitch, and I'm going to be trying it sooner or later because I don't think you're going to let go on your own. Rather it was sooner, let me know what I'm dealing with while I'm trying to save our asses. And that's an ace on the line."

"Krysty is one of us," the old woman said. "How you got her to give up her birthright is beyond me. And she's very strong."

"You brought us here," Ryan said, "and mixed us up in this. It wasn't any of our business."

"Couldn't die alone, because then everything I'd known would die with me. Chosen don't die alone, don't die far from home without returning." Her words slurred and became hollow, drifting away.

"You're losing her," Mildred said.

Holstering the SIG-Sauer, Ryan grabbed the woman. She fought against him weakly, then gave up. She spoke softly and sibilantly, and it took Ryan a moment to realize the same words were coming from Krysty across the room. They were two voices singing the same song.

Krysty lay there, her unseeing eyes directed at the ceiling overhead.

Chapter Eight

Without a word, Ryan backhanded Phlorin across the face, once, twice.

One of the men in the group started to get to his feet. "You can't do that to her," he protested.

Jak swung his .357 to cover the man, not saying anything. But with his ruby eyes glinting cold fire, he didn't have to say anything at all.

The man froze in place, making no effort to raise the .38 revolver he had. "Look," he said uncomfortably, "I don't want any trouble."

"You got a funny way of showing it," J.B. said.

"You fuckers are just as bad as them coldhearts," a skinny woman with ratted hair and a bruise under one eye snarled.

"Mary," the man who'd spoken up said, stepping over to shield the woman as she got to her feet, "you stay out of this."

"This woman," Ryan said, "has managed to hurt somebody I care about. Now you people, I don't even know. But I opened up the doors of this fort and let you in. And if there's a way to get you out of here, I aim to see you clear of this mess. You get in my way, though, and I'm going to put you outside."

"You can't do that," the woman said.

"Mary."

She turned to him, snatching at his shirt. "Clete, he can't do that. Don't you dare let him."

"Then we do what he says."

"You can't let him hurt that woman any more, either."

"Do you know her?" Ryan demanded.

Phlorin sat in pain from the blows, but she wasn't praying or singing anymore. Neither was Krysty, and that suited Ryan fine for the moment.

The noise of the chem storm drumming rain into the building sounded more hollow than ever in the silence that followed the question.

"No, mister," the man said, "we don't know her. Until today when them coldhearts jumped us and brought us here, we never saw her before."

"Anybody else?" Ryan flicked his one-eyed gaze from person to person, even looking at the children.

"I know of her."

Ryan pinned the speaker with his gaze.

The man stood only a little above Ryan's shoulder, thick set through his shoulders but tapered at the waist and haunches like a man accustomed to running or missing meals. He dressed in homespun hand-me-downs that didn't quite fit, a faded red cotton shirt and dungarees that had patches over them. His walking shoes were scuffed but serviceable, predark by the look of them instead of hand-made. Ryan guessed his age as late thirties, with unkempt dark hair shot with gray streaks hanging to his shoulders and two or three weeks' splotchy beard growth covering his seamed and weathered face. A knife blade had bisected his right eyebrow years earlier, rearranging the flesh so that it looked as if part of the brow were crawling up from his eye socket.

"Not her so much," the man said, "but what she is, mebbe."

"What do you know?" Ryan asked.

The man appeared hesitant. "Heard her calling herself one of the Chosen."

"That means something to you?"

"Heard of the Chosen. All women. All mutie women, from the way I been told. Got these strange powers, they say. That's why the Slaggers were so hard on her. Guess they heard some of the same stories."

"My dear fellow, what powers are you speaking of?" Doc, drawn out of the dementia that had almost claimed him, focused on the man.

The man shrugged. "Don't rightly know. I heard tell they know things before they happen. Heard they can see a lie the instant they been told it. I've also been told they can chill a man by just thinking about it if you get enough of them together."

"And precisely how are they supposed to do these things?" Doc persisted.

"If she's one of the Chosen," the man said, "she'll have a bag of simples."

"Simples? And what are they?"

Ryan looked at the clothing and packs the coldhearts' prisoners had brought with them. "Which pack is hers?"

THE SCARRED LEATHER BAG had a beadwork design on it. The bag was old, the leather fraying around the thick gut strings that held it together. Some of the beads were missing. Once, they'd been brightly colored reds, yellows, greens, blues, and they'd formed a pattern. Studying the pattern, Ryan thought maybe the design had once been of a quarter moon and a field of stars.

"Simples are potions," the man said. "Poultices. Mebbe even jolt that she uses to get her brain all frenzied up to do some of the big stuff. They carry herbs and such, too. And there's cards.''

Ryan went through the pack, finding the things that the man recited. The potions were in ceramic containers with corks, wrapped in layers of cloth to keep them from breaking. The poultices were in other containers and smelled strong and sour.

"Let me see those," Mildred asked.

Ryan handed them over, then returned his attention to the pack. Phlorin rocked, slowly and steadily nearby, her attention focused totally on him. He found herbs packed in homemade wax paper, the plants and flowers pressed neatly between the pages. And he found the cards in a drawstring leather pouch.

There were sixty or seventy of them. All of them had faces and figures painted on them. The art looked original, drawn from some kind of source, but not printed out the way they used to be in the predark ages.

"Hand painted," J.B. commented. "But there looks to be more than your regular fifty-two cards and jokers."

"There is." Ryan spread the cards out before him, contemplating the array of women featured on the cards. One showed a winged woman pouring from one cup to another, with a road leading up a mountain in the background. The legend at the bottom read Temperance. Another was of a woman with one hand on a wolf's head, the sun blazing high overhead. The legend on that one was Sun. The suits seemed to be broken down four ways, just like a normal deck. But the suits were moons, bowls, knives and spears. "I've seen something like this. When I was riding with Trader, we come upon this ville had an old woman in it who said she could tell the future with cards like these."

"The tarot," Mildred said. "Supposed to be a game from the Middle Ages. Maybe even further back than I can remember. Storytellers used them to help make up stories as they went from town to town. From there, I guess somebody got the idea of making those stories more personal and started telling futures.''

''Do not be so hasty as to dismiss the power of those cards, dear lady,'' Doc said. ''The great and learned minds of the Totality Concept had committed prodigious amounts of capital investment into the research and development of cogitation as regards to the black arts. Some were not so sure that those tales contained only the accoutrements of Joseph Campbell's myths.''

''Those cards are so much bullshit, Doc,'' Mildred argued. ''Good for slumber-party excitement.''

Ryan returned the cards to the drawstring leather pouch. ''What about those herbs and potions?''

''Purely homeopathic cures and aids,'' Mildred said. ''Some of them make sense. Like this plant.'' She held up a piece of bark wrapped in wax paper. ''Aloe. Helps with burns, as an antibacterial and as an insect repellent.'' She fanned out the other packages in front of her. ''Some of this stuff I can figure out, but there's a lot of it I'm not sure about.''

''Can we use the things in there?'' J.B. asked.

''Some. I don't know about all.''

''Make room in the packs for them,'' Ryan said. ''We'll sort it out later.'' They didn't pass up on meds when they could get them. Traveling as they did meant a lot of risk, and there were few healers along the way.

He glanced up at the man. ''What's your name?''

''Elmore. Franklin Elmore.''

''You ever heard of one of these Chosen taking over somebody else's mind?'' Ryan asked.

''No, but I'd believe it if you say it's true. I've even heard those women could fly.''

"Their society consists of women only?" Doc asked. "No men have evidenced these powers?"

Elmore nodded. "From what I've always been told."

"What about the men of their community?"

"There ain't any," Elmore answered. "Just women. A man tries to get too close to them, they chill him. Anybody who's been up and around this territory and come across any stories of the Chosen, they'll tell you that."

The comment started Ryan's mind spinning again, thinking about the things Krysty and the woman had said to him. That explained the way she'd treated him on top of the building, not wanting to touch him. And it explained Phlorin's statement that he'd taken Krysty's birthright from her.

"Ah, if you will pardon the seemingly insensitive nature of my asking," the old man went on, "but that begs the question of how such a society handles...procreation."

"They fuck like regular people," Elmore said. "Got the same equipment as any woman, and some of them are downright attractive. Only they don't like it so much. And there's a price they pay."

"What price?" Ryan asked.

"There's a few stories," Elmore said, "and I don't know if any of them are truth. But some say the Chosen only keep their powers as long as they keep their knees locked. First time she ruts with a man, she doesn't have her powers anymore."

"Then why fuck?" Ryan asked.

"Got to have more Chosen." Elmore grinned. "Otherwise they'd have run out of members a long time ago. I've heard they have some kind of gathering. A council, mebbe, somebody told me. They judge who's worthy and who's not worthy. The ones mebbe ain't so worthy, they become breeding stock."

"Oh, dear God," Mary whimpered, drawing in close to her husband.

Elmore turned to the woman and nodded. "Yes, ma'am, that's the kind of bitch you were trying to protect. But it gets worse. See, the Chosen capture men from time to time. Bring them into special camps quarterly, and have them lay with all the women selected as breeding stock. Takes place four times a year, based on the moon cycles."

"The equinoxes and solstices," Doc said.

"Don't know about that," Elmore replied, "but if you're talking about summer, spring, fall and winter, that's them."

"You know what kind of women we're talking about here, don't you, friend Ryan?" Doc asked. "The noble bard wrote about them a number of times, and their appearances were never to the good. Yon woman is a witch!"

Chapter Nine

"I've heard some call them that," Elmore admitted. "But don't you dare call one of them that to their face. I've heard they curse you, put a hex on you that can give a man anything from a few days' worth of rotten stomach to outright death. They're just the Chosen."

"What happens men who breed?" Jak asked. "Mebbe find one, talk him."

Ryan thought it sounded like a good plan, and he was aggravated he didn't think it through as clearly as the albino. But his head was still too jumbled from all the problems they had facing them. Leaving the junkyard fort without getting chilled was one of the biggest.

"They don't get away," Elmore said. "They get through using him, the Chosen sacrifice him. See, there's a purification process they go through to make sure his seed's ready before he puts his crank in any of them." He glanced at the women in the group. "Sorry if I've offended anybody. Just telling it how it is."

"In exactly what manner do they *purify* them?" Doc asked.

"Don't know. I just know that by purifying the man, the Chosen make sure the get of that fucking receives the powers of the Chosen. And that more'n likely it'll be a she-get rather than a he-get."

"And if the baby is a boy?" Mildred asked.

"They hold on to it," Elmore said, "till the next big

quarterly meeting. A week, three months, whichever it is. Then they have another sacrifice, this one supposedly more pleasing to whatever they pray to than anything else. After all, it's part of themselves they're offering up."

"Monsters," Mary hissed from her side of the room.

"Men make mockeries of us," Phlorin said weakly. "And you sit there, so weak. You hang on to that man beside you, and you never think to try to have your own life. You wait for old age to claim you and never realize your true station in this life. Women are bound to this world. Our cycles are like those of the moon, which affects everything on this world. Men are abominations, put here by the dark forces that rule the shadows. Men only know the hunger that stays forever in their bellies and their loins. Their imagination is only desire misnamed. Their lust has no conscience."

"You mean a hard dick has no conscience," Elmore said.

She spit.

"The Chosen's society takes care of its breeding stock?" Doc asked.

Elmore nodded. "Sure. Feed it. Clothe it. Keep it fucked and pregnant every quarter that it ain't. This purification process, it ain't always so gentle. Some of the get of these unions, they're mutie strain. Mindless monsters that receive some of the powers but no brains to use them with. Some of them are so deformed that it would be a burden on the Chosen to keep them."

"Chill, too?" Jak asked.

"Before they draw their first breath, way I hear it," Elmore answered. "A woman in the breeding stock, they pick her young enough that she can bear thirteen children. Some kind of mystical number to them."

"That again points back to the roots in witchcraft," Mildred said. "Not the Totality Concept."

"Not necessarily, dear lady," Doc argued. "Limiting replication is a self-serving design. What we're discussing here would severely curtail the gene pool available to these women. By the Three Kennedys, if they've been operating like this for any length of time, they could be carrying on disastrous DNA that would result in all kinds of birth defects and malformed children."

"The number of live births among them has been decreasing," Elmore said. "Which is why they been stealing kids the last five or ten years."

"You're not from here, are you?" Ryan asked.

"No. Farther west," Elmore replied. "Raised up by the Cific Ocean."

"Then why are you here?"

"Wasn't no paradise there." Elmore shrugged. "Guess I was just looking for someplace better. Lots of folks are. Problem is, I think we see each other in passing, but all we're doing is trading one set of problems for another. Folks get tired of that problem, they move on again."

Something about the man's answer didn't ring true to Ryan, but he couldn't pinpoint it.

"They steal people's children?" Mary asked. She held the little boy in the group close to her.

"Yes, ma'am," Elmore said. "But only girl-get. You got a boy. You got nothing to worry about. You'd probably come closer to losing your man than you would your child. Your man can fuck, and he's proved himself to any Chosen watching you all by fathering that boy. They'd take your man, leave you and the boy for dead."

"Why take the girl children?" Mildred asked.

"They got ways of knowing which ones have some of the power." Elmore pointed to the herbs and potions in front of her. "Probably some of them in there. Or mebbe they just mind-talk with them. Had a man tell me once that a Chosen could look in a young girl's eyes and know if she could be brought up their way."

"Widespread possibility of the psychic talents," Doc said. "Still think you're looking at a society founded totally on superstition?"

"Blow it out your ass, Doc."

"I find this all amazing to contemplate," the old man said. "At another time, I should like to advance further inquiries into this field of experience."

Elmore shrugged. "Told you about everything I know." He looked at Krysty rocking gently against the floor, her mouth silently moving to whatever words she was saying. "I'm just sorry it don't seem to help your problem none."

"Got a new problem," J.B. called from the window. "Rain's slacking up. Chem storm's about to pass over. The baron's men aren't going to wait around long before they decide to do something."

RYAN SAT AT THE WINDOW, peering over the sill. He kept the Steyr in his hands, taking small comfort from the solid feel of the sleek steel.

Phlorin lay against the back wall, her breathing sounding raspy and thin. Krysty still hadn't come out of the coma that had claimed her.

"Slaggers are still interested in how it goes down, too," J.B. said.

Ryan followed the line of the Armorer's pointing finger and spotted the coldhearts in hiding farther out, away from the junkyard. Some of the mongrels had put in an appearance, as well, requiring the baron's men to fire at will to prevent the hounds from closing in on them. As it was, Ryan knew of two men who were lost anyway. The dogs also succeeded in chasing nearly half the horses away after the baron's men had worked to keep them covered during the chem storm.

"We still got a few hours of daylight left," J.B. commented.

Ryan nodded. "That can work for us or against us, depending on how good the baron's men are in the dark."

"Home-ground advantage goes to the Slaggers, though." A crooked smile framed the Armorer's face. "And those bastard dogs."

"We got too many problems inside this fort," Ryan stated.

"I know."

"Trader'd think me a fool for putting up with all of them for so long. I need to find out what kind of hold that witch has over Krysty, and who of these folks the baron's men are after. Then I need to get us the hell out of here."

"Mebbe." J.B. took off his glasses and gave them a quick shine. "But I think back in those days when Trader was sharp, he'd have taken advantage of the rain, too."

"Rain's over," Ryan said. Outside, only a light mist hazed the air. But it was still enough to give a man pause about going out into it. If enough of the airborne caustic liquid was breathed in, lungs could become inflamed, a breeding ground for pleurisy or another respiratory ailment that would end up in a long, hard death.

J.B. put his glasses back on. "Which problem you going to deal with first?"

"Krysty."

"Could be hard going."

"Already is," Ryan admitted. "If I knew what to do, one way or the other, I could get it done."

"Best way to do anything," the Armorer said, "is to put the ace on the line and let the chips fall."

Ryan knew that was true, but he also knew that doing that was going to risk Krysty. Somehow, though, he knew she wouldn't want him to let the situation remained unresolved.

"ANY CHANGE?" RYAN ASKED.

Mildred shook her head. She sat next to Krysty's pallet, the red head lying in her lap. She brushed at the prehensile hair, trying to calm it from the bunch of frayed knots it had twisted itself into. "She's got a fever. Low grade and nothing's that's going to be dangerous, but it's wearing her out."

"How about the old woman?" Ryan cut his gaze over to Phlorin, who had woken and pierced him with her red-rimmed gaze filled with hate.

"Figured she'd be dead by now," Mildred admitted, "with that hole in her chest. We're talking about a lot of trauma to her system. She's a stubborn woman."

"If she dies, how do you think it's going to affect Krysty?"

"Not any more than the baron's men chilling her if they get their hands on her first. And she's going to die anyway, Ryan. No way to save her. Mebbe her dying will ease the hold she has on Krysty."

Ryan drew the panga. "Guess it's time to find out." He glanced at the old woman.

Phlorin stared back at him, a sarcastic smile somehow blossoming on the bloody lips through all the pain. "Come to me, man. Come ahead and do your worst. No matter what, I shall still survive!"

FOR A LONG TIME, Krysty knew she'd been floating in some kind of prison. It wasn't the land of geysers and sulfur stench that Phlorin had first put her in when she took over her body and nearly killed Ryan. The place she'd been kept had been a white room almost ten feet in all directions. There had been no furniture, no decorations, no way to tell what was a floor, ceiling or wall.

There hadn't been any gravity, either. At first, she'd run, slamming herself into the walls, the ceiling, the floor, whatever side of the cube she could throw herself at. She'd hoped she'd break something, find some way out. The walls had all held, and she felt that she was teetering toward madness.

In the background, always just within hearing, had been Phlorin's voice. And it had never sounded human again. The voice oozed words like an infected wound oozed pus into healthy tissue. Krysty was certain the voice was finding the weak spots of her mind, prying into every nook and cranny it could, then insinuating itself and taking root. At times she thought she could feel the voice actually inching deeper inside herself.

She no longer understood the words consciously. But she could tell that some part of her subconscious mind understood them. She still felt the way she had on top of the building, the knife in her hand as she tried to kill Ryan: herself, but one step removed.

Without warning, though, the voice became clear again.

Come see, Phlorin said. *Come see how your man plays into our little game. He's going to trap you forever, leave you to my mercy.*

Why are you doing this? Krysty demanded.

Because it is necessary. I am of the Chosen. I must survive. You have forsaken your birthright.

I didn't even know of you people, Krysty argued.

You knew that you were different. That alone should have started you on a quest until you found us, your sisters.

You're not my sisters.

Your mother was. The

Fear trembled inside Krysty then, and it reminded her of a moth's wings brushing frantically against her palms when she'd caught one as a child.

My mother was many things, she argued, *but she would never have been like you.*

You never really knew your mother. How can you be so sure?

Because Gaia has told me. In truth, during some of her prayers while she was growing up, Krysty had asked the earth goddess about her mother. There'd never been any definite answers, but Krysty had never had any cause to feel sad or scared. She was certain that whatever other secrets Mother Sonja might have had, she was a good person. At least at the time that she'd lived in Harmony ville.

You use the goddess's name in vain. Such sacrilege would normally be punished.

Then try. You've pushed me out of my own body, nearly chilled the man I love with all my heart. How do you think you can punish me any more?

The woman didn't answer, and the silence that followed the question was almost deafening, trapped as it was in the small white room.

Sensing the weakness, Krysty twisted in the air until she made contact with one of the walls again. The weightlessness here was confusing, and getting herself set was hard. Still, she managed, finally able to get into a kneeling position on the surface she'd chosen. Then she pushed herself outward toward the opposite wall. She put her bunched fists in front of her, screaming out her rage and frustration, temporarily blocking out that voice.

The room's walls exploded before her hands, tumbling away in jagged shards. Then she was inside the fort where the companions had holed up.

And she was looking down at her own body, her head in Mildred's lap.

No, she thought, instantly afraid of the implications.

Fool, Phlorin told her. *It isn't you who has died. But I am about to so that I may live.*

Krysty called out to Mildred, but her efforts went unheard. She reached for her friend, only to watch her hand pass right through Mildred's. Hastily Krysty turned her perspective point, focusing on Ryan as he squatted beside Phlorin.

Now it begins, the old woman said inside Krysty's mind. *This man of yours is stupe, but he is determined.*

The panga glittered in Ryan's hand, the edge pointed up.

Krysty crossed the room, having no sensation of walking, just suddenly appearing at Ryan's side. *Lover!*

Ryan stared at the woman. Krysty read in her lover's movements that he was there to kill the old woman. "Time's come to shit or get off the pot. You're only one step away from catching the last train headed West. Release Krysty."

Krysty reached for her lover, trying to cup her hand under Ryan's head and force him to turn to look at her.

Ryan froze, then slowly his head came around. His single eye widened, showing the full blue of the iris. "Krysty," he whispered.

Don't, Krysty tried to tell him. *You're playing right into whatever she's doing, lover.* Before, she'd managed to reach Ryan through some aspect of her gift. She guessed that it could happen again if she tried hard enough.

Ryan shook his head.

"What is it?" Mildred asked.

"I thought I heard Krysty call my name," he said.

Mildred shook her head. "Your imagination, Ryan. I've been with her the whole time and I haven't heard a word."

No! Krysty screamed. She reached for Ryan again, more
determined this time. Her hands and arms passed through
her lover's body as if he'd been made of smoke.

Ryan turned his attention back to the old woman. "Last
chance," he told her in a flat voice. "Let Krysty go, or I'll
chill you as you lay."

See how sure he is of himself, Phlorin taunted. *So brave,
so demanding. Men are pathetic. And they have the gall to
think that every problem can be answered with physical
violence.* She smiled in disdain, and Krysty didn't know if
the smile was meant for her or Ryan.

Then Ryan struck, as fast as any mountain cat back home
in Harmony that Krysty had ever seen. Despite his harsh
tactics, she knew her lover took no pride and no pleasure
in death. He struck to kill, plunging the panga deep into
the woman's heart.

Krysty felt the blade as though it entered her own body,
cold steel suddenly invading hot, pulsing flesh. She
screamed, but the pain in her voice paled beside the screech
that echoed in her mind from Phlorin.

The woman convulsed from the floor, grabbing at Ryan's
arm. Krysty watched, trapped by whatever bound her to the
old woman, and felt her lover's flesh through Phlorin's
hand.

Then the woman died, spitting blood onto Ryan as she
fought to hang on to her existence and bite him at the same
time. He caught her hair up in his free hand and shoved
her head back. Gradually her muscles relaxed, and she fell
away from him.

But Krysty felt the growth inside her own mind, more
deeply entrenched than ever. She screamed, realizing that
even though she'd escaped the cage she'd been confined
in, she was more trapped now than ever.

Before she could move, before she could think, she felt

something pulling at her. She turned to face it, then realized that she was being drawn to her own body. In an eye blink, she was back inside her own flesh. But she wasn't alone.

She also realized that she wasn't breathing.

RYAN GAZED DOWN at the corpse, his hand still gripped around the panga thrust into her chest.

"You shouldn't oughta done that," Mary wailed from the side of the house. "You shouldn't oughta done that to a witch."

"Shut her up," Ryan told the woman's husband. In truth, in the moment before he'd killed the woman, he'd felt an eldrich chill thrill through him, seeming to come through the knife handle itself. He believed in Krysty's premonitions, but he was no doomie himself. That feeling, though, had felt as close to any experience his lover had ever told him about.

"Ryan," J.B. called.

Ryan yanked the panga free and glanced at his friend, grateful for the distraction.

"Got a man out here waving a white flag at the end of a stick," the Armorer stated. "Want to hear him out, or do you want me to chill him where he's standing?"

Chapter Ten

"Step him back," Ryan said, gazing at the baron's man waving a piece of white rag from a wag antenna. "Gets close enough, he could heave a gren through the window if he's got one."

J.B. rattled off a quick 3-round burst that ripped through the acid-laced mud at the man's feet and threw clods back in the direction he'd come from.

Thinking he'd been shot, the man hurled himself to the side, dropping the makeshift white flag and himself into the mud. He started flopping and screaming at once as the acid residue from the chem storm ate into his flesh.

"Come get him if you want him alive," Ryan yelled out.

"How do I know you won't shoot them?" a man roared back.

"If I wanted you to think that," Ryan growled, "I'd have shot this poor stupe bastard. Didn't think he'd be fool enough to throw himself into the mud like that. And you're only risking two men."

"I got two men coming out," the man replied.

"I see any more than that moving," Ryan warned, "I'll chill every one I see."

Two men bolted from hiding among the wrecked wags. Neither carried weapons except for side arms. Both, however, had canteens. Cursing the man on the ground, they emptied their canteens over his face and hands. His skin pinked up from the caustic acidity left trapped in the ground. Once the man had control over himself, his two companions dragged him back to shelter. He never quit moaning.

"You cost me some water," the man yelled to Ryan.

"If we were on more friendly terms," Ryan said, "mebbe I'd feel bad about that. But it isn't anywhere close to that."

The man laughed, his voice sounding confident and loud in the canyons between the mounds of wrecked wags. "The way you sound, you'd think it was me between a rock and a hard place instead of you."

"I'm in here," Ryan said. "You're out there with the coldhearts and the dogs. Mebbe another chem storm the way the sky looks."

"Man can starve to death in there."

"Not with the rations we found," Ryan lied. "Figure we can wait in here, see whether we have to take on you or the coldhearts. Doesn't matter to us." His words drifted away into the ensuing silence.

"Ryan," Mildred called.

Glancing over his shoulder, Ryan watched as Krysty opened her eyes and looked around.

"HOW ARE YOU FEELING?"

Krysty looked up into Ryan's ice-blue eye, noting the worry that was in it. Her hand and arm felt as if it weighed a hundred pounds as she lifted it. She touched his face, dragging her fingertips across his mouth, across the scar that covered half his face. "Like I was hit by a wag," she said.

Ryan took her hand in his. "What about Phlorin?"

Krysty shook her head and regretted it immediately. "Don't know, lover. Mind's all a jumble right now." Inwardly she was cold, and she didn't know if that really was the answer or if Phlorin's presence was making her say that. Was the woman really dead and gone, or was she somehow still around? Krysty hated not knowing. The thing that Ryan had always had with her was trust—even when things were at their worst.

"We'll worry about that soon enough," Ryan told her. "Soon as we get out of here."

"When's that going to be?" Krysty wanted nothing more than to put the ville behind them. Then a meal from a self-heat and a night sleeping in Ryan's arms.

"Working on it now," Ryan told her.

A man called for attention from outside.

"Got to go," Ryan said.

Krysty nodded, then gazed around the room, seeing everybody that she'd seen earlier when Ryan had killed Phlorin. She didn't know how they'd come to be inside the building, or even where it was, and that inability to remember scared her. She trusted Ryan and the other companions, but she needed to be independent, too. Lying there like an invalid wasn't helping. She tried to sit up, but her stomach turned sick on her, revolving in wicked flips. She groaned.

Mildred put her arms around Krysty, helping her get steady. "Easy does it," the black woman said. "You've been through a lot. Don't rush it."

"Water," Krysty gasped, wanting to get rid of the sick taste in her mouth.

Mildred brought up a ring-pull and popped the top. She held the container as Krysty drank. "Go easy with that. Too much and you might make yourself sick."

Krysty sipped the contents, then settled back into the woman's arms. She glanced at Dean, who was lying with one ear pressed to the ground for some reason. She thought she'd ask him, but she didn't have the strength.

"WHAT'S YOUR NAME?"

"Cawdor," Ryan answered. "And yourself?"

"My name's Naylor."

Ryan scanned the terrain, watching the baron's men slither between the stacks of dead wags. Maybe Naylor was giving the appearance of stepping down his hostile actions, but he wasn't wasting any time in shoring up his position. The man had experience. "You a baron's man, Naylor?"

"Yeah. Working as sec chief for Baron Curtis Shaker."

"Don't know him," Ryan called back.

"Got a ville down south. Mebbe two weeks' ride from here as the crow flies."

"You got a reason for being in Idaho Falls?"

"I was sent here to find somebody."

"Can't be me," Ryan replied, looking back over the men and women assembled inside the building.

"Man I'm looking for owes the baron some blood," Naylor said. "If you stand in the way of me getting it back, there's going to be trouble."

"I don't like getting threatened," Ryan growled, but he cut his eye over the four men in the room. He automatically discounted Clete, the husband. If Naylor had been looking for a man with a wife, the sec chief would have said so.

"I'm not threatening, Cawdor," Naylor said. "Just laying the ace on the line so we all know what we're looking at."

Ryan kept his gaze on Elmore and the two other suspect men. "How do you know the man you're looking for was here?"

"Trailed him," Naylor replied. "Got a man here with me who knows him by sight."

"You don't?"

"No."

"How do you know you can trust him?" Ryan asked.

"I choose to," Naylor replied. "And me trusting him, that's pretty much my own lookout now, isn't it?"

"He's right about that," J.B. said quietly. The Armorer gave the appearance of being relaxed, but Ryan knew his friend was as tight as a bowstring, able to move faster than an eye blink.

"You don't owe them people in there anything," Naylor pointed out.

"No," Ryan replied, "you're right about that. But I gave them my word if they threw in with us, I'd see their way clear of this bastard situation."

"You're drawing to a hard hand if you think you can live up to that," Naylor said. "Fuck, I don't think you're going to get past those coldhearts. And I saw the woman you carried in myself. Been a stranger, you wouldn't have done that. Means you got one of your own wounded. Hate to see you hard up against it like that after all the chilling you did against these coldhearts."

"I usually do what I say I'll do," Ryan said.

"Mebbe we can cut a deal," Naylor said, "because I don't set too well with losing any more of my people, either."

Ryan kept watching the three men. "I'm listening."

DEAN LAY QUIET and still on the ground. He heard his father's voice and the exchange with the sec chief outside, but he also thought he heard something moving around inside the ground below the building.

At first, he'd thought it was just a vibration, maybe something settling outside after all the rain. Then, when it had kept up, he thought it could be something else.

He kept the Browning Hi-Power in his fist, and took out his turquoise-handled throwing knife. Holding it butt down, he slammed the heel of his hand against the ground. The knife's hilt plunged into the packed earth again and again, making him doubt what he'd heard.

Then the next blow he struck brought the hollow sound he'd been expecting to hear.

Rising to his knees, his heart thumping faster, Dean plunged the knife blade into the ground, searching.

"My dear boy," Doc said, his attention diverted for a moment from the three men he was watching, "whatever are you doing?"

"Hollow space under the ground, Doc," Dean said. "It's not natural." The knife blade slid deep without warning, running along the ground in a straight line for an instant. The knife's passing left a thin groove cut into the earth. As Dean watched, small bits of dirt fell into the groove and disappeared.

The vibration he'd been feeling grew stronger as he hooked the fingers of his free hand into the groove.

"GIVE ME THE MAN I'm looking for, and I'll provide you safe passage out of this ville."

Ryan gazed across the intervening space, aware that the sec chief's men were still moving. "Calls for an awful lot of trust on my part."

"Don't see any other way you're getting out of here alive."

"Who are you looking for?" Ryan asked.

"A man calls himself Ethridge."

"You want him alive or dead?"

"Living would suit the baron better. Don't want to have to explain how that man got himself chilled."

Ryan swept the three suspect men with his gaze, waiting to see which of them broke eye contact first. "Anybody want to step up and claim this one?" he asked.

None of them answered.

"Can you give me something more to go on?" Ryan asked. "None of the guys I've got in here appear to willing to fess up."

"Man's got a tattoo," Naylor called back. "On the inside of his forearm you'll find a big blue dot with lighter blue rings around it. Then there's two twisted lines of orange running through it."

The one-eyed man lifted the SIG-Sauer to point in the general direction of Elmore and the two other men. "One of you is lying, and I intend to have the man who is. Bastard quick."

Before anyone could reply, the ground under Dean seemed to erupt, and Ryan got a real good look at the maw full of fangs that lunged at his son's throat. "Dean! Get back!" Ryan brought his blaster around, knowing in his heart he was already too late.

Chapter Eleven

"Hot pipe!" Dean exclaimed, dodging back from the furred fury that boiled out of the tunnel he'd uncovered in the floor. Knowing he couldn't get clear to let his father use the 9 mm blaster, he rocked forward again and seized one of the animal's ears in his fist, narrowly avoiding the flashing teeth that snapped at his throat.

Throwing his weight against the dog, setting his shoulder beneath its jaw so it couldn't bite him, Dean landed on top of the animal. Then he brought the turquoise-hilted knife around in a short arc, driving it home between the ribs. Hot blood squirted over his hand, and he made sure he didn't loosen his grip so any of the liquid could make the knife hilt slippery. He pulled the blade free, then stabbed repeatedly until he was sure the dog was dead.

He was barely aware that his father had buried the long blade of the panga in the skull of the next dog trying to get into the room. But he heard the animal's final yelps. He'd hit his own attacker so hard that it hadn't had the breath left to growl or yelp or whine before it died.

"You okay?" Ryan asked, freeing his blade.

"Yeah." Dean pulled back from the dead dog and took a deep, shuddering breath. He cleaned his blade on the animal's fur. "Bastard dogs. Never thought they were down there for sure. Sounded small. Thought mebbe they were rats."

Ryan reached into the hole and dragged out the corpse

of the animal he'd killed. "You should have had somebody backing your play when you popped that bastard door. Think about what you're doing before you get us all killed."

"I thought I was," Dean protested. His emotions twisted inside him, not knowing how he was supposed to feel. The adrenaline still raced through his system because he'd found something his father and J.B. had missed, and because the dog had nearly taken his face off. Now he felt bad on top of it, because his father was right.

"If that had been a man in there with an automatic weapon," Ryan said, "we'd have all been chilled."

Dean kept the angry words from his tongue, and it made the burn behind his eyes even harder to take. "Wouldn't have let that happen to you. I'd have chilled him. Bastard dog surprised me, jumping like that. A man, he wouldn't have done that." He forced himself to meet his dad's unflinching gaze.

"Reckon you're right at that, Dean," Ryan said quietly. "You stood up and took that dog out before it could get loose in here."

"Slick," Jak agreed, waving a hand out steadily before him. "Like water over smooth pebble. Dog never had chance."

Dean took a long, rasping breath, smelling the stench of dog and dog turds coming from the open tunnel now. "Bastard dogs got in here somehow."

Ryan glanced back at the hole. "We need to find out where it goes. If it's something we can use. Looks like a dog run the coldhearts used at one time to mebbe send dogs out after anybody who holed them up in here. You feel up to finding that out?"

"Yeah," Dean answered, though he didn't feel so certain.

"Go with," Jak said, moving toward Dean. His leaf-bladed throwing knives gleamed in his hands.

Ryan nodded. "Not far. I don't have any plans on moving from here any too soon, but when we do, I don't want to have to come looking."

Dean glared down into the hole, but it was hard to see in the darkness. One thing was for certain—it wasn't very deep, maybe two and a half feet tall at best. He took an oil lamp from the shelves at the back of the room and lit it with a self-light from the gear he carried in his pockets. When he had the wick going well, he lowered the hand-blown hurricane glass around it once more.

He stepped into the hole and thrust the lantern out before him, chasing the shadowy darkness inside back little more than arm's length. It didn't leave much margin for error.

"Dog's eyes glow," Jak said softly in his ear, "you get close enough. See them coming."

"Yeah." Dean pulled the Hi-Power from its holster and got down on his stomach, promptly landing in piles of dog turds. Some of it was fresh. He swore at the stench and the greasy feel, but he made himself go forward into the tunnel he'd found. Taking on the Baron's men, followed by the coldhearts, was something none of the companions wanted to do.

Dog shit or not, the tunnel offered a way out. Dean kept crawling.

"CAWDOR!" NAYLOR BARKED from outside.

"Dammit," Ryan called back, "I'm checking arms. Give me a minute." He waved the SIG-Sauer meaningfully at the three men.

One of the men rolled his sleeves up without hesitation, revealing bare inner elbows.

"Sit down," Ryan instructed, moving on to Elmore and the other man.

"Was that a dog I heard in there?" Naylor demanded.

"Had one left over that recovered," Ryan replied. "Thought the bastard was dead. It is now."

"Hope he believes you," J.B. said quietly. "Otherwise we might have company."

"It'll be easier for Dean and Jak to find the other end of that tunnel than for Naylor or his people to find it."

"Mayhap," Doc said, wrinkling his nose against the sour stink that pervaded the room from the open trapdoor, "they would not want to traverse it even should they chance upon its location. The very pits of Hell should not be any worse, I would wager."

"Wouldn't have to go through it unless they just wanted to," J.B. said. "Put a man on the other end of it and have him shoot anybody trying to come out of it armed. Then it's a matter of who runs out of rations first."

"And there's always the coldhearts waiting in the wings," Mildred reminded them.

"Doesn't matter," Ryan said. "One way or another, we're not going to be here much longer." He pointed the pistol at Elmore. "Let me see your arm."

Elmore rolled up one sleeve and showed the scarred interior of his elbow.

"Now the other one," Ryan instructed.

"We need to talk," Elmore said.

Ryan rolled the hammer back on the SIG-Sauer, dropping the trigger tension down to near nothing. "I'll chill you and have a look myself if I have to."

"I thought you said if we threw in with you you'd stand by us," Elmore said. His eyes narrowed in anger and fear, and his throat tightened, giving a chopping rhythm to his words.

"I'll save who I can. Can't do any more than that." Ryan stared at him over the blaster's barrel, holding it to the center of the man's chest.

"They get their hands on me, they'll chill me."

"That's not my problem," Ryan said harshly. "Got myself in a whole world of trouble coming around here as it was. I'm ready to be rid of it."

Elmore rolled up his sleeve, revealing the tattoo.

"You're with the Heimdall Foundation," Mildred said.

Surprise filled Elmore's eyes, bringing glints of hope with it. "You've heard of the Heimdall Foundation?"

"Once," she answered.

"Then you know what they're trying to do there."

"No."

"Whitecoat stuff," J.B. stated. "And usually that's not a good thing."

Ryan knew that was true. In the companions' travels, most research facilities left over after the nukecaust had degenerated in their purpose or their personnel. And usually the whitecoats running the research labs were as cold-blooded and vicious as any baron.

"What we're trying to do is find out the truth about alien visitations to this planet," Elmore said. "It might help us understand more about what's happened here. You can't possibly understand how important that could be to our futures. *All* of our futures."

"My dear Ryan," Doc said calmly, "maybe we should barter with the sec chief. At least buy a little more time to find out if Jak and young Dean are, indeed, able to find a way from this structure that will not put us beneath the crosshairs of enemy weapons. I, for one, would endeavor to discourse with this man at length about the conspiracy theories he might have. When I visited the first future I was subject to, conspiracy theories were all the rage. No little of them were dedicated to aliens and abductions and numerous other phenomena.''

A red mist clouded Ryan's vision as he grew more angry. ''You're pissing in the wind, Doc,'' he told the old man, making sure Elmore understood him, too. ''I got a sec chief out there who says he'll go away if I give this man to him. This man isn't nothing to me.''

''And should this man Naylor not be as honest and forthright as he presents himself to be?'' Doc asked.

''Then I lose one man that's not one of us to be certain of that.'' Ryan hardened his resolve. ''Cheap enough buyin on a shaky play.''

''Heartless bastard, aren't you?'' Elmore asked.

''It keeps me breathing.'' Ryan motioned the man to the door with the blaster. ''If you want, I can chill you quick. All he wants is a body. I'll make sure you don't suffer.''

''Rather take my chances with him,'' Elmore said.

''Fair enough. Move along.''

Elmore started for the door. He paused before going through, looking at the woman, Mary. ''What about you, lady? Ain't you going to say something about this not being right?''

She turned her head into her husband.

''Surprising how self-survival puts things into perspective for most folks.'' Elmore gripped the door and opened it. Before he could move outside, Krysty screamed, and the pained shriek filled the small building.

KRYSTY TRIED TO STOP the second scream, but she couldn't. As with the first scream that ripped past her lips, the effort was beyond her control, like a muscle spasm. She doubled over, wrapping an arm around her stomach as pain shot through her. Mildred leaned in close, offering support and whispered words. Krysty wasn't able to make any of them out at all.

Her last glimpse was of Elmore frozen in the middle of the door, muted sunlight pooling across his boots. Then Krysty went blind.

"Krysty!"

She heard Mildred that time and tried to answer. But the words stayed locked up tight inside her, not going any further than her mind.

I'm still here! Phlorin shouted, and it sounded as if she came from a far distance. *Even in death, the Chosen are not truly helpless!*

Though she knew she was still blind in the physical world, could feel her eyes open and hear herself telling Mildred she was blind, a vision formed in Krysty's mind. She stood on a desolate mountaintop, wind battering her and howling like a mournful wolf. It wasn't cold and it wasn't hot; there was only the sensation of the wind.

Fog blew in from what she believed to be the east, covering over the sun just now borning from the bloody rim of the world. It was thick and grayish purple, the color of old bruises. Movement stirred within the depths of the fog. Incredibly Phlorin stepped into view less than ten feet from Krysty.

Where Krysty stood on the uneven terrain of the mountaintop, her boots rocking as the wind tore at her, the woman wasn't affected at all by the wind. And she stood on a wisp of fog, her sandaled feet never touching the ground. She wore a long green gown with intricate embroidery on it.

Get away from me! Krysty responded, looking down only to see the sheer face of the mountain spill away just below her boots. She felt the woman inside her head, like the inside of a beehive. It was a sticky, gooey feeling, the way the honeycomb had felt when she sometimes helped Uncle Tyas McCann rob beehives around Harmony to make honey.

There is no escaping me, Phlorin promised. *You have become my vessel, and you will do what I wish.*

No!

You have no choice, just as your man gave me none. Succeed or die! And that is the choice I put before you, Krysty Wroth. You will do as I need you to, or I will chill you.

I don't believe you.

Then I'll make a believer of you!

Before Krysty could take another breath, her heart stopped. She struggled to fill her lungs again, but they didn't react. She listened to the loud silence where the sound of rushing blood had once been, always taken for granted.

WHEN KRYSTY'S SCREAM reverberated through the tunnel, Dean instinctively went to ground. He dropped flat against the accumulated dog turds. He felt warmth along his chin and left cheek and knew that he was at ground zero for one of the areas the dead animals above had relieved itself before going toward the building. Thankfully his sense of smell seemed to have deserted him.

He ignored the caked feces on his face and body, and squirmed around to try to go back the way he'd come. Jak stopped him, his pale albino's face corpse-white in the dim light provided by the lantern. "What the hell are you doing?"

"Not back," Jak replied.

"That was Krysty screaming." Dean felt the anger boil in him, and he came close for a moment to hitting his friend.

"She's chilled," Jak said, "what good you back there?"

"She's not chilled." Dean's mind wouldn't let him accept that declaration despite the fear that had been in Krysty's voice. "She may need help."

"Best help we find other end of tunnel," Jak told him. "We start back and they coming." He shook his white-maned head. "No good anybody. All chilled mebbe."

Reluctantly Dean saw the wisdom in the albino's words. He made himself relax and turn, knees mashing through the offal beneath him. His back and shoulder ached from holding up the lantern, but he forced himself to keep it up. He kept the Browning in his other hand and hated the way the blaster was caked. He kept crawling, following the twist of the tunnel around.

Then, in the distance, he thought he spotted a rectangle of daylight.

Chapter Twelve

"She's not breathing!"

Ryan registered Mildred's words, watching as the woman slipped her hand under the back of the redhead's neck, tilting Krysty's head back. Then a bullet slammed into the door beside Elmore's head, the thunder of the shot following closely on its heels.

Elmore stood frozen, seemingly stunned by the events taking place in the building or the fact that he'd been shot at.

Knowing he was about to lose his only bargaining chip with the sec chief lying in wait outside, Ryan stepped forward and grabbed the back of Elmore's shirt and jacket. He yanked, pulling hard enough to throw himself and the man onto the floor.

More rounds cut the air above them as they fell and knocked the shelves from the back wall.

Reacting automatically, J.B. kicked the door shut, then fired across the street, drawing more blasterfire. He moved smoothly away from the window long enough to reach out and bolt the door again. "Dark night, that was close."

Ryan left Elmore where he lay, knowing the Armorer and Doc would keep the man covered. Crossing the floor in two long strides, Ryan dropped to his knees beside Krysty. "What's wrong?"

"I don't know." Mildred worked frantically, hooking a finger and running it down Krysty's throat. "She acted like she had a seizure of some kind, then keeled over.'' She brought her finger back out of Krysty's mouth. Specks of saliva and blood showed on Mildred's finger. ''There's no obstruction. As far as I can tell, the airway's open.''

''Then why isn't she breathing?''

''There's no reason for her not to be that I can see.'' Mildred brushed the prehensile red hair from Krysty's mouth. ''You hear me, girl? There's no excuse I'm taking from you for you not breathing. You're going to breathe.'' She kept Krysty's head tilted back, then looked at Ryan. ''Need you to do CPR on her while I breathe for her.''

''Fireblast!'' Ryan stared into his lover's eyes. They were both open, pools of green gazing emptily up at the ceiling.

''We haven't lost her yet, Ryan,'' Mildred told him in a strong voice. ''You hear me?''

''I hear you. Get on with it.'' Ryan straddled Krysty and placed his hands together over her heart, measuring with his fingers the proper distance along her breastbone. CPR wasn't anything new to him. He'd been taught by Trader while on War Wag One. A crewman got shot up or hit by electrical defenses on some of the redoubts they'd excavated and emptied didn't mean the Trader was going to accept losing that man.

''Count it down for me,'' Mildred ordered.

Ryan pushed against Krysty's diaphragm, willing his lover to start breathing again. When finished his reps, he pulled back and let Mildred breathe for her.

''It's that fucking witch,'' Elmore said hoarsely. He remained on the ground and spread-eagled, evidently not wanting to chance any movement on his part as going for a weapon.

''She's dead,'' Ryan growled.

"Two kinds of dead where they're concerned from what I've been told."

"And who told you?"

"Man named Donovan," Elmore said.

"Do it," Mildred ordered, pulling back and breathing hard.

Ryan returned his attention to the CPR, taking care to use enough force to make Krysty's lungs work without breaking any of her ribs. Puncturing a lung with a broken rib would have made matters even worse. Unless she was already dead. Even as he thought that, Ryan forced it from his mind. He wasn't about to accept that.

Mildred took over again.

"Who's Donovan?" Ryan asked.

"Project leader I worked for at the Heimdall Foundation." Elmore watched their efforts.

"He knows about the Chosen?"

"Studied them a lot. His mother was a breeder, one of the children they stole away. She managed to escape before she died, had Donovan in a ville and managed to live out her life. He doesn't have no love for them, that's for sure, but he knows they know things that most folks don't know."

"What's happening here?"

Elmore shrugged. "The Chosen got this way about those powers of theirs. They can swap memories with each other."

"My dear chap," Doc interrupted, "would you have us believe that these women are able to do that through some clairvoyance talent?"

"Don't know about that. I'm not even sure what clairvoyance means. But I know what I've been told. And Donovan told me he'd seen it done. That he came upon a dying

Chosen who was performing some kind of ritual with a younger Chosen.''

"Incredible."

"Ain't the half of it," Elmore assured him. "Got lots of stories about the Chosen, and Donovan told me the truth was even more unbelievable. And I'm a guy been over the mountain to see the elephant in my day."

Mildred pulled back from Krysty's face, her own features stained with perspiration. "It's okay," she said hoarsely, "Krysty's breathing on her own again."

Beneath his fingertips, Ryan felt the flutter of his lover's heart. As that registered, her eyes pulled down to his, focusing with effort.

"Lover," she said weakly.

"What happened?" Ryan asked.

"They're moving out there," J.B. called from the window. "Trying to fan out to get position on the front door. If they have a couple grens, they could come knocking real hard."

Ryan knew that, and his mind raced with the possibilities and problems that occupied his attention. Survival was first and foremost, but that meant Krysty's survival, too, and at the moment that appeared tied to Elmore.

"Phlorin's still inside my head, Ryan," Krysty replied. "She was talking to me. She made me go blind here, then stopped my heart to show me she could." She reached up for Ryan, trembling. "We've got to get her out of there. Can't stand not having my head not be my own."

"We will," Ryan replied, but fear touched him because he knew he didn't have the first idea how they were going to do that. The old woman was as dead as he knew how to make her. "Can you move?"

"Yes." Krysty nodded, then acted like she instantly regretted the effort. "I'll manage."

"Good enough." Ryan turned his attention back to Elmore as Doc continued questioning him.

"What would be the purpose of such a memory transfer?" the old man asked.

"The Chosen are broken down into groups," Elmore answered. "Donovan could tell you more, but I can tell you that. This woman was one of their scouts. An explorer. That beaded pack with all the designs on it told me that. The explorers don't travel back to their ville very often. They aren't allowed to. They get sent out to find what they can and make sure the information gets back to the others."

Ryan listened to the sound of Krysty's breathing as he went to join J.B. at the window. He took advantage of the cover the windowframe offered and scanned the area. Naylor's men were in motion, but there were few places for them to go.

"I asked Donovan about it once," Elmore said, "and he told me that if another Chosen comes up on a dead one soon enough, mebbe even within a few hours after, then they could still force a transfer."

"Then what happens?" Krysty asked, her voice cracking with emotion and exhaustion.

Elmore shrugged. "You mean what do they do with the information? Take it back to the others, I guess. You'd have to talk to Donovan about the rest of it."

"He knows about things like this?" Ryan asked.

"Only person I know of that would," Elmore admitted. He looked uneasy about saying that, and Ryan knew the man was wondering if he'd said too much. "Finding Donovan ain't easy."

"Saw a map once with Heimdall Foundation marked on it," Ryan said, laying the ace on the line. "A few days west of here, traveling by foot."

"He won't be there," Elmore said. "And that's assuming that map and your memory of it are right."

"Where'll he be?"

Elmore looked imploringly at Ryan. "Mister, I don't want to die. And if you turn me over to the baron's men out there, that's surely what's going to happen."

Ryan couldn't argue with that, and there wasn't time to investigate the matter between the two men any further at the moment. "Where's Donovan?"

"It's spring," Elmore answered reluctantly. "He'll be up in the mountains making sure of the water supply to the Foundation. Staying hidden like they do takes a lot of water to run things."

"If we take you out of here," Ryan said, "you can take us to Donovan?"

"Hell, yes."

Ryan looked at the man. "You try to fuck around with me, I'll chill you the first time I know it."

"Sure."

"Cawdor!" Naylor shouted from outside.

"I'm here," Ryan shouted back.

"We can still deal," the sec chief roared.

"Don't know about you," Ryan said, "but I'm kind of shy on trust at this end."

"One of my men got jumpy," Naylor explained. "Didn't mean nothing by it."

"A man under your command who doesn't follow orders isn't worth having," Ryan responded. "Man will never be able to carry his own weight, much less work into the position of being an asset."

There was a pause. "I see you've had some training."

"Enough."

"What about the man I want?"

"Make you another deal," Ryan said, "since you seem so keen on changing the one I thought we had."

Naylor paused, and the silence drew out. "Tell me," he said at last.

"Trot out the man who fired that shot," Ryan stated. "Then I want you to execute him in front of me."

"What?"

"You heard me. Call it a show of faith." Ryan glanced at J.B., making sure his friend was comfortable with the idea.

"Man might not feel so bad about chilling some poor bastard," the Armorer said, "who's already been wounded or is dead. Stake him out there, shoot him a couple times, make it look good."

"That's fine," Ryan said. "Every minute we get here gives Jak and Dean that much more time to get to the other end of that tunnel."

"You can't be serious about asking me to chill one of my own men," Naylor called back.

"I'm serious about it. If you don't want to chill him yourself, get him to that clearing and I'll chill him for you." He lined up the Steyr, gazing through the scope and sifting through the shadows he spotted around Naylor's position.

"I can't do that," Naylor said.

"That's too fucking bad," Ryan told the man. "Because you're not getting the man without doing it."

"Don't take the high hand with me, Cawdor. I've been looking at that building, noticing how much wood is in it. If you don't get burned to death in a fire, you'll at least be smoked out. Give me the man, and I'll make sure you get out of here alive."

"Mebbe there's something you haven't been considering," Ryan said laconically. "You walked into this situation and ended up between my people and the coldhearts. What makes you so sure you can just walk right back out of here when you get ready?''

"What the hell are you talking about?''

"Turn your back on me, and I'll chill you and your people every time I get a shot,'' Ryan promised. "I figure my chances here look better if you're trapped over there. The coldhearts waiting to pick up the pieces won't be quite so anxious to come back in here.''

"You're triple stupe!''

"I don't see the coldhearts charging in here,'' Ryan said. "And I don't think it's just because of the number of people I've got holed up in here with me.'' He put the Steyr's crosshairs over the first of two men he'd spotted. Only a sliver of the man's face was visible behind the wag wreckage where he took cover. The second man was attempting to scale the wags, avoiding the pockets of acid rain left in the dents in the rusted metal. Ryan put a round through the face of the first man, then managed a body shot to the second man before he could reach cover.

The first sec man flew backward, his brain pan emptied in a violent gush over the men behind him. The second sec man stretched out atop one of the ruined wags, his flesh sizzling in the pool of acid rain gathered on top. His hoarse screams echoed in the artificial canyons as he struggled to get out of the water.

A fusillade of shots slammed against the front of the building, driving Ryan to deeper cover. He took a moment to glance at Krysty, noting in satisfaction that the redhead was moving more smoothly now. Her face still contained pain and fear, and it hurt Ryan to see it.

"Stop firing!'' Naylor bawled. "Stop your bastard firing or I'll shoot the next man pulls a trigger myself!''

The blasterfire stopped, but the sec men challenged their

chief's decision with curses and questions. "Let's chill all those stupe bastards in there and be done with it," one man yelled. Most of the others agreed with the sentiment.

"Well," Ryan demanded during the lull, "how do you want to handle it, Naylor?"

"Fuck you, Cawdor."

"Something to think about," Ryan said. "We sit here chilling each other, those coldhearts out there may decide to pitch in and help."

"You think we can trust each other?" the sec chief asked.

"Mebbe a little more than before," Ryan said. "At least this way you know we aren't going to hesitate or back down."

"You're a hard man."

"You haven't seen hard yet," Ryan promised. "We end up stuck here past sunset and you haven't made up your mind, I intend to find out how good your men are in the dark. Of course, me and my people will only be a few predators out there among a bunch of others. You spotted all those skeletons out there, didn't you?"

Naylor didn't say anything.

"The coldhearts look like they've been feeding on human flesh when they had to or when they could get it," Ryan pointed out. "And they don't look to have been too particular about disposing of the leftovers. You can bet this place turns into a regular feedlot at night. And this close to rad-blasted areas, a lot of those night feeders are going to be muties. Mebbe some you haven't seen before."

"Dad." Dean's voice drifted up from the hole in the floor.

"Yeah, son. Come on through." He drew the SIG-Sauer and kept his finger on the trigger just in case Dean wasn't coming alone.

Chapter Thirteen

Dean eased up out of the hole. His hair was matted with dog shit and his clothing covered with it. He sat the lantern down on the floor, then raked pieces off his face with his fingers. "Found the other end. Comes out about 150 yards away."

"The river?" J.B. asked.

Dean nodded. "Real close."

"Where's Jak?" Ryan asked.

"Watching the other end. Some coldhearts are out there. Coming this way."

"Toward the tunnel?"

Dean shook his head. "Didn't look like it. That tunnel isn't where anybody would want to go unless they had to. Looks like it hasn't been used by anything but dogs. Mebbe they've even been kept in there for a while. Triple bad going through there, Dad."

"We don't have a choice," Ryan said.

"At least, after a bit the smell kind of goes away." Dean brushed at his clothes some more.

"My boy," Doc said, "you are sadly mistaken."

"Mildred," Ryan said, "you and Krysty get moving. Dean, help keep these youngsters moving along."

The woman, Mary, started to protest, pulling at her son protectively.

"Let Dean take him," Ryan told her. "He'll stand a better chance with him than with you. Dean knows where to move and when to move." He flicked his gaze over to the other man holding his daughter. "Same for your girl."

"I know it," the man said. "Seen this boy in action myself. I've lived roughing it in the past, but it's been a while ago."

Ryan turned to his son. "Take them, Dean. Stay close to Mildred and Krysty. We'll stagger the rest of them out."

Dean nodded and called the two youngsters to him. The boy went reluctantly, needing threatening from his father to get moving. His eyes filled with tears, but he went along. The girl, older than him by a couple years, took his hand and guided him as Dean helped them down into the tunnel.

Mary tried to go after her son.

"Wait," Ryan ordered, swinging the SIG-Sauer enough so that she caught the movement.

"That's my son," she protested.

"I know it," Ryan said. "And you need to stay back a ways. You crowd up on him, Dean won't be able to get him back to you if something goes wrong."

"He's right, Mary," her husband said, putting his hand on her shoulder. "Man knows what he's doing. Staggered line like this, we can cover for each other."

Ryan waited a bit, feeling the humidity press in through the windows.

"Cawdor!" Naylor sounded more anxious.

"Doc," Ryan said, "take the next group through." He pointed at Mary and her husband, then at one of the remaining women.

"I surely will, my dear Ryan, and how long before you join us on that road less traveled?" Doc grimaced as he peered into the tunnel.

"A few minutes," Ryan said. "J.B. and I are going to shut things down here."

"Do not tarry," the old man warned. "In her present

state of mind, I know Krysty will want you by her side."
He took another lantern from the shelves and lighted the
wick, adjusting it until it burned well.

"Get it done, Doc."

Doc dropped into the hole, then turned to help the
women down. "Dear ladies, I do so apologize for not doff-
ing my jacket as a true gentleman would to make the going
more palatable, but I fear it would be but a waste of my
raiment."

The women ignored him, not liking what they were having to do, but clambering into the tunnel all the same. Survival pushed most people through life, Ryan knew. The
husband followed them, then Doc crawled through, as well.

"Cawdor!" Naylor called again.

"What?" Ryan asked.

"It appears to me that we're both in a bad place."

"Man's kind of slow, isn't he?" J.B. asked with a mirthless grin. "Hadn't been so single-minded about getting Elmore back, he could have waited to see if we were going
to throw in with him, then chill us when we were least
expecting it."

"Already knew that," Ryan called out to the sec chief.
He motioned at Elmore and lowered his voice. "Take the
rest of them through."

Elmore nodded, then climbed up from the floor. He took
a lantern from the wall.

"If you aren't at the other end when I get there, you can
bet all your jack that I'll come looking. And I'm good at
hunting men." Ryan tossed the man the weapon they'd
taken from him.

Elmore caught the blaster and nodded grimly. "Figured
you would be."

"And I also don't intend to see anything happen to that
woman."

"I'll get you to Donovan," Elmore promised. "If we get out of here." He dropped down into the tunnel after the others.

"Cawdor?" Naylor called, sounding less sure than he had before.

"I'm listening," Ryan answered.

"Wasn't sure."

"What's your plan?"

Ryan gestured to J.B., pointing at the pockets where the Armorer kept his grens. "We'll leave them a going-away surprise."

J.B. nodded.

"There's safety in numbers," Naylor said. "Why don't you and yours come out, then we can get past those damn coldhearts."

"Convince me." Ryan caught the gren J.B. tossed him. He walked to the door and pulled the gren's pin. Working the gren, practiced in what he was doing, he jammed it between the bottom of the door and the floor, wedging it into place with a knife he got from one of the dead men. The gren balanced precariously, the plunger pressed tight against the door. Once it was opened, it would send the grenade spinning away, the 3-second delay fuse inside burning.

Naylor seemed at a loss for words, but he struggled through it.

J.B. slipped his gren onto one of the support struts at the back of the room, tying it into place with a rag he picked up from the floor. "When your blast goes off," the Armorer said, "it should free this one. Second blast will catch anybody coming through that door after the first one, or give them more cause to think about coming through so quick."

"Either way," Ryan said, "it'll buy us some time we

need." Before he could drop into the tunnel, blasterfire erupted outside. He returned to the window, puzzled when he didn't hear the slap of bullets against the building. As he watched, he saw misshapen brutes weaving between the stacks of wrecked wags.

"The ghoulies," J.B. said. "Guess they got tired of waiting for dinner."

"Bastards move through that wreckage smooth and quiet," Ryan said. "Good thing we didn't get caught out there."

J.B. silently agreed.

The ghoulies shattered Naylor's defensive line, driving his men out from cover. They fired into the muties, but it was almost like shooting at shadows. The ghoulies were too quick for the sec men, and they swung their axes and makeshift weapons with deadly accuracy.

Without warning, the sec men broke from cover and rushed toward the building where Ryan and J.B. were. There was nowhere else for them to go. The ghoulies stayed hot on their heels.

"Time to go," Ryan said grimly. He ran for the tunnel and dropped through the hole in the floor. The stench of the dog shit and wet fur filled his nose as his feet squished across the tunnel floor. He reached up to close the trapdoor, shutting the Armorer and himself into the darkness. Working to keep the Steyr clear of the muck below, he put a shoulder against one of the walls and started forward.

The first gren exploded behind him before he'd gone twenty paces. Screams of wounded and dying men rushed down into the tunnel, and the vibrations of the explosion rattled clods of earth from the tunnel's ceiling. Then all those sounds were temporarily swallowed up by the explosion of the second gren.

Ryan kept going forward as fast as he could. Even if

Naylor's sec crew didn't find the tunnel in the building, there was a chance the ghoulies already knew about it.

HARSH SUNLIGHT lanced into Ryan's eye as he emerged from the other end of the tunnel. He followed the SIG-Sauer out of the hole, coming up in a blind created behind stacks of wags. "Anything?" he asked.

Blasterfire still sounded in the distance behind him. Baying hounds punctuated the noise, along with the screams of men.

"We appear to be well out of sight here, my dear Ryan," Doc said. The humid wind whipped at his grayish locks, brushing them across his shoulders. "But I fear that such harbor is fleeting at most. We would best be served by setting about our course again. Whatever that is."

"The river," Ryan answered. "Double quick." He glanced at the men, women and youngsters he'd promised to help, resenting their presence now that he realized they would only slow the companions' efforts at saving themselves. "Saw some boat docks during an earlier recon. Mebbe we'll take one for ourselves, see how far we can get.

"J.B., I want you and Jak walking point. Keep each other in sight, with a forty-yard lead on the rest of us."

J.B. and Jak took off at once, already knowing from the sun's position which way the river lay.

"Elmore," Ryan went on, automatically redistributing his gear and weapons, "you go next. Dean, I want you on him. He makes a move to break free of the group, put a bullet in the back of his head."

Dean nodded.

Knowing he was putting his son in considerable danger, Ryan went on, "And if he makes a move to hurt you, chill him on the spot."

"Don't worry, Dad. I'll see it done."

Despite the argumentative look on his face, Elmore moved out, staying the agreed-upon distance back from J.B. and Jak. Dean fell in behind him, the Browning looking big in his hand.

"The rest of you fall in if you're going with us," Ryan said. "Keep up or we'll leave you behind. We're only going to live as long as we can move quick."

The group hesitated only a moment, then got under way. Ryan had Krysty and Mildred fall in next, and he brought up drag himself.

Even with the children, the group moved quickly. Jak and J.B. moved quicker, racing through the junkyard until they reached the high wooden wall securing the back. Most of the wall was constructed of old planks, but sheets of rusted tin and boards that looked different than the original wood covered areas where men or animals had broken through.

Jak and J.B. chose one of the tin-covered areas and hacked their way through with a camp ax. The blasterfire had died away, and no matter what had happened between the coldhearts and Naylor's sec team, Ryan figured it only meant bad news for the companions.

"Clear!" Jak called, throwing aside the last piece of tin. The albino led the way through.

Ryan hunkered down under cover, gazing back along the two aisles he could see between the wag wreckage. Perspiration clung to him, making the feces stuck to his clothes and skin feel even worse.

"The dogs," Krysty whispered from nearby as Doc urged his charges through the wall. Her green eyes looked haunted, fever bright.

"What about the dogs?" Mildred prompted.

"They've picked up our scents," Krysty said.

"How do you know?" Ryan demanded.

"I can...*feel* them." She shook her head, as if she didn't like the sensation. "It's Phlorin, lover. Her being in my head is affecting my powers, making them stronger."

Her words cut into Ryan's heart, but he shook it off. It was a waste of time worrying about something that he couldn't do anything about. Getting out of the ville—that would give them the breathing room they needed. Then they'd see what needed to be done.

Mildred and Krysty squeezed through the hole in the fence, and Ryan followed. With the dogs getting their scent, presumably the smell of the dog shit over all their clothes, as well, he knew there'd be little chance of throwing them off track.

THE LAND BROKE AWAY from the ville, falling into a rapid decline as the group neared the river. Judging from the amount of damage from water erosion, Ryan guessed that much of the surrounding land had been submerged at one time. The nukecaust had reshaped much of North America. Besides breaking off much of what had been California, it had also created a huge lake in the northwestern section of the Deathlands. The tidal waves that had rolled in as a result of the earthquakes and tsunamis that had swallowed the West Coast had continued on into the interior and created a huge lake. The overflow from that had evidently rolled through Idaho for a time.

Small wooden docks made of cast-off lumber jutted into the water. Some were higher than others, indicating the water level was subject to change. Judging from the docks he saw, the river was sometimes as much as thirty feet higher than what it was now, and pushed back over some of the tumbledown wreckage left of Idaho Falls.

Tall grass and cattails, still yellow and trying to make a

comeback from the earlier flood stages of the river, lined the sharp incline leading to the river. A handful of boats was tied up at the docks. The morning fishing was done, but men remained at the docks mending equipment and nets. Women and children stood around fifty-five-gallon drums filled with burning wood, smoking the fish that had been caught.

Wag engines roared in the distance, growing closer.

None of the boats, however, were equipped with engines. Masts stood proudly in all of them, the sails furled. Only two were big enough for the companions and the hangers-on they'd picked up.

Knowing they had no choice, Ryan commanded the others to ground behind the ville debris lining the riverbank, then waved Jak and J.B. to him. They went toward the long boat Ryan chose, walking in a loose triangle.

The afternoon sun beat down on the riverbank. The sand deposits scouring the sides of the incline were already nearly dry, as if the rainstorm that had come earlier had never happened at all.

The women and children spotted Ryan and the others first. They were poorly outfitted, dressed in patched home-spun that had faded from hard wear and too many wash-ings. Their faces carried scars, physical and emotional. Boning and scaling knives filled their hands, but they backed away. Mothers sent small children scampering to hide in the debris or in the nearby weeds.

Ryan didn't say anything because there was nothing to say. Even if the people didn't know what he was there for, they knew he was there to take something that wasn't his.

The sailboat had a tall mast that advertised plenty of room for sailcloth. With the wind blowing strongly and in the right direction, Ryan hoped it would be enough to push them quickly against the sluggish current of the greenish river.

Ryan brought up the Steyr, shoving the business end toward the bearded man mending a net on the rickety dock beside the sailboat. "Move away from the boat."

The bearded man was squat and powerfully built, probably not up to Ryan's shoulder, but almost half again as broad. He wore a faded gray sweatshirt with the sleeves hacked off, perspiration stains beading across his upper chest, and striped overalls that had been cut off at midthigh. His hair was dark brown but glinted red where the sun had washed the color out, the same as his beard. He wore a baseball cap that bore a picture of a leaping green fish.

"This is my boat, mister." The man motioned to the two teenage boys helping him with the net.

"Not now, it isn't," Ryan said. "Now it might be the only chance at escape my friends and I have got."

"My boat's the only way I got of making a living for my family. Take that from me, might as well shoot me right here."

"It'll be done," Ryan said. "I plan on dying last if I got a choice. And you stopping me now's the same as pulling a blaster on me."

The sailor stood slowly, a long gutting knife in his hand that looked like a short sword. Scars on his face and arms showed that he was no stranger to fighting or bladework.

The wag engines sounded closer, and Ryan knew they were running out of time. His finger tightened on the Steyr's trigger. He knew he'd kill the man if he had to. The boys spread out around their father, taking up defensive positions. Ryan had yet to see a blaster on any of them, but he didn't doubt he'd have to kill the boys if he killed their father. It didn't sit well with him.

But that boat was the companions' only way out of the trouble they were in. There was no choice about passing it up.

Chapter Fourteen

The sailor squinted past Ryan, gazing in the distance. His thumb nestled confidently on the broad-bladed gutting knife. It was turned edge up in his hand, the sawteeth glinting in the afternoon sunlight. "Slaggers?" he asked. "You got trouble with them?"

"They mean to put us on the last train headed West," Ryan said.

"Chill any of them?"

"Many as we could. You're wasting my time," Ryan growled.

"Got no love for the Slaggers," the sailor said with a mean grin, "but I love this boat, and I need this boat. I lose it, I lose myself, and there ain't no fucking around about that. You know how to handle it?"

"Sailed before." Even as he answered, Ryan remembered the storm-tossed seas in Georgia when he and J.B. had piloted a cabin cruiser along the Lantic coastline. He was more at home in an armored wag with plenty of fuel and ammo. It would have been his first choice.

"But you don't know this river," the sailor went on. "She's a tricky bitch, especially now. Stuff piled up on the bottom where you least expect it, and during the dry season like this, you don't know where those places are, you'll rip the bottom right out of her and not get away anyhow. Let me captain her for you, and you'll improve your chances on getting away. And I'll improve my chances on keeping my boat in one piece.''

"Makes sense," J.B. stated.

Ryan looked at Jak and got a nod of approval from the albino. "Cover him," Ryan told Jak.

The teenager put his .357 Magnum on the man. "Move," he ordered.

"My boys go with us," the sailor said. "I ain't leaving them here to take their chances with the Slaggers when they watch me sail out of here with you."

"You're getting mighty pushy for a man one bullet away from being chilled," Ryan said.

"Figure there's no better time," the man replied. "Still remains to be seen if you can chill me before I get close enough to open you up, take a look inside."

Ryan grinned at the man's confidence, appreciating it. "They go." He turned and waved to his companions, yelling at them to run. He could already see the dogs closing the distance, hear their baying echoing across the river.

In seconds, they'd loaded aboard the sailboat and ducked down out of sight. Blasterfire from the wags pelted the river and tore into the sailboat's sides.

Ryan took up a position aft, easing the Steyr into position on the railing. He led the first wag he spotted, then squeezed the trigger and rode out the recoil. The heavy bullet sheared through the broken windshield of the wag and exploded the face of the man beyond.

Out of control, the wag slewed crazily down the steep incline and into a small rowboat less than a dozen yards from the boat Ryan had chosen. The wag and rowboat went down at once, showing how surprisingly deep the channel had cut through the land throughout the years it had flowed through it.

Ryan managed to pick off two more Slaggers before the

coldhearts pulled back and formed a skirmish line. J.B. fell in beside him, but held fire for the moment. It was enough that the Slaggers knew they were armed.

Turning, Ryan watched the sailor's boys shinny up the masts like daring monkeys. They cut the sailcloth free in a heartbeat as their father cast off the lines. By the time they reached the decks, the wind was already starting to fill the sails and pull the boat into smooth motion.

J.B. cut loose with the Remington M-4000 three times. The hollow booms rolled across the boat and the water, but the knife-edged flétchettes ripped the dogs that raced down the dock to bloody tatters. Their corpses tumbled into the water.

The boat came about smoothly, taking to the water and charging upstream despite the current. The sailor kept his hand on the wheel, working the boom and calling out orders to his sons.

Ryan came down from the slightly raised prow and walked along the side facing the incline where the Slaggers raced on the bank. The coldhearts hadn't given up the chase, but with the lack of roads along the bank, they weren't having much success. Still, their bullets ripped across the sailboat's deck, ripping holes in the sailcloth.

The sailor cursed lustily as he saw the damage done to his sails. He ordered his boys to stay low. Ryan signaled to Doc to keep them under his eye. There was every possibility the man had weapons aboard his craft and might seek to redress his current situation.

A final volley managed to kill one of the women and two of the men aboard the sailboat, leaving Mary and her husband, and Elmore and one of the other women, as well as the children. The little girl screamed in anguish and held on to her dead father until Krysty took her into her arms and pulled her to safety. The men died instantly, but the woman died screaming, her guts blasted out of her and stringing across the boat deck.

In the end, Mildred held her tight, then slipped her ZKR 551 against the back of the woman's head and pulled the trigger to put her out of her misery. Blood sprayed into the air and dappled the belling sailcloth with crimson splotches.

When the woman was dead, Mildred shoved her over the edge. She hit the water with a splash, quickly falling behind the wake of the sailboat. For a moment, the body floated in the water, intestines strung out around her like a bloody spiderweb. Then the fish began to feed, nibbling at the rubbery trails of soft flesh and dragging it under in places.

During their earlier excursion through the river after arriving through the mat-trans unit, Ryan had discovered that the river held several forms of mutie fish. Some of them were damn near as big as a man.

"Bad place to go in the water," the sailor commented above the creak of the mast and the crack of sailcloth. "Docks attract scavenger fish and other things. Got mutie crawfish in there longer than a man's arm that have developed a real appetite for meat. Don't mind working for it, either. Seen men and women dragged under, they get too close to the water when they're fishing from the banks."

"I'll keep that in mind," Ryan said. He watched the Slaggers disappear to their rear. "What are the chances they'll be able to find us?"

The man smiled at Ryan.

"Think something's so damn funny?" the one-eyed man growled.

"Be kind of hard to hide the river, wouldn't it? And they know which direction we headed out in."

Ryan felt the back of his neck burn from anger. Too damn many things going on, and he wasn't thinking straight. Krysty's situation wasn't leaving him much room

for thinking about other things. She seemed to be getting
around better, but she still wasn't herself.

"Where are we going?" the sailor asked.

"Upriver," Ryan answered.

"Got a destination in mind?"

"Know it when we get there," Ryan said.

"Them Slaggers following us," the sailor said, "you go
far enough up this river till we reach the rough country,
they ain't gonna be so apt to follow. They live off the easy
pickings around Idaho Falls."

Ryan nodded, catching Jak's eye and letting the albino
know watching the sailor was his responsibility. The albino
gave him a short nod. Ryan reloaded the Steyr, noticing
how low his ammo was getting, then went back to join
Krysty. She still held the little girl as she cried.

"Her father," Krysty said, emotional herself.

"I know." Ryan looked down at the little girl but didn't
let emotion touch him. They were still running for their
lives, and getting overly involved could mean the death of
them all. He was surprised Krysty was so obviously over-
wrought.

"Not myself, lover." Krysty glanced up at him and
wiped at the tears on her cheeks. "Carrying a lot of extra
baggage in my head right now."

"It's okay." Ryan touched her shoulder, then resumed
scanning the river. "We'll fix it."

Krysty put her hand on the little girl's head for a moment, then grimaced. Abruptly the little girl passed out,
every muscle relaxing. "Better for her this way," the redhead said. "Took away her pain for a little bit. She'll sleep,
then mebbe we'll be in a better place."

"How'd you do that?" Ryan asked.

"Don't know, lover. Just knew that I could."

"Did you decide to do that, or did..."

"Phlorin?" Krysty supplied.

Ryan nodded.

"You know I've never done anything like that before in my life. It must have been Phlorin." Krysty smiled, touching the child's face with her fingers. "Hard to imagine a crusty old bitch like that caring enough to do something like this."

Ryan saw through to the darker side, though. "Being able to do something like that would make it a lot easier to steal children away in the dead of night," he pointed out. "Doesn't mean being able to do that is necessarily all good."

"Never really seen anything in the Deathlands that was all good." With the wind pushing at her, blowing her hair around her face, Krysty looked almost normal. But there was a haunted look in her bright green eyes. Mildred came and took the little girl away and went to join J.B., giving them room.

"I can't live like this, lover," Krysty said quietly.

"I know," Ryan said.

She turned to face him, placing a trembling hand against his scarred temple. "I mean what I'm saying, Ryan. If I have to live like this, I'll chill myself to get it overwith."

He didn't say anything, feeling the powerful emotion thinking of her loss triggered within him. It felt like somebody had strapped iron bars across his chest.

"Can't have anybody in my head like this," she went on. "And I can feel her. Wandering around in the back areas of my brain, learning everything she can. She'll use it against me when she gets the chance."

"I won't let that happen," Ryan said. He put an arm across her shoulders, pulling her close and holding her tight. "Long as you're with me, you're going to be safe."

But he had to wonder how true his words were.

"GOING TO NEED some ammo and supplies," J.B. said.

Ryan stood near the sailor, watching as the man handled the boat with ease. The green water of the river stretched out before them, alternately sandwiched in between stony banks and areas where pockets of trees and brush filled out in early summer growth.

"We'll get them," Ryan said. Nearly two hours had passed since they'd left Idaho Falls. There'd been no sign of the coldhearts or anyone else. The area upriver from the ville appeared pristine and uninhabited.

The Armorer took out his minisextant and took a reading from the sun. They were starting to lose the daylight now. When he finished, he made a few brief notations on a map of the area from his pack. "River's changed locations."

Ryan understood. They wouldn't be able to use the river as a marker to the other areas on the map. And coming back down the river past Idaho Falls to return to the redoubt they'd come through in wouldn't be a wise idea at the moment, not with the Slaggers marking territory.

"River changes every fifteen or twenty years," the sailor said as he piloted his craft around a sandbar that stuck out nearly to the center of the river.

"Every once in a while, the river even changes direction," the sailor went on. "Thirty years ago, when I was just a boy, it flowed the other way. And my grandpop, he told me that it changed direction when he was a boy, too. But quakes somewhere along the way shifted things so much that the river started going the other way. Made things interesting around the ville for a while because my da and grandpop salvaged a lot of predark things for a few years. Made a handsome living at it trading with folks."

"What's your name?" Ryan asked.

"Morse," the man answered. "My boys are named Bud and Sandy."

Seated ahead of the wheel, the boys both nodded at Ryan, but they didn't seem overly friendly about it. Their skin had been browned by the sun, and they were whipcord lean from the hard life they led. They'd stripped down to cutoff denims and carried broad-bladed knives at their waists in plastic sheaths. Their hair trailed well past their shoulders, done up in braids that kept it out of their faces.

"River still come from the north?" Ryan asked.

"There's a fork about forty miles north and east of here. Comes from north on into what used to be Montana there, and the other fork comes out of Wyoming."

"Those areas populated?" J.B. asked.

"Some," Morse said. "Mainly people who don't like being around other people. Get back in the woods, live by themselves, taking what they need from the land."

"That, old salt," Doc said, walking up, "does not sound like such a bad dream to hang on to whilst in this nightmare of apocalyptic life." The old man took a deep breath. "Why, friend Ryan and John Barrymore," Doc added, "I do believe the wind carries with it a freshness of the earth rather than the stench of the ville we so recently debarked."

Ryan took a breath and silently agreed. "What kind of supplies do you have on board?" he asked Morse.

Moving the wheel slightly to alter the sailboat's heading, Morse gave the one-eyed man a harsh stare. "Take my boat and steal from me, too? Fuck, we're going to have to talk about my wages at some point."

Ryan's anger gave way to the humor of the situation. The red mist cleared from his vision as he smiled. "You must have a set of brass balls big as your head."

J.B. gave a short grin, then doffed his hat long enough to wipe the sweat from his forehead. "Man's got a price in mind, usually first sign of a professional."

"You ain't going to find no son of a bitch knows this

river any bastard better than I do,'' Morse crowed. ''And that's a damn fact.''

Ryan glanced in the bow of the boat and spotted Elmore sitting with his back to the railing, gazing out at the trees and the lazy water passing him by. His eyes looked hungry but wary as he considered his options.

Dean sat across from him, his dark hair ruffling in the wind. The boy kept his Browning Hi-Power bared in his lap, his fist resting casually around it.

''You took my boat and the safety I had at Idaho Falls,'' Morse went on. ''Can't just take a man's home and expect him to be happy about it. Your problems weren't none of my own. Right?'' He looked at Doc, obviously expecting support.

''My dear fellow,'' Doc replied, ''you do a disservice to yourself by assuming that I have any sway with the gentleman who champions our little group. Though friend Ryan and I admittedly do not share the same perception of time, events or orchestration, it is through his savvy and strength that we have lived so long and adventured so much.''

''What about it?'' Morse pressed Ryan. ''Know you're a bad man from the way you carry yourself, the way you handle those blasters of yours, but are you an evil man?''

And in that moment, Ryan had to admire the man. Morse had grit. The Trader always cut a little slack for men who stood up for themselves, took a little off the bottom line when he sat down at a table to cut a deal.

''No,'' Ryan answered, ''I'm not an evil man by nature. Leastways, I'm not an evil man today. What kind of jack are you looking for?''

Morse grinned. ''Got a bottle of smooth-drinking whiskey down in the hold. If we're going to dicker, we ain't gonna do it dry. Let one of my boys go get it?''

"Sure," Ryan said. "Doc?"

"I shall accompany the lad, my dear Ryan."

"And take a look around at what's to be had for eating," Ryan advised. "Bastard self-heats right now don't sound good at all."

Chapter Fifteen

The whiskey burned the back of Ryan's throat as it went down, igniting a small fireball in his stomach. They drank from small ceramic cups molded by hand and fired in a postnukecaust kiln.

"Now, that's the stuff to set men's souls ablaze," Morse stated.

Ryan silently agreed. The whiskey possessed a rawness to it, but had been aged for a time somewhere in good barrels. He knew the difference from his time in his father's barony, and from the years spent on the road with War Wag One. And good whiskey barrels meant some kind of stability in a ville or small group of homes.

"Where's the boys' mother?" Ryan asked after drinks had been poured around again.

"You're thinking mebbe we left her in Idaho Falls?" Morse shook his head. "You'd have had to chill me to keep me from leaving any woman at the mercy of them Slaggers. Oh, those coldhearts gouge us for protection jack, as they term it, saying they keep most outlanders away from the ville. But they learned early on not to fuck around with any of Docktown. They came down a couple times, took some women and savaged them. Chilled one of them and fed her to those fucking dogs. Mebbe ate her themselves, way I hear it."

The sailboat glided across the water, hardly noticing any of the chop that settled across the river's surface. The shadows from the trees lengthened behind them as they headed east, stabbing shadowy branches into the water. Ryan had noticed a lot of game around the banks, winding between the trees and brush. It told him the water was good and the food plentiful. The companions definitely wouldn't go hungry.

"No," Morse went on, "I lost Sandy's ma to a tinker man. Came to the ville with knives and such. Predark nonsense an honest body wouldn't have a need for. But he was a good-looking man, and he had dresses the like of which that woman had never seen before. When he left after a few days, she left with him."

"Love never quite goes along the paths one wishes for it to," Doc lamented.

"Don't know about that," Morse replied. "Sandy's ma, she was quite a lay when she wanted to be. Got all wide-eyed and squealing when I let her ride me. But that woman could wear a strong man down to the bastard bone. Luckily most times she just put up with what I had to give her and wasn't trying to get her own. By the time she left, I was done playing slap-and-tickle with Bud's ma, and him already in the oven."

"Oh," Doc said.

Ryan could tell from the old man's face that Doc didn't know how to properly respond to the information, and smiled at his friend's discomfort. Doc's Victorian ways still showed through from time to time.

"Bud's ma, she ran as skipper on Dawson's boat. She was his daughter, but old Dawson, he liked to have his way with her. Didn't know it when I started sneaking around with her. Thought we was just hiding it from my first wife, but we was actually hiding out from her da. She turned out knocked up, Dawson knew it wasn't his because he went barren from a fever when he was just a young man. His wife got burned up in a fire down in Docktown. He figured why go looking for another woman when you already got one at home.''

Ryan listened to the story. It was like a lot of others a man could hear out in the Deathlands. Incest, though, remained a taboo in most societies, but not all. Even the baronies recognized the need for fresh blood in the gene pool. The story was too familiar to offer any strong reaction, but it still brought distaste.

''When Dawson found out his daughter was knocked up, he come at her with a knife. Cut her up some.'' Morse clucked his tongue. ''She got away from the fucker and come running to me. Dawson, he was stupe enough to figure he could take me. When I saw what he done, I broke his neck. Didn't chill him outright, though, just paralyzed him.''

''You let her chill the reprobate herself?'' Doc asked.

Morse shook his head. ''No. Junie, she was a good daughter. She wouldn't have chilled her old man no matter what. Probably might have even gone back to him if I hadn't chilled him. But I did. Took him out in the middle of the river down from Docktown, and propped him up in a cork-filled life preserver. Went fishing, using him as bait.''

''Paralyzed man good bait,'' Jak said knowingly. Ryan wasn't sure when the albino had joined them at the wheel. Jak sat on the railing, his body moving easily with the river current. ''Got tribe in bayous break necks of outlanders, use 'em troll for gators. Works bastard good.''

Morse nodded. ''Down where I took Dawson, they ain't got any gators. Only heard stories about them, but that place has got mutie catfish near to three hundred pounds. Fuckers don't come off the river bottom for much. But I cut the heels of Dawson's feet just enough that they'd bleed good without bleeding to death. And him squalling like a woman the way he was, he attracted a lot of attention from the local catfish population. Too big to fish for them with a line, but I got four of them with a bow before they took Dawson to pieces and gobbled him down.'' He grinned at the memory.

''So what happened to Junie?'' Doc asked.

Morse shrugged. ''We had some good years together. But she got kind of sick in the head. Mebbe it was all that shit her pa done to her, and mebbe it was the fact that she never did get over me taking him out and chilling him. But three years ago, she come up on me mad, waving a skinning knife in my face and telling me how she's gonna cut my balls off. I slapped her back off me before she could do any serious cutting, but she come at me again. Broke her arm that time.'' The sailor waved at his sons.

In response, the boys climbed the masts again and adjusted the rigging so that it better caught the breeze.

''Wind's changing,'' Morse said. ''Good in a way, though. Don't want to have to worry about the boat getting caught in a damn crosswind when we drop anchor tonight.''

''Nobody said anything about dropping anchor,'' Ryan told him.

''Be triple stupe to think about going on in these waters after dark,'' Morse stated. ''You haven't hardly seen any of the shit I've steered us clear of. And even with a good moon hanging overhead, we'd rip the body out of *Junie* for sure.''

''*Junie?*'' Doc inquired.

''Yeah. Named her after my second wife.'' Morse shrugged. ''Course I named her after my first wife and a few girlfriends before and after and in between, too. But today's she's *Junie*.''

"Pray tell me," Doc said, "what became of your second wife. You never mentioned. Unless I misremember."

"Chilled her," Morse replied. "Got to where she was creeping around at night. Caught her with a knife once, coming at me while I was asleep. I slept lighter than she knew."

"So you chilled her?" Doc repeated.

"Yeah. Fishing's hard work. Suck the life right out of a man, he ain't careful. Even with these boys, I bust my ass every day to bring a catch in. I don't need to be losing no sleep while I'm at it. A man gets tired, that's a man who makes mistakes. I'd sooner be without a wife than be without this boat."

"A man's got to have his principles, Doc," Ryan said.

"So you chilled your own son's mother." Doc shuddered at the thought.

"Did it right, though," Morse objected. "Slipped that boning knife between her third and fourth ribs right into her heart. She was gone before she knew she was going. Afterward, me and the boys took her out to the river and had a ceremony."

"Then used her for bait?" Doc asked dryly.

"Naw. Just dumped her in and went upstream to fish."

"And your boy Bud," Doc said, "he never came to you about any of this?"

Morse smiled. "Them boys, they like fishing more than anything else in the world. Reminds me of myself. I crewed aboard this ship when I was a boy for my da. And him for his before that. Ship's got a long history. Luck willing, I'll still have it to leave for my own sons."

"It and such an interesting history besides," Doc agreed somewhat sarcastically.

"Oh, and if it's stories you want, there's plenty of them about *Junie*, as well."

Before the storytelling could get any further, Ryan said, "You were asking about jack for the use of your boat."

Morse gave him a look filled with greedy interest. "I'm a working man. Going out of Docktown like this, I'm gonna miss a few customers on my regular rounds. Mebbe even lose some of them altogether. This taking my boat and taking me and my boys hostage, that's going to impact my business."

"Ah, the nomenclature of the would-be Wall Street tycoon," Doc said. "The me generation. And people thought all that had been left behind in the eighties. The 1980s."

"Noticed you and your boys didn't have any blasters when we came on board," Ryan said.

"No."

The man's answer was too short and too clipped to be the truth, and Ryan knew it. He was certain that somewhere aboard *Junie* was a hidden cache of one or more blasters. J.B.'s earlier investigation of the boat had turned up the bows and arrows kept in the small hold.

"You do a lot of salvage, though," Ryan went on.

"What I can," Morse agreed. "Not so much trade in it as there used to be. Most stuff me and the boys scull up from the bottom these days ain't worth having."

"J.B. doesn't see it that way. Says he spotted some blasters in the lockers belowdecks that he can fix."

"He thinks so?"

Ryan nodded. "Comes to weapons, J.B.'s an artist."

"He fixes those, you want to call it square on the jack you owe me for the boat?"

"Yeah. Only you're not getting all of the blasters."

Morse didn't look happy. "How many?"

"Half," Ryan answered. It was more than fair. Without being repaired, the blasters were useless. And fixed and ready to fire, they'd be worth more than anything Morse had ever laid his hands on. The others could be used by the companions to barter with.

"How far are we going?"

"Let you know when we get there." Ryan turned, leaving Morse in Jak's hands, and went back to join Krysty. She was asleep when he got there, her face turned in toward her arm. He settled in beside her and let the motion of the river lull him. His hand, though, never stayed far from the SIG-Sauer.

"YOU BELIEVE you can fix these, John?"

J.B. looked up at Mildred, his lap covered by the handblasters he'd found in the hold. There were eight of them in all, four Colt 1911 model .45s and four 9 mm Beretta Model 92-Ss. Two of the .45s had satin stainless-steel finishes, and the rest were all matte black.

"Can you fix a broken arm?" the Armorer asked.

"I don't fix a broken arm," Mildred replied. "I just set it and it fixes itself."

J.B. took one of the .45s from the military footlocker they'd been held in. "Don't fix these, either. But in my hands, they fix themselves." He knew his words, spoken in jest, were nonetheless almost the truth. There wasn't much he hadn't been able to fix back in Cripple Creek where he'd been born and raised, and the rest he'd learned even before he'd hooked up with the Trader.

"Best eat while you got the chance," Mildred said. "Keep your strength up."

"I'll get to it."

The light in *Junie*'s hold was dim. There were no portholes—mainly, J.B. figured, because much of the hold could be below water if she carried a heavy load.

The lantern he'd lit hung on a long hook attached to the wall, sticking out far enough that even though the lantern swung, it never connected. The pale yellow light ghosted the room, giving it a surreal quality. It was nowhere near natural light. But that was okay with J.B. because, if he'd had to, he could have fieldstripped and inspected the hand-blasters, and probably even fixed them in the blackest night.

The room held a small gas stove and kitchen. A warped table with benches screwed into the floor occupied the center of the room. And there was a mass of mattresses, sheets and pillows that served as a bed. Personally J.B. figured the bedding needed airing out in the worst way.

Mildred continued sitting, watching him. "Damn, but you smile like a little boy when you got your hands on a new weapon."

J.B. felt his smile get a little bigger. He couldn't help himself. Weapons had always been his top interest. Back when he'd been traveling with War Wag One and the Trader had given them permission to roam through a ville, most of the men had made for the closest gaudies to get laid as often and as soon as possible.

But J.B. hurried to visit the weapon smith in each ville they traded with. Sometimes they had shops, and sometimes they dealt out of saloons. And more times than not, the local weapon smith was just a guy or gal working out of his or her own home.

J.B. had learned to be a hell of a trader himself. It had been his job as armorer for War Wag One to keep the weapons up and dependable, and keeping extra parts on hand for some of the heavy machine guns had almost been a full-time effort.

When he hadn't been trading for parts the wags needed or might need, he'd traded blasters. He'd kept a fair selection aboard War Wag One, and always managed to have something to trade. He'd found that other weapon smiths were just as eager as he was to get their hands on something new and different, just to see if they could figure it out. J.B. would trade, sometimes coming out on the short end of the trade if it was a particular piece he hadn't had the chance to work with before, just for the privilege of working on it.

He'd taken a lot of busted blasters, pieces other weapon smiths had given up on. Nearly always he'd managed to find ways to fix them.

The blasters in the footlocker were going to be no challenge at all compared to some of the projects he'd taken on. Whoever had stored the blasters in the footlocker had removed the firing pins. It had been too much to hope that they would be in the footlocker, but if he had access to a machinist's shop for a day or two, he could get them all replaced. There'd be some repair work on the slides and other inner mechanisms, because there'd been some water damage. From the looks of the rust, he figured that the water damage had happened in the past couple of months, maybe when the footlocker had been dredged up by Morse and his sons.

Finding a machinist's shop, though, was going to be a problem.

And ammo. The footlocker was curiously bare of ammunition. J.B. guessed that Morse had cadged the ammunition and sold it, or stored it. Neither he nor Ryan believed that the boat was as defenseless as her captain would have them believe.

He looked up, pieces of the blasters strung across his knees and the surrounding floor. Mildred still sat there. He knew long minutes had passed as he disassembled the weapons, and though he didn't feel guilty about not talking to her, he knew she needed to talk.

"Krysty?" he prompted.

"Yeah." Mildred sat across from him, pulling her knees

in close and wrapping her arms around her legs. "I'm worried about her, John. What we're talking about here with this dead woman in her mind is like possession."

J.B. took off his glasses and cleaned them on the tail of his shirt. He had to work at it because they were still caked with feces. Mostly he kept his mind off of it because he'd been working on the blasters. He nodded.

"Possession," Mildred went on, "like with a ghost or something."

J.B. shook his head.

"Yeah, yeah, I know. You haven't ever seen a ghost. And mebbe I haven't, either, but that doesn't mean they don't exist. Shit, nobody back in the 1990s would have figured I could have been stuck in a cryogenic tank for a hundred years and woke up to find the whole world blown to hell. "Of course, it's probably hard for you to imagine the world before nukecaust."

J.B. went back to working on the blasters. What was hardest to imagine, what he sometimes still dreamed about, was walking into a sporting-goods store. He'd seen pictures in some old vids. Schwarzenegger stories, where the actor had just walked into a store and bought nearly any damn thing he wanted. He saw part of a vid where the man had walked into a military surplus store and picked up enough handheld weps to take out most armored wags.

That had been impressive.

And it was the stuff of fairy tales. Not ghosts.

"Used to be afraid of ghosts when I was a kid," Mildred admitted. "I went to movies just to be scared. Jason. Freddie. Michael Myers. Hell, we all went to those just to be scared. Poltergeists, they weren't that big a deal. Invisible for the most part. Just destructive. Rearranged furniture in houses, made shit fly through the air, sucked kids into televisions. But some of those movies about ghosts, they had them taking over people. Forcing them to do things they would never have done before. Never really thought about it before, about how bad it would be to be took over like that.''

"And now Krysty," J.B. said.

"I'm worried about her, and that's no lie. I guess I told you my daddy was a hellfire-and-brimstone preacher in his day.''

J.B. remembered as he scraped rust free of a .45's slide with a bit of steel wool he kept in his kit. Mildred's father had also been the victim of a firebombing, race-inspired violence that had been prevalent at the time, when she'd still just been a baby. She hadn't known him at all except through pictures and stories her family had told her.

"They said he did exorcisms in his church," Mildred went on. "Casting out demons and working against Satan himself.''

"Didn't know he was Catholic."

Mildred laughed. "Oh hell, no. He'd have probably been pissed if anybody had suggested that to him. But in the South back then, John, they still believed in demons and Satan working through people. Had to be cast out through prayer and fasting.''

"Mebbe that'd work for Krysty."

Mildred was quiet for a moment. "I don't know, John. But I do know what she's going through isn't easy. I'm going to pray for her and hope my daddy's looking out for me and my friends just a little these days. Sometimes a little faith is all you need.''

"Ryan isn't going to let anything happen to her."

"I know. But until he gets this thing figured out, I'd just like to know everything's going to be okay.''

J.B. took her hand into his and squeezed it. "Everything's going to be okay."

She smiled and kissed him, unshed tears glinting in her eyes. "I know it will be. I just wanted to hear you say it. I'm glad we can talk like this."

Chapter Sixteen

"Gonna be dark soon," Morse commented, squinting up at the darkening canopy of trees over the river.

Ryan stood next to the boat's captain and scanned the water. The color had gone from green to black as the sky lost the sun. "Is there a place nearby where we can put up for the night?" He'd taken Jak's place watching over the man, letting the albino grab a quick nap.

"Along here, we can put up damn near anywhere."

"We can't all sleep on the boat," Ryan pointed out. "Got to have defensible coastline wherever we put to." All of them sleeping on the boat wasn't what he wanted to do, either. It was one thing when the boat was under way; then they had the wind to push them along. At rest, the boat left little space on board to run to. Open terrain offered a better chance to flee or fight.

Morse nodded. "There's a cove farther ahead. But there's no chance of us getting there before dark."

Ryan glanced at the thick underbrush along the banks. Over the past hour, he'd seen snakes, insects and animals he wanted to keep plenty of distance from. "Then that's where we'll head."

Morse shook his head in disgust. "Make more and better sense to stay aboard *Junie* if you don't want to sleep out. Running in the dark is triple stupe. *Junie* ain't lighted for night running."

Ryan turned on the man, fixing him with his one-eyed

glare. "You do it or I do it. Either way, it gets done." Worrying about Krysty left him even more short-tempered than usual about having his decisions questioned.

"I'll do it," Morse said, "but I ain't gonna like it. Gotta get my boys to use poles as we go along. And running slow speed with the wind strong like this is triple hard."

Ryan ignored the man's comments with effort. If Morse and his knowledge hadn't been necessary, he'd have heaved the man overboard.

ELMORE LOOKED UP as Ryan approached, squinting through the darkness that had blanketed the river. Now that the sun had fully gone down below the western rim of the world, the temperature had cooled, drawing up a thick gray fog that surged restlessly in the pale moonlight.

"What do you want?" Elmore demanded. He'd remained taciturn since they'd left Idaho Falls, acting more like a prisoner than a freed man. Of course, it hadn't helped that Dean had kept such a close watch on him.

Ryan stopped in front of him, out of reach of a quick effort if Elmore decided to attempt to seize a weapon and take his chances overboard. "You never did say where we'd catch up with Donovan."

Elmore shook his head. "You're asking to take a peek at my hole card."

"No." Ryan stood with the Steyr canted on his hip. He and Jak had already spotted a dozen large amphibians crawling into the water in the boat's wake. Neither of them had been able to identify them properly, but they'd felt they were a mutie strain of raccoon. The creatures had possessed fur and the familiar mask of a raccoon, but they'd been nearly four feet long and had no problem going under water for long periods of time. "Heading up north the way we're going, things are liable to get dicey. Be good to know where we can look for Donovan." He paused. "In case."

"In case I get chilled?" Elmore asked. He laughed bitterly. "You're a hard man, Ryan. Got no reason to expect any sympathy from you. Nor even a fair shake."

"Wouldn't give it," Ryan said honestly. "Sympathy's a waste of time, a down payment on getting a ticket for a seat on the last train to the coast. A fair shake's out of the question when your needs conflict with mine or those of my friends."

"So as long as your woman's afflicted, I'm necessary?"

"Not even then," Ryan answered. "We got a general idea of where the Heimdall Foundation is. We could find it. So looking at it the way you are now, we don't need you to get there. What you can do is save us time. You need to keep that in mind."

"If you don't need me, then why not let me go?"

"I don't need you," Ryan pointed out, "but we're going to use you. You know Donovan by sight. Mebbe he'll listen to you long enough to get him to listen to us. People we bumped into that were with the Heimdall Foundation weren't real popular where we were. I reckon that's about the way it is anywhere up here." He gave the man a crooked, mirthless smile. "Baron Shaker's men gave me that impression, too."

"There are a lot of people who don't hold with where it comes to the Foundation," Elmore said. "But they're doing important work up there. Work that will mebbe answer some questions that happened during the nukecaust."

"What happened then doesn't mean a thing to me," Ryan told him. He stared hard at the man. "In case something did happen to you, where could we find Donovan?"

A sour look filled Elmore's face. "This time of year, he'll be up north and east of the compound. On the east side of the Rockies near a ville used to be called Anaconda. They call it Condaville these days, and it's a frontier boom-town of sorts. Got some people there who've used the river to make a big mill, and there's river trade along the Clark Fork River. People bringing in wheat they grow to be ground into flour. Not a big place, but one where you can get some things."

"What's Donovan doing there?"

"The Foundation's landlocked and it's in the mountains," Elmore said. "Best place for an observatory. And you can see folks coming for miles. Place is buttoned up tight, underground. You wouldn't know it was there—unless you knew it was there. Water supply gets to be a problem. Donovan's the guy that solved that problem. And that's where you'll find him. Along the Clark Fork River."

"Where? River's big."

"Don't know. Just somewhere along in there. We run into somebody we know, mebbe we'll find out more." Elmore's eyes darted nervously. "People you run into, they'll be more likely to talk to me than a stranger."

"I know."

"Just thought you might want to keep that in mind."

Ryan was more concerned about the distance involved, knowing that the companions were in for some hard traveling. It wasn't something they weren't accustomed to, but he had to wonder how much Krysty could take.

He left Elmore sitting against the railing and went forward into the prow. Sandy and Bud used long poles to feel for the river bottom as their father cut their speed to a crawl. Lanterns hung off stout supports from the prow, but the light did little to beat back the darkness.

"Cove!" Bud yelled, pointing.

Ryan looked ahead, following the direction of the boy's arm. There, nearly sixty yards ahead, he saw a jog along the riverbank that was almost hidden by low-hanging tree branches and brush.

Morse adjusted the sail, and *Junie* slowed a little more and pulled to starboard. "Drop anchor!" he called.

Sandy tossed the tripronged anchor over the side and started paying out the line. Bud joined him, and the boys wrapped the line around one of the prow cleats, paying it out grudgingly to slow the sailcraft still further. Their efforts were fluid and obviously practiced. In minutes, the boat butted into place in the shallows near the bank beneath low-hanging trees.

"Got a deeper draw here than you'd expect," Morse called, tying the wheel fast.

Ryan nodded, staring at the twenty feet of water separating them from the riverbank. Under the overhanging boughs, though, he could see the scars of past campsites, the vines and creepers not quite overgrowing the areas where campfires and pallets had been pitched. They had some work to do before they settled in for the night, but his chron told him it was only half-past eight. Dark still came early in the northern climes this early in the year.

"Gonna have to do some wading if you're gonna sleep on the bank," Morse said. He sniffed delicately. "Course, I don't see that it's gonna hurt them clothes none."

Ryan agreed. The thing that bothered him most was what the river might hold. Then and later.

"FUCK!" DEAN BELLOWED as he pushed himself out of the water and up on the other side. He pulled up a shirtsleeve. "Leeches! Bastard bloodsuckers!"

Ryan pulled himself up to wading distance, cutting through the water as quickly as he could while helping Krysty. He could already feel the leeches moving through his clothing, as well, tiny whispers of damp, cold movement that wouldn't be denied. The woman, Mary, screamed that they were crawling in her ears, which caused some consternation on her husband's part. The couple flailed in the water as he tried to ease her panic and check her ears.

"Dumb fucks," Jak commented, looking out at the pair. He'd brought their boy ashore after Ryan had assured Mary the albino could swim like a fish and would be safe with him. Neither Mary nor her husband, Jim, could swim well, and it showed. "They fuck around, drown." He put the boy on the ground and started stripping him out of the wet clothes.

The boy tried to squirm away.

Jak grabbed his young charge by the hair of the head and forced him to his knees. "Stand still, stupe!" the albino ordered. "Run into brush, might end up in something's belly. Get leeches off before make sick."

Reluctantly, obviously giving in to the pain, the boy stayed on his knees and didn't fight Jak.

The albino slipped out one of his leaf-bladed throwing knives and slid the point under one of a half-dozen leeches attached to the boy's back. He flipped them away with practiced ease, tossing them into the dirt and stamping them to death under his boot heel. He made occasional forays across his own body, flicking away leeches that came out into the open.

Mary and Jim finally had to be towed in from the water by a rope Bud threw to them. Sandy and Dean pulled them in, then used it again to draw Doc and the orphaned little girl across as quickly as possible.

J.B. came across with Mildred, dragging an oilskin pouch after him that Ryan felt certain contained the blasters he'd found. Morse ordered his boys into action, getting them to help him tie down the sailboat. Her rigging pinged metallically against the masts.

"Noise is going to give us away," Ryan said to Morse. He started skinning out of his clothes, Krysty stripping down beside him. Modesty was cheap in the Deathlands, and the companions didn't have a problem with it even in front of strangers.

The sailor grinned. "Might draw some of the two-legged varmints that ply these waters sometime, but it'll chase the four-legged kind."

"I must confess," Doc hollered as he pulled off his frock coat, "that those creatures that stalked us earlier have been somewhat worrisome on my mind."

"Wharf rats ain't nothing," Bud called out as he shinnied out of his clothes. "Purely come out at night. And they see the first sign of light, they go away. Put up a campfire, they stay away, too. Seen them eating dead things, but never attack nobody could take care of their self."

Stripped down, Ryan used a small knife to pluck the leeches from Krysty's fair skin, taking time to remind his lover with his touch that he hadn't forgotten about her. Everybody paired up, with Dean and Jak taking care of the two youngsters, then trading off on each other. Doc paired up with Elmore, while Morse had his sons strip him clear.

"Leeches are particularly bad this time of year," the sailor said. "Just into the breeding cycle for them, and ain't been any good floods yet to wash them away. Expect them anytime, though."

Ryan took charge of the camp, dividing the chores among the group. J.B. stayed at the campsite and cleared the brush so they'd have a defensible position and nothing would interfere with their line of sight. Ryan marked the area he wanted cleared with the panga, slashing through the heavy growth and small trees. Morse had brought over three machetes in his equipment, as well as ring pulls to cook with. He and his boys joined J.B. in clearing the undergrowth around the camp's perimeter, though the old sailor was vocal in his opinion that it wasn't necessary. One look from Ryan, though, and he'd gone straight to work.

Morse had also brought the bows and arrows from the boat. Ryan took the bows, keeping one for himself, then passing the others out to Jak and Dean. J.B. was good in the brush, as well, but he wanted the Armorer on hand in case Elmore or Morse decided getting the hell out of the area was in their best interests.

Doc busied himself with scavenging the local flora and fauna to add to whatever supper Ryan, Jak and Dean were able to bring down. Self-heats hadn't sounded good to anyone after they'd had them earlier in the day, and Ryan wanted something solid to put in Krysty's stomach to keep her strength up.

The others, under Krysty's and Mildred's supervision, were put to work gathering firewood.

Satisfied, Ryan led Jak and Dean into the thick forest surrounding the river. The bow wasn't his favorite weapon, but it allowed them to conserve the precious little ammo they had left and not announce their presence for miles.

Bud and Sandy had informed them that the local game included rabbits, quail, frogs and turkeys. Bears lived in the forest, as well, and a small type of mountain cat.

Ryan went naked except for the SIG-Sauer and panga belted around his lean hips, his boots, and the Steyr across his back. Mosquitoes were a problem, but Morse had a foul-smelling concoction in his kit that kept them away. After wearing dog shit for hours, the mosquito repellent was easy to put up with, although it left a greasy film that shone in the moonlight.

Jak and Dean were naked, as well, moving through the shadows like savages. Ryan was proud of his son; he was used to Jak not making any noise, but even Dean was soundless.

Less than five minutes into the brush, Ryan spotted a young tom turkey that probably dressed out near to fifteen pounds. The bird lurked in the shadows thirty feet away, only the bobbing of its head and the light band across its wings attracting Ryan's attention. The one-eyed man squatted beside a tree and nocked an arrow, breathing shallowly as he steadied himself for the shot.

Before he could release the bowstring, an arrow plunged through the night and burst through the turkey's head. The force of the shaft dragged the turkey's head sideways, pinning it to the side of a nearby tree.

The turkey beat its wings as it died, making only tiny noises because the shaft evidently lodged in its throat as well. Other sudden movement erupted around the turkey as more birds ran through the brush and tried to take flight.

Marking the other archer's probable location from the angle of the shot, Ryan loosed his shaft at a turkey hen leaping for a low-hanging branch. His arrow caught her in midflight, nailing one of her wings to her body. She screamed in pain as she fell, then flopped on the ground.

Dean slipped out of the shadows and squatted beside her to slit her throat with his knife, stilling her mournful cries. "Lot of noise, Dad," he admonished. "Should have aimed for the head."

Ryan grinned at his son, feeling proud. "I'll try to remember that in the future."

"Scare away the game," Dean said, "and it'll be hard feeding all those people."

"Yeah, I guess so." Ryan strode out into the clearing and used the panga to cut strips of young bark from the trees.

They used the bark strips to tie the turkeys by the feet

to branches above the ground, then cut their throats. It
would allow the bodies to bleed out, and keep them from
easy reach of other predators while they finished the hunt.

"There's a lot of meat here," Ryan said, meaning it as
a compliment.

"Mebbe," Dean said, "but if the hunting's good, might
as well make the most of it. Gonna be aboard ship for a
while. Mebbe we can jerk some of the meat down in the
kitchen, get it ready to travel."

"That's good thinking, Dean." Ryan dropped a hand on
the boy's shoulder and they melted into the night again,
two of the deadliest predators in the region.

A LITTLE OVER AN HOUR later, Ryan walked drag behind
Jak and Dean, his hand hard around the Steyr. Four good-
sized turkeys were slung over his shoulders. Their blood
streamed down his body, but he didn't care; it would wash
off easily enough.

Jak and Dean each carried another pair of turkeys, and
the albino had managed to get seven rabbits. They'd moved
lightning quick through the brush, but Jak had been death
in motion. Dean carried a pouch with close to two dozen
frogs in it that were eating size.

The brush around the campsite had been cleared, and the
companions sat around the fires. J.B. kept watch over Elmore, Morse and his sons and the others, the Remington
shotgun draped loosely across his knees. A big metal tub
sat on top of one of the two fires, the twisting flames licking
out from beneath it and scorching the metal black.

"Too many bastard fires," Ryan grumbled, dropping the
dead turkeys to the ground. "Light this place up and somebody else sees it, we're fucked."

"We keep running around without clothes," Mildred
told him, "we could be in trouble, too." She stirred the

contents of the big metal tub with a fresh-cut branch as thick as Ryan's wrist. "And wearing them all covered in dog shit is pretty stupe. Lot of animals like the smell of shit, and it's kind of hard to move around unnoticed."

"Thought about trying to wash the clothes out in the river, lover," Krysty said. "But that would have meant whoever did the washing would be fighting leeches the whole time. And the leeches would have been all through the clothes."

Ryan knew it was true and didn't say anything more. The scent of soaps and scouring powders tickled his nose. He crouched over one of the turkeys and started pulling feathers. Krysty joined him.

Jak and Dean both started gutting their kills, dropping the intestines into the river so the current would take them away. They also added everything that they wouldn't be cooking. Burning it or burying it in the ground was an option, too, but the river offered the cleanest way to get rid of it.

Krysty tore at the feathers with a vengeance.

"How're you feeling?" Ryan asked in a low voice that didn't carry any farther than between the two of them.

"I've got a headache that won't quit." Her face looked pale in the mix of firelight and moonlight. A slight tremble worked through her hands.

"Any voices?"

She shook her head hesitantly, and with care. "Phlorin's quiet for the most part now."

"Mebbe she's going away."

"I think mebbe she's just resting up, waiting for me to get a little weaker."

Ryan didn't like thinking about that. He took the panga out when they had the first turkey stripped clean, then carried the kill over to the river. He rasped the sharp blade against the big bird's ass to open up the body cavity, then reached inside and pulled the mass of coiling guts out. They splashed into the water, tangling out like bloody ropes that sank in places.

"Hot pipe, Dad!" Dean called. "Look!" The boy pointed out into the water, blood dripping red stains into the river from the tip of his knife.

It took Ryan a moment to see what Dean was talking about, expecting to see something breaking the river's surface. Instead, he spotted the luminous dots hanging suspended in the water despite the gentle current. Before he drew his next breath, he knew they were eyes.

As he watched, the luminous blue eyes glided toward the bank, drawn to the blood and waste. Large jaws distended, revealing long yellow fangs. They tore into the discarded intestines and body parts with savage relish, shredding flesh.

"You might want to watch yourself," Morse called out in his gruff voice. "Some of them damn piranha grew legs around here and learned how to come crawling out on the bank when they've a mind to."

"Now there's a cheery thought," Elmore grunted in disgust.

"J.B.," Ryan called.

"I heard," the Armorer responded.

"Let's make sure we let Doc know when he gets back."

"It'll make for interesting guard duty," Mildred commented sourly.

"Can you eat them?" Dean asked, as he continued watching the fish.

Ryan knew it was a sensible question, and probably one of the most directly related to their continued survival.

"Those bastard fish carry a poison with them," Bud said. "Get it from the contaminated water. Mebbe you get lucky and drink from the water and the worst you might get is a night of belly cramps. But you eat them fish, you're more than likely good as dead.''

''And there ain't no meat to speak of on them,'' Sandy interjected. ''Tough, worthless fuckers, you ask me.''

Ryan finished gutting the turkey, then took the next one Krysty handed over. He glanced up at the dark clouds scudding across the pinched face of the waning moon. ''Could rain again tonight. Let's get those tarps up, as well.'' He glanced at Krysty, seeing how pale she was and how her hands shook as she pulled feathers from the third turkey. He bitterly cursed the ill fortune that had found them, then pushed it away. They were doing all they could do. He just hoped it was enough.

Chapter Seventeen

Doc wandered back into camp less than an hour later, loaded down with vegetables and fruits he'd scavenged from the surrounding terrain. "Happily, my good friends," he said in a tired voice, "this hallowed ground does offer up a veritable cornucopia of victuals and refreshments. And you left the scent of yon fine birds basting in nature's juices over a slow fire to mark my way home." He made a production out of drawing in a deep breath through his nose, then sighed contentedly.

"What the hell's he saying?" Bud demanded.

"He's saying he found a lot of stuff and that the turkey smells good," Dean translated.

"Then why the fuck didn't he just say so?"

"He did," Dean said.

"And you understood him?"

"I've had some schooling." Dean said.

"You've had schooling?" Elmore asked from the other side of the fire.

"Sure," Dean replied. "Why?"

Elmore shrugged. "Just surprising is all."

"Heard of Nicholas Brody?" Dean asked.

"Seems like I have. Got a place down Colorado way."

"Went to school there for a while," Dean said. "Mebbe I'll go back some day."

Ryan swapped looks with Krysty, noting the thin smile

that filled her pale face. It was the first time the boy had ever said that.

"Schooling can be a good thing," Elmore stated. "Provided that ain't all a man puts in his head."

"Schooling's for pussies," Bud said derisively.

"Waste of fucking time," Sandy added.

Dean swiveled his gaze toward the brothers. "You know how to do anything more than read and write your names?"

"Don't know how to do that," Sandy said.

"Don't see how we're going to need to," Bud replied.

"Least you could make sure somebody spelled it right on your marker you do something stupe that gets you chilled," Dean told them. Color touched his cheeks, and Ryan knew his son was a little embarrassed to have taken pride in something the other boys were determined to ridicule.

"For pussies," Bud repeated.

Sandy flipped Dean off, shoving his middle finger defiantly into the air.

The turquoise-handled knife appeared like magic in Dean's hands. "Be glad to trim that finger off for you if you can't control it," he stated in a low, cold voice. "And shove it up your ass for you if you want to keep it as a souvenir."

Morse glanced at Ryan, as if expecting him to back Dean off. Ryan returned the man's gaze without expression. Dean was old enough to start picking the fights he was going to stand up in, and to choose the things he was going to be willing to fight over.

Bud and Sandy suddenly didn't look so sure of themselves when no adults took a hand in the brimming argument.

Obviously angry over the turn of events, Morse stood and walked over to his sons. He slapped each of them on the head with quick hands. "You fuckers stop acting so stupe and shut your damn mouths."

"He started—" Bud said.

Before the boy could say another word, Morse backhanded him to the ground. Blood trickled from a split lip.

"Don't make your last mistake, boy," Morse snarled.

Bud pushed himself back into a sitting position but didn't say anything. Morse continued on to the campfire and poured a fresh cup of coffee sub and returned to his place.

Ryan ignored the exchange, but realized that Morse was more afraid of them than the man let on. The sailor also resented it, not being a man used to fear.

J.B. got another coffee refill, as well, squatting close to Ryan and speaking only so they could hear. "Made yourself an enemy," the Armorer commented.

"Know it," Ryan said.

"Best if we parted company with him soon as we can."

"You feel comfortable piloting *Junie* along this river during rainy season?"

"Nope."

"Me, neither."

J.B. took a sip of the coffee sub. "Going to have to keep an eye on him. Man gets that fearful of you—"

"He'll stick a shiv in your back just to try to convince himself he's immortal again," Ryan finished. It was something the Trader had taught them back on War Wag One. And it had proved true on a number of occasions.

SINCE THE MODEST Doc had gone into the brush in only his long underwear, he'd had to improvise on methods to carry the vegetables and fruits he'd found. Using some of the long yellow grasses that grew abundantly in patches along the broken countryside, he'd twisted them into a webbed harness with small pouches that carried wild onions, garlic, blackberries, green apples, mushrooms, strawberries and herbs he'd recognized even in the moonlight.

With Mildred's and Dean's help, Doc removed the turkeys from the spits over the fire long enough to stuff them with the onions, garlic, apple slices and herbs. In moments, the aroma drifting off the cooking birds turned even more enticing.

Ryan's stomach growled in anticipation.

While they waited, the water heated up in a big tub that had been brought over from *Junie*. Steam curled up from the edges, letting them know it was hot enough to cook whatever leeches clung to the clothing. Washing got under way, with each person taking care of his or her own gear. Only two sets of clothing at a time could be washed before the water was so foul with dog shit that any further washing had to be postponed until more water was heated.

There was a moment of consternation when a group of piranha pulled themselves up on shore and came at the campsite. A flurry of blows from makeshift clubs and rifle butts killed them out quick enough, and Ryan made sure all the corpses were kicked back into the water. He didn't know if there was a way to drain the poison out of the fish, but he didn't want Morse to have the opportunity to use it against them later.

BY THE TIME the turkeys were ready, so were most of the clothes. Ryan opted to pull his on and let them dry on him rather than hang them from the branches the way Jak and Dean did. Being dressed made him feel more ready to move.

Metal and ceramic plates from *Junie*'s stores handled the food. There was also silverware. They all piled their plates high.

"Alas and alack," Doc moaned theatrically as he hunkered down with his back to a tree, "would that we might have been able to break bread with this meal."

"You'll be breaking wind soon enough after you stuff yourself," Mildred stated. "Judging from past performances."

Doc drew himself up. "Madam, you are ill-mannered."

"But truthful." Mildred smiled as she bit into a chunk of turkey breast she held in her fingers. "Anyway, if you had bread, you'd be moaning that you didn't have butter to go with it."

"In part," Doc admitted, "you are right. I should content myself on enjoying this fine repast we have managed for ourselves rather than lamenting what we do not have."

Ryan listened to the conversation but didn't take part. He ate with real appetite and turned his thoughts to what they were going to need to do to set things right. The meat tasted good, still managing to carry the flavor of the bird's own juices mixed in with the herbs and vegetables Doc had found. And the fruits carried clean, sharp flavors. He ate until near bursting, Krysty sitting beside him.

But they didn't talk. And Ryan was cognizant of the heavy silence between them even in the midst of the conversations circulating around them.

PHLORIN SPOKE. *This is only part of the heritage you carry now within you.*

For a moment, Krysty thought her mind had been bringing up an old nightmare. The witch's interjection, however, let her know the woman was controlling what she was seeing. She remembered lying next to Ryan, smelling the dampness that lingered in his clothes, making the detergent in them a little stronger. And she thought she remembered when he'd gotten up to relieve J.B. on watch.

But she wasn't sure about that now.

She stood in the middle of a street in a huge ville, a cancerous orange sun hanging overhead and peering fitfully through layers of indigo-and-charcoal clouds. Wags lined the streets, some of them resting against one another where they'd wrecked.

White-gray ash overlay everything like a blanket of snow. It was inches thick in places, piled deep on the wags, against the tall buildings, strewed across the bloated corpses. Tiny breezes carried whirling ash dervishes yards away. Nothing lived.

Krysty tried to stop her movement, struggled to stop walking through the deathscape rendered in ash and pain around her. But she couldn't; in the twisted nightmare, Phlorin controlled her body. Instead, Krysty turned her efforts to waking. She reached out for Ryan, feeling the emptiness that was there. Only the old woman living in the back of her brain didn't allow her to maintain that sensation.

This is your legacy, Phlorin said.

Not mine, Krysty argued.

You can't walk away from this. The Chosen are here to know.

To know what? Krysty scanned the death and destruction that lay in all directions around her. Despite all her experience with sudden death, with all the forms it could manifest itself in, these sights left her cold. There had been, she knew, life there in those streets only hours ago.

Now it was all gone.

She strode by a young man lying in the street, brickwork smashed around him from the nearby building. The swirling ash partially covered his face, but it hadn't completely filled in his open mouth or the gaping eye socket. His limbs were twisted mockeries of anything human, the flesh burned from them in places from a searing heat.

To know what was here before, Phlorin answered her question.

What was where?

Here. In Deathlands before it became called Deathlands.

If you can remember all of this, why can't you remember anything further back?

I can. I have the memories of my sisters to rely on.

The sensation of movement left Krysty dizzy. The scene before her blurred and changed. In moments, she seemed to be standing on the same street—or one like it—before the nukecaust had erupted and changed it forever.

The street was alive with movement and throbbed with an incessant noise like Krysty had never heard before. Wags raced along the street in both directions, clustered more tightly than an anthill, and people flowed along the sidewalks in dresses and clothing Krysty had seldom seen.

What is this place? Krysty asked.

A ville called Seattle. In its day, it was one of the largest villes in the predark times. It was drank down during the quakes that took the western coast.

How do you know about it? Krysty had seen fragments of vids concerning the ville. She'd even read about it in movie books that had survived the nukecaust and the intervening century. But never in all the vids and the images the books stirred up in her imagination had the ville ever seemed like this. She felt claustrophobic, lost amid the crush of people and wags, the noise and the smoke that burned the back of her throat.

One of the Chosen, an ancestor of mine, lived here at the time.

Krysty reached out for one of the people walking past her, wrapping her hand around the wrist of a man in a sharply fitted dark blue suit. She was surprised to realize she'd touched flesh over hard bone.

The man turned and gazed at her, cocking his head to one side. "Can I help you, miss?"

"No," Krysty told him. "No, thank you. I'm quite all right."

The man appeared uncertain for a moment, then moved on, rejoining the thronging flock that trudged along the sidewalk. She watched him go with mixed emotions.

How can you remember this? she asked.

Our memories go back generations. Our biggest concerns aren't how we remember, but how is it you don't.

No one can remember like this, Krysty protested.

We do.

How?

Someone has to keep records. Someone must learn the truth.

The truth of what?

Of how all this came to be, Phlorin said.

It happened because of the nukes, Krysty replied. *Governments stocked them before skydark. More than enough to kill the world a hundred times over.*

But who set off the nukes?

Krysty walked down the sidewalk, her eyes drawn to the shop windows filled with dresses, electronics, books and other merchandise. All of them seemed to glitter and appear ethereal.

If you talk to different people, you get different answers about that. And most people don't care at all anymore. It doesn't matter.

Not to place blame, but to simply know. That's what we need to hand down.

Krysty remembered some of the stories the companions had heard from the Heimdall Foundation men, Bernsen and Hoyle, while going back to Colorado to get Dean. Even after the nukecaust, the Foundation had dedicated itself to finding out what had truly happened to the world. *What good's the knowing?*

The truth shall set you free, Phlorin stated.

I'm not free, Krysty pointed out. *I've got a ghost wandering around in my head, forcing me to see things I'd rather not see, do things I'd rather not do.*

All will be explained when we return to my people.

That's not going to happen.

Oh, it'll happen. It'll happen, or I'll get strong enough eventually to stop your heart. Then we'll watch your man as you die.

You'll die, too.

If I don't get back to my people, Phlorin said, *I'm dead anyway.*

Silently Krysty hoped that Donovan's knowledge would be enough to free her from her predicament.

Donovan is only a man, Phlorin said in disgust, *and men know precious little as it is. Even before they start deluding themselves about their own grandeur.*

But Krysty heard the small tremor of uncertainty in the old woman's voice. It wasn't much, but it was enough to give her hope.

Evidently Phlorin sensed the emotion because the world changed around Krysty again, warping into a narrow corridor that led through a large house that reminded her of the Cornelius family's home in Louisiana. Dim light trickled into the corridor, and she thought she heard sibilant voices in the distance. A cold chill prickled her skin, running across her shoulders and making her spine feel brittle.

You don't like it here, do you? Phlorin taunted. And her voice seemed changed, as well, fitting into the creaking old manse as if it belonged.

No. Krysty froze in place, trying to ignore the slither of wet flesh cascading through the corridor behind her. It wasn't real, she told herself. None of it was real. But at one point, it had been all too real and she knew it.

You remember this place, don't you? You almost lost your man here.

Something lapped out, smacking against the wooden floor. Although she didn't want to, Krysty ran. It was survival. She didn't have a weapon in hand, and from the sound of the thing's progress, it was huge.

Thin gray light peeped out from a set of double doors ahead of her. She aimed for them. She couldn't remember if the doors or the room beyond them actually existed in the Cornelius house, but it fit with her memory of it now easily.

There's no hope. No hope at all. I'll be in your dreams, and I'll rob you of sleep. You will give in to me. It's only a matter of time.

Krysty burst through the double doors, a prayer to Gaia on her lips. The doors slammed back against the walls, revealing the dark room ahead of her. The back wall was taken up by the silver screen the companions had watched vids on. Before it were rows of folding chairs all orderly and neat.

The Cornelius family sat in the chairs, their heads swiveling to focus on Krysty as she skidded to a stop in the center of the room. All of them were there: Elric, Thomas, Mary, Norman and Melmoth—pale haired and fiery eyed, like Jak but much, much worse.

"Welcome," Elric said, rising to his six foot three inch stature. Wasp thin, he looked even paler in death.

And Krysty had no doubts they were dead. The companions had killed them all, ending the Cornelius family line. At least, as far as they knew.

"We wait to greet you properly," Elric said in those cultured, dulcet tones he'd had. But the words sounded hoarse—papery and thin, like words squeezed through the cracked timber of a coffin.

Krysty backed away, listening to the wet smack of heavy flesh hitting the wooden floor out in the corridor. The sound echoed inside the viewing room, but Elric kept approaching, acting as if he didn't hear it.

Krysty backed away from him. It was only a dream, she told herself. Not real. Not real at all. But she also knew she couldn't take that chance. With Phlorin inside her head, it could be so much more. She turned and looked back toward the double doors that had let into the vid room.

A huge crocodile lounged in the doorway, something she'd never seen in the Cornelius home. It was easily twenty feet long, its mouth a row of gaping white fangs. The beady black eyes carried a cold, reptilian intelligence. Krysty wouldn't have been surprised if it had spoken.

The other members of the Cornelius family spread out, coming for Krysty. They moved slowly, rocking back and forth like windblown saplings. They turned Krysty back, drawing closer. They reached for her, their fingers distending into vicious claws.

"You mustn't leave yet," Elric said in that hauntingly smooth voice. "We've not yet had the pleasure of having you for dinner." He opened his mouth, exposing the long canines.

Chapter Eighteen

Krysty turned, searching for a weapon but finding none. In desperation, she seized one of the folding chairs and threw it at Elric.

He brushed the piece of furniture aside casually, as though it were only a moment's inconvenience. The chair shattered into a hundred pieces, proof of the incredible strength that was housed in his rail-thin body.

Taking another step back, Krysty stepped up into the viewing area of the vid. The bright light hurt her eyes and blinded her, reducing the Cornelius family into ghostly gray apparitions that reminded her of the actors and actresses on the screen behind her.

Then she slipped, twisting violently to catch her balance as a gust of wind caught her. There was no explanation for the wind, and no explanation, either, for the way her arm suddenly plunged through the screen behind her.

At first she thought she'd ripped a hole in the screen. Instead, she noticed that her arm and hand had suddenly plunged into the room depicted in the vid. Filmed in noir black and gray, the term given to her by Doc and Mildred, the room was a large bar area. A man in a white jacket sat at the bar smoking a cigarette while watching a black man in a white jacket playing the piano.

Amazed, Krysty stepped into the vid screen and into the room. The swell of music surrounded her. Couples danced close to her, and on a handful of occasions stiff material touched the backs of her hands. This wasn't real, she told herself as she gazed around for a way out of the big room. It was hard to see through all the people.

It's real enough, Phlorin declared. *You haven't managed to escape—only to prolong the hunt.*

The Cornelius family moved through the vid screen after her, picking up speed.

Krysty rushed through the crowd, pushing through the dancers and drawing a flurry of angry curses. She ignored them all, searching frantically for an exit. Phlorin's control over her mind was like nothing she'd ever experienced.

From the corner of her eye, she noticed the white-jacketed man push away from the bar and come toward her. There was no way out of the big room and no place to hide.

Krysty stopped at the edge of the dance floor and turned to face the Cornelius family. *You're creating this out of my mind, Phlorin, out of my memories and out of my fears. Nothing more.*

Are you so certain, then, child?

Yes. Krysty stood her ground and let them come, her mind busy twisting the fabric of the dream. In some of the earliest days that she remembered Mother Sonja, her mother had taught her to banish bad dreams that plagued her. Krysty had never questioned where the bad dreams had come from as a child. Her mother had called them night terrors and seemed to be only a little concerned about them. Since learning the lessons Mother Sonja had given her, Krysty seldom had nightmares. Except for those produced by mat-trans jumps and premonitions.

This, she told herself, was neither. She forced herself calm, peering beyond the veil of emotions Phlorin created inside her subconscious.

Elric towered before her, his hand slashing out, filled with sharp claws.

Instinctively Krysty lifted her arm to defend herself. Burning pain filled her arm as Elric's nails sliced through her arm. She didn't look, using the pain as her focus. When Elric struck again, she didn't move at all.

The tall man's hand slashed through her without touching her. Angry, Elric stepped back, his lips twisted in a rictus as he hissed his displeasure.

Krysty closed her eyes, regulating her breathing, reaching inside herself to slow down her racing heart. Then she stepped out of the dream into wakefulness.

KRYSTY SAT UP in the cool, clean darkness of the night. She pulled off the covers and found out she'd started to get drenched with sweat underneath. She shivered, still feeling the hypnotic pull of the dream.

Next time, Phlorin called from within her, *it will get harder and harder to resist me.*

Ignoring the old woman's threat, Krysty pushed up from the ground, drawing Ryan's attention at once. She couldn't see him where he sat outside the perimeter of the campfires, but she knew he was there on watch. She sensed his attention on her at once, and his concern.

She knew J.B. had been scheduled for watch first, so she knew she'd gotten some sleep. Glancing around, she saw the companions and the others scattered across the ground, wrapped up in the blankets brought from the boat. No one stirred.

Gathering her own blanket, she crept through the campsite toward Ryan. Her movement didn't go completely undetected. With the enhanced perception that came as a result of the dream, she sensed that Jak, J.B. and Dean woke briefly and recognized her. With all the awareness, she felt like she had no privacy. Her mind was constantly buzzing.

"You should be sleeping," Ryan told her when she found him leaning against a tree just back of the campsite. He had the Steyr cradled in his arms.

"Couldn't, lover." Krysty stretched out and wrapped her arms around him. "Sleeping tonight might be the death of me."

"The old woman?"

"Yes." Krysty pulled him close, trying to get as much of her flesh in contact with his as she could.

"Won't be much longer."

One way or the other, Krysty couldn't help thinking. But she pulled back and looked up into Ryan's face. "I know." She slipped a hand inside his shirt, brushing her palm against the hard planes of his flat stomach and broad chest, drawing in his warmth. She'd always loved the feel of him, the unyielding presence he exuded.

"We'll be moving early in the morning," Ryan told her. "Sooner we shake the dust from us here, better off we'll be. Not going to leave much time for sleeping."

"I'll sleep on the boat if I'm able." Krysty put her head against his chest, listening to his heartbeat, slow and rhythmic. "Mebbe sleeping in the light will be easier."

His free hand came up behind her, threading his fingers through her sentient hair. Her hair coiled around his fingers in return, pulling him tight. Then she realized that his hand hadn't been placed there out of any tenderness. She sensed the withdrawal in her lover, a cold spot just beyond her reach.

It hurt her, feeling it and knowing it was there.

He doesn't trust you, Phlorin taunted in the back of her mind.

Ryan doesn't trust you, Krysty said. She held on to her lover harder. *You should know. He chilled you once.*

You, me. It's the same difference now, Krysty.

It's not going to stay that way.

You can't be sure of that. How do you know that I won't take over your arm at some point, have you pull out your blaster and blow a hole in this man?

Krysty shivered at the thought. She hadn't even considered that. But Ryan had. That was why his fingers were tangled in her hair. *Because Ryan won't let you.*

And he'd chill you before he let himself be chilled?

Yes. And the truth of her answer gave Krysty strength. Ryan was a survivor. He wouldn't let even her take his life without a fight, and he wouldn't be diminished. He'd still be every inch the fighting warrior she'd fallen in love with. The joy she felt burned her eyes, turned to tears that dripped across her cheeks. *You can't kill him. No one can.*

You're so sure.

"Cold?" Ryan asked.

"Just a chill, lover," Krysty said. "Somebody walking over my grave, like Doc would say."

"Wrap up in your blanket."

"Rather wrap up in you."

"I'm on watch."

"I promise not to be too distracting." Krysty's fingers unbuttoned the front of his trousers, feeling Phlorin retreat in the back of her mind. *Why don't you stay and play?* She had Ryan's cock in her hand, feeling the way it stiffened at her touch.

You're an abomination, Phlorin stated.

Krysty didn't argue, but took Ryan into her mouth, bathing his hot flesh in the heated caress of her kiss. Ryan kept his hand twisted in her hair but he quickly gave himself over to her touch. And for the first time in hours, Krysty felt truly at peace.

RYAN OPENED HIS EYE and stared up through the canopy of branches overhead. Dawn streaked the sky, threading it with orange and gold that slashed through the retreating purple.

He heard Jak walk over to him before he saw the albino.

"Time move," Jak said. "Wasting daylight."

Ryan nodded, then shifted gently to extricate himself from the arm and leg Krysty had draped over him in the night. She hadn't slept well, and he was surprised to find her asleep now. Cold fear touched him briefly when he thought her slumber might be something else. He placed his fingers against the side of her neck, and relaxed when he felt the thumping of her carotid artery.

He shook her slightly, watching her sentient hair pull back tightly against her scalp. As her eyelids flickered and she fought her way to sleep, he slid the SIG-Sauer from under his thigh and holstered it. He'd kept it in his hand the whole night against the possibility that Krysty might have lost herself in her slumber. He wouldn't have killed her, but the old woman trying to take over her mind might not have known that.

"Morning, lover," Krysty said in a tired voice. Her eyes cracked open reluctantly, exposing the bloodshot lines threading through them.

"Get much sleep?" Ryan asked.

"Some. I don't know." Still, she forced herself to her feet with effort and helped him gather the bedding they'd shared during the night. "Sorry. I know I kept you up."

That had been the truth in more ways than one. After she'd finished getting him off and he'd finished his turn at watch, she'd taken him to bed and had sex with him twice more.

Ryan hadn't thought she'd gotten much pleasure from the encounters herself. But she'd been driven, giving her all each time with a fierce abandon that had exhausted them both.

"Sore?" she asked.

"Feels like I spent the night in a rough-riding wag with busted shocks," Ryan admitted. His groin was tender to the pressure even from the weight of her leg lying across him. Her own passion had sparked his, and the anxiety filling both of them had found release.

She smiled, pleased with his answer. Some of the haunted look left her eyes for a moment. "Makes me feel good to hear you say that, lover. Been a while since we've had something like that."

Ryan rolled up the bedding and tied the restraining straps. "Made things better for you?" He hoisted the load to his shoulder.

"Gave me a little more control," Krysty admitted. "Phlorin doesn't care much for the sex. She's never had it."

"I guess she can't say that now."

"She still doesn't care for the idea of having shared it."

Ryan shook his head. "She's less than a fucking ghost. Whatever you think she shared, she won't be keeping that."

"Mebbe, lover. I hope so. But I also know that whatever she is inside my head, she's capable of taking my life away unless we do something about it."

"We're going to," Ryan promised.

Krysty knew she'd drawn the promise from him again in spite of the fact he'd already given it. He saw her brow wrinkle in displeasure, disappointed in her own weakness.

He reached out and touched her face. "It's going to be

okay,'' he told her. Red clouded his vision as the anger at his own inability to fix the problem now hit him for a moment.

"I know," she said, and her acceptance helped him curb his own emotions.

THE CAMPSITE CAME ALIVE slowly. Breakfast was a repeat of the previous night's meal, only gone cold. The only thing heated up was the coffee sub they had, and that only because the pot had been kept going all night to fuel whoever had been on watch.

Ryan joined J.B. and Mildred at the water's edge. The Armorer cleaned his glasses with his shirttail and looked at the murky brown water roiling with moss.

"Going to be bastard tricky getting back into the boat without getting leeches all over us," Mildred commented.

"Then there's the piranha," J.B. pointed out.

Ryan gazed into the black and evil eyes staring back up at him. The piranha glided easily through the water, schooling in lethal pools.

"Guess they took the feeding we dished out last night and decided to stay on," Mildred said.

Glancing around the campsite, Ryan called out to Jak, "Save some of that rope. We're going to need it."

The albino nodded, sorting it out from the gear they'd brought out from *Junie*.

"Climb over?" J.B. asked.

"We get a line across," Ryan said, "we can do it."

"Won't be easy with the children we've got tagging along," Mildred said.

Ryan glanced at the children and the others they'd rescued from the coldhearts.

Mildred looked hard at him. "We can't leave them here. These people were barely making it along whatever path they were taking. We abandon them here, we might as well bury them.''

Ryan felt the back of his neck grow hot. ''Fireblast, I know it. The situation we're in ourselves, taking on other responsibilities is a bastard nightmare.'' He turned his eye to the doctor. ''But I'm not going to cut them loose here. We'll see them off someplace safer—if we find one in these woods—and get clear.''

''YOU MISS, you're more than likely going to be fish shit by nightfall if you don't make it back to shore.''

Jak looked up at Ryan and nodded. They both stood in the big tree they'd chosen to rig up the ropes. They'd tied one end to a large branch above the albino, out as far as they could reach.

Grabbing the other end of the rope, Jak scampered back into the tree, choosing a branch that would give him enough of an arc to hopefully reach the boat. He stood on the branch barefoot, feeling the rough bark against the soles of his feet.

Ryan concentrated on swinging the panga, hacking small branches out of the way.

Jak knew they'd already removed all the ones that mattered, but he also knew the big one-eyed warrior was concerned about him. However, none among the companions was more able to achieve the feat that lay before him. He didn't feel any unease himself. If he couldn't have made it, he damn sure wasn't going to swing out over the piranha-infested waters.

''Make me promise,'' Jak said with a straight face.

Ryan looked up at him. ''What?''

''I fall in water, you shoot me in head. Gonna need relief.''

''Sure,'' Ryan replied, slipping the SIG-Sauer free of

leather. "In fact, if it looks like you aren't going to make it, I'll shoot you before you hit the water."

Jak thought about that, wondering how his joke had gotten lost in the translation. He tested the rope in his hands, pulling it taut and checking the pull of the branch it was tied to. "Joking, Ryan."

"Yeah," the big man said. "Me, too. Real fucking funny, wasn't it?"

Mentally Jak made a note that humor wasn't exactly something Ryan seemed capable of at the moment. Without another word, he took two running steps forward along the branch, then hurled himself out from the tree.

He kept the tension on the rope, transferring all his forward motion into a swing toward the moored boat. He checked the swing, letting his natural acrobat's ability guide him. The pull of gravity tugged at him, increasing his speed. In a heartbeat, he was out over the water.

His forward motion slowed, and he knew he couldn't risking losing all of it. Releasing the rope, he spread his arms wide in an effort to keep his balance as he hurtled toward the boat's prow. He was higher than he'd anticipated, coming down faster than he'd wanted. At least he was coming down near the boat.

When his forward motion stopped, he thought for an instant that he'd missed his target. The second rope had created more drag than he'd thought it would, or maybe he just hadn't gone as far out as he'd hoped. In the next instant, the bobbing deck was below him.

He landed hard, tucking into a roll and coming up on his feet. A feeling of exhilaration filled him as he turned to face the others. He smiled, then he started pulling the second rope across so they could rig the transfer.

IT TOOK ALMOST AS LONG to get the passengers aboard the boat as it did to rig up the ropes. Ryan glanced at the midmorning sun sourly. They'd lost much of the morning.

He stood back at the pilothouse with Morse, who bawled out orders to his sons. They raced up and down the rigging like monkeys as the other passengers and the companions settled in.

Junie slunk back into the river's current reluctantly, almost mired in the slow waters near the bank. Then the sails belled out and caught the wind. Her prow sheared through a low sandbar with a long grating sound that left Ryan wondering if she'd torn her bottom away.

Morse laughed as he worked the wheel. "Not to worry. Old *Junie,* she's a workhorse, not some nervous filly."

Ryan tightened his jaw and said nothing. He stood with a wide-legged stance that absorbed the pitch and roll of the boat as she cut to the heart of the river current. "Where's the nearest place we can do some trading for ammo and gear?"

"That'll be Annie's," Morse replied.

"How far?" Ryan asked.

Morse squinted against the breeze. "In a wind like this, if it stays with us, mebbe half a day. Be there before nightfall no matter what."

"How's she fixed for supplies?"

"Annie's a trader. Come by it natural born. Anything worth having anywhere near her, she'll have it if she wants it. Or she'll know where a fella can trade out of it."

"We're going to need ammo."

"She'll have it. She'll be willing to trade for blasters, so you can relax your brain about that. With the Slaggers in Idaho Falls getting fatter and bigger, a lot more people are wanting to get their hands on some firepower. If your friend can get those blasters fixed, she'll be willing to trade with both of us."

Ryan accepted that. Trading was only one of the options the companions had, and he knew it. With the condition Krysty was in, he wasn't going to be any more politic than he had to be.

Chapter Nineteen

"Back when I was around the Totality Concept whitecoats, my dear Ryan," Doc said softly, "they were experimenting with many things that were supposed to enhance a person's psychic ability. Drugs and electrical experiments. Even operations on the brain itself that involved transplantations from other brains and the insertion of microcomputers."

"Anything like this?" Ryan asked, looking at the nearby railing where Krysty slept like the dead. Her body rolled slowly with the motion of the boat. Only the slow rise and fall of her breasts let him know she was still alive. Dean sat nearby, keeping watch over her.

Doc shook his head, his long hair tangling in the breeze. "Not that I recollect. I made myself privy to as many of their goings-on as I could, but there was still much that I missed, as you are well aware."

"We're still days out from finding the Heimdall Foundation," Ryan stated. "After the problems she had last night, we need an edge to help her get past this."

"Doc and I talked last night," Mildred said. "We came up with a few possible solutions."

Ryan stood in the prow, feeling the breeze whisper past him and the sun beat down on him. The air was tainted with the smell of salt and minerals burning, coming from the galley below where Morse's sons had started up the water-purifying system they had on board. The water purification setup was cobbled together out of spare parts and copper tubing they'd scavenged, but Doc had pronounced it serviceable. Being able to filter water from the river made them dependent only on game from the riverbanks while they sailed. The previous night's haul would carry them for a few days.

"First option is to keep her hopped up on drugs," Mildred said.

"That'll mean carrying her with us," Ryan said. "We stay on the boat, that won't be much of a problem. Just one less blaster, which she almost is now. But once we leave, carrying her would be hard on the rest of us." And the truth also was that he couldn't tolerate the idea of Krysty mind numbed and not capable of taking care of herself. The beautiful redhead was independent and proud, qualities that had drawn him to her.

"We could," Mildred suggested, "leave her somewhere. With one of us."

Ryan shook his head. "We're in hostile territory, and splitting us up isn't something I'm going to do."

"Might not have a choice," Mildred pointed out.

"Make that choice when it's time," Ryan said. "Not before."

She nodded, accepting his decision. "Just playing devil's advocate, Ryan. You leave her behind unless there's just cause, you'll be leaving me behind, as well. We've been through too much to consider giving up now."

"What else?" Ryan asked.

"Hypnosis is a possibility I would be willing to consider," Doc said.

"What are you planning on doing with hypnosis?" Ryan asked.

"Perhaps I could help Krysty build a wall against the old crone's personality," Doc said. "By whatever means she employed to connive her way into Krysty's mind, she is only there because Krysty has not found a way to get rid of her.''

"Why not just hypnotize the woman?" Ryan asked. "Have her chill herself inside Krysty's head and leave Krysty alone?"

"Treating her like a multiple personality sounds like an answer," Mildred said. "But there's some problems with that."

"Exactly," Doc said. "At the moment, Krysty is the dominant personality of the two. We might upset that delicate balance by calling for the harridan that is possessing her. Once we get her to the forefront, she might not be so easily returned."

"What Doc wants to work on is breaking the communication between Krysty and the old woman," Mildred said. "Maybe if Krysty had more time and was in a quiet place, she'd be able to do it on her own."

"That's not going to happen now," Ryan said.

"No," Doc agreed, "it is not."

"There is one other option," Mildred said.

Ryan looked at her.

"We could perform an exorcism," she went on.

"Madam," Doc said, lifting his eyebrows in consternation, "I cannot believe you would suggest such a thing. How can you even entertain the notion of ghosts and call yourself a person of science?"

"Everybody believes in ghosts," Mildred said. "Or at least they admit to the possibility."

"I would in nowise agree to that blanket statement," Doc objected.

"No? But I'll bet you bought into every ghost story old Shakespeare ever wrote."

"I beg your pardon. The bard included ghosts only as

dramatic license, a plot device that kept a good story rolling along at a nice clip.''

''I'm not talking about ghosts,'' Mildred went on. ''I'm talking about belief systems. Maybe that old woman only has a toehold in Krysty's psyche because of her gifts and her belief in things supernatural. You ever talked to her about ghosts, Ryan?''

Ryan couldn't remember and said so. There were more important things they had to talk about every day than some threat that existed only in folklore.

''Maybe if we had an exorcism and Krysty believed hard enough, it would be able to help her build that wall against that old woman like Doc was talking about,'' Mildred said. ''We give her a crutch to believe in, maybe her own belief systems will kick in and deny the woman's existence.''

''Denying a problem's worse than facing it head-on,'' Ryan said.

''We're just trying to buy some time,'' Mildred explained. ''Your call.''

Grudgingly Ryan gave his acceptance. ''When?''

''After nightfall,'' Mildred said. ''By then maybe we'll be at this trader Annie's place and off the river for the night.''

Ryan nodded.

''And pray tell, dear lady,'' Doc said, ''how many exorcisms have you hosted?''

''This'll be my first,'' Mildred admitted.

''Fireblast!'' Ryan snarled. ''This isn't the time to be figuring out if mebbe you can and mebbe you can't.''

Mildred turned her dark gaze on him, anger burning in her eyes. ''I could have conducted forty of them before now. It doesn't mean it would work on Krysty now. An exorcism doesn't require me believing in it. It requires her believing in it.''

Ryan curbed his anger, and the red mist in his vision cleared somewhat. He glanced back at Krysty, seeing that she still slept.

"What bona fides do you have in this endeavor, madam?" Doc persisted.

"One of the college papers I did involved the creation of zombies in voodoo practices," she replied.

Doc shook his head. "More false mysticism."

"Ryan, listen to me." Mildred focused her attention on the one-eyed man. "Voodoo was very powerful in Haiti, New Orleans and other pockets of civilizations where the religion flourished. The darker side of voodoo involved blood sacrifices. We've seen muties who still practice it, and other things as we've knocked around. There were cases of zombie creation in the 1990s. They were documented studies. Pharmacological corporations sent teams down into South America and Haiti looking for the zombie powder. They were hoping to find a new anesthetic that was more potent than anything that had been found up to that date. Instead, they proved the existence of zombies."

"Dead men walking," Jak commented, approaching the group.

"You've heard of such things?" Ryan asked the albino.

Jak shook his head. "Seen 'em. Dead men crawl out graves in swamps. Made protect sacred areas, *bokor*'s secrets."

"*Bokor?*" Doc asked.

"Sort of a voodoo evil magician," Mildred said. "*Bokor*s raised the dead. Only they weren't really dead. The voodoo religion was so strong that the zombie powder convinced people it was given to that they were dead. What it really did was put them into a coma that lasted days. Then they were buried."

"Alive?" Ryan asked.

"Not so that you could tell it," Mildred replied. "There wasn't enough respiration to fog a mirror. No heartbeat that could be heard. For all intents and purposes, they were dead."

"Only they were truly in a coma," Doc said.

"Yeah. There was the belief among medical professionals, physicians and psychologists, that the afflicted person could still hear."

"While they were pronounced dead?" Doc queried.

"Right. It strengthened their belief that they would return as a zombie, that they were really dead. A funeral was held to further convince not only that individual, but also the community, that person was chilled. A few days later, the person was dug up and another drug was administered, or maybe the effects of the zombie powder wore off."

"Why didn't these people just go back to their lives?" Ryan asked.

"Because they believed they were zombies," Mildred answered. "That's what I'm telling you, Ryan. And it's one of the major differences between the Western practice of medicine versus the Eastern practice. Homeopathic medicine requires more belief on part of the patient than the Western style. But the success rates are on a par. Or were. Even Western doctors were convinced that after surgeries patients usually got better because they believed they would. Belief is a very strong thing."

"So if Krysty believes enough in this exorcism, mebbe it'll erase this woman from her head?" he asked.

"Perhaps it'll give her a better chance against that woman," Mildred commented. "We're still dealing with something we've had no experience in. We find this Donovan, maybe we'll know more."

"You talk to her first?"

Mildred nodded. "Get her thinking along the lines we

need her to first. Do the exorcism tonight when we have time to put on a show, do it right.''

"Only if she's got the strength,'' Ryan cautioned. He glanced down the river, shifting his body with the pitch of the sailboat. ''Even getting to the trading post, we're going to be on condition red. Don't trust Morse not to run us into a trap. Everybody keep your eyes peeled.''

"HOW MUCH FARTHER?'' Ryan demanded.

Morse called out sail changes to his sons and held on to the wheel. The river was swollen more now with the spring rains than before. ''Another ten, fifteen minutes should see us there.''

Ryan studied the riverbank. That morning, he'd been able to see where the waterline had been in weeks past. Dead grass and the clutter of broken branches and other debris had lined both banks, creating a definite line of demarcation. Now, the water was up against the green again.

And the river had picked up speed, sluicing whitecapped roils through the brown water.

"How many blasters at the trading post?'' Ryan asked.

"Don't know.'' Morse worked the wheel, putting his back into it. Muscle stood out in sharp slabs along his back, rippling with perspiration. ''Depends on how many Annie's putting up.''

"Putting up?''

Morse nodded. ''Built herself a couple cabins back of the trading post near twenty years ago. Likes her privacy, old Annie does. She's a reader. Got a lot of books the like of which I never seen before. Know one thing, though.''

Ryan surveyed the man.

"You bring Annie a book she ain't heard tell of before, you done won her heart.''

"Does she keep a standing sec force?''

"Not what you'd call a proper sec force. She's got a son, must be nearing fifty now, but he keeps meat on the table by foraging among the forest. Max, he's a silent one. Good with knives. Way I heard it, the mutie cougar Annie's got mounted over the bar was one Max took, and him with nothing more than a blade."

"What're the chances he'll be around?"

"Max knows when a boat's out on the water. He'll be there with Annie, waiting on us. Mebbe already spotted us from the forest in the last couple hours. She'll know who's coming before we get there."

Ryan glanced up at the wind-filled sails. "We've been making good time. Even with a horse, Max might not make it back in time."

Morse shook his head. "We're following the curve of the river, mister. That land on the leeward side of this boat is a half moon. Max cutting across the land is going to get to the trading post before we do. Can't be helped."

Ryan changed his gaze to the riverbank in question, thinking.

"You want to try to hedge your bet, mister," Morse said, "you go on and do 'er. But anybody you put on that riverbank now, you might as well say a few words over 'cause you ain't going to see them alive again. Max'll chill 'em and leave their bones to bleach in that forest."

"Might not go that way," Ryan pointed out.

"Mebbe," Morse grudgingly admitted, "but if we show up at the trading post before Max, Annie'll cut loose on us. Mebbe blow old *Junie* plumb outta the river."

"With what?"

"Got herself an artillery cannon mounted up in that trading post. Scavenged it from some National Guard unit after skydark. Been in her family for a couple generations, way

I hear it. Damn thing'll set up and belch out sudden death. Seen it happen myself.''

The idea of the cannon didn't sit well with Ryan, nor did the probability that any encounter with Max in the woods wasn't going to be beneficial to their cause. He didn't like the lay of the land at all, and that was a solid ace on the line. They had time, he knew he could figure a way out around it. But they didn't, and Krysty asleep and lying only a few feet from him was a constant reminder of that.

"Anybody else at the trading post regular?" Ryan asked.

"Just her grandson. Name's Jubal. He's the only child of her dead daughter, and that boy's been a retard since the day he was brought into this world."

"How often are the cabins occupied?"

"Often enough. And Annie don't let nobody stay there that wouldn't pick up a blaster in her defense." Morse pointed ahead of the boat. "See that grove of ash trees?"

"Yeah."

"We get around that," Morse said, "you'll be able to get your first look at the trading post."

Ryan nodded.

"Best you keep in mind, though," Morse cautioned. "Once you see that trading post, you remember you're also looking down the throat of an artillery cannon."

Chapter Twenty

"That's a regular fort," J.B. commented.

Looking at the trading post, Ryan had to agree. Knowing that an artillery cannon was aimed at them at the moment didn't set well, either. "Built it to last, didn't they?"

J.B. nodded.

The trading post sat on a hill on the north side of the river, cadged together out of tree trunks that looked nearly four feet across. They stood uniform, one end buried in the ground while the other end stretched upward at least twenty feet. The main interior structure sat in the center of the posts, well below the sight line. But a second story overlooked the river, constructed of the thick tree trunks, as well.

Ryan took out his binoculars and scanned the structure, focusing on the shiny bits atop the palisades. "Topped the timbers with glass and metal shards," he told the Armorer. "Man trying to go over's going to get cut up."

"Slowed, too," J.B. said. "Easy target."

The trees and brush had been cut well back of the palisade walls. White marks in the bark of nearby trees showed that the pruning was done on a constant basis. A narrow dirt trail led up to the front of the trading post, tucking in behind the tree line for a moment, then emerging along the edge of the overhang fronting the river. The bend there put it less than a hundred yards from the drop-off, which was sheer, falling nearly eighty feet to the river.

Ryan sharpened the focus on the binoculars and spotted the scars in nearby rocks from cannonshot. None of them looked recent. "Got the trail positioned so the artillery can take out any wags. One shot with anything of real size and the area would be cleaned, dropping the wag off into the river."

"Noticed that," J.B. agreed.

At the foot of the drop-off, a small pier jutted into the river, barely above the present flood stage. It was constructed of split logs rather than timbers, providing an uneven but serviceable surface. Rope ladders zigzagged back and forth across the drop-off, leading to the same point as the trail.

Morse called out instructions to his boys, cutting the sail. The vessel coasted closer to the pier, coming around expertly.

Ryan put the binoculars away, impressed with the construction and location of the structure. He also had the distinct impression someone was watching them.

"WHO BUILT the trading post?" Ryan asked as he stepped out onto the split-timber pier. The wood rang solidly below his boots.

"Annie did," Morse said, tying a thick hawser to one of the pier's support posts. "Came out here in a horse-drawn wag, saw the river and decided she wanted to live here. Took her a couple years to figure out how she was going to make a living. Trading came natural to her because her folks had been involved with it."

"They didn't come with her?"

"By then they were chilled. Never got the particulars of the tale. Some said they ran afoul of another trader—some said they sold snake oil that started a plague that damn near wiped out a ville. They got chilled. Annie survived, kept on moving.''

Ryan had unslung the Steyr, the safety off. He turned to the companions. ''While we're here, we're on condition red.''

They all nodded.

Wind trailed in off the river, bringing the scent of fish and sickness. A pair of corpses, bloated and dead for days, twisted and turned against a wooden dam built out into the water.

''Annie's,'' Morse explained, nodding at the dam. ''Uses it for salvage. Way the land floods around here and rivers take up new paths, she collects some good stuff every now and again that floats to the top or is carried along the bottom.''

''She knows we're here?'' Ryan asked.

Morse smiled. ''Ain't been fired on. That's practically an engraved invitation.''

Ryan gave the man a thin smile, then turned his attention to the series of rope ladders. ''Jak, you got the lead. I'll be the next man behind you.''

The albino nodded and started up the first ladder.

''Dean,'' Ryan went on, ''you'll follow me, with Krysty after you. Doc, you help with Krysty, in case she needs it.''

The redhead looked as though she was going to protest, then stopped, breaking her gaze away from her lover's.

Turning to the rest of the group that accompanied the companions, he commanded, ''The rest of you start along after Doc. Elmore and Morse, if you get any ideas about leaving sudden-like, I'll put you on the next train headed West myself. And you can take that as an ace on the line.''

Both men nodded.

''Mildred,'' Ryan said, ''you next. J.B., you're walking

drag.'' Keeping the Steyr at the ready, he turned to the rope ladders and started up.

They swayed and shook under his weight, but they held. The ropes looked in good condition, showing places where they'd been rebraided with new sections and repaired. The planks were handmade, cut from rough timber. Most of them were worn smooth because of heavy traffic, but a few—like the rope—showed where replacements had been made.

Halfway to the top, Ryan was covered in perspiration despite the wind blowing around them. The humidity that settled in over the area promised more rain to come, as well as hot temperatures.

As soon as Jak gained the top of the drop-off, he disappeared.

Ryan went up next, alert to the slightest sound or movement. He crested the top, his eye darting around the cleared space and the wag trail just beyond.

Jak stood at the trail's edge and stared at the trading post. The albino looked as tense as a bowstring. ''Don't like staying open. Too easy get shot.''

Ryan silently agreed, but knew there'd been no choice. The companions had to have supplies if they were going on. And there was no question about that, either.

''We'll try our luck at the trading post,'' he said.

A HANDMADE SIGN hung over the double doors cut into the palisade walls. Annie's Green Springs, it stated, crafted in bottle-green letters that had faded over the years. A brass bell hung beside the right door, screwed in tight to the tree trunk.

Ryan swung the chain attached to the clapper. The bell rang loudly, echoing out over the open space behind them. Standing this close to the trading post, he spotted the numerous bullet scars in the tree trunks. A history of violence clung to the trading post.

"Three people hold this place?" he asked Morse again.

"On a regular basis," the man replied. "Course, you gotta remember what I said about Annie having company. She usually does."

"People have tried to break in before."

"Sure. Even had a couple get through. Annie's got a lock-down inside the trading post. Hiding place nobody can dig her out of. Self-heats, source of fresh water. She wants, she can stay under for months. She's done it a couple times in the past."

"Did she lose much?" Doc asked.

"Salvaged stuff, but not her life. Annie always figures she can make a living if she just keeps on living. Dying's kind of hard on the profits. It would be hard to carry off all that she's accumulated over the years. The coldhearts who didn't get their asses shot off either coming or going didn't get away with much. And in most cases, they didn't get away at all. People who trade with Annie, they kind of take it personal when somebody jeopardizes the business. They've tracked coldhearts down, brought the stuff back they took. For a bounty, and Annie don't make no bones about paying it."

"Don't have many other places to go and trade around here, do they?" Ryan said, understanding at once.

"Mister, you got the right of it. Fella finds something worth trading, he might have to lug it around for months till he can find the person who can afford it or wants it. Annie opens him up an account here at the trading post, lets him get what he needs."

"And she takes a piece of the profits."

"Yeah."

Ryan reached for the bell and rang it again, louder and longer this time.

"Heard you the first time you rang that bastard bell," a woman's voice said. It was pitched low, sounding raspy. "What do you want?"

"To trade." Ryan glanced along the topmost section of the palisade, finally spotting the peephole created at the top of the tree trunks thirty feet to his left.

"Mebbe you want to, but I'm not sure I want to," the woman said.

"Are you Annie?"

"Been called that. Been called other things, too, but as long as I got my hand on this trigger, I don't have to put up with a lot of shit I don't want to."

"We're in a desperate way," Ryan said. "We've been run down and hunted. Short on supplies. Going back is out of the question, and pressing on isn't going to mean much unless we're better outfitted."

"You going to keep Morse's boat?"

"Hiring him on," Ryan said. "He's been paid." And it was true enough considering the blasters that J.B. had repaired to pay their way.

"He doesn't look too happy about it."

"If we'd had a boat, or didn't have a need for one," Ryan said, "we'd all have been happy. But we do, and I haven't chilled him yet."

"True enough," the old woman called back out. "But that's Morse's lookout. Don't owe him nothing, and he don't owe me enough to make it worth my while to take a hand in what you're prepared to deal out."

"We're going to have to trade," Ryan said, "one way or another." He let that sink in. "We don't have a choice about pressing on."

"Mister," the woman said after a brief pause, "words

like that could get you chilled in your boots, standing right there where you are.''

''There's been some who tried,'' Ryan said agreeably. ''Figure if you knew you had that locked down, you'd have already tried it.''

''You're a confident man.''

''Have to be. Otherwise, I'd have never climbed up this hill and rang that bastard bell.'' Ryan mopped a layer of perspiration from his forehead with his shirtsleeve.

''What have you got to trade?''

''Handblasters,'' Ryan answered. ''Four of them.''

''In good shape?''

''They are now. I've got a friend out here who can fix damn near any longgun or handblaster.''

''Talented man to have around,'' Annie stated.

Ryan didn't say anything; the old woman was just taking time now to decide if she was going to buy into the situation.

''Is what this man's saying true, Morse?'' she asked.

''It's the truth,'' Morse answered. ''I got some handblasters out of the deal myself.''

''Mil-spec?''

''Yeah.''

''No longguns?''

''No.''

''Mister,'' Annie called out to Ryan, ''assuming I let you inside, what are you going to want for those blasters?''

''Ammo,'' Ryan answered. ''Mebbe some self-heats, ring-pulls.''

''Got it all inside the post,'' she told him. ''We're only talking four handblasters, though, so you're going to have to come up with something else to even things out.''

''We ran into a sec team put out by a local baron,'' Ryan said. ''They had a few handblasters, but primarily they were outfitted with longguns. Handblasters are easy to carry out of sight. I don't think you'll have a hard time selling them. For what we're planning to trade for, your price will be covered.''

''Seem awful sure about yourself.''

''I am,'' Ryan replied. ''I'm no stranger to trading myself.''

''What kind of handblasters?'' Annie asked.

''Two 9 mm semiautos,'' Ryan called back. ''Two wheelguns.''

''How do I know they shoot true?''

''Test them yourself. If they don't, you don't have to make a deal.''

''By then, you might be inside.''

''It'd be hard for either one of us to get what we want if that doesn't happen.'' Ryan waited, letting the silence fill in the distance between them.

''I don't know that I want what you have to offer,'' Annie said. ''You have a lean and hungry look about you.''

Crimson misted Ryan's vision as the anger took him. He struggled for self-control as Doc stepped forward.

The old man struck an imposing stance and addressed the owner of the trading post. ''Madam, I should wonder if you pass that quote in telling jest, and not some happy chance of twisted words about you.''

''I don't know what you're talking about.''

''I think you do. The passage actually goes thusly, a scene from the first act of *Julius Caesar* by the immortal bard himself.'' Doc cleared his throat.

''Let me have men about me that are fat;/ Sleek-headed men, and such as sleep o' nights./ Yon Cassius has a lean and hungry look;/ He thinks too much: such men are dangerous.''

The old man's words rolled over the area, sounding powerful and resonant.

"Who are you?" Annie demanded.

Doc tucked his cane under his arm as he bowed with a flourish. "Dr. Theophilus Algernon Tanner at your service, madam." His wide smile showed his impossibly white teeth.

"You're a good-looking enough man to look at, Doc Tanner," Annie called back, "and you talk flowery."

"Why, thank you kindly."

"Pretty words and a nice smile don't mean you're going to get inside, though."

"Madam, let me assure you, we're here neither to harm nor rob you. Only to trade fairly and for things that we desperately need."

"I'm not known for giving out charity."

"Madam, I am reminded of some great words handed down by Sir Winston Churchill, who was also a hard man to deal with," Doc stated.

"You will make all kinds of mistakes, but as long as you are generous and true, and also fierce, you cannot hurt the world or even seriously distress her."

"You're an interesting man, Doc Tanner."

"Your generous nature is already showing, madam."

"I would like to talk to you at length, given the opportunity."

Ryan started to speak up, shifting to address the woman again. Krysty's hand came down on his arm. "Ease off, lover," she said softly. "Doc's making headway, and she's not going to be convinced by anyone else here."

Ryan studied the trading post, wondering how many blasters were inside. He caught J.B.'s eye, knowing the

Armorer was contemplating the same thing. No matter how Doc's discourse with the woman turned out, they weren't moving on without supplies. However they had to get them.

"By all means," Doc said, "I should be enchanted to enjoy your company. All that requires is your invitation."

"I'd extend it to yourself," Annie called back.

"Then," Doc replied, "I must regretfully forego the pleasure, as enticing as it sounds, for I shall not feel welcome where my companions are not."

"You're sure?"

"Yes, madam. Never more certain of anything in my life."

"What about you?" the woman called out. "The one-eyed, scruffy wolf."

"What?" Ryan growled.

"Would you send your man in if it might get you the provisions you wanted? At a fair price?"

"I don't know you at all," Ryan replied, "except from what Morse has said. For all I know, you'll take Doc inside, then ransom him back to us for what we brought to trade and more."

There was silence for a moment, then the woman's laughter pealed over them. "Morse, do you vouch for these people?"

"As much as I can," the sailor answered. "We've been kind of forced together."

"Have you suffered at their hands?"

"Not yet. But there's been some threats made."

"And our one-eyed wolf looks like just the sort of man who'd carry those threats out. Are you going to be willing to trade the blasters these men have repaired for you?"

"I've got a balance I already owe you," Morse grunted. "I don't see how you're going to let me take on the provisions we're going to need without trading."

"So you'll have eight handblasters," Ryan pointed out.

"What's your name, wolf?"

"Ryan. Ryan Cawdor."

"I've heard of you. For a time you traveled with the Trader. But I thought you were dead."

"Not hardly."

"I don't suppose you'd agree to laying down your weapons before you enter the trading post."

"No."

"Then come ahead, Mr. Cawdor, and be on your best behavior. Because if you aren't, we'll bury you, and you can believe that."

Ryan kept the Steyr at the ready as the huge twin doors opened in the palisade wall. Four armed men stood on the other side of the doors, weapons in their hands. All of them looked rough and showed the wear and tear of harsh experience lived on the land.

Chapter Twenty-One

Inside the palisade walls, the wag trail followed the natural incline of the land up to the main house. It was large and compact at the same time, full of rooms and each positioned carefully in the building. The natural finish of the wood had been left, and it had turned weathered and gray from exposure. Ryan also noted the way the main house cut into the earth, realizing there was at least one other floor beneath the ground level.

The interior of the trading camp was kept clean. No brush or trees grew up from the hard-packed ground. A large vegetable garden occupied the northwest corner of the trading post's interior area. Plants thrust up toward the afternoon sun, and strawberry bushes burgeoned with ripening fruit.

"Mr. Cawdor," the woman's smoky voice called out.

Ryan turned, tracking the voice up the ladder to the right. A catwalk jutted out from the inside walls. Three more men stood guard there, all watching the new arrivals. Two girls that didn't look to be out of their teens stood on the catwalk to the left of them, giving them a position to manage a cross fire. Both of the females dressed in revealing clothing.

Annie was a fit-looking woman in her late fifties or early sixties, Ryan judged, though she could have passed for ten or fifteen years younger. With her gray-and-black hair pulled back in a long ponytail, her body tight from hard living and a complexion the color of a fawn's coat, she was a handsome enough woman. The skin tone spoke of several possible heritages, or a mixture of them. She wore dungarees and a rawhide vest that clung to her ample bosom.

"By the Three Kennedys," Doc exclaimed in a low voice, "now, there walks a handsome woman."

"Put a lid on it, you randy old goat," Mildred snapped.

Doc shot Mildred a glower, but didn't say anything.

Annie approached Ryan without hesitation. She carried a sawed-off, double-barrel shotgun in the crook of her left arm, her right hand fisting the triggers. Both the hammers were eared back. "First sign of trouble from you," she told Ryan, "and I'll put you in the compost heap. That's a promise."

Ryan nodded. "We'll get our trading done, then be on our way."

"Keep your eye on business all the time, Mr. Cawdor?"

"Yeah."

"I like that in a man."

"Don't give a damn what you like," Ryan said. "One of Trader's hardest and most fast rules was to get business done ASAP. Once it was done, there was no reason to hang around unless somebody was fishing for information. Or wondering if they were big enough or bad enough to take you."

"Trader was a smart man. Come on inside the house. Hospitality can be quick, too, and I want to have a look at those blasters before we sit down to dicker too hard. Got some sipping whiskey inside that I brew myself. Make it out of potatoes, but it carries a hell of a kick."

"We'll see," Ryan said.

ANNIE LET THEM into the main house, and Ryan was surprised at the decor. Where the exterior of the house was rough, the interior showed the effects of considerable hard work. The floors were wood, but carpets covered them in places, all of them depicting outdoor nature scenes: woodlands and creatures, fish and rivers, snow-topped mountains. Looking at them, Ryan knew the influences had come from the land around the trading post.

He followed the woman through a narrow hallway off the main door, set between two rooms that had large Xs cut in them for blasterports. Evidently the woman took her security measures to heart.

As they stepped into the big room, he signaled to J.B. and had the Armorer step away to the right, then signaled Jak and Dean to step to the left. By the time they stopped, they formed a half circle around Annie and her people. Some of the trading post's gunners were still behind them, but they weren't bunched up.

The room was massive, filled with handmade furniture that sported overstuffed upholstery. Two of the walls held floor-to-ceiling shelves that were filled with books. A third wall was a taxidermist's dream, lined with the heads and bodies of wild game. Ryan scanned the assembled mountings, spotting bears, cougar, fish, snakes and other mutie animals that he wasn't so sure of.

There were also seven human heads. Five of them had belonged to men, and two to women. All of them looked terrified, and the flesh hadn't been as easily preserved as fur. Skin stretched taut over bone, and stitches showed on the faces of two men, showing where wounds had been closed up after death.

A huge fireplace occupied the fourth wall. There were no windows.

Annie stopped at a large table cut from tree trunks. Smooth river stones covered the tabletop, all of it leveled off by a flawless lacquer that held a suet-yellow color. She flipped a switch under the table, and electrical lights flooded the room.

"Make yourselves to home," Annie said. "Those that I let inside the trading post I take pride in showing hospitality to."

Ryan took a seat on one of the three large couches in the center of the room around the big table. J.B. sat across from him while Jak and Dean hung back. There were plenty of seats for Morse and his boys, Elmore and the others. Doc walked straight across to the shelves.

"Madam, I must say you have quite an eclectic collection of books," the old man said.

"Out here, Doc," Annie said, pouring drinks in glass jars, "I can't be too choosy about what I'm able to get. I take whatever I can get my hands on."

"Twain, Faulkner, King, Sheldon and names here that I am afraid I do not recognize, and I consider myself a learned man. Have you read them all?"

"As much as I've been able," Annie said. "As many as caught my eye and held my attention. I'm still a working woman, and I have to put in time every day if I plan on keeping this place together."

"Have you a favorite?"

Annie gestured to one of the men to hand out drinks. The man didn't look too happy about it, and used only one hand to carry the wooden platter of drinks. The other he kept on his rifle. "Jack London," she said. "I loved *Call of the Wild* and *White Fang*, and most of his other works. Brilliant writer."

"Why Jack London?" Doc asked.

"Man wrote about it the way it was," a new male voice said. "And the way it is."

Ryan glanced at the doorway and watched as a big man doffed his fur cap and entered the room.

"This is my son," Annie said. "His name's Max, and he's going to make sure the business we conduct is right and fair."

Max carried his mother's complexion, but most of the resemblance ended there. Ryan surmised that he had to have taken the majority of his looks from his father. Max had dark hair, plastered tight against his scalp from wearing the heavy fur cap, and tied into short braids. Nearly six and a half feet tall, he carried slabs of muscle on his broad frame. He wore leathers, all handmade and showing scars from hard wear.

"They come alone," Max said, taking one of the jars of liquor. He took a deep drink without showing any of the effects of the alcohol. He kept a long-barreled .44 Magnum Colt Model 624 in his fist. A camp ax hung by a thong from his belt, balanced by three throwing knives on the other side. He wore a bow over his shoulder and twin quivers of arrows on his back. Knife handles showed from his boot tops, as well.

"Was anyone left on the boat?" Annie asked.

"Empty."

"Anything on it they didn't tell us about?"

"Not that I could find." Max poured some more whiskey into his glass. "From what I saw, not all of these folks are together."

"I know about Morse and his boys."

Max nodded. "I watched those seven come up the hill together." He pointed out Ryan and the others. "They move like one. Been together a long time, and in dangerous places from the looks of them."

"You didn't have a reason to go on that boat," Dean stated angrily.

"Dean," Ryan said, "back off."

The boy's color remained mottled, and Ryan knew the

boy had inherited more from him than a mere physical resemblance. But the anger that resided in his son was going to have to be tempered if he was going to get a handle on it.

"It's not right, Dad," the boy said. "For all we know, this bastard set fire to the boat and burned it to the waterline."

If he was offended by the accusation, Max didn't show it. Instead, he seemed more amused than anything.

"We'd have seen the smoke," J.B. stated.

"The boat's still there," Max said as calmly as if they were discussing the weather. "I didn't do nothing more than look it over."

"I reserve the right, as always, to look out for my own welfare, young man," Annie said to Dean. "Your father knows this, and accepted it when he started up to this trading post."

That was the truth, and Ryan knew it. They couldn't have stayed with the boat and accomplished the trading. From the instant they'd left it behind, he'd been prepared to lose it. Now he recognized that Annie had read the commitment he'd made to getting the necessary supplies. It put them both on equal footing.

"There's something else you might consider," Annie told them.

"What?" Mildred asked. Her attitude showed that she didn't appreciate the high-handed way the woman had taken with them.

"There's a storm coming tonight," Annie said.

"How do you know?" Ryan asked.

The woman focused her attention on him, the dark slate eyes locking on his. "I've lived here almost all my life. I know the land, and I know the weather that surrounds it.

And I'm telling you now that there's a storm blowing in from the south that'll be here by nightfall.''

Ryan glanced at Morse, and the sailor gave him an abbreviated shrug.

"You're welcome to tie *Junie* up to the pier below," Annie stated, "but you're also welcome to stay up here at the trading post if you've mind to."

"I thought your guest houses were full up," Ryan said.

She nodded. "They are. But you're welcome to sleep in the barn if you'd like. It'd be better than trying to rest up out in that boat with the river running wild as it's gonna be."

"Getting off the boat for the night sounds good, lover," Krysty said. It was her way of letting him know she sensed nothing untoward about the offer.

Then again, Ryan had no reason to believe that her customary powers of deduction were what they usually were.

"I'll even add a little more to sweeten the pot," Annie stated. "The guest I've got staying with me even has his personal cook with him. He's rented my rooms and access to my larder. When he heard you folks were coming, he made me promise to ask you up to the table if you stopped by."

Doc turned to her and put on his most charming smile. "Dear lady, the mere thought of enjoying a delicious repast with you is fraught with the promise of exhilaration. I should think we would be delighted to join you. What say you, friend Ryan?"

"Sounds okay," Ryan replied. "But I want some idea of how much jack you're going to charge us before I accept your hospitality."

Annie grinned at him, her eyes blazing. "A practical man, Ryan Cawdor?"

"Always want to know if I can carry the freight before I heft it to my shoulder."

"Then I give you my word that the price you'll pay for the experience won't be anything you can't live with. My word on that. And I can vouch for the cook. He's been in my kitchen for the last nine days."

"Do you have a place we can wash up?" Mildred asked.

"There are horse troughs out in the barn," Annie said. "Got a hand pump out there, too, and a fireplace you can use to heat up water for baths. We get our water from an underground stream, not that shit out in the river, so you don't have to worry about diseases. It can be drank without purification or any fear of contaminants. There's tack you can use for bedrolls."

"When do we get to look at the supplies?" Ryan asked.

"If you want to do it now, Max will take you."

"I'd like to see what I'm getting."

Annie looked at her son, who nodded.

"Come with me," Max said.

"J.B.," Ryan called, "you come with me. The rest of you get down to the barn. We'll be along in a few minutes."

"Doc," Annie said, "I was wondering if you might spend a few minutes."

"I fear I really do not like shirking the work my fellow companions must be about in the barn," the old man said.

"It's okay, Doc," Ryan said. "We'll get things ready."

Doc looked vaguely surprised. "Well, if you are sure."

"I'm sure." Ryan followed Max and J.B. deeper into the huge house along another corridor. He marked two lefts, then they were in another windowless large room. Three big tables occupied the center of the room, surrounded by wooden stools that didn't look at all comfortable.

"Have a seat," Max said, pointing at one of the tables.

"I'll bring out some of the merchandise, give you a chance to look it over."

Ryan and J.B. sat while the big man walked over to the door to an adjoining room and fitted a key into the lock. He let himself inside without looking back.

"Got one guest staying in both guest houses," Ryan commented.

"Heard that," J.B. said.

"Brought his own cook. Must be a hell of a fucking guest."

"Some of those blasters facing us off when we stepped through the palisade doors were sec men."

Ryan nodded. He'd noticed the same thing. Sec men who'd spent time at their job developed a certain pattern of movement, a way of carrying themselves. "Going to be an interesting night."

"If we stay," J.B. said. "Don't have to do that."

"Play it as the hand is laid out. If a storm is coming, safest place for that boat is in some kind of harbor. That dock down below might not be much, but it's deep enough to keep the boat together if the water gets rough."

MILDRED TOOK CHARGE of the group back in the barn. She assigned Jak to watch Elmore, and she let the Heimdall Foundation man know he was on a short leash. Elmore wasn't happy about it, but he didn't try to slip off after the first time, either.

The barn stood nearly twenty feet tall, a big spacious building with a hayloft overhead. Stalls held eight horses with room for four more. Tack and saddles covered one wall, hanging from hooks. Loose straw lay over the hard-packed earth.

"Comfortable place," the ferret-faced man who'd

guided them to the barn said. "Tight and dry during the rainy season. Spent many a night here myself."

"You're not one of the guests Annie's got right now, are you?"

The man shook his head. "I'm one of Annie's regulars. Do my scavenging and trading with her 'cause she's fair to me. When times get lean, and they do often enough in the cold season, she stakes me, lets me stay in the barn if I got no other place."

"Where are you spending the night tonight?" Mildred didn't relish the idea of a bunch of strangers camping out among them. It was bad enough having Morse and his boys and what remained of the ex-prisoners of the coldhearts around them.

"Outside." The man hooked a thumb over his shoulder. "Got a tent, and Annie's giving me my meals for a few days."

"Is that normal?"

The man regarded her suspiciously. "Annie's done me enough favors, I don't kick much when she asks me for one." He excused himself and left the barn.

Mildred returned her attention to the barn. Dean laid out a fire in the stone fireplace, using wood that was neatly stacked up in a lean-to fifty yards from the barn. The horses whinnied and nickered as the people moved around among them.

"Horses used hard," Jak commented as he leaned against the wall and watched over Elmore.

"I noticed that," Mildred said. She hadn't exactly been a city girl all her life before being frozen in a cryo chamber and thawed after the nukecaust. But traveling with Ryan and the other companions had sharpened her eye.

The horses were leaned out from hard travel, their coats

not well taken care of. A few of them moved gingerly, as if their hooves had deep stone bruises.

"Horses shod, too," the albino said quietly. "Probably roadwork, not open range. Used to living in ville."

"Sec men and horses that have been pushed hard," Mildred said. "Kind of leads you to think that Annie's present guest wore out his welcome somewhere else, doesn't it?"

Jak grinned coldly. "Best we move early in morning."

Mildred nodded. "We'll make our own damn breakfast or skip it if Ryan and J.B. can push the trade through tonight. Being in the middle of somebody else's trouble is the last place I want to be." She moved off, intending to see to the placement of their people in case things turned bad.

"WE DO OUR OWN RELOADING where we can," Max said as he pushed boxes of ammo across to Ryan and J.B. "But the scavengers working the regions within trading distance around us still come across stuff like this often enough."

Ryan picked up a box of 9 mm ammo and slid it open. The bullets inside stood at rigid attention, gleaming from the thin oil coat that covered them. The noses were concave, letting him know they were hollowpoint. "Glasers," he commented. "These are some serious rounds."

Max nodded, staying out of reach, his hand never far from his blaster. "Annie wanted you people to have the best."

J.B. reached over for one of the bullets, rolling it appreciatively between his forefinger and thumb. "These bullets had a rep for one shot, one kill."

"I've used them," Max stated. "They live up to their name. I noticed you people packed 9 mm rounds, and you looked like you've been traveling hard for a while."

J.B. examined the round. "Factory made," he told Ryan.

"Got pellets suspended inside in liquid Teflon. You shoot something, they disburse inside it like a shotgun round. Tear the hell out of anything they hit. Pellets hit bone, ricochet around and follow the natural line of the bone till they rip out somewhere new." A smile curved his lips.

Ryan knew about the round. He'd come across them from time to time. It put him on edge that Max and Annie were so willing to part with ammo obviously worth so much.

Max had also brought rounds for J.B.'s shotgun. There was a mixture of fléchette, as well as double-aught. Again, like the 9 mm rounds, they were factory perfect.

"Noticed in some of the bandoliers on the sec men," the Armorer said, "they were carrying homegrown loads."

"Yeah." Max moved easily, transferring more boxes of ammo from the grease-stained mail pouch to the table. He returned Ryan's and J.B.'s gazes without flinching, but Ryan knew the man had realized he'd given away the fact that part of the group had been sec men.

"Who're they here with?" Ryan asked.

"Annie'll provide the introductions tonight." Max put the last box of ammo on the table and tossed the empty mail pouch onto the table, as well.

Ryan ran his eye over the factory boxes. There was ammo there for all the companions' weapons, including, oddly, Doc's Le Mat blaster. Max had memorized them all in the few minutes he'd been with them.

"Who's he running from?" Ryan asked.

"Nobody said anything about him running from nothing," Max answered.

"Didn't have to," Ryan replied. "You brought us back here and start passing out ammo like it's Christmas or something. Offer us the barn and a meal tonight. That indicates to me that you people want us here."

"Storm's coming," Max said flatly.

"I've been wondering about that, too." Ryan returned the man's level glare. At his side, he noted that J.B. already had his hand on his shotgun's grip, ready to swing it up. "I was thinking mebbe we should just finish up our trading, get the fuck out of here and take our chances with the storm."

"If the storm gets too rough tonight on that flooded river, you're going to get that boat swamped and lose it."

"Mebbe. But I'm wondering what we can expect to face if we stay around here."

"A dry bed and a good meal," Max said. "That much is certain."

"Yeah. But it's the entertainment you got waiting in the wings that leaves me wondering."

Max waved at the boxes of ammo. "Deal's on the table, mister, and staying the night's part of it."

"And if I choose not to stay?"

"Then you walk out of here the same way you walked in, and you get nothing from here."

J.B. took off his fedora and worked at the worn creases, taking time to get them as straight as possible. He worked one-handed, the hat in his lap and covering the fact that he'd raised the shotgun to waist level under the table.

"Fireblast," Ryan swore. "If we stay, it only makes sense that we know what we're up against."

"Nothing you ain't seen before probably dozens of times." Max paused. "Tell your friend to either use that shotgun or put it down before I push this to the edge. And don't get any fancy ideas about slipping out of here in that boat. You try it, you won't clear the river in it. Me and Annie, we ain't made it here all these years by rolling over. I figure you know where to draw the lines, too."

"I know where to draw them," Ryan said. "I hate having them drawn for me.'' He waved J.B. off. ''We can take the ammo now?''

Max nodded.

''Then let's have a look at the rest of it.''

''Later.''

Ryan's voice hardened and took on an edge. ''Now. You only make some of the rules around here, or we're going to find out if J.B.'s faster than you or not. And when we open the ball on this thing, a lot of people are going to get chilled. And that's an ace on the line.''

Max's face reddened. ''What do you want?''

''Some clothing,'' Ryan said. He picked up the ammo boxes and stuffed them back in the mail pouch.

''You staying?'' Max demanded, not moving a muscle.

''We'll spend the night,'' Ryan said. ''But I'm telling you now that tonight is the end of the bargain. You try to hold us another one, blood's going to be spilled. And that's a promise.''

Chapter Twenty-Two

"My favorite author, dear lady?" Doc asked, gazing into the woman's eyes.

"Yes." Annie sat across from him at a little table on a patio in back of the main house. A semicircle of wildflowers grew in the space provided between the wooden timbers used to make the patio and the path that led to the vegetable garden a little over fifty yards away.

"That would have to be Shakespeare," Doc answered.

"Why?"

The stripped down, no-nonsense question caught Doc off guard for a moment, but he appreciated it for its honest intent. In his travels after being trawled to the future, he'd seldom met those who could hold forth a proper discourse of Shakespeare's work. "Why do I like it?"

"Yes."

"How familiar are you with his work, madam?"

"I've read all thirty-seven plays," Annie said. "I've even got annotated versions of some of them. I'm familiar, though I'm no expert."

"Truly," Doc said, "I am impressed."

"I like the stories he tells. But why do you like him so much?"

"For several reasons actually," Doc said. "The stories themselves, though couched in archaic terms and words, considering our present state of affairs, are always timely. They are about the struggle between good and evil inside men and women, about the way they relate to their families and friends and the societies that surround them. Then there is the wordplay itself. Once you have gotten a grudging respect for this language we share, it is a marvel to see it used in the hands of a master. And Shakespeare isn't meant to be read, dear lady. It's meant to be heard. Have you never heard it read?''

"Never," Annie admitted.

"And never read it aloud to yourself?"

"Doc, I've got a dictionary. The words I didn't understand I looked up, but that doesn't mean I can make them sound right. And most of those lines seem like they're put together for a certain sound. Kind of like a song."

"Which is most true," Doc said. "There is a cadence in all of the immortal bard's works. His work was meant for the stage, and even so, more meant to be heard than to be seen. Would you mind if I borrowed a volume from your library and gave a dramatic reading from it?"

"I wouldn't mind at all," the woman replied. "Which play would you like?"

Doc held forth a hand. "Move not, dear lady. I know the way back to your sanctum sanctorum. I shall go get it myself and be back in but a moment. Perhaps, though, you could get us some water. Something cold and clear to drink. Something that will soothe the vocal cords."

"Tea with honey?" she suggested.

"That sounds divine." Doc excused himself from the table and walked back into the patio door. They'd come through the kitchen to get to the patio, but the book room was beyond that.

He deliberately took the wrong turn at the T juncture and snapped the swordstick open in his fists. One thing Ryan had always been insistent on was knowing as much about the terrain as was possible. His detour could add to their small store of knowledge about the trading post.

The corridor ran straight and true, then butted up against a locked door. Working the layout of the house in his mind, Doc knew a lot of space yet remained on the other side of the door.

Glancing at the lock, he knew it would take more time than he had to get past it. He turned and retraced his steps, then went into the book room. Searching the shelves, remembering where he'd seen the Shakespeare volumes, he selected a hardbound edition of *Macbeth* that had several scars in the leather binding.

He was the first to return to the table. He didn't take his seat immediately and turned his attention to the garden. Memory filed the names of the wildflowers as he stared at them.

"What?"

Doc turned, seeing Annie standing there with a teapot in one hand, a honey bottle and two cups held by their handles. "I am sorry, madam, what were you saying?"

"I asked you what you were saying. Sounded Greek to me."

"Latin, probably, dear lady," Doc said, realizing he had to have been talking out loud. "I was just admiring your garden."

Annie placed the teapot, cups and honey on the table. "I like the garden, but I made it where it's self-sustaining. Every year or two, I introduce something new or add a little more ground. The vegetable garden is the most important, so that's where I spend most of my free time."

Doc sat at the table across from her, taking the proffered cup of tea. "Thank you, madam."

"Add honey to taste. I've got some milk sub if you want."

Doc waved the offer away. "You manage the garden by yourself?"

Annie shook her head. "Two families help me tend it. Planting, weeding, harvesting and canning would keep me too busy to run the post. They get part of the harvest in exchange."

"But they do not live here?"

"You ask a lot of questions, Doc."

"That's because there is so much to ask questions about," Doc pointed out. "You'll note that I have not asked about your guests."

"You have now."

Doc gave her a small smile. "Touché."

"Ryan doesn't seem to be a man to let much pass him," Annie commented. "I suppose he'll be asking Max questions, as well."

"Ryan is not a man to let much pass him," Doc agreed. "Otherwise, he would be dead and buried in some nameless and forgotten grave. But he won't pry. That's not his way."

Annie drank her tea like a woman well accustomed to her own appetites, and not embarrassed about them at all. "He wouldn't get any satisfaction if he did. Max doesn't say much anyway, and our guest demands that his privacy be upheld."

"I see."

"Not yet, but you will tonight. In the meantime, read to me, Doc. Then we'll talk about a piece of strawberry pie I've been keeping back in the cold house in the cellar."

Doc opened *Macbeth*, cleared his throat and began, setting the stage with narrative exposition based on the play and adding to it from his store of memory of stages he'd seen and the performers who'd put the story on.

THE TRADING POST also had a large assortment of clothing and footwear. Ryan and J.B. knew the sizes of all the companions, as everyone in the group did. Scavenging meant knowing what was needed without guessing, without having to pack around extra gear that might or might not fit.

They got everyone a change of clothing, sticking with jeans and shirts in the same colors the friends preferred. They even found fatigue pants, something Mildred favored. Strangely socks and underwear seemed to be in shortage, but Ryan and J.B. managed to get enough to go around.

Max didn't say anything about the quantity they were taking. In fact he didn't say much about anything. Ryan was of the opinion that outside of J.B., Max was about the most taciturn man he'd ever seen.

They put their selections in plastic bags, double and triple bagging them to insure that they didn't break and drop through.

"What about the price?" Ryan asked Max when they were finished.

The man worked a whetstone across the hand ax's blade. "You need what you got there?"

"Wouldn't have taken it if we didn't," Ryan said.

"Saw the shape of your crew," the big man said. "I think you need it, too. Looks like you been needing it for a while."

"Hard traveling." Ryan shifted his burden.

"There ain't no other kind." Max ran the whetstone across the ax's edge again. "Don't worry about the price. Annie'll be fair with you."

RYAN SPOTTED Dean in the barn's hayloft while he was sixty yards out. The boy had snuggled down in the loose straw there and was nearly invisible in the camouflage he'd chosen. Ryan hadn't even seen the glint of gunmetal in the retiring afternoon sun.

Dean gave him a small wave as he got nearer, somehow knowing his father had seen him. Ryan lifted his chin and dropped it quickly, acknowledging the wave. The hayloft was a good choice for posting security. With its back and left side put up nearly against the palisade wall, the only attack that could come from inside the trading post could be covered from the hayloft.

The smell of fresh horse dung greeted Ryan as he strode into the barn. He noticed at once that the survivors from the coldhearts in Idaho Falls had separated themselves from the companions. Morse and his sons formed another small pocket against the wall opposite the horse paddocks. Elmore was the odd man out and obviously not happy about it. Jak kept him under guard, the albino sitting back on his haunches less than twenty feet from him.

"Did you get everything we needed, lover?" Krysty asked, coming up to help Ryan with the packages.

She looked washed out, thinner than he'd ever remembered. Dark circles hung under her emerald eyes. And for the first time since he'd known her, her sentient hair didn't lie neatly in place. The strands were kinked in places, and uneven.

"Everything they had that we could use," Ryan answered. He started passing the ammo out first, then parceled out the new clothing.

Mildred poured another bucket of water into the horse trough she'd selected to use as a bath. She'd laid a fire along one side of it, burned it down to coals so the heat would be there without an abundance of flames. "I filled it," she said, "so I get the first one."

No one argued with her.

J.B. took the bucket from her hands. "I'll finish filling if you want to get in."

Mildred started stripping off. The horse trough was partially shielded from view in one of the paddocks, out of sight of the Idaho Falls people. When she was naked, she stepped into the water, lying back gingerly. She sighed in satisfaction as she immersed herself. "Don't bring that water on too fast, John," she instructed. "Water's feeling just short of too hot, and after all this traveling, I don't want to miss out on it."

J.B. worked the pump handle and quickly filled the bucket with only a few short strokes. "Well water," he told Ryan. The Armorer dipped his fingers into the bucket and tasted them. "Heavy mineral content, and cold as a gaudy slut's heart in January."

"It's not coming in off the river, then," Ryan said.

J.B. shook his head, agreeing.

"Means they tapped an underground stream feeding into the river." Ryan sat on a small farrier's bench only a few inches off the ground. He stretched his legs out before him. Tapping the underground stream in more than one place, because he was sure there was at least one or two other hand pumps located in the main house, meant the trading post had no shortage of water. It could literally seal itself off from the rest of the world for months.

At least, they could do that as long as the walls held. Thinking of that, though, reminded Ryan of Annie's mystery guest who'd taken up both guest houses. The thought coiled uneasily through his mind.

"What are you thinking about, lover?" Krysty sat cross-legged across from Ryan.

"Staying or going," Ryan answered in a low voice. "Trying to figure out which would be less likely to get us chilled." He gestured at the clothing before him, then broke open one of the boxes of 9 mm ammo and started filling his extra clips for the SIG-Sauer. "They didn't take any jack for this stuff. Said we'd settle up later."

"Jak and Dean ran a head count on the people here at the trading post," Krysty said. "Besides Annie and her son, there's nearly thirty other men and women here at the trading post."

"Where are they put up?"

"In the guest houses."

"Any sign of the guest?" Ryan asked.

"No."

Ryan turned his attention to the albino. "Jak."

The teen shifted his focus to Ryan. "Yeah."

"How good a look did you get at those men in the guest house?"

"Thirty, forty feet at closest. Could see plain enough."

"Sec men?"

"Move like. Got organization. Got man checking posts regular."

"Any markings?"

Jak shook his head. "Stripped clean. Saw places where mebbe had them before."

Ryan thought about that. It wasn't unusual for a sec force to have markings to identify itself in a more heavily populated ville. The effort saved on having to kill ville inhabitants who didn't recognize the local authority standing before them. It also meant that the mystery guest was probably a baron, which didn't sit well with Ryan at all. Barons nearly always meant trouble.

"HOW'S YOUR HEAD?" Ryan asked.

"Still hurts, lover," Krysty answered after a minute. "I can still feel Phlorin crawling around back there. Every now and then, I can hear her voice. But I think I'm getting better at blocking her out.''

Even if Krysty was, Ryan knew the effort was quickly sapping her strength. He'd seen her hands shaking as she'd worked a self-heat to get Vienna sausages for both of them. Ryan kept himself centered, but it hurt him to watch her struggle to keep it together. He and Mildred had decided that any attempt at exorcism would have to be postponed, given the uncertainty of their situation at the fort.

"We could leave at dusk," Krysty pointed out. "That's not more than a couple hours away."

Ryan shook his head. "Sky's darkening up. The old woman was right about the storm coming." He'd spotted the clouds brewing when he'd scanned the trading post, wondering when Doc was going to make his way to them. "And we have no way of knowing when Doc's going to make it back."

"Do you think that woman's holding him hostage?"

"Mebbe."

"If she is doing it to keep us here, why?"

"They have thirty blasters," Ryan said. "We make another seven. Upscaling their forces by twenty-five percent, that's reason enough."

"Nearly forty weapons," Krysty stated. "What can they be up against?"

"I don't know. But I figure we're going to know soon enough." Ryan touched her face with his fingers, trying not to show that he'd seen her involuntarily draw back at first.

She captured his hand in hers, then kissed the center of his palm. "Mebbe the night, wherever we spend it, won't be all bad."

Ryan nodded, but he wasn't able to ignore the threat that hung over them all. He pulled Krysty to him, knowing she needed the feel of him against her. He captured one heavy breast in his palm, out of sight of the others, and kneaded it until he felt her nipple grow erect in his fingers. His thoughts drifted back to Doc despite Krysty's presence. But he knew it was because her being there made the thought of escape even more enticing.

Only they couldn't leave without Doc. Wherever the hell he was. Ryan cursed beneath his breath and kept holding Krysty.

Chapter Twenty-Three

"Mebbe this could be a good resting point, Theophilus," Annie suggested.

"Madam, I assure you that my reading voice is as strong as ever." Doc glanced up from the pages, then drank the dregs of tea from his cup. Truth to tell, he'd lost himself in the play, drawing on all those past experiences of watching the play on stage till reality had faded around him. He'd given himself over to the machinations of Macbeth and his lady, and the foreknowledge of the price they were both going to pay for their treacheries.

Annie smiled good-naturedly. "Your voice is good, and strong and vibrant. And I'm enjoying the story, but you've interested me in other things, as well."

Doc slipped a finger into the pages of the book, holding his place. "Pray tell, what other things, dear lady?"

She laughed at him, a full-throated guffaw that she gave herself over to. "I thought we might start with a bath."

Doc's face flamed in embarrassment, and he was at a loss for words.

Annie mistook his inability to speak. "Unless—you're not able for such playing."

Doc found his voice. "Dear lady, I am flattered by your offer, truly."

"You trying to tell me you're not interested? I know I don't look the way I did when I was a girl, but I thought I could still turn a man's head."

Placing the book on the table, Doc hesitantly reached ou
for Annie's work-roughened hands. He smiled reassuringl
at her, surprised at the thin threads of insecurity in her eyes
"You do turn my head, Annie, and do not let this snow o
the mountain fool you." He brushed at his long gray-whit
hair. "There is still a fire down below."

"Mebbe you'd like to prove that." Her voice turned he
words into a mocking challenge.

Doc found himself strongly attracted to the woman. H
lifted a hand and ran the backs of his fingers along the sid
of her face, coming in toward her eye. Her flesh felt ho
against his. "You have strong cheekbones, and a fine face
Lips that are full, as well as full of promise."

"I've lived a lot of hard years," she said in a softe
voice. "They show."

"All the years that are left to any of us are hard," Do
countered. "You will feel better after that bath."

"I don't want you to get the wrong idea," Annie said
"I'm not in the habit of offering myself to just any ma
that comes along. Mebbe I'm even making a fool of mysel
with you. Could be you'll get me off to myself and slip
knife blade between my ribs."

"No," Doc replied.

"I have my own reasons for my generosity, for openin
the trading post and its store to you and your friends."

"My companions and I are already aware of that."

"I know. Damn me if I know what makes you so dif
ferent than all the other men I've seen."

Doc shrugged.

"So, you think you'd really like to have that bath wit
me?"

"At the moment, dear lady, I can think of nothing mor
that I'd want to do."

Annie approached him and took his hand. "Then come with me."

"Madam," Doc said earnestly, "I have every intention of doing just that." Her touch was electric.

RYAN JOINED DEAN in the hayloft. The boy shifted slightly, making room. He kept his Browning Hi-Power in his fist.

"Anything?" Ryan asked. He stared down into the inner courtyard of the trading post. The sec men floated in loose, easy circles on the elevated boardwalk built on the palisade walls.

"They keep moving around," Dean said, "but mainly they're just checking the perimeter. Keeping things buttoned down. Guys act like they're on condition red."

Ryan silently agreed. He lay on his stomach and surveyed the sec men.

"It would be better," Dean said, "if we could just get out of here now."

"Yeah."

"Can't do that without Doc, though. And I don't think Krysty's up to traveling tonight if the river's going to be rough."

"You're right." Ryan glanced back inside the barn. Krysty was in the horse trough below, soaking in the water. He'd helped her bank the fires around the trough, bringing the heat back up. J.B. brought new buckets of water as the water started to steam more forcibly. Krysty's skin pinked up with the heat of it.

None of the Idaho Falls survivors had interacted with the companions and stayed huddled in their group. They'd been given self-heats from the provisions Ryan had taken from Max, and were working their way through them.

Morse's oldest boy had gotten up from the place where he'd been sitting and was casually making his way around

the barn's interior. His path was gradually bringing him
closer to the stall where Krysty bathed in the trough.

It was one thing, Ryan knew, for the companions to see
each other undressed. That was just naked. It happened
when a person took his or her clothes off, and there were
plenty of reasons to take clothes off. But the Morse boy's
interest wasn't to be tolerated.

Ryan signaled, catching Jak's eye.

The albino cut his gaze to the approaching Morse boy.
Jak slipped one of his leaf-bladed throwing knives from
inside his clothing. With a quick flick, still from a seated
position, he threw it at the Morse boy.

With a squall of real pain and fear, the boy jerked his
head back, raising a hand to his face. When his fingers
came away bloody and he saw it, he screamed again.

Morse jumped to his feet, turning toward Ryan in rage.
"Cawdor, what the fuck are you doing?"

"Your boy's nose was getting too long for his own
good," Ryan said. "Took a bit of it off for him."

Morse grabbed his boy when he came close enough,
peering in consternation at the wound. Maybe a quarter
inch of the boy's nose had been removed at the end of his
face, sliced cleanly, giving it a whole new tilt.

"You had no call to do that!" Morse screamed.

"Could have chilled him then and there," Ryan said.
"Still can if I want to. The boy's eyes were wandering too
much for his own good. I could have had those taken instead of a bit of his nose."

Morse glowered at Ryan, then bellowed at his other son
to go get water and rags.

"Use some kerosene on his nose," Ryan said. "You
don't want infection to set in. His face'll rot off if you're
not careful."

Finished with her bath, and maybe self-conscious because she figured out what the event had initiated, Krysty got out of the trough, dried herself and dressed. "Ryan," she called out when she finished.

"Be there in a little bit," Ryan called back. "Want to take a look around first." He turned to his son. "Dean, you go on down and get a bath."

Dean didn't look happy about the prospect.

"Go on," Ryan said, "and make sure you get clean."

Reluctantly Dean clambered down the ladder leading up to the loft. He hooked his feet on the outside edges and slid down.

No longer worried about being spotted by the sec men roving through the trading post, Ryan stepped out of the hayloft and grabbed the outer edge of the roof. He pulled himself up onto it with a smooth roll of muscle. Gaining his feet, he carefully moved across the sharply slanted roof. In winter the slant would aid in keeping snow off the roof, but now it made the way treacherous. Still, the roof got him close enough to the boardwalk around the interior of the palisade fence to jump the distance.

He landed hard, one hand still clutching the Steyr. He kept walking toward the river side of the trading post, knowing he'd drawn the attention of the roving sec men. His new boot heels gripped the rough bark of the half-cut trunks making up the boardwalk, and the sound of them hitting echoed around him. As he neared the river, he heard the thunder of it, louder than he remembered when they'd put in at the small pier at the bottom of the drop-off.

When he reached the palisade wall, he peered down.

The river had swollen a lot more since they'd arrived at the trading post. The water level was now up high enough to run over the top of the pier, spilling whitecapped runnels across the surface like a spiderweb. The boat yanked at her mooring lines and anchor, bucking restlessly, like a live thing in a trap as it sought to follow the river's course.

Getting away from the trading post by boat was out of the question, Ryan knew. Even if *Junie* survived the effort, there was no guarantee that they would be able to stay aboard and work the sails.

He turned away from the river and made his way back to the barn. At the moment, they were all trapped by their needs.

He wondered what was keeping Doc.

Chapter Twenty-Four

Annie's quarters inside the main house included a huge bathroom with a large tub. The walls maintained the same wooden finish as the rest of the house, but here scented cedars had been used, creating an atmosphere that was immediately different than the rest of the house.

The tub had been crafted of colorful ceramic tiles no bigger than two-inch squares, some of them broken and chipped to create the contours for the corners. The tub was over three feet deep and over nine feet across.

"My extravagance," Annie stated. "Took me over a year to build it. My husband thought it was totally useless and refused to bathe here. But I made it into my place."

Doc walked around the room, noticing the carvings made into the wood. They were meticulously done, displaying forest scenes from rough and rugged country. There were snowcapped mountains and dogsleds, small cabins and lonely campfires. He ran his fingers along the edges, amazed at the detail and obsession with the same.

"My tribute to the stories by Jack London," Annie stated. "Got a lot of wall space left to me, but during the winters, when trading's down and there's not much to occupy my attention here, I work on it."

"Dear lady," Doc said, meaning what he was saying, "this is truly fabulous."

"My husband considered this a waste of time, as well." She stood in the center of the room, her arms around herself, almost looking embarrassed. "Outside of Max and Jubal, less than a handful of people have seen this room."

"Then I shall indeed consider myself fortunate." Doc turned to her. "If you'll show me where the buckets are, I shall endeavor to draw a bath for us."

"It'll be easier than you think. I constructed a cistern on the roof to hold water. Over a hundred gallons, all of it warmed by the sun. I use a hand pump up there to keep the cistern filled. That way I don't have to waste a lot of time heating the water. Winters, of course, I have to lay in a fire to bring it up to a more reasonable temperature."

She walked to one of the walls and opened up a section, revealing a length of coiled hose inside. After pulling the hose out and laying the end in the tub, she opened a faucet. The tub filled rapidly.

Doc watched the water swirl into the tub with fascination. "A remarkable achievement."

"I put down roots here," Annie said, "and I meant for my life to have some pleasantries. That's not too much to ask, is it?"

Doc shook his head. "Indeed not. Cleanliness is next to godliness, I have always heard."

"Don't know about godliness," the woman replied. "Haven't seen much of that except for a wandering Bible thumper every now and again. Didn't have much use for them, but some did have nice stories to tell. Wars and killings and such like that. I've always enjoyed the story of Moses, but I never could figure out why God cut David so much slack."

Reaching into the tub, Doc found the water to be quite warm. It was also already nearly a foot deep and showing no signs of slowing.

"Temperature okay?" Annie asked.

"It's fine."

"Good, 'cause we don't want any shrinkage, do we?"

Doc turned to the woman and grinned, even more amused to see the red flush creeping into her features. She broke eye contact with him self-consciously.

"Sorry about that," she said. "Mebbe joking wasn't exactly called for."

"Laughter is the very essence of life," Doc argued, drawing his hand from the water. In the large room, with the sound of running water in his ears, he was even more aware of her sexuality. Part of him felt torn, knowing he should be back with Ryan and the others, planning on their departure. But he was drawn to the wild, restless woman before him, attracted by the hard exterior she exuded, and by the mixture of the parts that made her up. "We could never have too much of that."

"Not much left in the world these days."

"It only makes you enjoy it the more," Doc replied.

"You have a strange way of looking at things. Not like any man I've encountered before."

"Then I will tell you I am flattered," Doc told her.

"Your friend Ryan Cawdor," she said, "men like him I've known all my life. He's rough and hard, used to getting what he wants, wanting not much more than to survive with no thoughts of any too far-off tomorrow, and willing to die to see himself free and able to do the things he wants."

Doc nodded agreeably. "I think that is an entirely fair summation of him. And I will tell you now that it has been those qualities that have kept our little group alive during some mean circumstances."

"You're more of a dreamer, Theophilus."

"Sometimes," Doc said, feeling his voice thicken as he thought of the dementia that occasionally took him into its seductive embrace, "I am too much of a dreamer."

"One of these days, I'd like to hear about those dreams."

He thought of his lost wife and children, and the melancholy that was so much a part of his existence. A twinge of guilt struck him as he looked at the woman before him. His wife had been good with her hands around the house, as well, using her skills to turn it into a home.

"Those dreams, madam," he said, "are too often filled less with laughter than sadness. You might not like hearing about them."

She turned her head, looking at him. "You're nursing old wounds."

Doc gave her a grin, but it felt weak. "I would say that anyone who attained our age has more than a few regrets and disappointments."

"And tragedies? Like the ones Shakespeare wrote about?"

"Those, too. Though I think if the bard had lived at these times, he'd see what true tragedy really was. This canvas that is the world around us now is pared down to the basest of emotions and desires. But our mere living our lives, with effort to conduct them the way we want to, has to be considered a triumph. Take this trading post you've built. Not many people would have invested so much of themselves into such a structure."

"Lot of back-breaking work went into the construction of this place."

"And a lot of heart, as well." Doc ran his fingers along the carving on the wall.

"Couldn't leave this place if my life depended on it," Annie told him. "Got too much invested here."

Doc nodded. "You say that, but if it came to it, I think you would survive. Despite our best intentions, those of us strong enough find ways to survive no matter what we experience."

Annie crossed the distance between them and took Doc into her strong arms. "Bath's ready. If you're ready."

"Yes," he replied.

She reached into the wall beside him and turned the faucet off. Then she placed a hand on the front of his trousers and stroked his erection.

The pressure against his groin surprised Doc because he hadn't noticed exactly when the erection had sprung into being. The aroma of the cedar in the wet environment had grown stronger, flooding his senses. He bent his head and crushed his lips against hers, tasting the honeyed tea on her breath.

"You're ready," she declared. Her hands fumbled with the buttons on his pants but couldn't quite manage the feat.

Gently Doc stepped back from her, then undressed her first. Despite the age and the extra pounds, she maintained a womanly figure. Her breasts were larger than he'd expected, capped with brown nipples too big for him to encircle between his thumb and forefinger.

He bent his head to them, taking the first into his mouth. He tasted the perspiration that clung to her, the saltiness on his tongue mixed in with some kind of herbal scent. Her nipple came erect at once, and she moaned in a low voice as her pleasure took her. He nibbled at both her breasts, noting the scarlet flush that crept under her skin. She held him tightly, pulling his mouth against her breast.

His hand crept down, slipping between her thighs. At first, she tried to block his progress.

"Can't," she breathed huskily. "You touch me there, and I'm going to go off. Been too long since the last time, and I don't remember a touch ever being so gentle."

"Good," Doc told her. "But if you do, do not worry about it. There will be other times."

She pulled his head back from her breasts. "Are you sure? I don't want to waste this one building."

Doc chuckled good-naturedly. "I'm sure, dear lady. We have only just begun."

Her thighs parted, allowing him to touch her inner recesses. Doc's fingers slipped into her at once, exploring the depths and finding her surprisingly tight. His thumb brushed against her clit, locating the throbbing pulse of her lust beneath the pubis mound.

Without warning, she erupted, gasping and trembling. Doc felt the extra moisture trickle through his fingers and spread heat across his hand.

"I've got to sit," she said, fighting against buckling knees.

Doc guided her to the edge of the tub and helped her sit. Her body still quivered from the aftereffects of the climax.

"Are you all right?" he asked.

She smiled at him. "More right than I've felt in a long time." Her hand dropped to his erection and worked it vigorously.

Doc's response came unbidden, his buttocks suddenly pulsing with a life of their own as he bucked against her hand. Still, he managed to hold himself back. He breathed in the scent of the woman's sex between them, discovering the scent of cedars might have been a kind of aphrodisiac.

He gently disentangled her hand.

She looked confused. "Am I doing something wrong?"

"No, dear lady. But I must insist on a modicum of control from myself. I am no teenage boy on a lark. Together, we'll build your desire, then we'll find mine."

"I'm afraid I'm through," she said.

Doc smiled at her. "You may not realize it, but you've only just begun." He gently guided her into the tub's warm water. She waited in the center of the tub while Doc stepped in. She took him by the erection at once, leading him to one of the seats that allowed him to lie back against the tub wall and keep his head above water.

"Are you ready now?" she asked.

"Incredibly ready," Doc admitted. He pulled her to him, helping her straddle him. His cock stood up erect, grazing across her wet flesh, feeling the coarseness of her pubic hair against his underside.

Then she had his diamond-cutter where it would do the most good, tucking its head just inside the lips of her sex. She sank down on him, covering his erection with her hot, moist center. She bucked against him, and Doc met her stroke for stroke, not taking a break until it felt like the top of his head blew off.

LATER, LYING in the big upholstered bed in the bedroom adjoining the bathroom, Doc lay in blissful surrender. A warm lassitude filled him, draining away all the days of hard travel, making his arms and legs feel heavier than anything human should have.

The room was growing dark as dusk settled over the trading post. It was small and compact, with everything in its place. More books lined one of the walls in the room, and magazines depicting home and garden decor. The varied collection of reading materials revealed even more of the dreamer that Annie was.

"Dear lady," Doc said, his gaze heavy lidded as he regarded her strong, handsome face, "I feel as though I have died and gone to heaven."

She had her hand on his cock, pumping hopefully, and Doc was surprised to find himself reacting. "Well, if you're in heaven, mebbe you won't mind if I blow old Gabriel's horn for you."

Before he could respond, she took his cock into her

mouth. Her tongue swam around it, igniting the passion that seemed insistent on taking over his body and mind.

He fumbled for her breasts, finding the nipples and tweaking them into full hardness with his soft touch.

"No," she said, pushing his hands away from her body. "Don't want you distracting yourself from what I want to give you. You just lay back and enjoy this one."

"Your wish is my command, dear lady," Doc whispered, not knowing if he could speak plainly. He gave himself over to his own lust, feeling it pool quickly in his loins. He knew it wouldn't take long, and that it would be just as shattering as the previous climax he'd had.

Long minutes later, when the departing sun had drawn even longer shadows on the wall, Doc came, losing control and grabbing the back of Annie's head, pulling the woman's mouth down on him hard. He apologized profusely afterward, shocked at his own loss of control.

Annie smiled and licked her lips. "It wasn't a problem. Kind of liked seeing you lose that control you seem to be so proud of."

"Still, no gentleman—" he began.

"Theophilus, you've been every inch the gentleman." She traced a forefinger against his chest. "Tell me, do you really like the garden and the tub and this place?"

"What is there not to like?" Doc replied. "You have poured your heart and soul into this trading post. It is a good home. You have every right to be proud."

"Built up a fine trade, too."

"Yes."

She seemed a little hesitant to go on, her eyes no longer quite meeting his. Tears glittered unshed.

"What is it, dear lady?" he asked. "Have I erred in some wise that I did not notice?"

"No," she insisted, "you did everything right. Mebbe that's the problem."

"I seem to still have hurt you," he said. "And I never meant to do that."

"You haven't hurt me," she said. "I'm hurting myself. You've stirred up a lot of emotion in me in one afternoon."

"Is there something I can do?"

She looked at him, lying naked on top of the bedsheets that were twisted around them both. "Have you ever thought of settling down?" she asked.

Chapter Twenty-Five

"Somebody's coming, lover."

Ryan woke at once from the semidrowse he'd dropped into after bathing, his fist coiling around the butt of the SIG-Sauer blaster lying across his stomach. "Who? Sec man or one of the traders?"

"Looks like a scavenger," Krysty said.

Rolling to his feet, Ryan gazed through the hayloft where he and Krysty had retired to when he'd finished his bath. He was dressed in new clothes, feeling better in some respects than he had in weeks. If only Krysty hadn't had a dead woman lodged in her brain and they hadn't been trapped at the trading post by the coming storm.

The temperature had cooled off, and darkness had swaddled the countryside, damping the light like a candle censer. Only a few lanterns burned around the trading post, providing bare trails to those who knew the grounds intimately.

Ryan spotted the man approaching the barn easily enough because the scavenger carried a lantern. The glowing bubble of light was turned down, not giving away much. The man also carried a double-barreled shotgun in his other hand. He came to a stop some twenty feet from the barn.

"Hello, the barn," the man called out.

"What do you want?" Ryan asked. He stood at the edge of the hayloft opening.

"Dinner's about to hit the table," the man replied. "Annie wanted me to let you know you should get yourself up to the main house."

"What if we don't feel like coming?"

The man shrugged, the response magnified by the bobbing oil lantern. "Don't know. Don't care. Want me to tell her you're not coming?"

"We can't stay here, lover," Krysty said quietly. "It'd be best to play along since we're here."

Ryan knew that, and he admitted he was also curious about the baron who was staying at the trading post. "Tell her we're coming," he yelled back.

"Make up your fucking mind," the man snarled, then turned and walked back to the main house.

"J.B.," Ryan called out, knowing the Armorer would be up and around.

"Yeah."

"Elmore and Morse go with us. The others can stay behind if they want." Ryan helped Krysty to her feet, feeling the weakness in her. "Do you feel like going?"

"More than staying here," she replied. "I don't want to be left by myself, lover, because I'm not really by myself right now. I don't know what Phlorin's capable of."

"We'll only stay as long as we have to. Then we're gone come hell or high water."

"Good enough."

RYAN SURVEYED the heavily laden tables in the banquet room. The room wasn't all that fancy. Folding tables were surrounded by folding chairs, not all of them in good shape. Some effort had been spent to spruce everything up, cloths put over the tables and fresh-cut flowers in plastic vases.

But the food almost stunned Ryan.

It was hard remembering back to when he'd seen so many different kinds of foods, and so much of it. A whole pig stretched out across one folding table all by itself. Long roasting had burned the skin black in places, causing it to crack and peel and glisten with the released fats and oils. An apple lodged its jaws open, revealing long yellow teeth.

On the tables around it were platters with turkeys and chickens, venison and beef. Vegetables garnished them and filled other large bowls. Soups steamed in tureens along with gravies.

"You people grab chairs and sit where you're able," a big sec man with a burn scar on his neck said. He wore his dark hair cut short, looking like brush. "Baron Shaker's feeling generous tonight."

Ryan recognized the baron's name at once as the man who'd sent the riders into Idaho Falls after Elmore. "Baron Shaker's here?"

The big man's eyes narrowed. "You know Baron Shaker?" A line of men formed behind him, their hands on their blasters.

"Heard of him," Ryan acknowledged.

"You people outlanders?"

"Travelers," Ryan corrected. *Outlanders* was an accepted term, but in a lot of places in Deathlands it was synonymous with enemy.

"What are you doing here?"

"They are here at my request," Annie's voice rang out. She swept through the line of sec men with Max plowing the way ahead of her. Judging from the sec men's obvious haste, Max had proved his prowess to them. "You'll do well to treat them kindly, Loomis, because they're my guests before they're in any way responsible to the baron."

What surprised Ryan even more was Doc walking into their midst with the woman on his arm. The old man had a well-relaxed air about him, and looked like a dandy in his freshly cleaned frock coat and new shirt and pants.

"Baron Shaker's welfare—" Loomis began.

"Is completely dependent on my generosity tonight," Annie stated. "Unless you'd rather take your chances out there in the chem storm that's brewing."

Loomis's eyes hardened as he turned to face the smaller woman. "Mebbe you need to remember that we'll fucking well stay here if we want. Got more blasters here than any of your people."

Before Loomis had time to blink, Annie whipped out a snub-nosed S&W .38 Airweight Bodyguard blaster and settled it between his eyes. Her finger was tight on the trigger. Since it was hammerless, there was no indication how much pressure she'd put on the trigger.

"This is my house, you arrogant, stupe bastard," Annie said, her voice raw with emotion. "I built it from the ground up, poured my blood and sweat into it, and no fucking man's going to come in here and even think about telling me what I'm gonna do or not gonna do under my own roof."

Loomis's eyes focused on the Airweight's barrel.

Ryan took a step to the right, noticing J.B. was automatically going to the left to balance out their firezone. However it went, he was ready to back the woman's play.

Doc grinned widely.

"What the fuck you grinning at, you old turd?" Loomis demanded. But the effort didn't come across very well with the blaster centered on his big nose.

"My dear chap," Doc said blithely, "I find myself amused at the circumstance you find yourself in. Combating an abbreviated blaster with a deviated septum is not trouble you would ordinarily beckon. Shall we say, this is not the caliber of competition that you should embark on?"

Loomis shifted only slightly, not enough to get his feet under him, but enough to try to save face.

Ryan felt certain that if Loomis had moved too much, Annie would have killed him then and there. The one-eyed man touched the SIG-Sauer's butt with his fingertips.

"Loomis, you'll stand down this instant or I'll chill you myself." The voice carried over the room full of people.

Loomis's shoulders rounded, and his weight settled more squarely on his heels. "Yes, sir," he barked.

The crowd parted again, flowing back into place around the tall man who strode through them. Annie kept her small blaster centered on Loomis's head. The audience was mostly quiet, but Ryan heard the rumble of discord that flowed through the whispers. There was still a definite danger of violence breaking out in the trading post as the two groups split between sec men and scavengers.

Baron Shaker stood tall and broad, heavily muscled from more than day-to-day survival. His skin was dark, a bronze coloring that hinted at a mixed ancestry, but his hair was dark copper, curled in tight ringlets, echoed by the short beard he wore cropped close to the skin. He was dressed in a red silk shirt, tight across the trunk but loose in the sleeves, black denim pants and black riding boots that nearly went up to his knees. He was one of the youngest barons Ryan had ever seen, surely no older than his mid-twenties. But his control was never in question in the room.

"What are you going to do?" Shaker asked Annie. He peered at her intently, arms relaxed at his sides.

"I'm thinking about reserving a seat on the last train to the coast for this triple-bastard stupe," Annie replied. "Do you have any problems with that?"

"None," Shaker replied without hesitation. "This man offered an effrontery to your guests without provocation."

"And if I drop him right here?" the woman asked.

Ryan scanned the sec men, surprised when there were

no pleas for Loomis's life to be spared, or threats for the same. Shaker's control over his men was strong.

"If you choose to drop him right here," Shaker said, "then I'll have my people drag his body out and throw it into the river."

"Just like that?"

"Just," Shaker said, "like that."

Annie's breath came tightly, and Ryan knew the woman was thinking of shooting the man more than releasing him.

"Annie," Doc said softly at her side, "shooting him would put a damper on the night's festivities. And the baron's chef has gone to great trouble to provide a repast fit for courts and kingdoms. I am thinking that being generous this night might not be such a bad thing."

"It's not in my nature to be overly generous, Theophilus," Annie told him.

"There is an alternative punishment to chilling Loomis for his ill manners," Doc said.

"I'm listening."

"Send him to bed without his supper," Doc said.

Turning to Doc at her side, Annie suddenly burst out laughing. When she got hold of herself, she said, "That's got to be the most asinine thing I've ever heard."

"It is less messy," Doc stated, "and wouldn't hamper the appetites that surround these tables."

Ryan also knew it would force Shaker to take an even firmer stand with his men, pushing the situation to a head between the two groups. He waited tensely.

"Mebbe you're right," Annie said. She returned her angry glare to Loomis. "Get your ugly face out of here, you stupe fucker, 'cause you'll not eat at my tables tonight."

Loomis didn't move, glancing at Shaker.

The baron nodded toward the door.

Like a well-heeled dog, Loomis turned and went. The

other sec men jeered at him, drawing angry curses from Loomis. But he took the punishment without an unkind word to Annie or Ryan.

"Again," Shaker said to Annie, "I offer my humblest apologies, Annie. My men are quite used to living in the rough, and they don't often acknowledge the finer behaviors of civilization."

Annie lowered the blaster and put it away. "Your apology's accepted, Baron Shaker. But you tell that asshole if he looks at me crossways during the time you're here, I'm going to put a bullet in both his eyes."

"Of course," Shaker replied. "Trust me when I say that you'll never see him again."

Annie turned to face the group. "Then what are you people waiting for? Let's eat."

The men fell to with gusto.

RYAN SAT at a table with the companions. Morse and Elmore sat at the far end, out of sight of Shaker and his sec men in case any of them recognized the Heimdall Foundation man, or *Junie*'s captain from Idaho Falls. So far, they hadn't drawn a second glance.

As a precaution, Ryan kept the SIG-Sauer in his left hand under the table, managing his meal with the right. J.B. kept the Uzi out of sight under the table, but he was ready to move, as well.

Baron Shaker held court at one of the center tables. Doc and Annie were seated with him, listening to the big man's stories. He seemed to be well-read, because most of the conversation between the three of them centered on works of literature. Ryan recognized some of the names.

"What do you get about him?" Ryan asked Krysty.

She shook her head, and he noticed that she was only picking at her food. He couldn't remember if she'd eaten a self-heat in the barn. "Not much, lover," she answered in a whisper. "He's here for definite reasons that he feels very strongly about, but I can't fathom what they are."

"Anybody recognize Elmore?"

"Not that I've noticed." She looked at him, her emerald eyes threaded with red. "But I can't be sure, Ryan. Keeping Phlorin locked away in the back of my mind could be interfering with my gift."

"It's okay," Ryan said. But it bothered him that she couldn't be sure. Her gift had saved them countless times, and he didn't realize how dependent they'd become on it. "Figure we'll have an early supper and leave as soon as we can."

"I think that's best. I'd like to get some sleep if I could."

"We'll get back under way first thing in the morning," Ryan told her. "Elmore says we should catch up to Donovan in four more days."

"That won't be anytime too soon," Krysty stated.

Ryan glanced at her plate. "Food's good. Better than we've seen in a long time. You should eat more."

Krysty pushed at the piece of pork on her plate, running it through the red-pepper gravy and pearl onions on her plate. "I've tried, but I can't. My stomach keeps twisting around on me like it's my time of the month or something."

"Is there anything I can do?" Ryan asked.

She touched his face. "If there was, I'd let you."

Ryan accepted that because he had to, but it didn't set well with him. He didn't like being confronted with something that needed doing and him with no way of doing it.

BEFORE THE MEAL went on much longer, Annie put on entertainment in the form of music. A CD player was brought out, along with an electrical cord. The lantern lights were muted somewhat, but candles on the tables kept the diminishing stock of foodstuffs well illuminated.

Ryan took that moment to go for another cup of coffee sub, corralling Doc at the table where the drinks were kept.

"You haven't been back, Doc," Ryan said. "We were getting worried about you."

"No worries, my dear Ryan," Doc said. "I have been amply entertained by our generous hostess."

Ryan kept his voice low so that no one else could hear. The music spilled from speakers inset in the walls of the dining room. "You could have got word to us."

"Actually she's taken up all of my time since we got here."

"She say anything about why Shaker's here?"

"Not one word." Doc looked at him. "I suppose I could ask."

"No." Ryan felt irritated. Doc clearly had lost focus on the situation they'd found themselves in at the trading post. "You remember Shaker, don't you, Doc?"

"Clearly. He's the baron in charge of the men we crossed swords with in Idaho Falls."

"That's right, so that means at this very minute we're squatted down feeding our faces in the camps of a potential enemy."

"They have not recognized us."

"Yet. That can change. And it bothers me that these people are holed up in here like Texans at the Alamo."

"Perhaps it's only the coming chem storm."

"And mebbe it's something else. Shaker's got a lot of men here. Take a lot to chase him inside. The other thing that's bothering me is that Annie hasn't set a price on the supplies we've taken so far."

"Mayhap she is only being generous."

"A person being overly generous with goods or information is a person looking to put a hand in your pocket or slit your throat when you aren't watching,'' Ryan replied. "That's something I've found to be true more times than not.''

"I am afraid that I have no concrete answers for you. You will have to rely on your own judgment in this matter. However, I must tell you that my own instincts are to trust her.''

Ryan filled his cup with coffee sub. "What about you, Doc? Where does Annie figure into all of this for you?''

Doc appeared uncomfortable, scratching at the back of his neck, which was red enough to see even in the dim light. "She has evidenced a certain interest in me.''

"No shit,'' Ryan said.

"And she has asked me to stay here with her.''

"Why?''

Doc pulled a surprised look on his face. "I gather that she somewhat fancies me.''

"And what do you fancy, Doc?''

The old man shook his head, peering into the glass of wine he'd poured himself. "I must admit, it is a tempting offer. There are all the books she has, all the physical comforts this place has. And she is a very handsome woman, with, ah, a certain whole-hearted enthusiasm.''

"Nobody'd blame you if you stayed,'' Ryan said. But he knew he'd miss the old man. Doc was one of the loyalest and truest friends he'd ever had.

"However tempting it might be,'' Doc said, "I find that I must follow my heart. There is this current problem with Krysty, and I have known no true home in Deathlands except at your side. It is there that I shall stay, dear Ryan, long as we may both yet live. Or perhaps until I find a way to return to the bosom of my family.''

"Wouldn't be the same without you,'' Ryan told him.

"So when you get ready to sally forth into the hinterlands, simply let me know." Doc cut a salute with his swordstick. "I shall be at your side."

"It'll be soon. Mebbe come morning if the storm isn' too rough."

"Until such time," Doc said, "I shall stay with the lady as long as I can, taking and giving what comfort that . may."

"Always heard the best comfort was the high and hard kind," Ryan said with a grin. "Frequent is good, too." He left Doc standing there, nearly glowing with rad intensity in his embarrassment.

THE CHEM STORM BROKE at 8:15 p.m. according to Ryan's chron. It filled the air with the flash of lightning and the stink of ozone, and thunder shook the trading post's main house.

Ryan watched the poisonous rain spill from the leaden indigo sky from a windowed room off the dining area. He had his arm around Krysty. They'd almost left the house and headed back to the barn before the storm burst loose. For the moment, they were trapped in the main house.

"Spectacular, isn't it?"

Turning, keeping one hand on Krysty to aid her in speed if necessary, Ryan dropped his hand to the SIG-Sauer blaster and looked at the speaker.

Baron Shaker walked into the room. Three sec men flanked him, but he waved them off as he approached Ryan.

Chapter Twenty-Six

"I didn't catch your name," the baron said. He seemed even more imposing in the shadows, bigger and colder.

"Didn't throw it. Name's Ryan."

"Have you another name?"

"Ryan'll do."

"My name's Curtis Shaker." The big man peered through the window at the rampaging storm. "That's a hellish thing to be caught out in. Lucky for us, Annie's trading post is here."

Ryan didn't say anything. Too many hard years had trained him to be silent until all the cards were on the table. Or at least as many of them as he could get a look at.

"You came by the boat tied up at the pier below," Shaker said.

"Yeah."

"It's not your boat, though."

"No. Hired the boat's skipper and his sons."

"I also heard there were more people with you than just the ones at the tables inside."

"Is that any business of yours?" Ryan asked. "Or are you just taking a census?"

"I've always been of curious nature," the baron said, not taking any offense. But he had to check the sec men who'd stepped forward at the perceived disrespect. "Now I find myself curious about you."

"I was always told," Ryan said, "that if a man's business extended much past his nose, he often found himself in over his head really sudden-like.''

Shaker smiled thinly. ''Wise words. Under other circumstances, mebbe I'd listen to them. But not now.''

''What is it that you want?'' Krysty asked.

''To know more about you,'' Shaker replied, switching his gaze briefly to the redhead.

''We're scavengers,'' Krysty said.

''Looking for what?''

''Whatever we can find. We brought blasters in to trade with Annie.''

''So I'd heard. But in my experience, scavengers tend to hang around a certain area, mining whatever rumors and half truths they can find.''

''I'm more fiddle-footed than most,'' Ryan said. ''But getting back to the curiosity part, you asking so many questions makes me curious about you.''

Shaker spread his hands. ''Why not? I'm in a magnanimous mood. Good food and creature comforts have always brought that out in me. What do you want to know?''

''What're you doing here?'' Ryan asked. ''Most barons I've heard about seem more content to stay at home than wandering the countryside. Still got a lot of rad areas around here, chem storms and muties. Why not stay at home?''

''Because I'm a searcher, Ryan,'' Shaker said. He paced, but carefully remained out of the firezones necessary to his sec men. ''I was brought up by a very idealistic father compared to most of the power mongers you see in Deathlands. He taught me to read, taught me a love for the history books concerning the time before the nukecaust. He was convinced that something more happened a hundred years ago than just the genocide of the world.''

The line of thinking reminded Ryan of the talks he'd had with the Heimdall Foundation people.

"I've spent time and part of the considerable wealth my father has left me, and to which I've added, in the pursuit of certain knowledge."

"About things before the nukecaust," Krysty said. And the way she said it let Ryan know she hadn't sensed any lies in the man's words.

"Exactly," Shaker confirmed.

"Don't see that it would matter one way or another," Ryan growled. "Time's going forward, not backward."

Shaker took no offense, shrugging off the comment. "Once, when I was young, I thought in the same fashion. But I've changed my mind. Think of it, Ryan, if we could recover but a fraction of the knowledge that was lost during the nukecaust, so much could be gained."

"By you?" Ryan asked softly.

A fork of lightning flared outside the window, washing all the subdued color out of the darkness, illuminating the room in electric white.

"By anyone who takes the time to learn," Shaker said. "By me."

"You ever think mebbe all that knowledge was what brought about the nukecaust in the first place?" Ryan asked.

"There's some who believe mebbe the nukecaust was brought about by an outside force," Shaker stated.

"It was war that destroyed the world," Krysty said. "Paranoia fed by a nuke arsenal."

"I don't know if I completely believe that."

"Then what do you believe?" Ryan asked.

"I believe that a few months ago an abandoned space station fell from the sky," Shaker said. "Its orbit decayed, and it fell from the heavens, breaking up as it reentered the atmosphere. I've been told that one of the pieces landed very near this place. Mebbe only a little farther north. Do you know anything about that?"

Ryan lied. "No. But you pay attention at night, you see lots of things burning up as they come down. How sure are you that it didn't just burn up? Even if you're right?"

"Because I've recovered one of the pieces," Shaker said. "And I want the others."

"We don't have any."

"Just letting you know," Shaker said. "There are others out trying to get those pieces. Some of them work for the Heimdall Foundation. They're not taking my interest in the pieces very well."

Ryan returned the baron's inquisitive glance full measure, registering nothing about the name.

"You ever heard of the Heimdall Foundation?"

"No."

Shaker hesitated, as if trying to figure out his next line of attack.

"Ryan," J.B. called from the other end of the room. The Armorer stood in the doorway of another room that led into the room where Ryan confronted Shaker. "Time to go. Rain's letting up, and we need shut-eye. No telling when it'll start again, or when it'll let up next time." J.B. stood with his Uzi peeking from under his jacket.

Ryan nodded. "Guess we'll be going."

The baron's sec men started to move forward on an interception course. Shaker waved them down. "Another time."

"Mebbe," Ryan said. He put Krysty beside and behind him, using his body to shield her. Then he left the room, following J.B.

"Everybody's ready to quit the ball," the Armorer said. "Except Doc."

"He'll be along," Ryan said. A glance behind him showed that Shaker and his people were making no attempt to follow.

"SHAKER WAS TELLING the truth about the space station," Krysty said. She lay beside Ryan in the quiet dark of the barn. He'd chosen to make their bed in the hayloft where they had a view of the trading post's inner courtyard.

"As far as he knows it," Ryan agreed. "Did he believe we didn't know anything about it?"

"No." Even though Ryan was lowering his voice, listening to him made Krysty's head ache even more fiercely than it had an hour ago. She hadn't mentioned it, but the dinner had been spent in sheer agony.

Ryan shifted behind her, pressing his crotch against her buttocks. She felt his erection through the material, and her own sudden lust pushed some of the pain away inside her head. She reached for him without turning, running her palm against his erection hard enough to make his hips buck in anticipation.

"You feeling up to this?" he asked hoarsely.

"Yes." Krysty rolled over into his arms, listening to the rain drumming on the barn's roof, hearing it slapping against the pools already gathered out in the courtyard.

In minutes, their new clothing was spread out across the blankets they made their bed on, and across the loose straw in the loft. Giving in to the hunger that drove her, Krysty rolled Ryan over and straddled him, feeling the cool air breeze across her erect nipples.

She slid forward until her sex was poised over his face, then wrapped her silken thighs about his head, covering him like a saddle. She locked her hands behind his head and pulled his face into her.

She felt his tongue slither into her, parting her delicate

folds with its hard, probing intensity. He licked at her, not gentle in his approach, attacking her sex and driving her toward a climax. Her juices ran freely, surging when her orgasm took her with shuddering force.

Ryan pushed her back from his face, breathing hard from his passion. She helped him scoot her back, feeling his cock brush against her ass, riding briefly against the wet cleft, driving her crazy as it brushed against her clit.

She reached between them, riding him as his body pushed against her. Her hand found his diamond-cutter, then guided it into her wet center.

Rising and falling, Krysty urged Ryan toward his orgasm, feeling him grow steadily harder inside her. Then Phlorin's voice echoed inside her mind, sounding faraway, the words not intelligible. Krysty closed her eyes and hammered her hips down across Ryan, using her extraordinary vaginal muscles to draw him even deeper. Her breath powdered her lover's chest in slight gusts.

Take your triple-bastard lover then, bitch! Phlorin shouted inside Krysty's head. *Take him and love him all you can and turn your back on your ties to the Chosen.*

Krysty tried to ignore the dead woman's voice and concentrate on Ryan's coming climax, feeling the loss of control in her lover's movements. She gave herself over to her efforts, hoping Phlorin would be shamed to the back of her mind.

Keep up with your immoral ways. Turn your back on the beliefs of the Chosen. But you can't turn your back on me. You have no birth control, and I can tell that you're fertile now.

Krysty didn't want to believe the woman. With her mutie powers, she'd always been able to tell when it was possible for her to become pregnant, and she'd been able to prevent it.

Not this time, Phlorin warned. *This time when your man's seed enters your body, I'll make it quicken. I'll let you hear the heartbeat of your newborn child within your womb. And when you link your heart to its heart, I'm going to kill it and let you listen to its mind as it dies.*

Sick with the callousness of the threat, and the uncertainty of the woman's ability to carry it out, Krysty lunged sideways, yanking Ryan out of her. She cried out in fear and loathing, unable to stem the sudden nausea that turned her stomach over and over.

"Krysty?" Ryan reached for her.

Automatically Krysty drew away from his touch. "Can't, lover." She threw up again, shuddering with the nausea.

"What's wrong?"

"That bitch," Krysty gasped. "That fucking bitch inside my head." She surrendered herself to Ryan's touch. "I'm sorry, lover. Truly I am."

"It's okay," Ryan said, smoothing her hair. "We're not going to let this beat you. You just hang on and we'll find a way out of it."

Krysty let herself cry silently on Ryan's shoulder, not wanting to wake anyone else. Dry heaves rocked her body. Even in his arms, with him holding her tight, she felt more alone than she ever had in her life.

THE ATTACK CAME just before dawn.

Ryan woke with the first harsh rattle of gunfire, grabbing for the Steyr. He pulled out of Krysty's tight grip and reached for his pants with his free hand. Crouched at the edge of the hayloft opening, he gazed out toward the southern wall, toward the river where the sounds of battle seemed to be coming from.

The trading post's inner courtyard jumped with activity. Sec men ran to man the defensive areas atop the catwalk along the palisade walls. Most of them clustered along the south wall, firing as soon as they fell into position. The rain during the night had left the ground muddy, and large pools of water shimmered in the light breeze.

Krysty struggled to wake. During the night, she hadn't slept well, if at all. Her blaster filled her hand as she pulled clothes on.

"J.B.," Ryan called.

"Up," the Armorer responded.

Ryan buttoned his pants, then pulled on his shirt. "Get everybody else up. We're going to have to move."

"See anything?"

"Attack's coming from outside." Ryan left his shirt open, then jammed his feet into his boots, leaving them unlaced for the moment. He shouldered the leather pouch that held extra rounds for the Steyr and the extra magazines he had for the SIG-Sauer.

"That's where we left the boat," J.B. called back.

"I'm going to check it. Be back quick or not at all."

"We'll be ready."

"Careful, lover," Krysty said, taking his free hand and squeezing it gently.

"Can't afford to lose that boat," Ryan told her. "We try going overland on foot, it'd take us weeks to get where we're going. Mebbe too late by then." He slung the Steyr and leaped up from the hayloft opening, grabbing the roof's edge. He hauled himself up and leaped from there to the catwalk.

Max swarmed up a nearby ladder, bristling with weapons. He glanced at Ryan.

"What's going on?" Ryan asked.

"Rival party that's been hunting Shaker and his group," Max replied. "Don't have a name. Doesn't matter. Annie gave her protection, that's how it's going to stand." He grinned evilly as he pulled himself onto the catwalk. "Now you're going to earn all that ammo and clothing you were given."

Ryan didn't say anything and continued running toward the south wall, unslinging the Steyr.

Bullets ripped through the tops of the palisade wall posts, throwing splinters into the air. Before he reached the site, two of Shaker's sec men were hit and thrown from the catwalk. Only one of them lived long enough to scream on the way down.

Reaching the wall, Ryan stayed well clear of the knot of sec men and peered over the top. He scanned the hundred yards of trail and rough terrain that led to the precipice over the pier area. Nearly three dozen men were scattered throughout the zone, barely showing in the graying pre-dawn light breaking over the eastern horizon.

"Make way for the baron!" someone roared.

Ryan glanced over his shoulder as Shaker climbed onto the catwalk. The baron started shouting orders at once, positioning and urging his men on at the same time. The firing by the sec men became more systematic, dropping their adversaries in the broken land before the trading post.

Shouldering the Steyr, Ryan briefly aided the sec men in putting down a rush by the enemy forces. As soon as he lowered the rifle's telescopic sights over one target and squeezed the trigger, he moved on to the next.

A bold roar rose up from the sec men as they scattered their attackers before their withering fire.

Ryan felt the celebration was premature. He reloaded the Steyr's magazine, then ran back along the catwalk to the barn.

All of the companions except Doc stood outside, their gear already packed.

"The boat?" Mildred called up.

"Still there as far as I know," Ryan answered from above. "But at this point, I don't know much. Can't see the boat from up here."

"If those people get their asses handed to them," J.B. said, "they'll be looking for a quick way out. Storm the way it was last night, there's probably not much chance they came by a boat of their own with the river running like it had to have been. Might not be any too safe right now."

Without warning, the distinct, hollow boom of a cannon pealed out over the trading post, splitting the air.

Ryan looked up and spotted the cannon atop the main house, the long snout poking through the roof. Judging from the way it was set up, he guessed that the weapon was mounted on some type of elevator system that raised and lowered it through the house. With the way the house was designed, he didn't doubt that it was normally kept in the basement level and raised all the way to the roof when needed.

"What do we do, lover?" Krysty asked.

"We leave," Ryan answered. "Despite Annie's willingness at the moment to protect us, I don't trust that to stay. So we're not staying, either. Get Morse and his boys out here. And Elmore. They're going with us."

"What about the people we took with us from Idaho Falls?"

"They make their own way from here," Ryan replied. "It'll be safer than where we're going."

The crackle of autofire, muted just for an instant by the roar of the cannon, underscored his words. Whatever enemies Baron Shaker had made, they were strong, relentless ones.

Chapter Twenty-Seven

Doc raced through Annie's private rooms, the Le Mat blaster in his hand. With the sound of the first few shots, Annie had leaped from the bed they'd shared during the night. Doc had been slower, his head dulled somewhat by the wine from the previous night's party and from the physical exertion of keeping pace with the woman's libido.

The next room had been converted into an art studio. Paint pots and carving tools covered the workbenches and shelves. Then Doc spotted the section of wall that wasn't quite flush with the rest. He pressed against the wall and it opened wider, sliding back on well-greased hinges.

The darkness beyond the yawning mouth was broken by a light from above.

Doc stepped inside and peered around. A shaft sank through the floors above and below. Feeling the cool gust of wind from below, he deduced that it went all the way into the basement. Pulley ropes hung in the center of the shaft.

Glancing up, Doc saw the platform above, watched it shudder and heard another report from the cannon. A ladder was built into the wall to his left, constructed simply of pieces of wood nailed across the wooden wall braces. He tucked the Le Mat through his belt and climbed the ladder.

Annie sat on the platform next to a 20 mm cannon converted to work with elevation and peripheral controls. The woman occupied a chair beside the cannon and made adjustments with wheels that controlled jagged-toothed cogs that moved the blaster.

Then she fired again.

Doc pulled himself up to her platform, still clinging to the makeshift ladder. The detonation of the cannon round was loud inside the rooftop area. He tracked the cannonfire, spotting the men ranged in front of the palisade wall at the front of the trading post.

The 20 mm round exploded against the ground less than thirty yards distant from the palisade wall. It opened up a small crater in the earth and flung two corpses to the ground yards away.

"By the Three Kennedys!"

Annie jacked another round into the cannon. She sat in the chair without a stitch of clothing on. "Glad to see you up and around, Theophilus. Thought I'd chilled you with last night's loving." She fired again.

"Madam, I'll warrant that you put your best efforts to the task, and indeed I found myself sluggish recuperating, but I am still here."

Only a few rifle bullets struck the rooftop, but the gunners were too harried by Baron Shaker's sec men and the other scavengers to be accurate.

Doc stayed low anyway.

Annie continued firing and reloading, working the 20 mm cannon with grim authority. Her accuracy punched holes in the attack.

Concerned, Doc turned his attention to the barn, wondering how the companions were faring. He had no doubts that Ryan would have them up and moving, but they were separated.

"What's wrong?" Annie asked.

"Dear lady, I am wondering about my companions' welfare. We have traveled down many hard and harsh roads together.''

''I saw them moving around a minute ago.''

''Did you see in which direction they headed?''

''I was kind of busy,'' Annie replied.

A fresh hail of rifle bullets scored on the rooftop. This time two of them punched through the opening and tore splinters on the walls around Doc and Annie.

''Goddamn!'' the woman roared, ducking instinctively. ''Where the fuck did that come from?''

Doc scanned the line of attackers, searching for any that might be in position to shoot more properly at them. ''There,'' he said. ''There is a sniper in the tree out beyond the perimeter you have blazed. To the left of the trail to the gates.''

''I see him, I see him.'' Annie worked the cannon's controls, elevating the muzzle as she racked another round into the chamber. She fired almost as soon as the cannon muzzle leveled.

The 20 mm round slammed into the treetop, tearing branches and the sniper loose. The dead man dropped to the ground in a crumpled heap.

''Excellent shooting, dear lady!'' Doc stepped forward again and swept the inner courtyard for some sign of the companions. They couldn't have left him. Could they?

Yet, at the same time, Doc knew he wouldn't have blamed them. It had been his choice not to stay with them while they'd been camped out in the trading post.

''What's on your mind?'' Annie asked.

''My companions.'' Doc peered out at the river, knowing Ryan's first impulse would have been to get to the boat.

''I thought you were staying here.''

''Dear lady, as much as that thought warms the very cockles of my heart,'' Doc told her as diplomatically as possible, "my future is surely bound in theirs as long as they have need of me." And he still hadn't completely given up hope of finding a way back to his own time, back to his family. Time trawling still existed in certain redoubts.

"Sorry to hear you say that."

"But if there was a place in Deathlands where I would stay were things different..." Doc started.

"No need going on about it, Theophilus. You got your mind made up. I could tell yesterday when I was foolish enough to ask you to stay." Annie threw up a hand and pointed. "There're your friends."

Doc peered across the inner courtyard and saw the companions running toward the main house.

"Not exactly what I had in mind when I outfitted them," Annie said. "Figured at least they'd stand and fight with us."

Anger surged through Doc, but he kept it in check. "Do not underestimate them, madam. Our boat lies in yonder direction. Ryan will not be leaving here without it."

Annie glanced at him, not looking any too sure about his statement.

"DOC UP THERE."

Ryan twisted his head, following the line of Jak's pointing finger. He saw Doc in the rooftop opening of the main house, then lost him for a moment as the cannon blasted again. "Doc!" he yelled up.

"Yes, my dear Ryan!"

"Coming?"

"I shall endeavor to join you precipitously."

Ryan shifted his gaze over to the woman. "Those people may decide to take the boat while they have the chance. I'm not going to see that happen. While Shaker and your people hold the front wall, we're going to come up beside those bastards and shoot the hell out of them until we see a way clear to the boat.''

"That's a dangerous piece of work," Annie called back. "Be triple stupe to go out there."

"Got to be done," Ryan said, "if we're going to save that boat. Don't save that boat, we're going to be in more trouble than we know what to do with. When you know we're out there, ease up with that blaster unless you know for sure what you're shooting at."

"Count on it."

RYAN LED THE WAY over the north wall at the back of the trading post, swarming up the ladder and using the rope J.B. had brought from the barn to lower himself over the side.

"Look out, Ryan!" Krysty yelled, opening up with her .38-caliber blaster.

Releasing the rope halfway up, Ryan dropped just as bullets cut the air over his head. Before the hollow sounds of the rounds smacking into the posts died away, Ryan was rolling across the ground, searching for the men who'd come up behind the trading post. He heard J.B.'s Uzi stutter to life, joining Krysty's blaster.

Ryan guessed there had to have been a half-dozen men positioned in the forest's edge beyond the cleared area next to the trading post. He unleathered the P-226 and fired at the nearest man, punching three full-metal-jacket rounds through the man's chest, blowing his lungs to shreds and tearing big holes through his back.

Before the corpse toppled from its position beside a gnarled oak tree, Ryan had his second target in his sights. The first two rounds cut the leafy branches above the woman's head, spooking her and driving her out into the open. A quick burst from J.B.'s Uzi turned her into a twisting, jerking marionette. She didn't die at once, and her screams echoed through the forest.

Jak came down the rope with the agility of a monkey. Before he touched the ground, he leaped off and threw himself into a diving roll. Bullets broke the ground where he'd been.

Ryan shifted his blaster, picking up one of the coldhearts shooting at Jak. One of the three rounds he fired in the man's direction cored through the coldheart's skull, emptying his brain in a heartbeat.

By then, Jak had disappeared into the foliage. Ryan charged, running flat out while the other companions provided covering fire. He put away the SIG-Sauer and raised the Steyr as he took up a defensive position beside a thick-boled tree, spotting two coldhearts in brief flashes through the brush. They were moving, as well, falling back from their positions. He ignored the telescopic sights at such close range, and used the open rings beneath.

One man held a position behind a boulder. Ryan tried to aim at him, but the eruption of gunfire drove him to cover. Dodging to the other side of the tree he was using for cover, he squeezed the trigger twice quickly.

The bullets cored through the man's head, yanking him out of cover. He windmilled his arms, trying in vain to get his balance, but he was dead before his body came to a stop.

The second man sprinted through the forest, pulling back and sweeping toward the west side of the trading post. Ryan led him slightly, anticipated the break in the tree line then squeezed off a trio of shots. At least two of them caught him in the chest, throwing him sideways.

The wounded woman finally stopped screaming as the rest of the companions climbed over the wall and followed Ryan into the forest. As he led the way, he found two more men with Jak's familiar leaf-bladed knives embedded in them. Ryan retrieved the knives and tucked them into his pockets. He knew Jak ranged somewhere ahead of them, scouting out the way.

Mildred and J.B. brought up the rear, guarding Elmore, Morse and the two boys. Dean and Doc stayed with Krysty.

Once everyone was in the forest, moving through the brush with the ease and skill they were accustomed to, Ryan picked up the pace. He caught occasional glimpses of Jak as the albino teen allowed him. Ryan was good in the brush, but Jak was every bit as much the ghost as he looked in the trees.

They swept around the front of the trading post, angling steadily toward the river and the pier where the boat was. Ryan reloaded his weapons automatically as he moved, firing when he had certain targets. As they came into the terrain in front of the trading post, still deep within the tree line, Ryan kept the companions close to ground to avoid the blasterfire of the baron's sec men.

Jak left a swath of death behind him.

Ryan collected more of the leaf-bladed throwing knives, stashing them in his pockets. Coming up on the albino's freshest kill, he heard a man say, "Whitey. Whitey, where the fuck are you?"

Pulling up behind a shelf of rock, Ryan froze into place. Behind him, Doc, Dean and Krysty stopped, then waved the other companions into hiding. Unable to see the approaching man, Ryan listened instead, focusing on the man's breathing and movements, separating them from the crash of blasterfire all around.

The man stayed low, but he chose to go over the rock shelf. Pebbles dropped onto Ryan's back amid a shower of dirt, letting him know the man was above him. Keeping the SIG-Sauer in one fist, he reached up with the other and grabbed the man by the hair. He put all his weight into the yank that brought the man down with him.

The coldheart screamed in pain and fear, and fought against Ryan. Before the man could get himself set, Ryan slapped the side of his head with the muzzle of the 9 mm blaster. The skin broke, and blood sprayed over Ryan's hand.

"Fireblast," Ryan snarled, rubbing as much of the blood on his pants as he could. He didn't want it running inside his grip and loosening his hold on his blaster.

The man tried to bring up his rifle.

Ryan slapped it away with his forearm, then kicked the man in the crotch with his steel-toed boot.

All the fight in the man drained away, and he spilled to the ground in a limp heap.

Ryan seized the rifle and threw it into the brush. If he'd been able, he'd have taken it and used it to barter someplace else. But now it would only serve to slow him. A dead man couldn't trade.

"Who are you?" Ryan asked the man.

The coldheart's eyes flared in pain. The one on the left was already turning red from the broken blood vessels spewing into it. "Jenkins."

"What're you doing here?"

"Come after Baron Shaker," Jenkins answered. "Hired on with a man named Callton a few months back. We been hunting Shaker ever since."

"Why?"

The man shook his head, holding one hand to his temple. "Mister, I don't know. Callton, he collects things. Found out Shaker does, too. A couple times, we weren't hunting Shaker—he was hunting us. Same reason."

"What kind of things are they collecting?"

"Predark stuff. Comp progs. High-tech stuff that doesn't

even work no more. Doesn't make sense if you ask me, but Callton keeps the jack coming on time.''

"If I let you go," Ryan offered, "you get the fuck out of here.''

"Sure thing, mister." Hope dawned in the coldheart's eyes. He scrambled to his feet when Ryan let him go, then moved uncertainly toward the trading post.

For a moment, Ryan thought the guy was going to leave. But in the end, pride or stupidity laid the final ace on the line and he dived for his rifle.

Ryan put a bullet in his brain for his trouble, tearing out the side of the coldheart's head that he'd already brutalized. Ryan was already moving again when the corpse fell.

Chapter Twenty-Eight

Ryan came across Jak less than fifty yards on. The albino lay low in the tall grass, choking the life from a mutie snake nearly six feet long that wrapped around the youth's arm.

"Bite you?" Ryan asked.

Jak snorted derisively. "Never had chance. Got him before got me." He nodded ahead of them. "Run out of cover."

Ryan scanned the tree line as Jak threw the dead snake away. They were at the outer perimeter. Beyond it was the open space leading to the drop-off where the rope bridges to the boat were.

"Got no choice," Ryan said as the rest of the companions came up around them. "Without the boat, we're too far away from anywhere we want to be."

"You planning on going out there?" Elmore asked incredulously.

"Yeah."

"Going to get us all chilled."

"No. Going to get us out of here." Ryan gave instructions, spreading the companions out and building a skirmish line. Callton's sec forces had dug themselves into the forest on the other side of the clearing, and in the area more toward the trading post in the area where Ryan and the companions were.

Three coldhearts bolted from the forest on their side. J.B. opened up with the Uzi as they started firing and yelling to the others, attracting attention. The Armorer's vicious figure eight lifted the three men from their feet and sent them spinning away.

"Cat's out of the bag now," Mildred said, picking off two more coldhearts who'd turned their attention on the companions. "We move, or we die right here." She moved her ZKR 551 and fired again, taking out a third man.

"Jak," Ryan growled, "you got the lead. Chances are some of the coldhearts are aboard the boat, holding it in case they have to retreat."

The albino grinned thinly. "Not hold it long."

"Doc, you're next. We can use that big blaster of yours to clear the way. Mildred, J.B., you're bringing up drag. Dean, Krysty, keep the others moving along."

Elmore pulled a sullen face. "You can't make me go out into that."

More bullets from Callton's men were starting to rip bark from the branches and tree trunks nearby. Other men crept through the forest, closing in on their position.

Ryan looked at his son. "If that triple-stupe bastard doesn't move when you tell him, you put a round through his head, make sure he's chilled."

"I'll do it, Dad."

"Now get them up and let's move." Ryan pushed himself up, bringing the Steyr to his shoulder. He fired into the approaching line of coldhearts, putting two men down immediately and causing the others to go to ground.

Jak broke cover and stayed low, followed immediately by Doc. Callton's men shot at them at once, but Ryan, J.B. and Mildred blasted into them, their bullets finding targets with unerring precision. At the same time, the gunners manning the trading post caught their attackers in a cross fire. In the next instant, Annie laid down a fierce barrage with the 20 mm cannon. The big rounds chewed holes in the ground and toppled trees, breaking some of them and leaving trunks four or five feet tall.

Ryan held his position until J.B. and Mildred got clear. Jak plunged over the edge in the distance, racing down the rope ladder. The sounds of blasterfire slammed up from below, letting Ryan know he'd been correct in assuming there'd be men positioned there.

He reloaded the Steyr, then raced after the companions. Instead of heading for the bridge area, he stayed along the tree line, driving his feet hard against the ground.

Two coldhearts pursued him. They whipped through the underbrush, closing on him like hounds scenting the kill. Ryan raced on, ignoring them for a moment. Running like they were, they weren't able to effectively use their weapons.

Reaching the edge of the precipice overlooking the pier, Ryan threw himself down in a diving roll. He came up on one knee, pulling the Steyr to his shoulder. When the open sights underneath the telescopic lens centered on the lead man's chest, Ryan squeezed the trigger and rode out the recoil.

The bullet smashed through the man's heart, tearing out a section of his spine as it punched through.

Ryan moved to the second target, tracking the man's efforts to take cover. The coldheart dived into the brush headfirst. Unable to get a clear shot at the gunner's head, Ryan settled for shooting him twice in the groin. Even if the man lived, he'd be too busy holding himself together to do much more fighting.

Rolling on toward the precipice, Ryan peered down. The boat was still tied up at the pier, a promising sign in its own right. But coldhearts were aboard it, shooting at the companions as they made their way down the rope ladders.

Ryan had expected the attempted ambush, and he'd

known the companions were going to be vulnerable. But there'd been no choice.

He pulled the Steyr to his shoulder and aimed at a gunner aboard *Junie* as a 20 mm cannon round exploded close enough to shower him with dirt. He ignored it, concentrating on picking up the targets aboard the boat.

Bullets ripped through the rope ladders, splintering some of the planks and making others jump like live things.

Ryan's first round took the man in the throat, nearly decapitating him before he fell overboard. Two more rounds were necessary to take out the gunner riding the unruly prow as the boat bucked in the raging torrent of the river. Whitecaps danced on the water, twisting and turning before going under and reappearing.

J.B. accounted for a third as Ryan made the shift. The Armorer's rounds tracked across the deck, throwing up splinters and leaving pockmarks behind, then smashed into the gunner.

The fourth man hid back by the wheel as Ryan chased him into cover. Jak was on the final set of steps leading to the pier when the thick black smoke curled up from the boat.

"Fireblast!" Ryan snarled. He didn't have a chance to see how bad the fire was before bullets drove him to cover himself. He cursed some more, feeding shells into the Steyr. Glancing back at the trading post, he discovered the attack by Callton's coldhearts had all but broken off. Dead men draped the broken terrain.

Judging by the sudden interest the coldhearts had in him, Ryan decided he'd been selected as a consolation prize.

Down the precipice, Jak had reached the boat. The albino dashed belowdecks and came back up with a water bucket. He ran across the two corpses left on deck and dipped up a bucket of water. By the time he sluiced it across the deck, trying to combat the flame, the coldhearts had closed in on Ryan.

There was nowhere to go.

KRYSTY'S VISION BLURRED from the pain throbbing inside her head. She heard Phlorin's voice whispering in the back of her mind, but she didn't understand a thing the dead woman said.

She knew at once that Ryan was in danger, though. She felt it with every fiber of her being. Pausing on the last set of rough timber steps, she peered back up at the drop-off.

"Dear lady," Doc said from in front of her, "is something wrong?"

"Ryan," she replied in a dulled voice, struggling in vain to pull her vision into focus. "He's in trouble."

As if to bear out her words, a riptide of shots opened up above. In the next moment, Ryan's body came tumbling over the edge, arms and legs flailing.

"Oh, Gaia!" Krysty's breath locked in her throat as she watched Ryan fall, then disappear under the raging river. Then she felt Doc's hand on her forearm, tugging her along, Dean behind her, pushing forward.

"No time," Dean said. "He's going to be all right, but that river's going to pull him along. We've got to get the boat moving. It's his only chance."

He's dead, whore, Phlorin cackled in the back of Krysty's mind. *Dead and gone. You're never going to see him again. He's never going to have the chance to defile you again, never have the chance to defile one of the Chosen again.*

Krysty refused to believe that. If Ryan was dead, she'd know. Her gift would allow her that. Gaia would see to it that she knew.

But she stared out at the rushing water and felt only icy cold hope nestled around her heart.

"Krysty," Doc said gently.

She let him lead her, managing the steps with real effort. Somehow Doc got her into a run, and she felt the rope ladder sway beneath her feet. Only then did she notice the smoke aboard the boat.

RYAN PLUMMETED into the river feetfirst, absorbing most of the shock through his boot heels. The water, though, was still cold enough to take his breath away. His left shoulder was on fire. Before he'd managed the leap from the dropoff, a bullet had found him. He didn't know how bad the wound was, but the pain was enough to cause him problems with the arm.

His gear and the Steyr slung over his back worked to drag him under. Water filled his boots, near freezing in intensity. For a moment, he figured he was going to smash into the river bottom, not knowing for sure how deep it was where he'd been able to jump, and not knowing how far down his drop would put him.

By the time his downward momentum was spent, his lungs felt like bursting, burning for the need for oxygen. He looked up but he couldn't see through the dirty water enough to know where the surface was.

He made his left arm work, stroking upward. With the current carrying him along, he knew he wasn't going to come up anywhere near the boat. In fact, after struggling with the river, he thought it was going to be a miracle if he came up at all. The current seemed intent on dragging him five or six feet forward for every foot he pulled himself up, dragging him back down again.

Black spots were floating in his vision when he made it to the surface. He wheeled desperately, trying to get his bearings. As deep as he was, tossed by the current and savaged by the cold, he spotted the boat's masts. But they were staying put and he was moving away from them fast.

"KEEP THEM COVERED, Millie," J.B. said.

Mildred knew the Armorer wasn't talking about the cold-hearts pouring down the rope ladders. Bullets peppered the water and the boat, but Morse and his boys were the ones J.B. was talking about.

"Get the boat moving," J.B. ordered.

"I move out there, I'm going to get shot," Morse protested, hiding by the door to belowdecks.

"You stay where you are," Mildred promised, "I'll shoot you myself."

The Armorer stepped up to the man and backhanded him, turning his head completely to the side even with the short blow. "And if she doesn't do it," J.B. put in, "those fuckers coming down those ladders will do it. Now get your ass in gear."

Morse yelled at his boys, staying low as he started unfurling the sails. Bullets chopped at them, delaying their work.

Dean stayed with Krysty and kept his blaster leveled on Elmore.

"You've got to find Ryan, J.B.," Krysty said in a weak voice.

"Going to," J.B. replied. He slipped one of the machetes mounted on the boat's railing free, then ran to the mooring rope holding the prow to the pier.

Mildred kept the .38 loose, watching as J.B. slashed through the mooring ropes, prow and stern, and through the rope holding the anchor, as well. The boat was swept out into the river's current at once, almost listing sideways, stopping just short of capsizing as the rushing water took it into its embrace.

Hanging on to the railing, Mildred watched as the river water surged up, slopping over the side. Her feet were drenched, turning cold at once. She no longer had to cover the Morse family; they were all locked into survival together.

"Do you see him?" J.B. asked.

Mildred strained to see across the river as the next current caught them and boosted them up. "No. Dammit, can't see much of anything."

"Bastard river's taken him downstream," J.B. replied.

The sails filled overhead, cracking in the breeze. Mildred felt the boat surge, like a horse fighting the tether.

"There!" Doc called. "I see him!" He stood, holding Krysty tight at his side.

Looking farther down river, Mildred spotted Ryan. The one-eyed man disappeared under the water for a moment, then came bobbing back up. "Get us over there," she ordered Morse.

"This current," Morse replied, "ain't making this boat any too easy to handle."

Still, he managed to get *Junie* close enough to Ryan for J.B. to hand down one of the sheared remains of a mooring rope. Ryan somehow found the strength to hang on as they hauled him up.

Mildred got some blankets from belowdecks and draped them across Ryan's shoulders. She also found and popped a self-heat of chicken-noodle soup. By that time, the boat was well into the current, running for all she was worth.

The threat of the coldhearts died away, as they were pounded further into submission by the trading post's 20 mm cannon.

Crossing the deck to where Ryan lay, Mildred dropped

to her knees, her body rolling with the frantic pitch of the boat. She looked at his injured shoulder, at the blood spreading across the shirt material. She unbuttoned the shirt and pulled it back.

"Ruined the shirt, didn't it?" Ryan asked.

"Got your old one in the gear." Mildred examined the bullet hole. The round had cored through the outer deltoid muscle atop Ryan's left shoulder. It was more messy than damaging. "Through and through. You got lucky."

"Real lucky, Dad," Dean said. "Thought that bastard river had taken you for sure. Glad it didn't."

"Me, too." Ryan tried to sit up, managing it with help from Mildred and Dean.

Mildred pulled the blanket tighter around Ryan, noting his pallid complexion. It wasn't from the shock of the wound; it was the chill of the water. "Eat your soup. Get your temperature back up before you get the chills or end up getting sick. I've got to pack that wound, get the bleeding stopped."

Ryan did as he was instructed, ignoring the spoon he'd been given and drinking the soup straight from the container.

Mildred took gauze from the first-aid supplies and plugged the entry and exit wounds on the one-eyed man's shoulder. Ryan, being the indomitable hardass he was, didn't say a word during the whole procedure.

"After exposure to that water, I'm going to pump you full of vitamin B, too." Mildred took one of the few ampoules they'd found in a recent visit to a redoubt and injected him. "You might run a slight fever with this, but you'll be okay."

RYAN SAT BESIDE KRYSTY, nursing another self-heat of chicken-noodle soup as he watched her sleep. Hours had passed, and he'd slept some of them himself, but for a few minutes here and there, he'd talked with Krysty and with the other companions.

After his rescue, Ryan had instructed Morse to turn up-river again. The coldhearts were no longer a threat, and the companions passed the fort without incident. The river had calmed as they'd sailed, but with the sun hanging so low in the sky and the coastline so uncertain, there was no choice about dropping anchor for the night. Too much debris washing down from upriver created hazards. Morse had already had his boys working to patch the leaks from the bullet rounds that had cored through the decks. The boat had taken on a foot and a half of water before they'd been able to get most of them stopped. The boys, spelled by Jak, Dean, Doc and J.B., worked a hand bilge pump to clear the water. Ryan had even taken a couple turns himself, not wanting his wounded arm to stiffen too much.

"Got any of that soup left, lover?" Krysty croaked.

"Yeah." Ryan handed it over, but she was too weak to sit up and take it.

"Sorry," she said. "Stomach's rolling. I'm hungry, but I'm too weak to take care of it myself."

Ryan helped her sit, then patiently spoon-fed her. "Talked to Elmore earlier," he said. "We're mebbe four days out from where Donovan's supposed to be up in the mountains around the Heimdall Foundation."

"Long time," Krysty said. "And a long way."

"Seen longer times and longer ways," Ryan replied. "We'll see this one through just the same."

"Wish I believed that as much as you do, lover. But I hear that bitch's voice in the back of my mind just eating at me. It could be that by the time we get there, there won't be much of me left."

"You have a hard time believing in that," Ryan told her,

keeping his voice strong, "then you just believe in me. I ain't never let you down before."

"Haven't, lover," she corrected him gently. "You haven't ever let me down."

"Haven't," he said agreeably. "And I ain't about to start now." He thought she might correct him again, but instead she was asleep in his arms. He held her despite the pain it caused in his wounded shoulder, knowing it would be nothing like the agony he'd feel if he lost her.

Four days, but they could measure a lifetime—Krysty's. He concentrated on her breathing as he held her, hearing it even above the constant smack of waves against the boat's hull and the crack of sailcloth.

Chapter Twenty-Nine

The four days passed hard for Ryan, and being forced to stay aboard the boat for the duration was intolerable. He was a man used to making his own way.

The wounded shoulder healed well, with only a slight case of infection. He'd lanced it himself with the heated blade of the panga. The other companions struggled with the claustrophobic feelings inspired by life on the boat. J.B. was the only one who handled the time without strain, but that was because the Armorer had room to spread out all the companions' weapons and give them a proper cleaning.

Morse and his sons had grown increasingly belligerent about manning *Junie*. Morse himself had a lump on his jaw and behind his ear where Jak had pistol-whipped him with the .357 Magnum when the man had tried to jump Dean. To Dean's own credit, he'd resisted killing the man outright.

The deeper they got into what had once been the state of Montana before the nukecaust, the more hopeful Elmore had become. Evidently the man believed the Heimdall Foundation was going to get him out of his present predicament one way or another.

Ryan knew that wasn't going to happen until after he'd gotten help for Krysty. His lover had remained asleep most of the trip, plagued by the sickness that wrenched her guts, and by the dead woman feeding her twisted dreams. She'd told Ryan some of them during the times she'd been awake, and even he'd been sickened. There'd been no loveplay even though Ryan had tried to instigate it to bring her relief The woman's threats to kill whatever seed quickened ir Krysty's belly had frightened her too much.

On the evening of the fourth day, they found Michae Donovan, the Heimdall Foundation man they'd come deep into Montana to find.

Trouble was, others had found him first.

"THAT'S DONOVAN'S BOAT," Elmore said.

The river here was becalmed and placid. J.B. had founc some old maps aboard the boat that listed the river in Montana as the Jefferson River. At least, that was the location the Armorer's minisextant indicated.

Donovan's boat was nearly twice the size of *Junie,* strung with rigging that looked as delicate as a spiderweb. She looked as though she'd cut through the water like a knife blade through butter once her sails were gathering the wind.

But not now.

Now the big boat was listing in the wind, the few sails she had up catching the breeze the wrong way. Around her were seven smaller craft that Ryan could see through his binocs. Four of them were small motor craft, and three of them looked like water bikes.

The sound of blasterfire echoed flat across the river.

"Who are they?" Ryan demanded.

"River pirates," Elmore stated. "Get them through here a lot. Especially during the rainy season. Come down to see what they can find washed up on shore. If they don't feel like doing the work themselves, they take stuff they want from other folks already took the time to salvage it."

"Why doesn't Donovan have a bigger crew if he knows these coldhearts are going to be out here?" J.B. asked.

"Probably does have a bigger crew back at the main campsite," Elmore said. "He likes to do his own exploring."

Ryan put his eye back to the binoculars, reeling the attack back into focus. "Man's got to be out of his mind to go anywhere alone if he's got an army to go with him."

"I think, my dear Ryan," Doc spoke up, "that the more appropriate nomenclature at this juncture would be *navy*. That Donovan has a navy at his back."

"If we don't step in," Ryan stated, "Donovan's going to have the life expectancy of a mosquito stuck to flypaper." And with the man might go any chances of helping Krysty.

He glanced over at Morse. "Get us in there."

THE BOAT'S SPINNAKER unfurled when Morse released it. The material belled out into the breeze, swelling to its full size in seconds. The boat surged forward, cutting deep into the flat planes of the river.

Ryan commanded the others into position, taking the prow himself. He pulled the Steyr to his shoulder, favoring his wounded arm.

"They see us now," J.B. called out from Ryan's right. "Going to try us."

Before the Armorer's words died away, three of the motor craft peeled away from the savaged sailboat and raced for *Junie*. Bullets from the approaching river pirates created dozens of impact areas in the water ahead of the boat. In a few more seconds, the bullets slapped into the boat around Ryan.

He aimed and fired smoothly, plucking the man working the tiller on the powerboat from his seat. The powerboats were small fishing boats with rear-mounted motors that whined like deep-throated bumblebees.

Donovan's vessel looked to be taking on water, listing roughly to its left, unable to break away now that the attention of the river pirates had been diverted.

The powerboat with the dead driver went out of control, pulling around in a hard circle. The men aboard the boat scrambled, working against one another as they tried to get control of the outboard. Ryan fired twice more, aiming at the engine, which exploded as the gas tank ruptured. The flames spread over the passengers, as well as the boat, and threw black smoke into the air.

Bullets from the other boats drilled into *Junie* and cut the air around Ryan. Before he had a chance to aim at another of the pirate boats, they were past him. He stepped from the prow to the starboard railing, bringing the rifle to his shoulder again.

J.B. accounted for one of the racing water bikes by shooting the gas tank with a fléchette round from the M-4000. The tank erupted into a fireball that enveloped the driver. The passenger, protected by the driver's body, dived into the water. When he came back up, the Armorer blasted another round into his head. The decapitated body swirled briefly in the water as the final nervous spasms jerked through it, then sank.

Mildred picked off two more pirates from another boat before being driven to cover by return fire.

The river pirates turned in concert, cutting white plumes through the water as they came around for another pass.

Ryan laid down heavy fire, squeezing through his rounds as he aimed at the lead craft. His bullets holed the metal hull of the canted prow, then smashed on into two of the men beyond. The misshapen bullets tore huge wounds in the flesh and blood. Ryan heard the screams of the men over the outboard as the boat broke off the attack and sped past them.

Dean managed to get one more of the water bikes with his Browning Hi-Power before they disappeared farther down the river. The youngster crowed in savage delight.

"Reload your weapons," Ryan ordered. "Chances are we haven't seen the last of them."

The companions complied, taking up positions around *Junie* so they could keep watch in all directions. Now that they'd made themselves known to the river pirates, they'd taken on the role of prey, as well.

"Morse," Ryan yelled.

"What?"

"Bring us alongside that other craft."

Morse called out the adjustment to the sails to his sons and steered *Junie* closer to the foundering ship.

Ryan studied the bigger sailboat. She listed more deeply in the water now, making no headway at all even with the tug of her sails. Despite the slight breeze flowing all around him, Ryan's face was covered with perspiration, and his clothing was soaked with it from the heat of the sun.

With Morse's expert handling, *Junie* pulled alongside the other craft, staying out a good thirty feet. Stern heavy now, the bigger boat's prow lifted well above the normal waterline. Her name was painted on the port side in green letters against the faded blue hull—*Calypso*.

"Ahoy, the boat," Ryan called out. He lowered the Steyr, but kept it in both hands.

"What the hell do you want?" a rough voice shouted back. In the stillness left after the blasterfire and the sounds of the outboards had died away, the words sounded unnaturally loud.

"Looking for a man named Donovan," Ryan said.

There was a pause. "And if you found him?"

Ryan turned over his shoulder, fixing Elmore with his gaze. "Let them know who you are."

Hesitantly Elmore stepped up to the railing. "Donovan, it's Elmore. You remember me?"

Nobody moved on *Calypso,* but the few blasters aboard shifted to take in the new target.

"We don't mean any harm," Ryan said, "unless it's offered to us first."

"River pirates done cleaned us out of everything worth having," the man shouted back.

Ryan saw him now, a medium-built man with a shock of black hair dropping to his shoulders. A white streak of hair matted one temple in a jagged line. He was burned nut brown by the constant exposure to the sun and the elements, and went bare chested, wearing only shorts and lace-up boots. He held a Marlin .22 rifle easily in one hand.

"Not here for anything except Donovan," Ryan said.

"Why do you want him?"

"Information."

"About what?"

"Want to talk to him about the Chosen," Ryan called out.

"What about them?"

"Had some trouble with them. Still do. Figure mebbe Donovan can help."

A debate seemed to ensue aboard *Calypso,* the black-haired man taking on other survivors aboard the boat.

"You people figure on jawing about your situation much longer?" Ryan shouted out harshly.

"Find ourselves in a bad way," Donovan shouted back. "We aren't too keen on making it any worse."

"You're aboard a boat that isn't going to make it to shore," Ryan said, "and those river pirates may return at any minute to finish the job they started just out of sport. Mebbe you can abandon ship and swim to shore, but you're still going to be vulnerable when you do it. Your situation gets any worse, you'll have to get chilled to do it. Where I'm sitting, that may not be that far way."

"All right." Donovan lowered the rifle and stepped to the railing, making a big target of himself if it went that way. "We're about out of choices."

"You're Donovan?"

"I am." Despite his situation, the man seemed to take pride in acknowledging his identity.

Ryan gave him a half smile, recognizing the fact that the man faced them without fear and that he'd be a dangerous enemy. "Get your people off that boat and we'll take you aboard."

"Boat's salvageable," Donovan said.

"Not by me," Ryan replied.

"Save me, save my boat. Like you pointed out, I've got the option of swimming to shore."

"There's some deadly mutie fish in this river," Elmore called out loud enough for Ryan to hear. "He goes in, there's a chance he won't be coming back out."

"You got any bilge pumps aboard that boat?" Ryan asked.

"Two. Both of them gasoline powered. Neither one of them working right now. Pirates saw to that when they scuttled the boat after taking our cargo. They'd have opened bigger holes in her if we'd let them. But after we saw they meant to chill us anyway, we fought back. If we'd tried to fight back any earlier, we couldn't have done it."

"Why?"

"Mister," Donovan said, "there were a lot of bastard pirates here. And they aren't going to take too kindly to you people chilling the ones you did, or destroying their transport. Salvaging one of those predark watercraft is hard, even up here where water activities seemed to be pretty big."

Ryan glanced farther downriver. "If there were so many pirates, mebbe it'd make better sense if you got off that goddamn boat and came aboard."

"No way," Donovan said. "This boat's my life. Spent more time aboard her these past ten years than anywhere else in my life. Leaving her is not an option."

Ryan tried staring him down across the expanse of dirty water as a corpse floated between them. He didn't think it was one of the bodies of the river pirates they'd killed, so it was mute testimony to the fate the Heimdall Foundation people had ahead of them if they stayed with *Calypso*.

Donovan showed no signs of giving in.

"Fireblast," Ryan swore. Then he turned to Morse. "Get us alongside so we can tie on."

Morse clearly wasn't happy about the prospect. "That boat will drag us under with it. She's near twice as big as mine."

Ryan glared at him. "I didn't say you had a choice. Get it done. *Now*."

ONCE RYAN'S COMMITMENT to help the stricken ship became definite, the crew aboard *Calypso* galvanized into action. Ropes from both boats were used to tie the bigger ship behind the smaller one. Jak and Dean helped the Morse boys bring up the hand-crank bilge pump from belowdecks and transferred it to the Heimdall Foundation craft.

Within twenty minutes, they were ready to attempt to move the boat. The borrowed bilge pump didn't equal the amount of water flooding *Calypso* belowdecks, but at least it managed to slow the water it was taking on.

Morse looked at the lines lashing them to the other boat with disgust and vehement hatred. "*Junie*'s going to handle like a fucking fat-assed mud turtle trying to haul that bastard boat."

"Get it done," Ryan ordered.

"I am, I am." Morse surveyed the ropes himself, then called out new orders to *Calypso*'s crew to trim their sails the way he wanted. "But you better hope those pirates don't come rushing back with reinforcements. Even without that boat tied to us, we couldn't outrun them."

Ryan knew that, and he hoped it as strongly as he dared.

Chapter Thirty

"Bring up the sails!" Morse bawled.

His sons, working with sailors from the Heimdall Foundation boat, pulled on the lines and sent sailcloth spinning up *Junie*'s masts. They filled at once, sucking in the breeze with greedy need.

Ryan stood in the prow, clear of *Calypso* so he had a view downriver. Donovan stood beside him, a couple inches shorter and moving with a seaman's gait as *Junie*'s deck bowed and shivered in protest of the load she was taking on.

Donovan had pulled on a sleeveless light blue shirt decorated with scarlet-and-green parrots, but Ryan suspected it was more for the shirt's ability to hold his pipe and tobacco than for any creature comfort. The Heimdall Foundation man looked as if he could weather any elements. Scars crisscrossed his body, mute testimony to the rigorous trials he'd been subjected to.

Slowly, inexorably, *Junie* stole *Calypso* from a watery grave. They traveled with the river but headed for the eastern bank. Donovan had pointed out the various tributaries feeding into the river, and Ryan had confirmed them with his binocs. Even with the river level up, Donovan also gave Morse directions to steer clear of certain areas of the river because of underwater wreckage.

"When the river lowers after the rainy season," he said to Ryan, "you get a better chance of seeing most of them.

ut there's others, if you haven't explored this river, that ou won't know about until you've ripped the underside of our boat out. Ask me how I know. This isn't the first time 've had to put *Calypso* back together.''

'WE'VE GOT A CAMPSITE farther up this tributary,'' Donovan said.

Ryan kept his eye on the men in *Calypso*'s crow's nest. So far, neither of them had spotted the returning pirates. He knew it was possible that the pirates had decided to cut their losses, but he didn't trust that. With full dark coming less than an hour away, the pirates may have decided to hole up for the night on familiar terrain. Come first light, Ryan figured they'd be hunted again.

"What's the campsite for?" Ryan asked.

Donovan shook his head. "Just a base camp. You don't even need to take us there. Just put us ashore farther up this stream, and we'll see our own way clear.''

"It isn't going to happen like that," Ryan said. Then he told Donovan about Krysty and their encounter with the Chosen.

'HOW ARE YOU FEELING?'' Donovan squatted beside Krysty and gently peeled her eyelid back.

"Like I'm just short of catching the last train headed for the coast," Krysty croaked. It was a struggle for her to sit up on her own against the side of the boat.

"You still hearing the woman's voice?"

"Louder all the time. Can't hardly keep her away these past few days."

Donovan released her eyelid, and it slowly closed. "Well, you keep holding her back. Keep eating your soup and work on saving your strength. We'll see you clear of this."

"You can get her out of my head?" Krysty asked.

"Not me," Donovan replied. "But I know someone who
can."

"I can't wait," Krysty said. "There's not room enough
for both of us in here."

"HAVE YOU SEEN this before?" Ryan asked when they
were back in the prow, away from Krysty.

Donovan nodded. "Twice. Both of them were women
who'd come up on Chosen with death rattling in the backs
of the throats. One of them was a gaudy slut over in Tay-
lorville south and east of here. Rough trade ville, purely
sport and gaudies, folks living out hard days there and
spending their nights taking whatever they can from other
folks, staying there just because they think they can keep
ahead of folks taking from them. Gaudy slut had slit the
throat of one of the Chosen, then she got her mind grafted
for her trouble."

"Grafted?"

Donovan nodded and sucked on his pipe, streaming fra-
grant smoke. "The Chosen's term, what they call what they
do. A lot of their skills with their minds they'd only started
exploring right before skydark."

"In the Totality Concept," Ryan said.

Donovan's head snapped around. "What do you know
about the Totality Concept?"

Ryan shook his head. "I'm not here to say what I know.
Want to know what you know."

"But if you can add to our store of knowledge about the
Totality Concept..."

"That's not what I'm here to do," Ryan said.

"How much do you know about the Heimdall Foundation?" Donovan asked. "I talked with Elmore. He said you
knew some of it."

Ryan had let Elmore join the other crew aboard *Calypso*. "No."

"Mebbe I could be as tight-lipped about what I know about the Chosen."

"That's not a game you want to play with me," Ryan told the man harshly. "I saved your ass back there. Now I'm saving your boat. Way I see it, the scales here are way out of balance."

"But you do know something."

"Something," Ryan admitted. "But not what you're looking for. All the stuff I've gotten to know, the Heimdall Foundation's the first place I've heard of that's got an idea that skydark was brought about by aliens from another world."

"ETs," Donovan said automatically.

"ETs what?" Ryan asked.

Donovan removed his pipe from his mouth. "Sorry. ETs are extraterrestrials. Aliens. We know a little about the Totality Concept. Supposed to have been a division, called Department Thirteen we think, that had made some kind of contact with an alien race."

"And you believe that?"

"Enough that I've given my life over to finding out whether it's true."

"Waste of time."

"What makes you say that?"

"Had some kind of ETs here," Ryan said, "you'd have known about them before now."

"Not so sure about that."

"You ever seen an alien?" Ryan asked.

"Of course not. If we had, there wouldn't be such a desperate need to know."

"Then how can you believe in them?"

"I want to believe."

"Friend I used to know had a saying. Want in one hand and shit in the other. See which one gets fullest first."

"Whether you're ready to deal with it or not, Ryan," Donovan said harshly, "it happened. The world was on the brink of an alien invasion, and it was them who started the nukecaust that blew up the world."

"Don't give a damn about that," Ryan said. "I'm here now, and I got my own problems. I want to know what we're going to do about Krysty."

"There's someone I can send for. I've got a lot of friends in out-of-the-way places."

"What's this friend going to do?"

"We'll have to see. First we get my boat to shore and set up camp for the night. Then you and I have got some more dickering to do."

"About what?"

"About what you're going to do for helping me get your lady friend's ass out of the sling it's in."

"Saved your life," Ryan said. "Saved your boat. You owe me big time."

Donovan gave him a hard stare. "That's one of the Chosen dancing around in your lady friend's head. You can't save her, and she can't save herself. She's knocking on death's door right now. Don't know how she hasn't gone under before now. But she hasn't. Mebbe she still has a chance. But to give her that chance, I'm going to have to call in a marker that's owed me, mebbe give one back that's going to be pure hell to pay. And I'm the one going to have to pay it back."

Ryan glared at the man, not trusting himself to speak. But he knew Donovan was right; he didn't know the price the man was going to have to pay. And Ryan was willing to pay whatever price was asked. It was a seller's market.

"If you could have done something," Donovan reminded him in a gentle voice, ''you'd have done it before now. All you got left is the best you can do.''

Ryan said nothing because he had nothing to say.

THEY PUT IN TO THE RIVERBANK just before dark descended on the mountainous terrain the stream cut through. They'd made good time because the wind had been with them, but going against the flow of the stream pulling the foundering ship behind them had slowed them considerably.

Ryan wasn't at all comfortable with the distance they'd managed to put between them and the pirates, but he ordered everyone off *Junie,* including Morse and his sons, and established a watch rotation among the companions.

The Heimdall Foundation people spread out along the bank, making do with the sodden camp gear packed aboard *Calypso.* Donovan organized his people, setting up a work team to continue pumping the boat out during the night. Ryan wasn't happy about the lanterns the work team operated by. Even within the belowdecks of the boat, the soft yellow light diffused over the dark landscape and was reflected in the stream. But he knew they had no choice if they were going to save the boat. Left untended, the boat would have sunk to the bottom of the stream where they anchored for the night.

Donovan also put out hunting teams, and Jak and Dean volunteered to go with them, anxious to get away from *Junie*'s confines.

At first, Ryan was reluctant to let them go. Allowing them away from the group put them at risk as being taken captive or killed by the Heimdall Foundation people.

Donovan saw his indecision. ''Let them go. I give you my word that you don't have anything to worry about from me.''

''I don't know that your word is worth anything yet.''

"Those boys look able to take care of themselves out there. And you're going to have to trust me to some degree at some point if you're going to save your lady friend."

"Man's right," J.B. said at Ryan's elbow. The Armorer had come up so quietly Ryan had never heard him. "Jak and Dean aren't going to get in so deep with this bunch that we can't get them out. Donovan here appears purely motivated about saving his boat."

Ryan knew that was true, and he knew J.B. was hinting about the explosives he'd made on the journey.

"Better to find out now, while we're not in it up to our necks, how much you can trust him," J.B. pointed out.

Jak and Dean had disappeared from camp as soon as they'd been told.

"YOU NEVER SAID what your cargo was," Ryan said. He stood belowdecks in *Calypso,* watching as Donovan shone a bull's-eye lantern around the interior of the sailboat.

Donovan stood in waist-high water, the rhythmic crank of the hand-powered bilge pump echoing all around him. "Piece of a space station that come down a few months ago."

"*Shostakovich's Anvil?*" Ryan asked.

Turning, Donovan was careful to keep the main intensity of the lantern from Ryan's face, but he draped part of the glow over him. "You know about it?"

"Saw it come down," Ryan answered.

"Where were you?"

"In the Smoke Creek Desert."

Excitement flared in Donovan's face. "The space station broke up somewhere over that area."

Ryan nodded. "You ever recover any pieces of the space station?"

"No. We sent teams in there, but no one ever found an

impact area. The piece of *Shostakovich's Anvil* that I was carrying came over from what used to be Washington State. The people tracking the space station's breakup charted it, then traded with a bunch of scavengers who'd located it. I was making the final haul with it back to the Heimdall Foundation when the river pirates jumped me.''

"A big piece of the space station went down in the Smoke Creek Desert," Ryan said.

"We knew it had, but we didn't find an impact area. Figured muties carried it off, mebbe. Some of them seem to have an affinity for predark tech. Can't use and don't seem to understand it, but they worship it all the same. Recovered some nice pieces from them over the years. Or we thought it might have been scavengers.''

Ryan scanned the damage he could see to the boat's hull. It looked like axes had been used on the planks, creating crosshatches of white-scarred wood. "Where it fell," he said, "it would take a mighty determined man to get it out.''

"Where?''

Ryan looked at the man and shook his head. "If we get Krysty back to herself, I'll tell you. You're not the only feller playing with a hole card here.''

Chapter Thirty-One

"A couple days' work should see us clear of most of the damage."

Ryan sat on the other side of a campfire from Donovan. The Heimdall Foundation man lounged back against a tree that had been felled to provide firewood.

"We can even do most of it while we're being towed," he went on. "Troy tells me he's managed to save one of the gasoline-powered bilge pumps, and it'll be working come morning. With the hand-cranker you've let us borrow, we should be able to make a real move on getting *Calypso* dry. Got men cutting new timbers now that'll serve us till we can put up in dry dock back at the Foundation."

"How big is this place?" Doc asked. He held a thin branch with a piece of turkey meat on the end, browning in the campfire. All of them had eaten big meals, mixing the self-heats from the stores of both boats, as well as the meat the hunting party had brought back.

"The Foundation?"

"Yes."

"It's a big place," Donovan replied. "Other than that, I'm not going to say too much. We've survived this long by keeping our secrets secret."

"Of course, my dear fellow," Doc said unctuously, "but having some interests in the scientific research area myself, I find myself intensely curious."

"Mebbe someday you'll get up to the Foundation and have a look yourself."

"Mayhap I will. Ryan has told me you're aware of some of the ramifications of the Totality Concept."

"Sure. What areas were you most interested in?" Donovan asked.

"Why the experiments regarding—"

"No," Ryan interrupted, not wanting to give Donovan any more information than he already had.

Doc ceased speaking, glancing at Ryan in owl-eyed curiosity. "Have I spoken out of turn?"

"Man's leading you on, Doc, wanting to find out how much you know," Ryan commented. He stroked Krysty's hair. She'd insisted on coming to sit by the campfire with him but hadn't been able to remain awake. He missed talking to her, missed the way she was able to help him keep his thoughts all untangled. It felt as though he had knots in his head now.

"Surely there can be no harm in telling him some of what we have found out," Doc said.

"Another time," Ryan replied. "Man's holding out information on us, we're not going to be doing him any favors real soon."

Donovan grinned, shifting into a cross-legged position. "So you have the location of *Shostakovich's Anvil* and more information about the Totality Concept."

"For trade," Ryan agreed. "Once we get Krysty back on her feet."

"Ryan said you'd known of two other cases like this," Mildred spoke up.

"That's right. Both of them involving Chosen who were about a flat minute from being chilled. They put their personality in other people, forced them to do the things they wanted them to."

"Which was?"

"Return to the Chosen."

"But they didn't get there?"

"No. I saw them both. A family held the first woman, hoping something good would come of it, that mebbe the personality would wither away."

"But it didn't?" Mildred asked.

Donovan shook his head. "Gaudy slut was put in jail. Went crazy and chilled the man she's working for. She kept trying to escape."

"What happened to them?"

"Not much. Took them a couple weeks, but they both died." He glanced at Krysty. "Glad she was sleeping when you asked that."

But from the way Krysty moved against him, Ryan knew she hadn't completely been asleep. She'd heard.

THE GROUP AWAKENED the next morning as the sun started to gray the eastern sky. The Heimdall Foundation people took a long time to rise. Ryan and Donovan had to pass through them, kicking at exposed feet until they got them up and moving. They reluctantly crowded back aboard *Calypso* until Donovan reminded them that walking back would have been a hell of a lot farther and harder.

Ryan didn't bother trying to hide the remnants of the campsites. It would have taken too long, and if the pirates followed them they needed all the head start they could manage.

Breakfast was self-heats and leftover meat from the night before, as well as loaves of bread that had been salvaged from the Heimdall Foundation's stores.

Ryan put Jak on watch in the crow's nest aboard *Calypso*. He had the sharpest eyes of all the companions, and

Ryan trusted him more than anyone in the Heimdall Foundation's ranks.

With the bilge pumps both operating and crew to use them, *Calypso* was riding higher in the stream by midmorning. The wind came in from the west, northwest, and pushed them even faster to the east. *Calypso* was able to use her sails to lighten the strain, as well, enabling them to achieve greater speed.

J.B. dropped a bucket into the stream and hauled it up near Ryan. He stuck a hand into it and pulled it back out, tasting the water drops on his fingers. "Fresh," he said, "and good. Can't taste any chems."

Mildred stood at his side and cupped a hand, drinking from the bucket, as well. "Damn, it's as good tasting as it is pretty. This water's pure, clean and healthy. Not like that sludge pumping through that river we left."

"Comes down out of the mountains," Donovan said. He'd been consulting area maps, some of them Ryan had noticed from the predark, and some that looked handmade. "Got to catch it early in the spring, when the snows melt."

"Usually the snows are fouled, as well," Mildred pointed out.

"I know," Donovan agreed. "Usually has some kind of residue you have to deal with. Some of it around here is tolerable in its own right, but this tributary—and a few others like it—is virgin pure. Problem is if you don't get it early enough, it peters out during the hot part of the summer. There's times in July and August that this streambed isn't more than a foot or two deep."

Looking at the sixty-foot-wide river, knowing from the depths called out by Morse's sons that they were presently in twenty to twenty-five feet of water at any given time, Ryan had a hard time believing that.

"Part of this water comes from snowmelt," Donovan

went on. "But some of the researchers at the Foundation think it has something to do with a fluctuating water table in this area, as well. Everything has to be working in accordance to get the water this way."

"An artesian well system," Doc suggested. "Underground springs that are fed from the snowmelt, then filter out the impurities through stratum before passing the water on."

"Mebbe. I'm not much into water. But I do know if we don't get a full ration of water in the spring, the Foundation struggles for the rest of the year."

"How do you get it?" Doc asked.

"We dam up the stream," Donovan answered. "Block it up for two, three months, however long it takes, then release it, forcing it to go in the direction we want it to."

"You reconfigure this stream?" Doc asked.

"Have to."

"Why not just build the Foundation near the stream?" the old man asked.

"Logistics," Ryan answered. "They build the Foundation on the river, it's more likely to be found. So they build it somewhere it won't be as likely to be found and pull the water in."

"You dammed this stream?" Mildred asked.

"As well as we could," Donovan said.

"What did you use?"

"Timbers, rock. It's not watertight, but it allows us to build up the water supply."

"And there's still this much water left over?" Doc asked.

"Yeah. Gotta be real careful about dam building. Don't try to hold back enough and we run short of water. Try to hold back too much, have it break the dam down, run even shorter of water and mebbe get some folks chilled for their trouble. Seen it work out both ways. Trick is to get it just right.''

"THIS IS BEAUTIFUL COUNTRY, lover."

Ryan held Krysty in his arms as he sat against the railing. He felt her shake in his embrace as though she had a chill. He wrapped the blanket he'd gotten for her more tightly about her.

The terrain had turned definitely more mountainous. He couldn't remember reading if it had always been that way, or if the present landscape was the direct result of the nukecaust and all the earth pounders. Spruce and fir dotted the mountaintops, spilling into thick forests below.

"Nice to look at," Ryan agreed.

Krysty took his hand. "Make me a promise, lover." She turned, looking with both her emerald eyes into his single ice-blue one.

"What?"

"If I die somewhere up in this rough country," she began.

"You're not going to die."

"No arguments. Just something I've got to say."

Ryan swallowed hard but didn't say anything.

"If I should die up here," Krysty said, "promise me that if you're able, you'll find me a grave site up in those mountains and leave me there to rest."

Ryan couldn't speak around the hard knot lodged in his throat.

"If you can't say it," Krysty said, knowing him so well, better than anyone ever had or ever would again, "just nod."

Ryan gave her a single, tight nod. But it was more than an agreement with her; it was an acknowledgment that he might have come this far still only to fail. He cursed himself for ever letting that thought cross his mind.

THE STREAM GOT increasingly narrow, finally getting down to something less than thirty feet across. It held steady at a depth of fifteen feet, plenty of room for the boats to pass.

By early evening, they'd entered a canyon area that reached between forty and sixty feet above the stream. Ryan glanced up at the high-walled rock, cool in the shadows that stretched out over him.

Less than a quarter mile in, the canyon rounded out, forming a natural cistern that had to have been a hundred feet across. It was a natural harbor site for boats, protected from the wind and most of the elements.

Besides the channel they'd followed up from the Jefferson River, Ryan noted three other channels on the north side of the cistern. Streams followed each one of those, as well.

The dam blocked the stream directly in front of them. It was huge, constructed of timbers fifteen feet across and stacked over a hundred feet tall. Groups of men worked near the top, laying in new logs cut to fit.

"By the Three Kennedys!" Doc exclaimed, gawking up at the construction.

"Dark night," J.B. breathed.

"It can be impressive to look at," Donovan admitted. "I don't think I'll ever get used to them even after all the ones I've built."

"How many have you built?" Mildred asked.

"This is my ninth year as construction chief. Worked on the ones before, as well. Saw a lot of bad things happen. Personally I'd rather be out during the months it takes to construct the dam, but I've got a knack for building the things."

Scanning up the dam, Ryan admitted that Donovan was speaking the truth. Even though it was dammed, the stream leaked water between the timbers, spilling twisting and lunging strings and sprays of water that splattered against the flat surface of the cistern pool below.

"Still a couple weeks from having it full," Donovan said. "But we're getting there."

"Pirates not come here?" Jak asked.

"No. This year they've come farther upriver than I'd ever expected. Area where you found me gets real dangerous. Lot of tributaries feed into the Jefferson, bringing all kinds of scavenging material. Trouble is, the river's so forceful at times in that area that it can send something through a boat. And you get a lot of chop. The small watercraft the pirates use would break up when the water's really rough."

"They've never been here?" Ryan asked.

"No. But they've never all been working with Barbarossa."

"Who's Barbarossa?"

"Leader of the pirates," Donovan answered. "Until this spring, I'd never seen so many pirates working together. I saw him today, though, and there was no doubt who was in charge."

"What changed things?"

"For the pirates? Barbarossa went after the pocket groups, started with a few groups last spring from what I heard. Took them over, then proved it was worth their time to stay with him. Evidently he's gotten even more aggressive about consolidating the other water scavengers around here. Didn't expect what I ran into today."

"He's got all those gasoline-powered craft," Ryan said. "Where's he getting the fuel?"

"This is Montana territory," Donovan replied. "Got a

lot of mineral resources around here. You know where to look, you can find places where gasoline's been stockpiled. A few other places manufacture their own. There's coal mines in operation, too, and slavers operate those. This is a rough land.''

"And the Chosen live here, too?"

"Some of them."

A SHANTYTOWN OF TENTS and semipermanent lean-tos crowded the narrow ledge on the south side of the cistern. Few plants and trees grew along the stony soil where the campsite was, and even fewer sprouted from the steep incline leading to the mountains above.

Morse bawled out orders and cut the sails, aiming both boats into the pier that extended out into the cistern.

"How deep's the water here?" Morse asked.

"Forty, fifty feet," Donovan replied. "There's been groups in here before, drawn by the freshwater fish. They dredged the cistern during the hot season when it sank low. Unfortunately they killed the fish they were here to live off.''

"Wrecked the ecology," Mildred said.

"Yeah. Took years for the fish to come back, but they're here.''

"Hot pipe, Dad," Dean shouted in obvious delight. "Come look at this." He stood near the railing in *Junie*'s prow, looking down into the water.

Ryan joined him, peering down through the startlingly clear liquid. He recognized the schools of trout, whitefish and grayling as they cut through the water beneath the sailboat.

"There's no shortage of game here," Donovan said. "Besides the fishing, there's also moose, goat, elk, deer, bighorn sheep and antelope. You want bird? You got your choice between pheasant, duck and grouse. One thing about this cistern—it attracts wildlife. A man doesn't go hungry unless he's too lazy to go hunt it down or fish for it.''

"How many people do you have here?"

"Probably about sixty. We lost seven men when the pirates boarded *Calypso*.''

RYAN SAT on an empty wooden barrel on the cistern ledge. The barrel had once held nails but now only showed the signs of long use as a seat. He gazed out at the piers. Besides *Calypso*, there was one other sailcraft only a little larger than *Junie*. Then there were nearly a dozen outboard boats.

"We use the small boats for exploration and supply craft," Donovan explained. "Carry gasoline for them on *Calypso* and *Ariel*.''

Ryan glanced at the top of the mountains ringing the canyon. The sun was dipping below the western horizon. Outside the cistern, some of the light was still visible, but in the bowl all light was gone and total darkness had descended. Lighted torches ringed the area, creating bubbles of illumination for the group.

The dam workers had distanced themselves from Morse and the companions, but Elmore circulated freely within them, telling all he knew.

Jak and Dean were down at the water's edge with their poles in hand. Despite the tension of the situation, they'd been drawn to the fishing with the other dam workers. Their efforts hadn't gone unrewarded.

"What a wonderful ambrosia!" Doc exclaimed, approaching their group.

"You talking about the fish stew, Doc?" Donovan asked. Each one of the campfires was festooned by a large stainless-steel pot hanging over the flames.

"Yes, indeed."

Donovan snorted. "Not so wonderful after you've been eating it for months."

"Well, sir, I have not been given that opportunity. Nor, of late, for the pan-fried bread I see in ample supply."

Grinning, Donovan said, "Feel free to help yourself. There's plenty here, and the crew doesn't mind sharing."

Doc touched his hat. "Ryan, if I'm not needed here, I think I will sample what there is to be had, in order to fill that growing hollow pit leaching at my backbone. I shall, of course, be ever ready to stand at your side."

"Enjoy," Ryan said.

"I'm going to get Millie a plate myself," J.B. said. "Mebbe sit with Krysty awhile to spell her."

Ryan nodded, waiting until J.B. stepped away. He'd been with the Armorer for years, and J.B. knew how to make himself scarce, giving Ryan time to talk to Donovan on his own.

"Time for us to get down to the nut cutting," the one-eyed man stated. "What's it going to take for you to help us with Krysty?"

"That's simple." Donovan spread his hands. "I want you to help me get that chunk of *Shostakovich's Anvil* back from the pirates."

Chapter Thirty-Two

Ryan carried a lantern, following Donovan up the rope
scaffolding that led to the top of the canyon near the dam.
The Heimdall Foundation man carried a lantern, as well,
playing his light over the rough-hewn rock.

"Thought mebbe you'd like to take a look at the dam
itself," Donovan said. "Give you more of a perspective of
what you'll be fighting for."

In truth, the view was awe inspiring. The moon hung
orange and full in the sable heavens, reflected in the dark
pool of the basin below. Stars glittered around the moon,
light glass bits embedded in the night.

"I've got enough to fight for," Ryan answered. "I'd
walk through mutie slime pits for that woman back there."

"Knew you would. I saw it in your eye when you were
telling me the story."

"Something else you should know," Ryan said. "If you
lie to me and don't get help for her the way you said you
would, I'll chill you. And that's an ace on the line."

Donovan stopped, meeting Ryan's level gaze without reserve. "I believe you. If that section of the space station
wasn't out there in the hands of Barbarossa and the pirates,
if I hadn't been told how important it was, I'd probably
still help your woman. Mebbe for nothing at all. But I need
your help, and I mean to see you give it. Gonna cost me
plenty in getting you that help, though you might not be-

lieve that right now. I've seen your kind of man plenty of times before, Ryan.''

Ryan didn't say anything, feeling the heat of Donovan's lantern brushing across his face.

''Once you get what you need, or what you want, you'll be gone. Won't matter what anyone else needs or wants. You believe in very little outside yourself.''

''I've found that's the best way to be,'' Ryan replied lightly.

''Not up to me to try changing your religion. Just my effort to keep the record square.'' Donovan turned and headed on up the grade, following the trail.

''I BELIEVE IN THE WORK the Heimdall Foundation is doing,'' Donovan said when they reached the top of the dam. ''Whatever future Deathlands has in store, part of it's going to be guided by institutions like the Foundation, people working hard to look backward so they can look forward again.''

''It was institutions like the Foundation that put the world in the shape it's in.'' Ryan studied the dam. The logs had been hewed to fit, staggered in an alternating double-stacked layer like rounds in an M-16 clip. They'd been bricked up with mud, which helped slow the water's eventual erosion of the dam.

The blocked water stretched out behind the dam for over two hundred yards, at least half that in diameter. The water was still, eddying smoothly, reflecting the sky overhead.

''How long will this water last?'' Ryan asked.

''We get lucky,'' Donovan said, ''all year.''

''How do you get it to the Foundation?''

''We dam the other end of the cistern before we release the water. When it has nowhere else to go, it flows along the northern channels.''

"And one of them leads to the Foundation?"

"Yeah. Pretty much. There's more to it. Most folks wouldn't be able to trail the water. Goes underground in places. It's no easy process, and it took years for us to figure out a way to get it to the Foundation without being traced or contaminating it. One of these days, you'd have to see the Foundation."

"Mebbe." Ryan's wanderlust had driven him the length and breadth of Deathlands, first as a young man, then as a lieutenant on War Wag One with the Trader. When he'd first heard about the Heimdall Foundation while going to check on Dean at Nicholas Brody's school, he'd wanted to journey to the Foundation and see it for himself. That inclination was still in him.

But now wasn't the time. Not with Krysty in the shape she was in.

"How do you release the water?" Ryan asked.

"Same way we close down the other end of the cistern— use explosives. After all these years, we know where to place them."

Ryan filed that bit of knowledge away.

"Got something else to show you," Donovan said, "if you're not too tired."

"What? I've got a feeling morning's going to come bastard early if we're going to get at those pirates."

"You're right. But I think this is going to interest you. Since you've heard of the Totality Concept, I'm certain you've also learned they left redoubts scattered around Deathlands."

Ryan looked at the man.

"We found one here," Donovan said. "Want to go look?"

IT TOOK Ryan and Donovan almost half an hour to trek back farther upstream along the mountain ridge. By that time, he'd worked off most of the small amount of supper he'd eaten back at the campsite. Seeing Krysty sick as she was had left him without an appetite, but it was making up for lost time now.

"Hungry?" Donovan asked, offering a cloth-wrapped bar.

"What's that?"

"Trail-mix bar. Kind of like an old-style journeycake, only this has a lot of raisins, nuts and dried fruits in it. Standard Foundation issue, along with self-heats and ring-pulls. Too much work to chew to put any fat on you, but they keep your energy up."

Ryan took the bar, unwrapping it and smelling it. Satisfied with the odor, his stomach growling in sudden anticipation, he took a bite and began the unexpectedly long task of chewing. It was good, but as Donovan said, it took real work to get it down.

Only a few minutes farther on, they arrived at the redoubt.

The massive steel door was inset in the rock face, sheltered and partially hidden by a low-hanging shelf. Huge boulders and brush around it served to further mask the door's presence.

Judging from the brush and the loose rock in front of the entranceway, it had never been opened. Ryan experienced the familiar excitement thrilling through him when he thought about what might be on the other side of the huge door.

"Been inside?" he asked.

Donovan shook his head. "Only redoubts I've ever seen were blown open or wrecked during a quake. Looted so long ago nothing worth anything was left behind."

Ryan stepped toward the door, wary for any traps that

might have been left behind. The Totality Concept staff sometimes left wicked traps behind; other times it was frustrated looters. Satisfied nothing was there, he flipped open the cover on the keypad.

"Keypad's active," Donovan said, "but nobody's ever found a way in."

Ryan punched the proper key sequence. The keypad lights went from red to amber to green. An instant later, the door slid sideways.

"Son of a bitch!" Donovan exclaimed. "How the fuck did you do that?"

"Got lucky." He adjusted the lantern he carried, turning up the illumination. Taking the SIG-Sauer blaster in his free hand, he walked into the redoubt.

Donovan followed him.

THE REDOUBT WAS small compared to many of those Ryan had seen. There were two rooms. One held a mat-trans unit with bright blue armaglass sporting dark green diagonal stripes.

"Is that a gateway?" Donovan asked, pointing at the mat-trans unit.

"What do you know about them?" Ryan asked.

"Read about them in some of the materials at the Foundation. Supposed to transport something or someone from one place to another by a light beam bouncing off a satellite or something. Does it?"

Ryan only gave the man a small smile.

The second room held more promise, turning out to be a small but complete armory. He played the lantern light over the weapons, grinning as he realized J.B. was going to have the time of his life.

"Fuck me!" Donovan exploded, holding his own lantern up and moving closer.

"Ready to go into the pirate-chilling business?" Ryan asked.

"LOVER."

Ryan turned his head tiredly and gazed at Krysty. She was huddled under her blankets, her skin as pale as death. "Yeah."

"I don't remember you coming to bed last night. Mebbe I missed it."

"Didn't get there," Ryan said. He squatted near her, drinking coffee sub from a ceramic mug Donovan had given him.

"What's going on? I thought I heard power tools earlier."

"You did," Ryan assured her. "We've been busy." He gestured out toward the six boats he and J.B. had worked on with volunteers from the dam builders. They'd mounted a .50-caliber machine gun from the redoubt on each boat. The arsenal still contained another six, as well as rifles and handblasters that were being passed out to the Heimdall Foundation people. Ryan had easily let the weapons go, after restocking their own ammo needs, because the companions couldn't take them.

He had, however, locked the redoubt door behind them. The mat-trans unit still offered a back door out of the area—after Krysty was taken care of properly.

Krysty forced herself up to one elbow and surveyed the dock. "What's going on, lover?"

Ryan told her about the agreement to help recover the satellite section from the pirates.

"Shouldn't have done that," Krysty objected, her face going crimson as her hair. "You're trying to take on too much weight to take care of me."

"Has to be done to close the deal."

"That's not much of a deal, lover."

Ryan turned his single eye on the beautiful redhead. "I'd make a deal with the devil himself if I had to."

RYAN RODE with Donovan in the lead powerboat, feeling the engines throb through the entire craft and the slap of the river against the hull. Eight other men occupied the boat with them, all of them armed and scanning the river. The early-morning sun rose to their right, burning through the thin layer of fog that lay over the water and reduced visibility.

"Reports we've had lately are that Barbarossa has put up a campsite here." Donovan laid a forefinger on the handmade map he held.

The map was well made, and seemed to cover the river's current course, more or less. In the powerboats, the trip back to the river from the cistern took only a couple hours.

On the map, the river cut a lazy S downstream and north of their present position. The pirate base was located on the second hump of the S.

"Are you sure they're still there?" Ryan asked.

"No." Donovan folded the map and put it away. "This is just my best guess."

LITTLE MORE than an hour later, Donovan's information and guess, however, proved correct.

Ryan lay on his belly, his binocs to his eye as he surveyed the pirate camp. J.B. and Donovan lay on either side of him, field glasses to their eyes, as well.

Dean and Jak stayed behind them with three other men that Ryan had designated as the land-based attack team. Doc and Mildred had stayed at the base to care for Krysty. Ryan hadn't liked splitting their forces, but Krysty couldn't make the trip and he wasn't going to leave her there alone.

The pirate base showed none of the semipermanency of the Foundation base. Few tents stood along the riverbank, leaving men sleeping out on the open ground wrapped in thick woolen blankets or in tattered sleeping bags. They clustered around low-burning campfires, few of which showed any signs of being cared for during the night.

"Sleeping deep," J.B. observed.

"Local hootch," Donovan replied. "Got a small ville called Snockers farther downstream that has a potato-whiskey still set up. Most folks working this river find something Snockers can use and trade for the whiskey. Snockers has overland traders set up to trade farther in-country. To them, Barbarossa and his filth are just another customer."

Ryan didn't comment as he raked the binocs across the riverbank. The land tumbled down out of the mountains, remaining rough and broken all the way to the water's edge. It also provided a lot of cover in the form of brush and tall grasses, which Ryan had counted on after studying the shoreline. He'd left their boat a half mile back, cutting across the land and keeping the river in sight to mark their bearings.

More than two dozen water bikes floated in the harbor area the pirates had chosen, tethered by ropes, chains or leather thongs to boats, rocks, trees and small anchors. Nearly four dozen bigger boats, all of them in deteriorating condition, also bobbed in the water. Together, they constituted an impressive armada.

And Ryan's plan called for direct action, his six boats against the numbers before him.

Scanning the boats, Ryan saw that only a few of them had mounted weapons. The machine guns they'd raided from the redoubt held more firepower than most of the pirate craft. The biggest boat in the group was a sixty-foot powerboat that had faded Montana Lake Patrol insignia on it coupled with State Police running along the bow.

The sixty-footer sported a black flag with a white skull and crossbones that looked handmade. It drooped now in the light breeze, hardly unfurled at all. The sixty-footer was the only craft big enough to hold the recovered space-station section, according to Donovan. A tarp covered a lump taller than Ryan and nearly twice a long. The weight caused the sixty-footer to sink lower in the water than she was supposed to.

Ryan couldn't help wondering how the heavy load was going to affect the sixty-footer's performance. Speed remained a big part of their survival plan.

"Got them outgunned when it comes to quality of fire-power," J.B. commented quietly.

"But there's no getting around the numbers," Ryan said. "They'll chase us. And with that load—"

"Well," the Armorer said, cleaning his glasses on his shirttail, "that's what we're planning for. If we get enough of a head start, it'll be enough."

"It'll have to be," Ryan said. He looked at Donovan. "Unless you want to back off on this."

The Foundation man shook his head. "This isn't the risk-iest thing I've ever done. If we didn't have the blasters, I'd back us off. But that space-station piece is too damn important to just go away. And I'll still line our boat pilots up against theirs anytime."

"Guess you're going to be doing just that." Ryan put the binocs away. "Time to get about it." He turned to Jak and Dean and the three men with them. "We go in quiet. No blasters used until they use them first." He eyed the three Foundation men. "You understand me?"

They nodded.

"You pull a blaster before they do, mebbe risk getting

the rest of us chilled, I'll punch your ticket for the last train to the coast myself."

"They understand," Donovan said defensively. He'd picked the men in the party himself, vouching for their skill and their nerve.

"I mean what I say," Ryan growled. "Me, Jak and J.B.'ll go first. I count five guards that are up and moving. We'll go in, take care of those. The rest of you get down to the riverbank. Wilcox, you get on that sixty-footer, make sure you can get the engines started when we need them. Otherwise, we're all dead meat. Dean, you're with him. Cover fire. But only after all hell's broke loose."

Dean nodded.

"When we get to the river," Ryan went on, "the rest of you put as many boats out of commission as you can. Quiet. Slash the gas lines, put river mud in the tanks, cut the electrical wires or any other thing that comes to mind. The fewer of them we have chasing us, the better off we're going to be. Don't know how fast that big boat can go, but those water bikes will for damn sure be faster."

Chapter Thirty-Three

Ryan led the way into the brush, Jak and J.B. at his heels. Leaving the SIG-Sauer leathered, he drew the panga, the steel glistening in his hand. He stopped, chest flat to the forest floor less than three feet from a man sitting guard on a toppled tree covered in orange fungus.

The guard was dressed in worn clothing like most of Barbarossa's group. He carried a single-shot 12-gauge that sat across his knees as he sucked on a sugar stick.

Ryan came out of the brush as soundless as a big cat stalking game. Reaching around the man, he drew the panga across his victim's throat. Warm blood doused his hand, and the man thrashed in his grip, kicking out his life in seconds. Ryan kicked sand over the spilled blood and left the corpse propped up in a sitting position with the shotgun.

Pulling back into the brush, Ryan located his next target. A woman stepped into the tree line carrying a lever-action .30-30. She was thin and slatternly, black hair cut short around her face.

Ryan almost lost her in the thick trees for a moment, but she wasn't moving quietly. The sound of her footsteps gave her away. He didn't know how many of the pirates were women, but a good number of them were. Donovan had mentioned Barbarossa hadn't been too selective in choosing the people who followed him.

But they were all dangerous.

And all it took at the moment to be deadly was a single scream.

Trailing the woman, Ryan watched her select a tree, then kick the brush. Satisfied that nothing crawled, slithered or crept through the nearby brush, the woman lowered her trousers and squatted.

Pale flesh gleamed against the dusty black leathers she wore. She rested her head on her crossed arms atop her knees, gazing up at the treetops as she pissed.

Ryan closed on her. He struck while she was still squatted, clapping his hands on her head and twisting it viciously. Her skull separated from her spinal cord with a single, definite pop.

He kept her in a squatted position so her dying reflexes wouldn't kick the brush and make noise. When she was still, he shoved her forward. She fell facedown in a heap.

Ryan glanced over his shoulder and saw the Armorer tucking a corpse into the brush less than a dozen feet away. They moved back toward the camp.

Sunlight started to streak the tops of the trees around them, showing signs of invading the campsite.

Another guard walked a perimeter, obviously restless and not too pleased with his assignment. Heavy lidded and young, he looked as if he'd rather have been asleep. Ryan reached out from the tree line, grabbed him by his long hair, twisting him as he pulled him into the brush.

His free hand wrapped around the hilt of the panga, Ryan slashed the heavy blade at the man's throat. The sharp edge cleaved through cleanly, for a moment exposing the white bone of the spine at the back of the man's throat. Then blood wept into the cut.

Ryan dragged the body farther into the trees, almost finishing decapitating the dead man in the process. He felt

nse as he returned to the camp, automatically locking on
the female guard closest to his position.

She sat at a campfire, picking at a piece of meat she
armed at the end of a stick. Two women and three men
ept at her feet, coiled tightly in their blankets. Vomit
rings hung from one man's mouth as he snored.

Ryan closed on the woman and slipped the panga be-
veen her third and fourth ribs, not stopping until he
ierced her heart. She gave a few spasmodic jerks and died
n his arms.

For good measure, Ryan slit the throats of the five pirates
round the campfire, holding them down while he was un-
een.

Then a shot rang out, a single blast that echoed within
ne enclosed space of the campsite.

"Fireblast!" Ryan swore, glancing out into the make-
hift harbor. The Foundation men had managed to put down
few of the pirates' boats, but there were still many left.
Ie sheathed the panga and slipped the Steyr off his shoul-
er. For close work, the rifle also made a good blunt in-
trument.

The pirates came awake sluggishly, showing the effects
f a night spent with the home brew.

Breaking into a run, Ryan spotted Jak and J.B. sprinting
or the pirate flagship. Blasterfire started slowly at first, then
;ained in intensity.

Ryan fired the rifle dry, picking his targets more or less
.s they were presented. Almost to the water when the as-
ault rifle fired dry, he slung it over his shoulder and drew
he SIG-Sauer.

"Got you now, you stupe bastard!" a pirate yelled, step-
•ing out from behind a tree in front of Ryan. He brought
ip a sawed-off double-barreled shotgun.

Pivoting, Ryan threw himself to the right in a long dive,

aiming himself at an A-shaped tent. The shotgun explode
behind him, and a couple pellets struck him in the leg
knocking him off balance.

The tent collapsed when he hit, coming loose from the
thin support poles that gave way instantly. Ryan went down
in the canvas, flailing for balance, the wound in his shoul
der tearing open again. The whine of outboard motors and
diesels sounded out in the harbor. The escape plan was to
get the hell out of the area as soon as possible. No one
figured on waiting.

Ryan rolled, lost for a moment in the canvas. Someone
inside the tent surged up against him, trying to get out from
under. Still in motion, unable to get free of the canvas
Ryan turned his attention to the shotgun-toting pirate. The
SIG-Sauer came up in line with his eye, and he squeezed
off three rounds into his adversary's chest.

The pirate managed to pull off his second round, but the
spread dug into the ground, throwing up a blinding cloud
of mud. The 9 mm hollowpoints drilled through the pirate's
chest, tearing huge chunks of flesh out his back. He stum-
bled back, squatting with a surprised look on his face.

The man trapped inside the tent brought up his weapon,
cursing. "Fuck you!" he screamed. "Get off me!"

Still struggling himself, Ryan spotted the shape of the
man's head through the canvas. He pressed the blaster's
muzzle against the head shape and pulled the trigger twice.
Blood blew through the holes the bullets made in the tent,
throwing a sheet of crimson and gray across the canvas.

Ryan pushed himself into a run as the dead man kicked
out his life, already shrouded in the tent.

Ahead J.B. ran through the water toward the pirate flag-
ship, keeping his knees and the M-4000 scattergun clear.
Dean pulled himself over the bow, attracting the attention
of the gunner on the flying deck. The pirate turned, bringing

is rifle into target acquisition. Dean fired without hesita-
on, a double-tap burst the way his father and J.B. had
aught him.

The pirate slid sideways as the rounds hammered the
center part of his body.

Dean slid up the side of the bow and onto the flagship's
eck as the corpse toppled into the water. By then Jak was
p the side, rolling over in a wet rush of flying water.

Ryan lost them then, turning his attention to his own
roblems. The ground became spongy underfoot, slowing
im. Unable to reload the Steyr, he had to depend on the
SIG-Sauer. When the blaster ran dry, he used it like a club
nd drew the panga.

"Get those bastards!" a loud voice roared. "A case of
whiskey to every man who brings me a head!"

Less than ten feet from the water's edge, Ryan spotted
a giant of a man flanked by two women manning a .30-
caliber Browning Automatic Rifle. The big man handled
he machine gun with ease, cradling it on one big arm while
 one woman kept the belts clear.

"Get them, Brutus!" the other woman encouraged. She
gripped a .357 Magnum blaster in both hands, popping off
rounds in quick succession at one of the Foundation men
lumping mud into a boat's gas tank.

The Foundation man staggered when he was hit in the
back of the head, then pitched into the water. Pirates
swarmed out into the river, racing for their boats and water
bikes.

Ryan halted at the crest of the rise, thinking he might
have a chance to reload. A bullet burned along his side,
coring through his jacket, ripping through the flesh just
above his hip. Warm blood trickled into his pants, bringing
a fiery agony with it.

Some of the bullets cut through the branches over the

heads of the big man and the two women, tearing leave
loose. The woman feeding the ammo belts to Brutus's BAR
ducked and looked back. "You stupe fuckers watch where
you're—" She froze when she spotted Ryan.

Seeing the line of pirates charging toward his position,
Ryan threw himself forward, at Brutus and his women.

Moving surprisingly fast for a big man, Brutus wheeled
around, trying to bring up the BAR. He tore the ammo belt
from the woman's hands.

Desperate, trapped and in a hard place and knowing it,
Ryan head-butted the big man in the face. Brutus's nose
broke with a vicious snap, blood dripping from the flattened
nostrils.

Brutus roared with rage and pain, going down backward.
His finger lay heavy on the trigger, and the unaimed bullets
chugged into the air.

Working quickly, Ryan slashed at the big man's blaster
wrist with the panga. Flesh parted in a spray of blood. The
heavy blade cleaved the ligaments to the hand, releasing
the BAR.

The ammo woman threw herself on Ryan's back, a knife
flashing in her hand. Brutus grabbed at the one-eyed man
with his good hand, his face a mask of blood.

Ryan moved as quick as a mutie rattler. He jerked his
arm back, smashing his elbow into the knife-wielding
woman. She shrilled in agony as her cheekbone crumpled.
He followed through with the panga, slashing her across
both eyes, releasing the liquid cores onto her pale face.

The other woman brought her pistol up from less than
ten feet, both hands wrapped around the butt. The muzzle
sight centered between her cold, hard eyes.

Stepping into Brutus, Ryan hefted the SIG-Sauer, slamming its butt into the side of the big man's face. Flesh
peeled back to reveal bone, covered quickly by blood. Ryan

raised his arm again and levered his forearm into Brutus's sweat-soured armpit. Using sheer strength, he spun the pirate around as a shield just as the woman fired.

She screamed in rage when she saw what Ryan had done, but she kept firing until the revolver emptied.

Brutus's body shivered with the impacts of the bullets. His yells turned to sibilant hissing as the rounds perforated his lungs.

Shoving the dead bulk from him, Ryan sheathed the panga and SIG-Sauer, then scooped up the BAR from the ground. The woman dropped her blaster and grabbed for a .22-caliber target pistol tucked in her belt at the back.

Firing the BAR from the hip, Ryan stitched a handful of the heavy rounds across the woman's breasts, punching through her heart. He knelt and quickly attached another ammo belt from the plastic box, then turned back to the line of approaching pirates, aware of the ground pocking around him.

He fell forward onto the ground, the BAR levered in front of him. The bipod at the barrel's end flipped out at his touch, and he squeezed the trigger, keeping it down and chewing through the belt and a half of ammo as he raked the line of pirates from left to right.

Bodies—both dead and wounded—dropped out of the line of pirates, leaving long and frequent gaps. The charge broke before the echo of the BAR's barrage faded away.

Ryan threw down the weapon and ran out into the water, heading toward the flagship. He ejected the empty clip from the SIG-Sauer, pocketed it and shoved a fresh one in.

A pirate on a water bike roared at Ryan, bringing his blaster to bear.

Lifting the SIG-Sauer, Ryan shot the man in the face from ten feet out. The water bike spun out of control, the throttle stuck even after the dead man toppled from the craft. It slammed into a nearby outboard, striking the engine. Both vehicles erupted in a black-and-orange explosion.

Ryan slogged through the water, ignoring the heat wave that roiled over him. Twin white spumes spurted out from the rear of the flagship.

"Dad!" Dean yelled. He maintained a low profile as he fired the Hi-Power at the pirates following Ryan into the river. "Hurry!"

Donovan hauled himself aboard the flagship, dripping wet and slipping across the deck. J.B. stood on the flying deck, working the controls. Only one of the other Foundation men had made it to the vessel.

Ryan ran as best he could, his breath burning his lungs. The river, even with the gentle current here, made the going hard. The water rose to his chest by the time he reached the flagship. He reached up and caught the built-in stepladder, then pulled himself aboard.

Donovan emerged from belowdecks.

"You find it?" Ryan asked.

"It's there."

"Hang on," J.B. roared over the twin diesels.

Ryan nearly fell as the Armorer threw the engines to full ahead, too much weight shifting to his wounded leg. His boots, filled with water, hampered his movements, as well.

Already mired by the weight of the space-station section aboard, the boat wallowed in the river like a mud pig on a hot day as the screws churned the water. Then it gained speed as it moved forward, rising inches as the hull hydroplaned.

Several of the pirates made their way toward the vessel.

Taking the brief respite to reload the Steyr, Ryan shouldered the rifle and started firing. He aimed for people, as well as exposed engines, creating instant havoc among the pirates.

Bullets holed the flagship and chopped long splinters from the deck, revealing the white wood beneath. More bullets whined off the brasswork and cracked through the Plexiglas windows on the flying deck.

Ryan reloaded and watched J.B. shove the shotgun forward. The Armorer fired, then grabbed for the wheel again.

"Dean, Jak," Ryan called out.

"Yeah, Dad," Dean answered.

"Yeah," Jak said.

"Hold the position here. I'm going up topside with J.B." Both youths nodded, and he crossed the deck as fast as he was able. Bullets chased him up the ladder to the flying deck.

Once there, Ryan peered out at the harbor. Several of the pirates' vessels sat stranded in the water, put out of commission by Jak, Dean and the Foundation men. But several more of them cut through the water. Seven of the boats formed a blockade line across the narrow mouth of the harbor. The pirates aboard them opened up with their weapons, creating a sheet of bullets that slapped into the flagship in a savage tattoo.

The remaining pieces of the Plexiglas windows on the flying bridge disintegrated, and the frame warped under the sustained assault.

"Dark night!" J.B. said, removing his beloved fedora.

"If your hat gets a hole in it," Ryan observed, "it'll probably be in your head, too." He took the time to reload the Steyr.

"On the off chance it isn't," the Armorer said, "I want to keep the hat of a piece. What do you want to do with the blockade?" He kept the lever at half speed but maintained the course toward the boats.

"Pick the weakest point," Ryan said, "then run over them."

"Could lose this boat," J.B. warned.

"Stay in this harbor much longer," Ryan said, "they'll shoot it out from under us anyway. They're picking up on accuracy."

"Noticed that. Do it now?"

"Now." Ryan pulled the Steyr into position, staying only enough above the edge of the Plexiglas window to see his targets. He kept the rifle's barrel off the frame, trying to keep it steady with his body.

"Between the third and fourth boats?" J.B. asked.

"Yeah." Ryan squeezed off a shot, missing the outboard engine on the third boat from the left by inches. The water spumed up a foot high. He fired again, getting closer, then waited a moment as J.B. buried the speed controls.

Chapter Thirty-Four

The sixty-foot powerboat lunged forward again, the prow lifting even higher from the river.

Ryan fired three more times, believing he hit the outboard engine at least twice. It ruptured, catching fire in a small explosion. But the gasoline spread, pooling in the bottom of the boat and catching fire, as well. The pirates broke ranks and evacuated the boat, diving into the water.

The one-eyed man yelled a warning to Jak, Dean and the Foundation men, sending them to cover, then he doubled over and butted into the padded console of the vessel himself.

The impact screamed as Fiberglas slammed against Fiberglas and shuddered through the sixty-foot powerboat. The collision also hammered Ryan against the console. Despite the padding, the wind left his lungs, and his face smashed into something hard and unyielding. He tasted blood, felt a tooth loose in its socket.

Then they shot past the blockade.

Looking back, Ryan saw the twisted wreckage of two boats in their wake, one of them in flames. The other boats in the blockade created a trap for the remaining craft trying to get out of the harbor.

Donovan joined Ryan and J.B. on the flying deck. "We didn't put as many of them down as we'd hoped," the Foundation man said.

"Mebbe we got enough," Ryan replied. "We'll see how

things go up ahead.'' The trap with the six machine-gun-outfitted boats waited around the second lazy curve of the river.

For now they had the jump on the pirates, and the sixty-foot powerboat had more speed than Ryan had hoped. He retreated down the ladder to the stern to help defend against the front line of the pursuing pirates.

GLANCING AHEAD as they rounded the second curve of the S, Ryan saw the tattered green shirt flying from an oar on the east side of the river. He lifted the Steyr and fired off three rounds, signaling the shore teams to get the first phase of the trap ready.

Ryan had chosen the spot when he'd first seen it. Leafy trees hung low, out over the river, providing plenty of cover for anyone coming from the north against the current. Three of the boats occupied either side of the river, their motors running.

After the sixty-foot powerboat rushed through the area, a span of fishing net lifted in the water. The net held remote-controlled plas-ex packs J.B. had put together from supplies the Foundation people had back at the dam site. One of the Foundation sec men in the six boats held the remote control in case Ryan and the others hadn't made it back out.

The first pirate water bike hit the net and instantly got tangled up. It flipped end over end, spilling the rider into the river. Two more rammed into the net, as well, with the same results. The fourth water bike managed to curve away in an effort that left a white roil of water in a semicircle that washed through the fishing net.

The first boat crashed through the net, tearing it free, pulling it along.

"Open fire!" Ryan roared. Even though the range wasn't

the best, and the uneven jarring of the flagship's deck made marksmanship impossible, they laid down a heavy firezone, burning through ammo. The noise of the attack, with the gunshots rolling over the flat planes of the river, covered the sounds of the machine guns mounted on the Foundation powerboats when they started firing.

Caught in a vicious cross fire between the .50-caliber machine guns, the pirate boats became confused, bumping into one another. Even more confusion ripped through their ranks when the remote-controlled plas-ex blew.

Giant spumes of white water twisted high into the air over the group of pirates with enough explosive force to twist the water into a brief tsunami. Several of the craft turned over or submerged. Three of the boats and two of the water bikes were caught outright and destroyed in the string of explosions that went off in a prolonged sequence.

Before they recovered, the six Foundation powerboats sped on either side of them. The big .50-caliber machine guns opened fire in sustained bursts. The heavy bullets raked the pirates' craft, ripping them to shreds.

The six boats with Ryan's team engaged the stalled attack effort and continued the blistering .50-caliber fire. A secondary wave of explosions erupted as the smaller packages J.B. had constructed blew, even more damaging than the first. The first wave of explosions had scattered the secondary ones in a wide circumference, some of them landing in the pirate boats.

"That's worked out well," Donovan said to Ryan, shouting to be heard above the carnage.

"Hasn't stopped all of them," Ryan pointed out.

And it was true. Though the river was filled and bottlenecked by stricken boats and water bikes, the pirates were already working to get through the area.

"It'll take them a while to get their courage up," Ryan said.

"But they'll follow us?" Donovan asked.

"No doubt about that. You took the space-station section back and killed a lot of them. If Barbarossa is as interested in building his private navy as you say he is, he can't afford to take this kind of beating without getting his pound of flesh back."

Donovan glanced back at the twisted wrecks and the roiling water of the Jefferson River. "Used up a lot of our stashed plas-ex. Going to have to hump a fresh load in from the Foundation."

Ryan showed the man a thin grin. "I think you can tell whoever runs the Foundation that it was well spent." He reloaded the Steyr, watching as the six Foundation powerboats pulled up alongside the flagship.

"Going to be a big race back to the dam, isn't it, Dad?" Dean asked.

"Yeah," Ryan said. "And even going at full speed, it's going to take over an hour to reach it." He squinted against the rising morning sun, at the sparkling water spread out over the river. He knew before the sun set again there'd be a lot more bodies piled up and waiting for the last train to the coast.

SEVENTY-EIGHT MINUTES LATER by Ryan's chron, J.B. piloted the pirates' flagship into the mouth of the narrow canyon leading to the oversize cistern the Foundation people used as a base. The Armorer kept the power on full ahead, skimming across the water as the diesels pushed them toward their final destination.

Ryan stood with difficulty on his wounded leg, which throbbed now, and had started to swell from all the damage and stress. Days were going to pass before he felt anywhere near normal again. His other wounds were dull aches.

The pirates maintained the distance, swapping occasional shots with the Foundation boats. Donovan had lost three more men, and Dean had gotten nicked along the left thigh.

Ryan stood now with J.B. on the flying deck. He managed the Steyr with greater ease. Aiming on the crest of the waves, even as fast as they came at the speed they traveled, had become easier.

The pirates had learned to stay back, and J.B. had offered the opinion that they were assuming the role of hounds in a long and arduous chase. They intended to run the Foundation boats to ground and kill everyone aboard.

When they entered the narrow canyon, the pirates struggled to form a single line. They also got braver, thinking the race was almost run.

Ryan hung on to the railing and braced the Steyr against his shoulder. He fired three rounds, all of them coring the lead boat behind them. Sparks jumped from the powerboat's metal trim, and the boat pilot tried a defensive maneuver.

The wake left by the flagship and the six Foundation powerboats slopped up high on the sides of the canyon. Hitting the wake wrong, already trying to overcontrol his craft, the boat pilot slammed the powerboat into the side of the canyon. The hull ripped out of her, spilling her passengers into the river. They promptly got hit by the boats behind.

Ryan glanced ahead again just as the pirate flagship roared through the canyon into the broad expanse of the cistern. He glanced along the top of the canyon, spotting the Foundation people on the edge around the dam. Donovan had judged it to be the safest place.

J.B. only geared the throttles down at the last minute.

Even then the flagship roared up onto the rocky ledge where the Foundation people had made their campsite.

"Hold on!" J.B. shouted in warning.

Ryan gripped the railing as the hull ripped out from under the big boat. It listed, turning over on its side. The one-eyed man forced himself to his feet, standing on the console as the boat slid sideways.

When the flagship came to its final rest, the prow caved in where it struck a huge boulder. Ryan vaulted onto the rocky ledge in time to watch the other six powerboats race to shore, as well.

"Get your asses over here!" Donovan roared, waving to the teams.

Two men stayed with each boat, taking the .50-caliber machine guns loose from the side rails. The extra men from each group raced over to the pirate flagship. Men atop the dam lowered a huge fishing net with attached cargo hooks. Donovan and some of the men climbed into the sixty-footer's belowdecks with the hooks and nets, attempting to salvage the piece of space station.

Ryan and J.B. set up a firezone, then liberated disposable LAWs they'd found inside the redoubt.

The pirates showed up minutes later, obviously delayed by the boat Ryan had shot up. By that time, Donovan and his men had freed the space-station piece from the flagship. The Foundation man shouted up the side of the dam, and men above began hauling up the cargo net.

"I've got the first shot," J.B. stated quietly.

"Go," Ryan said.

The Armorer waited only a little longer, then he fired the LAW. The 94 mm warhead sped just over the top of the cistern water and collided with the second boat back in the cluster that had spotted the rocky ledge.

The resulting explosion took out three boats and threw

a wave of fire over the others. Confusion swept the pirates' ranks.

"Get those people up the dam," Ryan ordered Donovan.

The Foundation man and his teams wasted no time in scaling the rope ladders that had been thrown from the top of the dam. Ryan ordered Jak and Dean to go next.

Shouldering the tube-shaped weapon, Ryan fired it at the largest cluster of pirate boats he saw. The impact threw fiery remnants into the air. He didn't wait to see any more, sprinting for the nearest rope ladder, with J.B. at his side.

As he made his way up the dam, half dragged and half climbing, he saw the pirate boats get organized again. Given how many he spotted, he knew the ones they'd seen in the small harbor earlier hadn't been all of them. Barbarossa had evidently split his forces. Forty, maybe fifty watercraft had crowded into the cistern.

Just over halfway up the dam, Ryan told Donovan to blow the canyon walls on the other side of the cistern. The man hesitated only a moment, looking down and obviously thinking Ryan and J.B. weren't going to make it. His voice was ripped away by the wind, but the instant detonations behind Ryan told him the command had been given.

Glancing over his shoulder, Ryan watched a mass of rock slide into the canyon that bottlenecked the cistern. In seconds, the thunderous mass blocked the canyon, sealing off the pirates who were inside from the ones who hadn't made it. Ryan knew there had to have been only a few of them who hadn't come into the killing zone.

Less than thirty feet remained to be climbed to the top of the dam. Ryan shouted at Donovan to blow the dam.

There was no hesitation at all this time.

The dam blew in an earthshaking explosion, releasing a thundering cascade of water that leaped out into the cistern like a live thing. It surged over the pirate vessels, smashing and overturning them as if they were a child's toys.

Without warning, a part of the wall of water draining into the cistern whipped over, giving testimony to how much pressure the dam had actually held back. The cascade nearly ripped Ryan from the rope ladder. He clung to it, his shoulder screaming, feeling the rope burn his palms as it slid through his hands.

Then the water was gone, joining the rush that continued to spill from the broken dam.

Ryan took a deep breath and finished climbing, joining Krysty at the top of the dam.

The beautiful redhead rushed to him, holding him tight in spite of the wet clothing. "Thought for a minute there I'd lost you, lover."

Ryan shook his head. "Not yet." He peered down into the cistern, watching the water pour over the pirates.

At first, the Foundation people had cheered the destruction of their enemies. But watching the avalanche of water pull the pirates under so effortlessly gave them all pause.

Even Ryan, as inured as he was to the toll exacted by Deathlands, felt a chill that wasn't the cause of the water drenching him.

As the cistern filled, it flooded into the four canyons at the side, at least one of them running into the hidden water reserves of the Foundation.

Ryan suspected there'd be few survivors. He didn't wait to see. There was definitely not going to be any pursuit.

He approached Donovan. "Fulfilled my part of the bargain. Time to handle your end."

Epilogue

The Chosen witch joined the companions just after dusk at the new campsite the Foundation people set up that evening.

"My sister," Donovan said as a way of introduction when he brought her over to where Krysty sat on a sleeping bag. "Her name's Dora."

Ryan knew at once she was one of the Chosen from her style of dress and the distant look in her dark eyes. But she was lean and curved, surely no older than nineteen or twenty, pretty enough to turn the heads of men. "What's she going to do?" Ryan asked, his hand resting on the SIG-Sauer's butt.

Darkness fell all around them, complete and unforgiving. Rain clouds blotted out the moon and stars.

"She's going to withdraw the dead Chosen from Krysty's mind," Donovan said.

Dora knelt in front of Krysty and put her hands on the redhead's temples and began to chant in a low melodious voice. Krysty reached out and took Ryan's hand, squeezing it tightly.

Without warning, the two women propelled away from each other, both knocked backwards.

"It's done," Dora said, wiping bloody spittle from her mouth with the back of her hand. She glanced up at Donovan. "Remember our bargain, brother."

Donovan gave her a tight nod as he helped her to her feet.

Heart pounding with fear, Ryan glanced at Krysty.

She looked up at him. "It's true, lover," she said hoarsely. "Nobody in here now but me. All alone again. Thank Gaia." Then she slept.

Ryan held her hand while everyone left them alone together, and he held it for a very long time after that.

"AFTER SEEING how easily you open these redoubts," Donovan said the next morning, "there's people at the Foundation who aren't going to be too happy to know I let you go."

"We had a deal," Ryan reminded him.

"I know," Donovan said sourly. "But you didn't have all your cards on the table."

Ryan gave him a thin grin. "I never do."

"I guess this is goodbye, then. Unless I can talk you into coming up to the Foundation."

Ryan shook his head. Truth to tell, he'd like to see the place. "Mebbe another time."

"Still curious," Donovan said.

"What?"

"How you could know that you could trust me to let you go."

"Didn't trust you," Ryan said. "Trusted ourselves. During the raid on the pirates, Jak put a plas-ex bomb on the space-station section. If we'd needed it, there'd have been a way out." He left Donovan standing there with his mouth open. He stopped at the door of the redoubt and gave the man a brief salute before keying in the code to open the doors and disappearing inside.

Ryan made his way to the mat-trans and shut the door, automatically activating the sequence that would send them

omeplace else. After glancing around at the other com-
anions who'd already prepared for the jump, he took a
eat on the floor beside Krysty. The familiar fog lifted from
he glowing metal plates and obscured the view through the
olored armaglass. He turned his attention to his lover.
'Feeling better?''

"Yeah, lover, and after things calm down at the other
nd of this jump, I'm going to show you just how much
etter I'm feeling.'' Krysty squeezed his hand.

Feeling the transfer blotting out his senses, Ryan closed
is eye.

James Axler

OUTLANDERS™

NIGHT ETERNAL

Kane and his fellow warrior survivalists find themselves launched into an alternate reality where the nukecaust was averted—and the Archons have emerged as mankind's great benefactors.

The group sets out to help a small secret organization conduct a clandestine war against the forces of evil....

Book #2 in the new Lost Earth Saga, a trilogy that chronicles our heroes' paths through three very different alternate realities... where the struggle against the evil Archons goes on...

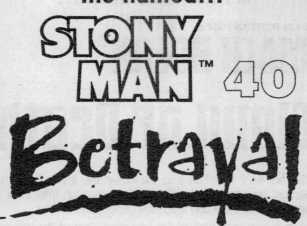

A wave of terror paves the way for the millennium...

DON PENDLETON's
MACK BOLAN®

Cloud of Death

After his fiery initiation into the covenant, Mack Bolan is stunned by what he pieced together based on intel from a former cult disciple and a Justice Department insider.

Bolan is one man against the next move toward the end—a cataclysmic nerve gas attack. But to stop the coming nightmare, he must evade the cult's powerful paramilitary leader....

Book #2 in The Four Horsemen Trilogy, three books that chronicle Mack Bolan's efforts to thwart the plans of a radical doomsday cult to bring about a real-life Armageddon....

Available in April 1999 at your favorite retail outlet.

Chiun's been charmed by a cult,
leaving Remo to defend the free
world alone...

THE
Destroyer™

#115 Misfortune Teller
Created by

WARREN MURPHY
and RICHARD SAPIR

When Chiun watches an infomercial produced by Man Hyung Sun and his group of Loonies, he revels in the leader's sales pitch about the Sun Source and the upcoming conversion of all humanity into Koreans. After all, what could be more divine?

While the leader lights the fuse on an international incident, Remo and Chiun are headed toward an incident of their own, as the Master of Sinanju grows tired of his disciple's lack of respect for "Seer Sun." What follows is the mother of all battles, in more ways than one....

Available in May 1999 at your favorite retail outlet.